Classic American Short Stories

17 Stories from Hawthorne to Fitzgerald

Edited by
Clarence C. Strowbridge

DOVER PUBLICATIONS, INC.
Mineola, New York

Copyright

Bibliographical Note

This Dover Large Print Classics edition, first published in 2002, is a new anthology of seventeen short stories reprinted from standard sources.

Library of Congress Cataloging-in-Publication Data

Classic American short stories : 17 stories from Hawthorne to Fitzgerald / edited by Clarence C. Strowbridge.
p. cm. — (Dover large print classics)
ISBN-13: 978-0-486-42251-0
ISBN-10: 0-486-42251-8
1. United States—Social life and customs—Fiction. 2. Short stories, American. 3. Large type books. I. Strowbridge, Clarence C. II. Series.

PS645 .C584 2002
813'.0108—dc21

2001058422

Manufactured in the United States by LSC Communications
42251811 2017
www.doverpublications.com

This Large Print Book carries the Seal of Approval of N.A.V.H.

Contents

Rappaccini's Daughter

by Nathaniel Hawthorne

We do not remember to have seen any translated specimens of the productions of M. de l'Aubépine,—a fact the less to be wondered at, as his very name is unknown to many of his own countrymen as well as to the student of foreign literature. As a writer, he seems to occupy an unfortunate position between the Transcendentalists (who, under one name or another, have their share in all the current literature of the world) and the great body of pen-and-ink men who address the intellect and sympathies of the multitude. If not too refined, at all events too remote, too shadowy, and unsubstantial in his modes of development to suit the taste of the latter class, and yet too popular to satisfy the spiritual or metaphysical requisitions of the former, he must necessarily find himself without an audience, except here and there an individual or possibly an isolated clique. His writings, to do them justice, are not altogether destitute of fancy and originality; they might have won him greater reputation but for an inveterate love of allegory, which is apt to invest his plots and characters with the aspect of scenery and people in the clouds and to steal away the human warmth out of his conceptions. His fictions are sometimes historical, sometimes of the present day, and sometimes, so far as can be discovered, have little or no reference either to time or space. In any case, he generally contents himself with a very slight embroidery of outward manners,—the faintest possible counterfeit of real life,—and endeavors to create an interest by some less obvious peculiarity of the subject. Occasionally a breath of Nature, a raindrop of pathos and tenderness, or a gleam of humor, will find its way into the midst of his fantastic imagery, and make us feel as if, after all, we were yet within the limits of our native earth. We will only add to this very cursory notice that M. de l'Aubépine's productions, if the reader chance to take them in precisely the proper point of view, may amuse a leisure hour as well as those of a brighter man; if otherwise, they can hardly fail to look excessively like nonsense.

Our author is voluminous; he continues to write and publish with as much praiseworthy and indefatigable prolixity as if his efforts were crowned with the brilliant success that so justly attends those of Eugene Sue. His first appearance was by a collection of stories in a long series of volumes entitled *Contes deux fois racontées.* The titles of some of his more recent works (we quote from memory) are as follows: *Le Voyage Céleste à Chemin de Fer,* 3 tom., 1838. *Le nouveau Père Adam et la nouvelle Mère Eve,* 2 tom., 1839. *Roderic; ou le Serpent à l'estomac,* 2 tom., 1840. *Le Culte du Feu,* a folio volume of ponderous research into the religion and ritual of the old Persian Ghebers, published in 1841. *La Soirée du Chateau en Espagne,* 1 tom., 8vo, 1842; and *L'Artiste du Beau; ou le Papillon Mécanique,* 5 tom., 4to, 1843. Our somewhat wearisome perusal of this startling catalogue of volumes has left behind it a certain personal affection and sympathy, though by no means admiration, for M. de l'Aubépine; and we would fain do the little in our power towards introducing him favorably to the American public. The ensuing tale is a translation of his *Beatrice; ou la Belle Empoisonneuse,* recently published in *La Revue Anti-Aristocratique.* This journal, edited by the Comte de Bearhaven, has for some years past led the defence of liberal principles and popular rights with a faithfulness and ability worthy of all praise.

A young man, named Giovanni Guasconti, came, very long ago, from the more southern region of Italy, to pursue his studies at the

University of Padua. Giovanni, who had but a scanty supply of gold ducats in his pocket, took lodgings in a high and gloomy chamber of an old edifice which looked not unworthy to have been the palace of a Paduan noble, and which, in fact, exhibited over its entrance the armorial bearings of a family long since extinct. The young stranger, who was not unstudied in the great poem of his country, recollected that one of the ancestors of this family, and perhaps an occupant of this very mansion, had been pictured by Dante as a partaker of the immortal agonies of his Inferno. These reminiscences and associations, together with the tendency to heartbreak natural to a young man for the first time out of his native sphere, caused Giovanni to sigh heavily as he looked around the desolate and ill-furnished apartment.

"Holy Virgin, signor!" cried old Dame Lisabetta, who, won by the youth's remarkable beauty of person, was kindly endeavoring to give the chamber a habitable air, "what a sigh was that to come out of a young man's heart! Do you find this old mansion gloomy? For the love of Heaven, then, put your head out of the window, and you will see as bright sunshine as you have left in Naples."

Guasconti mechanically did as the old woman advised, but could not quite agree with her that the Paduan sunshine was as cheerful as that of southern Italy. Such as it was, however, it fell upon a garden beneath the window and expended its fostering influences on a variety of plants, which seemed to have been cultivated with exceeding care.

"Does this garden belong to the house?" asked Giovanni.

"Heaven forbid, signor, unless it were fruitful of better pot-herbs than any that grow there now," answered old Lisabetta. "No; that garden is cultivated by the own hands of Signor Giacomo Rappaccini, the famous doctor, who, I warrant him, has been heard of as far as Naples. It is said that he distils these plants into medicines that are as potent as a charm. Oftentimes you may see the signor doctor at work, and perchance the signora, his daughter, too, gathering the strange flowers that grow in the garden."

The old woman had now done what she could for the aspect of the chamber; and, commending the young man to the protection of the saints, took her departure.

Giovanni still found no better occupation than to look down into the garden beneath his window. From its appearance, he judged it to be one of those botanic gardens which were of earlier date in Padua than elsewhere in Italy or in the world. Or, not improbably, it might once have been the pleasure-place of an opulent family; for there was the ruin of a marble fountain in the center, sculptured with rare art, but so wofully shattered that it was impossible to trace the original design from the chaos of remaining fragments. The water, however, continued to gush and sparkle into the sunbeams as cheerfully as ever. A little gurgling sound ascended to the young man's window, and made him feel as if the fountain were an immortal spirit that sung its song unceasingly and without heeding the vicissitudes around it, while one century imbodied it in marble and another scattered the perishable garniture on the soil. All about the pool into which the water subsided grew various plants, that seemed to require a plentiful supply of moisture for the nourishment of gigantic leaves, and, in some instances, flowers gorgeously magnificent. There was one shrub in particular, set in a marble vase in the midst of the pool, that bore a profusion of purple blossoms, each of which had the lustre and richness of a gem; and the whole together made a show so resplendent that it seemed enough to illuminate the garden, even had there been no sunshine. Every portion of the soil was peopled with plants and herbs, which, if less beautiful, still bore tokens of assiduous care, as if all had their individual virtues, known to the scientific mind that fostered them. Some were placed in urns, rich with old carving, and others in common garden-pots; some crept serpent-like along the ground or climbed on high, using whatever means of ascent was offered them. One plant had wreathed itself round a statue of Vertumnus, which was thus quite veiled and shrouded in a drapery of hanging foliage, so happily arranged that it might have served a sculptor for a study.

While Giovanni stood at the window he heard a rustling behind a screen of leaves, and became aware that a person was at work in the garden. His figure soon emerged into view, and showed itself to be that of no common laborer, but a tall, emaciated, sallow, and sickly-looking man, dressed in a scholar's garb of black. He was beyond the middle term of life, with gray hair, a thin, gray beard, and a face singularly marked with intellect and cultivation, but which could never, even in his more youthful days, have expressed much warmth of heart.

Nothing could exceed the intentness with which this scientific gardener examined every shrub which grew in his path: it seemed as if he was looking into their inmost nature, making observations in regard to their creative essence, and discovering why one leaf grew in this shape and another in that, and wherefore such and such flowers differed among themselves in hue and perfume. Nevertheless, in spite of this deep intelligence on his part, there was no approach to intimacy between himself and these vegetable existences. On the contrary, he avoided their actual touch or the direct inhaling of their odors with a caution that impressed Giovanni most disagreeably; for the man's demeanor was that of one walking among malignant influences, such as savage beasts, or deadly snakes, or evil spirits, which, should he allow them one moment of license, would wreak upon him some terrible fatality. It was strangely frightful to the young man's imagination to see this air of insecurity in a person cultivating a garden, that most simple and innocent of human toils, and which had been alike the joy and labor of the unfallen parents of the race. Was this garden, then, the Eden of the present world? And this man, with such a perception of harm in what his own hands caused to grow,—was he the Adam?

The distrustful gardener, while plucking away the dead leaves or pruning the too luxuriant growth of the shrubs, defended his hands with a pair of thick gloves. Nor were these his only armor. When, in his walk through the garden, he came to the magnificent plant that hung its purple gems beside the marble fountain, he placed a kind of mask over his mouth and nostrils, as if all this beauty did but conceal a deadlier malice; but, finding his task still too dangerous, he drew back, removed the mask, and called loudly, but in the infirm voice of a person affected with inward disease,—

"Beatrice! Beatrice!"

"Here am I, my father. What would you?" cried a rich and youthful voice from the window of the opposite house,—a voice as rich as a tropical sunset, and which made Giovanni, though he knew not why, think of deep hues of purple or crimson and of perfumes heavily delectable. "Are you in the garden?"

"Yes, Beatrice," answered the gardener, "and I need your help."

Soon there emerged from under a sculptured portal the figure of a young girl, arrayed with as much richness of taste as the most splendid of the flowers, beautiful as the day, and with a bloom so deep and vivid that one shade more would have been too much. She looked redundant with life, health, and energy; all of which attributes were bound down and compressed, as it were, and girdled tensely, in their luxuriance, by her virgin zone. Yet Giovanni's fancy must have grown morbid while he looked down into the garden; for the impression which the fair stranger made upon him was as if here were another flower, the human sister of those vegetable ones, as beautiful as they, more beautiful than the richest of them, but still to be touched only with a glove, nor to be approached without a mask. As Beatrice came down the garden-path, it was observable that she handled and inhaled the odor of several of the plants which her father had most sedulously avoided.

"Here, Beatrice," said the latter, "see how many needful offices require to be done to our chief treasure. Yet, shattered as I am, my life might pay the penalty of approaching it so closely as circumstances demand. Henceforth, I fear, this plant must be consigned to your sole charge."

"And gladly will I undertake it," cried again the rich tones of the young lady, as she bent towards the magnificent plant and opened her arms as if to embrace it. "Yes, my sister, my splendor, it shall be Beatrice's task to nurse and serve thee; and thou shalt reward her with thy kisses and perfumed breath, which to her is as the breath of life."

Then, with all the tenderness in her manner that was so strikingly expressed in her words, she busied herself with such attentions as the plant seemed to require; and Giovanni, at his lofty window, rubbed his eyes and almost doubted whether it were a girl tending her favorite flower, or one sister performing the duties of affection to another. The scene soon terminated. Whether Dr. Rappaccini had finished his labors in the garden, or that his watchful eye had caught the stranger's face, he now took his daughter's arm and retired. Night was already closing in; oppressive exhalations seemed to proceed from the plants and steal upward past the open window; and Giovanni, closing the lattice, went to his couch and dreamed of a rich flower and beautiful girl. Flower and maiden were different, and yet the same, and fraught with some strange peril in either shape.

But there is an influence in the light of morning that tends to rectify whatever errors of fancy, or even of judgment, we may have incurred during the sun's decline, or among the shadows of the night, or in the less wholesome glow of moonshine. Giovanni's first movement, on starting from sleep, was to throw open the window and gaze down into the garden which his dreams had made so fertile of mysteries. He was surprised, and a little ashamed, to find how real and matter-of-fact an affair it proved to be, in the first rays of the sun which gilded the dew-drops that hung upon leaf and blossom, and, while giving a brighter beauty to each rare flower, brought everything within the limits of ordinary experience. The young man rejoiced that, in the heart of the barren city, he had the privilege of overlooking this spot of lovely and luxuriant vegetation. It would serve, he said to himself, as a symbolic language to keep him in communion with nature. Neither the sickly and thought-worn Dr. Giacomo Rappaccini, it is true, nor his brilliant daughter, were now visible; so that Giovanni could not determine how much of the singularity which he attributed to both was due to their own qualities and how much to his wonder-working fancy; but he was inclined to take a most rational view of the whole matter.

In the course of the day he paid his respects to Signor Pietro Baglioni, professor of medicine in the university, a physician of eminent repute, to whom Giovanni had brought a letter of introduction. The professor was an elderly personage, apparently of genial nature and habits that might almost be called jovial. He kept the young man to dinner, and made himself very agreeable by the freedom and liveliness of his conversation, especially when warmed by a flask or two of Tuscan wine. Giovanni, conceiving that men of science, inhabitants of the same city, must needs be on familiar terms with one another, took an opportunity to mention the name of Dr. Rappaccini. But the professor did not respond with so much cordiality as he had anticipated.

"Ill would it become a teacher of the divine art of medicine," said Professor Pietro Baglioni, in answer to a question of Giovanni, "to withhold due and well-considered praise of a physician so eminently skilled as Rappaccini; but, on the other hand, I should answer it but scantily to my conscience were I to permit a worthy youth like yourself, Signor Giovanni, the son of an ancient friend, to imbibe erroneous ideas respecting a man who might hereafter chance to hold your life and death in his hands. The truth is, our worshipful Dr. Rappaccini has as much science as any member of the faculty—with perhaps one single exception—in Padua, or all Italy; but there are certain grave objections to his professional character."

"And what are they?" asked the young man.

"Has my friend Giovanni any disease of body or heart, that he is so inquisitive about physicians?" said the professor, with a smile. "But as for Rappaccini, it is said of him—and I, who know the man well, can answer for its truth—that he cares infinitely more for science than for mankind. His patients are interesting to him only as subjects for some new experiment. He would sacrifice human life, his own among the rest, or whatever else was dearest to him, for the sake of adding so much as a grain of mustard-seed to the great heap of his accumulated knowledge."

"Methinks he is an awful man indeed," remarked Guasconti, mentally recalling the cold and purely intellectual aspect of Rappaccini. "And yet, worshipful professor, is it not a noble spirit? Are there many men capable of so spiritual a love of science?"

"God forbid," answered the professor, somewhat testily; "at least, unless they take sounder views of the healing art than those adopted by Rappaccini. It is his theory that all medicinal virtues are comprised within those substances which we term vegetable poisons. These he cultivates with his own hands, and is said even to have produced new varieties of poison, more horribly deleterious than nature, without the assistance of this learned person, would ever have plagued the world withal. That the signor doctor does less mischief than might be expected with such dangerous substances, is undeniable. Now and then, it must be owned, he has effected, or seemed to effect, a marvellous cure; but, to tell you my private mind, Signor Giovanni, he should receive little credit for such instances of success—they being probably the work of chance,—but should be held strictly accountable for his failures, which may justly be considered his own work."

The youth might have taken Baglioni's opinions with many grains of allowance had he known that there was a professional warfare of long continuance between him and Dr. Rappaccini, in which the latter was generally thought to have gained the advantage. If the reader be inclined to judge for himself, we refer him to certain black-letter tracts on both sides, preserved in the medical department of the University of Padua.

"I know not, most learned professor," returned Giovanni, after musing on what had been said of Rappaccini's exclusive zeal for science,—"I know not how dearly this physician may love his art; but surely there is one object more dear to him. He has a daughter."

"Aha!" cried the professor, with a laugh. "So now our friend Giovanni's secret is out. You have heard of this daughter, whom all the young men in Padua are wild about, though not half a dozen have ever had the good hap to see her face. I know little of the Signora Beatrice save that Rappaccini is said to have instructed her deeply in his science, and that, young and beautiful as fame reports her, she is already qualified to fill a professor's chair. Perchance her father destines her for mine! Other absurd rumors there be, not worth talking about or listening to. So now, Signor Giovanni, drink off your glass of lachryma."

Guasconti returned to his lodgings somewhat heated with the wine he had quaffed, and which caused his brain to swim with strange fantasies in reference to Dr. Rappaccini and the beautiful Beatrice. On his way, happening to pass by a florist's, he bought a fresh bouquet of flowers.

Ascending to his chamber, he seated himself near the window, but within the shadow thrown by the depth of the wall, so that he could look down into the garden with little risk of being discovered. All beneath his eye was a solitude. The strange plants were basking in the sunshine, and now and then nodding gently to one another, as if in acknowledgment of sympathy and kindred. In the midst, by the shattered fountain, grew the magnificent shrub, with its purple gems clustering all over it; they glowed in the air, and gleamed back again out of the depths of the pool, which thus seemed to overflow with colored radiance from the rich reflection that was steeped in it. At first, as we have said, the garden was a solitude. Soon, however,—as Giovanni had half hoped, half feared, would be the case,—a figure appeared beneath the antique sculptured portal, and came down between the rows of plants, inhaling their various perfumes as if she were one of those beings of old classic fable that lived upon sweet odors. On again beholding Beatrice, the young man was even startled to perceive how much her beauty exceeded his recollection of it; so brilliant, so vivid, was its character, that she glowed amid the sunlight, and, as Giovanni whispered to himself, positively illuminated the more shadowy intervals of the garden path. Her face being now more revealed than on the former occasion, he was struck by its expression of simplicity and sweetness,—qualities that had not entered into his idea of her character, and which made him ask anew what manner of mortal she might be. Nor did he fail again to observe, or imagine, an analogy between the beautiful girl and the gorgeous shrub that hung its gemlike flowers over the fountain,—a resemblance which Beatrice seemed to have indulged a fantastic humor in heightening, both by the arrangement of her dress and the selection of its hues.

Approaching the shrub, she threw open her arms, as with a passionate ardor, and drew its branches into an intimate embrace,—so intimate that her features were hidden in its leafy bosom and her glistening ringlets all intermingled with the flowers.

"Give me thy breath, my sister," exclaimed Beatrice; "for I am faint with common air. And give me this flower of thine, which I separate with gentlest fingers from the stem and place it close beside my heart."

With these words the beautiful daughter of Rappaccini plucked one of the richest blossoms of the shrub, and was about to fasten it in her bosom. But now, unless Giovanni's draughts of wine had bewildered his senses, a singular incident occurred. A small orange-colored reptile, of the lizard or chameleon species, chanced to be creeping along the path, just at the feet of Beatrice. It appeared to Giovanni,—but, at the distance from which he gazed, he could scarcely have seen anything so minute,—it appeared to him, however, that a drop or two of moisture from the broken stem of the flower descended upon the lizard's head. For an instant the reptile contorted itself violently, and then lay motionless in the sunshine. Beatrice observed this remarkable phenomenon, and crossed herself, sadly, but without surprise; nor did she therefore hesitate to arrange the fatal flower in her bosom. There it blushed, and almost glimmered with the dazzling effect of a precious stone, adding to her dress and aspect the one appropriate charm which nothing else in the world could have supplied. But Giovanni, out of the shadow of his window, bent forward and shrank back, and murmured and trembled.

"Am I awake? Have I my senses?" said he to himself. "What is this being? Beautiful shall I call her, or inexpressibly terrible?"

Beatrice now strayed carelessly through the garden, approaching closer beneath Giovanni's window, so that he was compelled to thrust his head quite out of its concealment in order to gratify the intense and painful curiosity which she excited. At this moment there came a beautiful insect over the garden wall; it had, perhaps, wandered through the city, and found no flowers or verdure among those antique haunts of men until the heavy perfumes of Dr. Rappaccini's shrubs had lured it from afar. Without alighting on the flowers, this winged brightness seemed to be attracted by Beatrice, and lingered in the air and fluttered about her head. Now, here it could not be but that Giovanni Guasconti's eyes deceived him. Be that as it might, he fancied that, while Beatrice was gazing at the insect with childish delight, it grew faint and fell at her feet; its bright wings shivered; it was dead,—from no cause that he could discern, unless it were the atmosphere of her breath. Again Beatrice crossed herself and sighed heavily as she bent over the dead insect.

An impulsive movement of Giovanni drew her eyes to the window. There she beheld the beautiful head of the young man—rather a Grecian than an Italian head, with fair, regular features, and a glistening of gold among his ringlets—gazing down upon her like a being that hovered in mid-air. Scarcely knowing what he did, Giovanni threw down the bouquet which he had hitherto held in his hand.

"Signora," said he, "there are pure and healthful flowers. Wear them for the sake of Giovanni Guasconti."

"Thanks, signor," replied Beatrice, with her rich voice, that came forth as it were like a gush of music, and with a mirthful expression half childish and half woman-like. "I accept your gift, and would fain recompense it with this precious purple flower; but if I toss it into the air it will not reach you. So Signor Guasconti must even content himself with my thanks."

She lifted the bouquet from the ground, and then, as if inwardly ashamed at having stepped aside from her maidenly reserve to respond to a stranger's greeting, passed swiftly homeward through the garden. But, few as the moments were, it seemed to Giovanni, when she was on the point of vanishing beneath the sculptured portal, that his beautiful bouquet was already beginning to wither in her grasp. It was an idle thought; there could be no possibility of distinguishing a faded flower from a fresh one at so great a distance.

For many days after this incident the young man avoided the window that looked into Dr. Rappaccini's garden, as if something ugly and monstrous would have blasted his eyesight had he been betrayed into a glance. He felt conscious of having put himself, to a certain extent, within the influence of an unintelligible power by the communication which he had opened with Beatrice. The wisest course would have been, if his heart were in any real danger, to quit his lodgings and Padua itself at once; the next wiser, to have accustomed himself, as far as possible, to the familiar and daylight view of Beatrice,—thus bringing her rigidly and systematically within the limits of ordinary experience. Least of all, while avoiding her sight, ought Giovanni to have remained so near this extraordinary being that the proximity and possibility even of intercourse should give a kind of substance and reality to the wild vagaries which his imagination ran riot continually in producing.

Guasconti had not a deep heart,—or, at all events, its depths were not sounded now; but he had a quick fancy, and an ardent southern temperament, which rose every instant to a higher fever pitch. Whether or no Beatrice possessed those terrible attributes, that fatal breath, the affinity with those so beautiful and deadly flowers which were indicated by what Giovanni had witnessed, she had at least instilled a fierce and subtle poison into his system. It was not love, although her rich beauty was a madness to him; nor horror, even while he fancied her spirit to be imbued with the same baneful essence that seemed to pervade her physical frame; but a wild offspring of both love and horror that had each parent in it, and burned like one and shivered like the other. Giovanni knew not what to dread; still less did he know what to hope; yet hope and dread kept a continual warfare in his breast, alternately vanquishing one another and starting up afresh to renew the contest. Blessed are all simple emotions, be they dark or bright! It is the lurid intermixture of the two that produces the illuminating blaze of the infernal regions.

Sometimes he endeavored to assuage the fever of his spirit by a rapid walk through the streets of Padua or beyond its gates: his footsteps kept time with the throbbings of his brain, so that the walk was apt to accelerate itself to a race. One day he found himself arrested; his arm was seized by a portly personage, who had turned back on recognizing the young man and expended much breath in overtaking him.

"Signor Giovanni! Stay, my young friend!" cried he. "Have you forgotten me? That might well be the case if I were as much altered as yourself."

It was Baglioni, whom Giovanni had avoided ever since their first meeting, from a doubt that the professor's sagacity would look too deeply into his secrets. Endeavoring to recover himself, he stared forth wildly from his inner world into the outer one and spoke like a man in a dream.

"Yes; I am Giovanni Guasconti. You are Professor Pietro Baglioni. Now let me pass!"

"Not yet, not yet, Signor Giovanni Guasconti," said the professor, smiling, but at the same time scrutinizing the youth with an earnest glance. "What! did I grow up side by side with your father? and shall his son pass me like a stranger in these old streets of Padua? Stand still, Signor Giovanni; for we must have a word or two before we part."

"Speedily, then, most worshipful professor, speedily," said Giovanni, with feverish impatience. "Does not your worship see that I am in haste?"

Now, while he was speaking there came a man in black along the street, stooping and moving feebly, like a person in inferior health. His face was all overspread with a most sickly and sallow hue, but yet so pervaded with an expression of piercing and active intellect that an observer might easily have overlooked the merely physical attributes and have seen only this wonderful energy. As he passed, this person exchanged a cold and distant salutation with Baglioni, but fixed his eyes upon Giovanni with an intentness that seemed to bring out whatever was within him worthy of notice. Nevertheless, there was a peculiar quietness in the look, as if taking merely a speculative, not a human, interest in the young man.

"It is Dr. Rappaccini!" whispered the professor when the stranger had passed. "Has he ever seen your face before?"

"Not that I know," answered Giovanni, starting at the name.

"He *has* seen you! he must have seen you!" said Baglioni, hastily. "For some purpose or other, this man of science is making a study of you. I know that look of his! It is the same that coldly illuminates his face as he bends over a bird, a mouse, or a butterfly, which, in pursuance of some experiment, he has killed by the perfume of a flower; a look as deep as nature itself, but without nature's warmth of love. Signor Giovanni, I will stake my life upon it, you are the subject of one of Rappaccini's experiments!"

"Will you make a fool of me?" cried Giovanni, passionately. "*That,* signor professor, were an untoward experiment."

"Patience! patience!" replied the imperturbable professor. "I tell thee, my poor Giovanni, that Rappaccini has a scientific interest in thee. Thou hast fallen into fearful hands! And the Signora Beatrice,—what part does she act in this mystery?"

But Guasconti, finding Baglioni's pertinacity intolerable, here broke away, and was gone before the professor could again seize his arm. He looked after the young man intently and shook his head.

"This must not be," said Baglioni to himself. "The youth is the son of my old friend, and shall not come to any harm from which the arcana of medical science can preserve him. Besides, it is too insufferable an impertinence in Rappaccini thus to snatch the lad out of my own hands, as I may say, and make use of him for his infernal experiments. This daughter of his! It shall be looked to. Perchance, most learned Rappaccini, I may foil you where you little dream of it!"

Meanwhile Giovanni had pursued a circuitous route, and at length found himself at the door of his lodgings. As he crossed the threshold he was met by old Lisabetta, who smirked and smiled, and was evidently desirous to attract his attention; vainly, however, as the ebullition of his feelings had momentarily subsided into a cold and dull vacuity. He turned his eyes full upon the withered face that was puckering itself into a smile, but seemed to behold it not. The old dame, therefore, laid her grasp upon his cloak.

"Signor! signor!" whispered she, still with a smile over the whole breadth of her visage, so that it looked not unlike a grotesque carving in wood, darkened by centuries. "Listen, signor! There is a private entrance into the garden!"

"What do you say?" exclaimed Giovanni, turning quickly about, as if an inanimate thing should start into feverish life. "A private entrance into Dr. Rappaccini's garden?"

"Hush! hush! not so loud!" whispered Lisabetta, putting her hand over his mouth. "Yes; into the worshipful doctor's garden, where you may see all his fine shrubbery. Many a young man in Padua would give gold to be admitted among those flowers."

Giovanni put a piece of gold into her hand.

"Show me the way," said he.

A surmise, probably excited by his conversation with Baglioni, crossed his mind, that this interposition of old Lisabetta might perchance be connected with the intrigue, whatever were its nature, in which the professor seemed to suppose that Dr. Rappaccini was involving him. But such a suspicion, though it disturbed

Giovanni, was inadequate to restrain him. The instant that he was aware of the possibility of approaching Beatrice, it seemed an absolute necessity of his existence to do so. It mattered not whether she were angel or demon; he was irrevocably within her sphere, and must obey the law that whirled him onward, in ever-lessening circles, towards a result which he did not attempt to foreshadow; and yet, strange to say, there came across him a sudden doubt whether this intense interest on his part were not delusory; whether it were really of so deep and positive a nature as to justify him in now thrusting himself into an incalculable position; whether it were not merely the fantasy of a young man's brain, only slightly or not at all connected with his heart.

He paused, hesitated, turned half about, but again went on. His withered guide led him along several obscure passages, and finally undid a door, through which, as it was opened, there came the sight and sound of rustling leaves, with the broken sunshine glimmering among them. Giovanni stepped forth, and, forcing himself through the entanglement of a shrub that wreathed its tendrils over the hidden entrance, stood beneath his own window in the open area of Dr. Rappaccini's garden.

How often is it the case that, when impossibilities have come to pass, and dreams have condensed their misty substance into tangible realities, we find ourselves calm, and even coldly self-possessed, amid circumstances which it would have been a delirium of joy or agony to anticipate! Fate delights to thwart us thus. Passion will choose his own time to rush upon the scene, and lingers sluggishly behind when an appropriate adjustment of events would seem to summon his appearance. So was it now with Giovanni. Day after day his pulses had throbbed with feverish blood at the improbable idea of an interview with Beatrice, and of standing with her, face to face, in this very garden, basking in the Oriental sunshine of her beauty, and snatching from her full gaze the mystery which he deemed the riddle of his own existence. But now there was a singular and untimely equanimity within his breast. He threw a glance around the garden to discover if Beatrice or her father were present, and, perceiving that he was alone, began a critical observation of the plants.

The aspect of one and all of them dissatisfied him; their gorgeousness seemed fierce, passionate, and even unnatural. There was hardly an individual shrub which a wanderer, straying by himself through a forest, would not have been startled to find growing wild, as if an unearthly face had glared at him out of the thicket. Several also would have shocked a delicate instinct by an appearance of artificialness indicating that there had been such commixture, and, as it were, adultery of various vegetable species, that the production was no longer of God's making, but the monstrous offspring of man's depraved fancy, glowing with only an evil mockery of beauty. They were probably the result of experiment, which in one or two cases had succeeded in mingling plants individually lovely into a compound possessing the questionable and ominous character that distinguished the whole growth of the garden. In fine, Giovanni recognized but two or three plants in the collection, and those of a kind that he well knew to be poisonous. While busy with these contemplations he heard the rustling of a silken garment, and, turning, beheld Beatrice emerging from beneath the sculptured portal.

Giovanni had not considered with himself what should be his deportment; whether he should apologize for his intrusion into the garden, or assume that he was there with the privity at least, if not by the desire, of Dr. Rappaccini or his daughter; but Beatrice's manner placed him at his ease, though leaving him still in doubt by what agency he had gained admittance. She came lightly along the path, and met him near the broken fountain. There was surprise in her face, but brightened by a simple and kind expression of pleasure.

"You are a connoisseur in flowers, signor,"

said Beatrice, with a smile, alluding to the bouquet which he had flung her from the window. "It is no marvel, therefore, if the sight of my father's rare collection has tempted you to take a nearer view. If he were here, he could tell you many strange and interesting facts as to the nature and habits of these shrubs; for he has spent a lifetime in such studies, and this garden is his world."

"And yourself, lady," observed Giovanni, "if fame says true, you likewise are deeply skilled in the virtues indicated by these rich blossoms and these spicy perfumes. Would you deign to be my instructress, I should prove an apter scholar than if taught by Signor Rappaccini himself."

"Are there such idle rumors?" asked Beatrice, with the music of a pleasant laugh. "Do people say that I am skilled in my father's science of plants? What a jest is there! No; though I have grown up among these flowers, I know no more of them than their hues and perfume; and sometimes methinks I would fain rid myself of even that small knowledge. There are many flowers here, and those not the least brilliant, that shock and offend me when they meet my eye. But pray, signor, do not believe these stories about my science. Believe nothing of me save what you see with your own eyes."

"And must I believe all that I have seen with my own eyes?" asked Giovanni, pointedly, while the recollection of former scenes made him shrink. "No, signora; you demand too little of me. Bid me believe nothing save what comes from your own lips."

It would appear that Beatrice understood him. There came a deep flush to her cheek; but she looked full into Giovanni's eyes, and responded to his gaze of uneasy suspicion with a queen-like haughtiness.

"I do so bid you, signor," she replied. "Forget whatever you may have fancied in regard to me. If true to the outward senses, still it may be false in its essence; but the words of Beatrice Rappaccini's lips are true from the depths of the heart outward. Those you may believe."

A fervor glowed in her whole aspect, and beamed upon Giovanni's consciousness like the light of truth itself; but while she spoke there was a fragrance in the atmosphere around her, rich and delightful, though evanescent, yet which the young man, from an indefinable reluctance, scarcely dared to draw into his lungs. It might be the odor of the flowers. Could it be Beatrice's breath which thus embalmed her words with a strange richness, as if by steeping them in her heart? A faintness passed like a shadow over Giovanni and flitted away; he seemed to gaze through the beautiful girl's eyes into her transparent soul, and felt no more doubt or fear.

The tinge of passion that had colored Beatrice's manner vanished; she became gay, and appeared to derive a pure delight from her communion with the youth not unlike what the maiden of a lonely island might have felt conversing with a voyager from the civilized world. Evidently her experience of life had been confined within the limits of that garden. She talked now about matters as simple as the daylight or summer clouds, and now asked questions in reference to the city, or Giovanni's distant home, his friends, his mother, and his sisters,—questions indicating such seclusion, and such lack of familiarity with modes and forms, that Giovanni responded as if to an infant. Her spirit gushed out before him like a fresh rill that was just catching its first glimpse of the sunlight and wondering at the reflections of earth and sky which were flung into its bosom. There came thoughts, too, from a deep source, and fantasies of a gemlike brilliancy, as if diamonds and rubies sparkled upward among the bubbles of the fountain. Ever and anon there gleamed across the young man's mind a sense of wonder that he should be walking side by side with the being who had so wrought upon his imagination, whom he had idealized in such hues of terror, in whom he had positively witnessed such manifestations of dreadful attributes,—that he should be conversing with Beatrice like a brother, and should find her so human and so maiden-like. But such reflections were only momentary; the effect of her character was too real not to make itself familiar at once.

In this free intercourse they had strayed through the garden, and now, after many turns among its avenues, were come to the shattered fountain, beside which grew the magnificent shrub, with its treasury of glowing blossoms. A fragrance was diffused from it which Giovanni recognized as identical with that which he had attributed to Beatrice's breath, but incomparably more powerful. As her eyes fell upon it, Giovanni beheld her press her hand to her bosom as if her heart were throbbing suddenly and painfully.

"For the first time in my life," murmured she, addressing the shrub, "I had forgotten thee."

"I remember, signora," said Giovanni, "that you once promised to reward me with one of these living gems for the bouquet which I had the happy boldness to fling to your feet. Permit me now to pluck it as a memorial of this interview."

He made a step towards the shrub with extended hand; but Beatrice darted forward, uttering a shriek that went through his heart like a dagger. She caught his hand and drew it back with the whole force of her slender figure. Giovanni felt her touch thrilling through his fibres.

"Touch it not!" exclaimed she, in a voice of agony. "Not for thy life! It is fatal!"

Then, hiding her face, she fled from him and vanished beneath the sculptured portal. As Giovanni followed her with his eyes, he beheld the emaciated figure and pale intelligence of Dr. Rappaccini, who had been watching the scene, he knew not how long, within the shadow of the entrance.

No sooner was Guasconti alone in his chamber than the image of Beatrice came back to his passionate musings, invested with all the witchery that had been gathering around it ever since his first glimpse of her, and now likewise imbued with a tender warmth of girlish womanhood. She was human; her nature was endowed with all gentle and feminine qualities; she was worthiest to be worshipped; she was capable, surely, on her part, of the height and heroism of love. Those tokens which he had hitherto considered as proofs of a frightful peculiarity in her physical and moral system were now either forgotten or by the subtle sophistry of passion transmitted into a golden crown of enchantment, rendering Beatrice the more admirable by so much as she was the more unique. Whatever had looked ugly was now beautiful; or, if incapable of such a change, it stole away and hid itself among those shapeless half-ideas which throng the dim region beyond the daylight of our perfect consciousness. Thus did he spend the night, nor fell asleep until the dawn had begun to awake the slumbering flowers in Dr. Rappaccini's garden, whither Giovanni's dreams doubtless led him. Up rose the sun in his due season, and, flinging his beams upon the young man's eyelids, awoke him to a sense of pain. When thoroughly aroused, he became sensible of a burning and tingling agony in his hand,—in his right hand,—the very hand which Beatrice had grasped in her own when he was on the point of plucking one of the gemlike flowers. On the back of that hand there was now a purple print like that of four small fingers, and the likeness of a slender thumb upon his wrist.

Oh, how stubbornly does love,—or even that cunning semblance of love which flourishes in the imagination, but strikes no depth of root into the heart,—how stubbornly does it hold its faith until the moment comes when it is doomed to vanish into thin mist! Giovanni wrapped a handkerchief about his hand and wondered what evil thing had stung him, and soon forgot his pain in a reverie of Beatrice.

After the first interview, a second was in the inevitable course of what we call fate. A third; a fourth; and a meeting with Beatrice in the garden was no longer an incident in Giovanni's daily life, but the whole space in which he might be said to live; for the anticipation and memory of that ecstatic hour made up the remainder. Nor was it otherwise with the daughter of Rappaccini. She watched for the youth's appearance, and flew to his side with confidence as unreserved as if they had been playmates from early infancy,—as if they were such playmates still. If, by any unwonted chance, he failed to come at the appointed moment, she stood beneath the window and sent up the rich sweetness of her tones to float around him in his chamber and echo and reverberate throughout his heart: "Giovanni! Giovanni! Why tarriest thou? Come down!" And down he hastened into that Eden of poisonous flowers.

But, with all this intimate familiarity, there was still a reserve in Beatrice's demeanor, so rigidly and invariably sustained, that the idea of infringing it scarcely occurred to his imagination. By all appreciable signs, they loved; they had looked love with eyes that conveyed the holy secret from the depths of one soul into the depths of the other, as if it were too sacred to be whispered by the way; they had even spoken love in those gushes of passion when their spirits darted forth in articulated breath like tongues of long-hidden flame; and yet there had been no seal of lips, no clasp of hands, nor any slightest caress such as love claims and hallows. He had never touched one of the gleaming ringlets of her hair; her garment—so marked was the physical barrier between them—had never been waved against him by a breeze. On the few occasions when Giovanni had seemed tempted to overstep the limit, Beatrice grew so sad, so stern, and withal wore such a look of desolate separation, shuddering at itself, that not a spoken word was requisite to repel him. At such times he was startled at the horrible suspicions that rose, monster-like, out of the caverns of his heart and stared him in the face; his love grew thin and faint as the morning mist, his doubts alone had substance. But, when Beatrice's face brightened again after the momentary shadow, she was transformed at once from the mysterious, questionable being whom he had watched with so much awe and horror; she was now the beautiful and unsophisticated girl whom he felt that his spirit knew with a certainty beyond all other knowledge.

A considerable time had now passed since Giovanni's last meeting with Baglioni. One morning, however, he was disagreeably surprised by a visit from the professor, whom he had scarcely thought of for whole weeks, and would willingly have forgotten still longer. Given up as he had long been to a pervading excitement, he could tolerate no companions except upon condition of their perfect sympathy with his present state of feeling. Such sympathy was not to be expected from Professor Baglioni.

The visitor chatted carelessly for a few moments about the gossip of the city and the university, and then took up another topic.

"I have been reading an old classic author lately," said he, "and met with a story that strangely interested me. Possibly you may remember it. It is of an Indian prince, who sent a beautiful woman as a present to Alexander the Great. She was as lovely as the dawn and gorgeous as the sunset; but what especially distinguished her was a certain rich perfume in her breath,—richer than a garden of Persian roses. Alexander, as was natural to a youthful conqueror, fell in love at first sight with this magnificent stranger; but a certain sage physician, happening to be present, discovered a terrible secret in regard to her."

"And what was that?" asked Giovanni, turning his eyes downward to avoid those of the professor.

"That this lovely woman," continued Baglioni, with emphasis, "had been nourished with poisons from her birth upward, until her whole nature was so imbued with them that she herself had become the deadliest poison in existence. Poison was her element of life. With that rich perfume of her breath she blasted the very air. Her love would have been poison,—her embrace death. Is not this a marvellous tale?"

"A childish fable," answered Giovanni, nervously starting from his chair. "I marvel how your worship finds time to read such nonsense among your graver studies."

"By the by," said the professor, looking uneasily about him, "what singular fragrance is this in your apartment? Is it the perfume of your gloves? It is faint, but delicious; and yet, after all, by no means agreeable. Were I to breathe it long, methinks it would make me ill. It is like the breath of a flower; but I see no flowers in the chamber."

"Nor are there any," replied Giovanni, who had turned pale as the professor spoke; "nor, I think, is there any fragrance except in your worship's imagination. Odors, being a sort of element combined of the sensual and the spiritual, are apt to deceive us in this manner. The recollection of a perfume, the bare idea of it, may easily be mistaken for a present reality."

"Ay; but my sober imagination does not often play such tricks," said Baglioni; "and, were I to fancy any kind of odor, it would be that of some vile apothecary drug, wherewith my fingers are likely enough to be imbued. Our worshipful friend Rappaccini, as I have heard, tinctures his medicaments with odors richer than those of Araby. Doubtless, likewise, the fair and learned Signora Beatrice would minister to her patients with draughts as sweet as a maiden's breath; but woe to him that sips them!"

Giovanni's face evinced many contending emotions. The tone in which the professor alluded to the pure and lovely daughter of Rappaccini was a torture to his soul; and yet the intimation of a view of her character, opposite to his own, gave instantaneous distinctness to a thousand dim suspicions, which now grinned at him like so many demons. But he strove hard to quell them and to respond to Baglioni with a true lover's perfect faith.

"Signor professor," said he, "you were my father's friend; perchance, too, it is your purpose to act a friendly part towards his son. I would fain feel nothing towards you save respect and deference; but I pray you to observe, signor, that there is one subject on which we must not speak. You know not the Signora Beatrice. You cannot, therefore, estimate the wrong—the blasphemy, I may even say—that is offered to her character by a light or injurious word."

"Giovanni! my poor Giovanni!" answered the professor, with a calm expression of pity, "I know this wretched girl far better than yourself. You shall hear the truth in respect to the poisoner Rappaccini and his poisonous daughter; yes, poisonous as she is beautiful. Listen; for, even should you do violence to my gray hairs, it shall not silence me. That old fable of the Indian woman has become a truth by the deep and deadly science of Rappaccini and in the person of the lovely Beatrice."

Giovanni groaned and hid his face.

"Her father," continued Baglioni, "was not restrained by natural affection from offering up his child in this horrible manner as the victim of his insane zeal for science; for, let us do him justice, he is as true a man of science as ever distilled his own heart in an alembic. What, then, will be your fate? Beyond a doubt you are selected as the material of some new experiment. Perhaps the result is to be death; perhaps a fate more awful still. Rappaccini, with what he calls the interest of science before his eyes, will hesitate at nothing."

"It is a dream," muttered Giovanni to himself; "surely it is a dream."

"But," resumed the professor, "be of good cheer, son of my friend. It is not yet too late for the rescue. Possibly we may even succeed in bringing back this miserable child within the limits of ordinary nature, from which her father's madness has estranged her. Behold this little silver vase! It was wrought by the hands of the renowned Benvenuto Cellini, and is well worthy to be a love-gift to the fairest dame in Italy. But its contents are invaluable. One little sip of this antidote would have rendered the most virulent poisons of the Borgias innocuous.

Doubt not that it will be as efficacious against those of Rappaccini. Bestow the vase, and the precious liquid within it, on your Beatrice, and hopefully await the result."

Baglioni laid a small, exquisitely wrought silver vial on the table and withdrew, leaving what he had said to produce its effect upon the young man's mind.

"We will thwart Rappaccini yet," thought he, chuckling to himself as he descended the stairs; "but, let us confess the truth of him, he is a wonderful man,—a wonderful man indeed; a vile empiric, however, in his practice, and therefore not to be tolerated by those who respect the good old rules of the medical profession."

Throughout Giovanni's whole acquaintance with Beatrice, he had occasionally, as we have said, been haunted by dark surmises as to her character; yet so thoroughly had she made herself felt by him as a simple, natural, most affectionate, and guileless creature, that the image now held up by Professor Baglioni looked as strange and incredible as if it were not in accordance with his own original conception. True, there were ugly recollections connected with his first glimpses of the beautiful girl; he could not quite forget the bouquet that withered in her grasp, and the insect that perished amid the sunny air, by no ostensible agency save the fragrance of her breath. These incidents, however, dissolving in the pure light of her character, had no longer the efficacy of facts, but were acknowledged as mistaken fantasies, by whatever testimony of the senses they might appear to be substantiated. There is something truer and more real than what we can see with the eyes and touch with the finger. On such better evidence had Giovanni founded his confidence in Beatrice, though rather by the necessary force of her high attributes than by any deep and generous faith on his part. But now his spirit was incapable of sustaining itself at the height to which the early enthusiasm of passion had exalted it; he fell down, grovelling among earthly doubts, and defiled therewith the pure whiteness of Beatrice's image. Not that he gave her up; he did but distrust. He resolved to institute some decisive test that should satisfy him, once for all, whether there were those dreadful peculiarities in her physical nature which could not be supposed to exist without some corresponding monstrosity of soul. His eyes, gazing down afar, might have deceived him as to the lizard, the insect, and the flowers; but if he could witness, at the distance of a few paces, the sudden blight of one fresh and healthful flower in Beatrice's hand, there would be room for no further question. With this idea he hastened to the florist's and purchased a bouquet that was still gemmed with the morning dewdrops.

It was now the customary hour of his daily interview with Beatrice. Before descending into the garden, Giovanni failed not to look at his figure in the mirror,—a vanity to be expected in a beautiful young man, yet, as displaying itself at that troubled and feverish moment, the token of a certain shallowness of feeling and insincerity of character. He did gaze, however, and said to himself that his features had never before possessed so rich a grace, nor his eyes such vivacity, nor his cheeks so warm a hue of superabundant life.

"At least," thought he, "her poison has not yet insinuated itself into my system. I am no flower to perish in her grasp."

With that thought he turned his eyes on the bouquet, which he had never once laid aside from his hand. A thrill of indefinable horror shot through his frame on perceiving that those dewy flowers were already beginning to droop; they wore the aspect of things that had been fresh and lovely yesterday. Giovanni grew white as marble, and stood motionless before the mirror, staring at his own reflection there as at the likeness of something frightful. He remembered Baglioni's remark about the fragrance that seemed to pervade the chamber. It must have been the poison in his breath! Then he shuddered,—shuddered at himself. Recovering from his stupor, he began to watch with curious eye a spider that was busily at work hanging its web from the antique cornice of the apartment, crossing and recrossing the artful system of interwoven lines,—as vigorous and active a spider as ever dangled from an old ceiling. Giovanni bent towards the insect, and emitted a deep, long breath. The spider suddenly ceased its toil; the web vibrated with a tremor originating in the body of the small artisan. Again Giovanni sent forth a breath, deeper, longer, and imbued with a venomous feeling out of his heart: he knew not whether he were wicked, or only desperate. The spider made a convulsive grip with his limbs and hung dead across the window.

"Accursed! accursed!" muttered Giovanni, addressing himself. "Hast thou grown so poisonous that this deadly insect perishes by thy breath?"

At that moment a rich, sweet voice came floating up from the garden.

"Giovanni! Giovanni! It is past the hour! Why tarriest thou? Come down!"

"Yes," muttered Giovanni again. "She is the only being whom my breath may not slay! Would that it might!"

He rushed down, and in an instant was standing before the bright and loving eyes of Beatrice. A moment ago his wrath and despair had been so fierce that he could have desired nothing so much as to wither her by a glance; but with her actual presence there came influences which had too real an existence to be at once shaken off; recollections of the delicate and benign power of her feminine nature, which had so often enveloped him in a religious calm; recollections of many a holy and passionate outgush of her heart, when the pure fountain had been unsealed from its depths and made visible in its transparency to his mental eye; recollections which, had Giovanni known how to estimate them, would have assured him that all this ugly mystery was but an earthly illusion, and that, whatever mist of evil might seem to have gathered over her, the real Beatrice was a heavenly angel. Incapable as he was of such high faith, still her presence had not utterly lost its magic. Giovanni's rage was quelled into an aspect of sullen insensibility. Beatrice, with a quick spiritual sense, immediately felt that there was a gulf of blackness between them which neither he nor she could pass. They walked on together, sad and silent, and came thus to the marble fountain and to its pool of water on the ground, in the midst of which grew the shrub that bore gemlike blossoms. Giovanni was affrighted at the eager enjoyment—the appetite, as it were—with which he found himself inhaling the fragrance of the flowers.

"Beatrice," asked he, abruptly, "whence came this shrub?"

"My father created it," answered she, with simplicity.

"Created it! created it!" repeated Giovanni. "What mean you, Beatrice?"

"He is a man fearfully acquainted with the secrets of nature," replied Beatrice; "and, at the hour when I first drew breath, this plant sprang from the soil, the offspring of his science, of his intellect, while I was but his earthly child. Approach it not!" continued she, observing with terror that Giovanni was drawing nearer to the shrub. "It has qualities that you little dream of. But I, dearest Giovanni,—I grew up and blossomed with the plant and was nourished with its breath. It was my sister, and I loved it with a human affection, for, alas!—hast thou not suspected it?—there was an awful doom."

Here Giovanni frowned so darkly upon her that Beatrice paused and trembled. But her faith in his tenderness reassured her, and made her blush that she had doubted for an instant.

"There was an awful doom," she continued, "the effect of my father's fatal love of science, which estranged me from all society of my kind. Until Heaven sent thee, dearest Giovanni, O, how lonely was thy poor Beatrice!"

"Was it a hard doom?" asked Giovanni, fixing his eyes upon her.

"Only of late have I known how hard it was,"

answered she, tenderly. "Oh, yes; but my heart was torpid, and therefore quiet."

Giovanni's rage broke forth from his sullen gloom like a lightning flash out of a dark cloud.

"Accursed one!" cried he, with venomous scorn and anger. "And, finding thy solitude wearisome, thou hast severed me likewise from all the warmth of life and enticed me into thy region of unspeakable horror!"

"Giovanni!" exclaimed Beatrice, turning her large bright eyes upon his face. The force of his words had not found its way into her mind; she was merely thunderstruck.

"Yes, poisonous thing!" repeated Giovanni, beside himself with passion. "Thou hast done it! Thou hast blasted me! Thou hast filled my veins with poison! Thou hast made me as hateful, as ugly, as loathsome and deadly a creature as thyself,—a world's wonder of hideous monstrosity! Now, if our breath be happily as fatal to ourselves as to all others, let us join our lips in one kiss of unutterable hatred, and so die!"

"What has befallen me?" murmured Beatrice, with a low moan out of her heart. "Holy Virgin, pity me, a poor heart-broken child!"

"Thou,—dost thou pray?" cried Giovanni, still with the same fiendish scorn. "Thy very prayers, as they come from thy lips, taint the atmosphere with death. Yes, yes; let us pray! Let us to church and dip our fingers in the holy water at the portal! They that come after us will perish as by a pestilence! Let us sign crosses in the air! It will be scattering curses abroad in the likeness of holy symbols!"

"Giovanni," said Beatrice, calmly, for her grief was beyond passion, "why dost thou join thyself with me thus in those terrible words? I, it is true, am the horrible thing thou namest me. But thou,—what hast thou to do, save with one other shudder at my hideous misery to go forth out of the garden and mingle with thy race, and forget that there ever crawled on earth such a monster as poor Beatrice?"

"Dost thou pretend ignorance?" asked Giovanni, scowling upon her. "Behold! this power have I gained from the pure daughter of Rappaccini."

There was a swarm of summer insects flitting through the air in search of the food promised by the flower-odors of the fatal garden. They circled round Giovanni's head, and were evidently attracted towards him by the same influence which had drawn them for an instant within the sphere of several of the shrubs. He sent forth a breath among them, and smiled bitterly at Beatrice as at least a score of the insects fell dead upon the ground.

"I see it! I see it!" shrieked Beatrice. "It is my father's fatal science! No, no, Giovanni; it was not I! Never! never! I dreamed only to love thee and be with thee a little time, and so to let thee pass away, leaving but thine image in mine heart; for, Giovanni, believe it, though my body be nourished with poison, my spirit is God's creature, and craves love as its daily food. But my father,—he has united us in this fearful sympathy. Yes; spurn me, tread upon me, kill me! Oh, what is death after such words as thine? But it was not I. Not for a world of bliss would I have done it."

Giovanni's passion had exhausted itself in its outburst from his lips. There now came across him a sense, mournful, and not without tenderness, of the intimate and peculiar relationship between Beatrice and himself. They stood, as it were, in an utter solitude, which would be made none the less solitary by the densest throng of human life. Ought not, then, the desert of humanity around them to press this insulated pair closer together? If they should be cruel to one another, who was there to be kind to them? Besides, thought Giovanni, might there not still be a hope of his returning within the limits of ordinary nature, and leading Beatrice, the redeemed Beatrice, by the hand? O weak and selfish and unworthy spirit, that could dream of an earthly union and earthly happiness as possible, after such deep love had been so bitterly wronged as was Beatrice's love by Giovanni's blighting words! No, no; there could be no such hope. She must pass heavily, with that broken heart, across the borders of Time; she must bathe her hurts in some fount of paradise, and forget her grief in the light of immortality, and *there* be well.

But Giovanni did not know it.

"Dear Beatrice," said he, approaching her, while she shrank away as always at his approach, but now with a different impulse,—"dearest Beatrice, our fate is not yet so desperate. Behold! there is a medicine, potent, as a wise physician has assured me, and almost divine in its efficacy. It is composed of ingredients the most opposite to those by which thy awful father has brought this calamity upon thee and me. It is distilled of blessed herbs. Shall we not quaff it together, and thus be purified from evil?"

"Give it me!" said Beatrice, extending her hand to receive the little silver vial which Giovanni took from his bosom. She added, with a peculiar emphasis, "I will drink; but do thou await the result."

She put Baglioni's antidote to her lips; and, at the same moment, the figure of Rappaccini emerged from the portal and came slowly towards the marble fountain. As he drew near, the pale man of science seemed to gaze with a triumphant expression at the beautiful youth and maiden, as might an artist who should spend his life in achieving a picture or a group of statuary and finally be satisfied with his success. He paused; his bent form grew erect with conscious power; he spread out his hands over them in the attitude of a father imploring a blessing upon his children; but those were the same hands that had thrown poison into the stream of their lives. Giovanni trembled. Beatrice shuddered nervously, and pressed her hand upon her heart.

"My daughter," said Rappaccini, "thou art no longer lonely in the world. Pluck one of those precious gems from thy sister shrub and bid thy bridegroom wear it in his bosom. It will not harm him now. My science and the sympathy between thee and him have so wrought within his system that he now stands apart from common men, as thou dost, daughter of my pride and triumph, from ordinary women. Pass on, then, through the world, most dear to one another and dreadful to all besides!"

"My father," said Beatrice, feebly,—and still as she spoke she kept her hand upon her heart,—"wherefore didst thou inflict this miserable doom upon thy child?"

"Miserable!" exclaimed Rappaccini. "What mean you, foolish girl? Dost thou deem it misery to be endowed with marvellous gifts against which no power nor strength could avail an enemy,—misery, to be able to quell the mightiest with a breath,—misery, to be as terrible as thou art beautiful? Wouldst thou, then, have preferred the condition of a weak woman, exposed to all evil and capable of none?"

"I would fain have been loved, not feared," murmured Beatrice, sinking down upon the ground. "But now it matters not. I am going, father, where the evil which thou hast striven to mingle with my being will pass away like a dream,—like the fragrance of these poisonous flowers, which will no longer taint my breath among the flowers of Eden. Farewell, Giovanni! Thy words of hatred are like lead within my heart; but they, too, will fall away as I ascend. O, was there not, from the first, more poison in thy nature than in mine?"

To Beatrice,—so radically had her earthly part been wrought upon by Rappaccini's skill,—as poison had been life, so the powerful antidote was death; and thus the poor victim of man's ingenuity and of thwarted nature, and of the fatality that attends all such efforts of perverted wisdom, perished there, at the feet of her father and Giovanni. Just at that moment Professor Pietro Baglioni looked forth from the window, and called loudly, in a tone of triumph mixed with horror, to the thunder-stricken man of science,—

"Rappaccini! Rappaccini! and is *this* the upshot of your experiment?"

The Cask of Amontillado

by Edgar Allan Poe

The thousand injuries of Fortunato I had borne as I best could; but when he ventured upon insult, I vowed revenge. You, who so well know the nature of my soul, will not suppose, however, that I gave utterance to a threat. *At length* I would be avenged; this was a point definitively settled—but the very definitiveness with which it was resolved, precluded the idea of risk. I must not only punish, but punish with impunity. A wrong is unredressed when retribution overtakes its redresser. It is equally unredressed when the avenger fails to make himself felt as such to him who has done the wrong.

It must be understood, that neither by word nor deed had I given Fortunato cause to doubt my good-will. I continued, as was my wont, to smile in his face, and he did not perceive that my smile *now* was at the thought of his immolation.

He had a weak point—this Fortunato—although in other regards he was a man to be respected and even feared. He prided himself on his connoisseurship in wine. Few Italians have the true virtuoso spirit. For the most part their enthusiasm is adopted to suit the time and opportunity—to practise imposture upon the British and Austrian *millionaires.* In painting and gemmary, Fortunato, like his countrymen, was a quack—but in the matter of old wines he was sincere. In this respect I did not differ from him materially: I was skilful in the Italian vintages myself, and bought largely whenever I could.

It was about dusk, one evening during the supreme madness of the carnival season, that I encountered my friend. He accosted me with excessive warmth, for he had been drinking much. The man wore motley. He had on a tight-fitting parti-striped dress, and his head was surmounted by the conical cap and bells. I was so pleased to see him, that I thought I should never have done wringing his hand.

I said to him: "My dear Fortunato, you are luckily met. How remarkably well you are looking today! But I have received a pipe of what passes for Amontillado, and I have my doubts."

"How?" said he. "Amontillado? A pipe? Impossible! And in the middle of the carnival!"

"I have my doubts," I replied; "and I was silly enough to pay the full Amontillado price without consulting you in the matter. You were not to be found, and I was fearful of losing a bargain."

"Amontillado!"

"I have my doubts."

"Amontillado!"

"And I must satisfy them."

"Amontillado!"

"As you are engaged, I am on my way to Luchesi. If any one has a critical turn, it is he. He will tell me—"

"Luchesi cannot tell Amontillado from Sherry."

"And yet some fools will have it that his taste is a match for your own."

"Come, let us go."

"Whither?"

"To your vaults."

"My friend, no; I will not impose upon your good nature. I perceive you have an engagement. Luchesi—"

"I have no engagement;—come."

"My friend, no. It is not the engagement, but the severe cold with which I perceive you are afflicted. The vaults are insufferably damp. They are encrusted with nitre."

"Let us go, nevertheless. The cold is merely nothing. Amontillado! You have been imposed upon. And as for Luchesi, he cannot distinguish Sherry from Amontillado."

Thus speaking, Fortunato possessed himself

of my arm. Putting on a mask of black silk, and drawing a *roquelaire* closely about my person, I suffered him to hurry me to my palazzo.

There were no attendants at home; they had absconded to make merry in honor of the time. I had told them that I should not return until the morning, and had given them explicit orders not to stir from the house. These orders were sufficient, I well knew, to insure their immediate disappearance, one and all, as soon as my back was turned.

I took from their sconces two flambeaux, and giving one to Fortunato, bowed him through several suites of rooms to the archway that led into the vaults. I passed down a long and winding staircase, requesting him to be cautious as he followed. We came at length to the foot of the descent and stood together on the damp ground of the catacombs of the Montresors.

The gait of my friend was unsteady, and the bells upon his cap jingled as he strode.

"The pipe?" said he.

"It is farther on," said I; "but observe the white web-work which gleams from these cavern walls."

He turned towards me, and looked into my eyes with two filmy orbs that distilled the rheum of intoxication.

"Nitre?" he asked, at length.

"Nitre," I replied. "How long have you had that cough?"

"Ugh! ugh! ugh!—ugh! ugh! ugh!—ugh! ugh! ugh!—ugh! ugh! ugh!—ugh! ugh! ugh!"

My poor friend found it impossible to reply for many minutes.

"It is nothing," he said, at last.

"Come," I said, with decision, "we will go back; your health is precious. You are rich, respected, admired, beloved; you are happy, as once I was. You are a man to be missed. For me it is no matter. We will go back; you will be ill, and I cannot be responsible. Besides, there is Luchesi—"

"Enough," he said; "the cough is a mere nothing; it will not kill me. I shall not die of a cough."

"True—true," I replied; "and, indeed, I had no intention of alarming you unnecessarily; but you should use all proper caution. A draught of this Medoc will defend us from the damps."

Here I knocked off the neck of a bottle which I drew from a long row of its fellows that lay upon the mould.

"Drink," I said, presenting him the wine.

He raised it to his lips with a leer. He paused and nodded to me familiarly, while his bells jingled.

"I drink," he said, "to the buried that repose around us."

"And I to your long life."

He again took my arm, and we proceeded.

"These vaults," he said, "are extensive."

"The Montresors," I replied, "were a great and numerous family."

"I forget your arms."

"A huge human foot d'or, in a field azure; the foot crushes a serpent rampant whose fangs are imbedded in the heel."

"And the motto?"

"Nemo me impune lacessit."

"Good!" he said.

The wine sparkled in his eyes and the bells jingled. My own fancy grew warm with the Medoc. We had passed through walls of piled bones, with casks and puncheons intermingling, into the inmost recesses of the catacombs. I paused again, and this time I made bold to seize Fortunato by an arm above the elbow.

"The nitre!" I said; "see, it increases. It hangs like moss upon the vaults. We are below the river's bed. The drops of moisture trickle among the bones. Come, we will go back ere it is too late. Your cough—"

"It is nothing," he said; "let us go on. But first, another draught of the Medoc."

I broke and reached him a flagon of De Grâve. He emptied it at a breath. His eyes flashed with a fierce light. He laughed and threw the bottle upward with a gesticulation I did not understand.

I looked at him in surprise. He repeated the movement—a grotesque one.

"You do not comprehend?" he said.

"Not I," I replied.

"Then you are not of the brotherhood."

"How?"

"You are not of the masons."

"Yes, yes," I said, "yes, yes."

"You? Impossible! A mason?"

"A mason," I replied.

"A sign," he said.

"It is this," I answered, producing a trowel from beneath the folds of my *roquelaire.*

"You jest," he exclaimed, recoiling a few paces. "But let us proceed to the Amontillado."

"Be it so," I said, replacing the tool beneath the cloak, and again offering him my arm. He leaned upon it heavily. We continued our route in search of the Amontillado. We passed through a range of low arches, descended, passed on, and descending again, arrived at a deep crypt, in which the foulness of the air caused our flambeaux rather to glow than flame.

At the most remote end of the crypt there appeared another less spacious. Its walls had been lined with human remains, piled to the vault overhead, in the fashion of the great catacombs of Paris. Three sides of this interior crypt were still ornamented in this manner. From the fourth the bones had been thrown down, and lay promiscuously upon the earth, forming at one point a mound of some size. Within the wall thus exposed by the displacing of the bones, we perceived a still interior recess, in depth about four feet, in width three, in height six or seven. It seemed to have been constructed for no especial use in itself, but formed merely the interval between two of the colossal supports of the roof of the catacombs, and was backed by one of their circumscribing walls of solid granite.

It was in vain that Fortunato, uplifting his dull torch, endeavored to pry into the depths of the recess. Its termination the feeble light did not enable us to see.

"Proceed," I said; "herein is the Amontillado. As for Luchesi—"

"He is an ignoramus," interrupted my friend, as he stepped unsteadily forward, while I followed immediately at his heels. In an instant he had reached the extremity of the niche, and finding his progress arrested by the rock, stood stupidly bewildered. A moment more and I had fettered him to the granite. In its surface were two iron staples, distant from each other about two feet, horizontally. From one of these depended a short chain, from the other a padlock. Throwing the links about his waist, it was but the work of a few seconds to secure it. He was too much astounded to resist. Withdrawing the key I stepped back from the recess.

"Pass your hand," I said, "over the wall; you cannot help feeling the nitre. Indeed it is very damp. Once more let me *implore* you to return. No? Then I must positively leave you. But I must first render you all the little attentions in my power."

"The Amontillado!" ejaculated my friend, not yet recovered from his astonishment.

"True," I replied; "the Amontillado."

As I said these words I busied myself among the pile of bones of which I have before spoken. Throwing them aside, I soon uncovered a quantity of building stone and mortar. With these materials and with the aid of my trowel, I began vigorously to wall up the entrance of the niche.

I had scarcely laid the first tier of the masonry when I discovered that the intoxication of Fortunato had in a great measure worn off. The earliest indication I had of this was a low moaning cry from the depth of the recess. It was *not* the cry of a drunken man. There was then a long and obstinate silence. I laid the second tier, and the third, and the fourth; and then I heard the furious vibrations of the chain. The noise lasted for several minutes, during which, that I might hearken to it with the more satisfaction, I ceased my labors and sat down upon the bones. When at last the clanking subsided, I resumed the trowel, and finished without interruption the fifth, the sixth, and the seventh tier. The wall was now nearly upon a level with my breast. I again paused, and holding the flambeaux over the mason-work, threw a few feeble rays upon the figure within.

A succession of loud and shrill screams, bursting suddenly from the throat of the chained form, seemed to thrust me violently back. For a brief moment I hesitated—I trembled. Unsheathing my rapier, I began to grope with it about the recess: but the thought of an instant reassured me. I placed my hand upon the solid fabric of the catacombs, and felt satisfied. I reapproached the wall. I replied to the yells of him who clamored. I re-echoed—I aided—I surpassed them in volume and in strength. I did this, and the clamorer grew still.

It was now midnight, and my task was drawing to a close. I had completed the eighth, the ninth, and the tenth tier. I had finished a portion of the last and the eleventh; there remained but a single stone to be fitted and plastered in. I struggled with its weight; I placed it partially in its destined position. But now there came from out the niche a low laugh that erected the hairs upon my head. It was succeeded by a sad voice, which I had difficulty in recognizing as that of the noble Fortunato. The voice said—

"Ha! ha! ha!—he! he!—a very good joke indeed—an excellent jest. We will have many a rich laugh about it at the palazzo—he! he! he!—over our wine—he! he! he!"

"The Amontillado!" I said.

"He! he! he!—he! he! he!—yes, the Amontillado. But is it not getting late? Will not they be awaiting us at the palazzo, the Lady Fortunato and the rest? Let us be gone."

"Yes," I said, "let us be gone."

"For the love of God, Montresor!"

"Yes," I said, "for the love of God!"

But to these words I hearkened in vain for a reply. I grew impatient. I called aloud—

"Fortunato!"

No answer. I called again—

"Fortunato!"

No answer still. I thrust a torch through the remaining aperture and let it fall within. There came forth in return only a jingling of the bells. My heart grew sick—on account of the dampness of the catacombs. I hastened to make an end of my labor. I forced the last stone into its position; I plastered it up. Against the new masonry I re-erected the old rampart of bones. For the half of a century no mortal has disturbed them. *In pace requiescat!*

Bartleby

by Herman Melville

I am a rather elderly man. The nature of my avocations, for the last thirty years, has brought me into more than ordinary contact with what would seem an interesting and somewhat singular set of men, of whom, as yet, nothing that I know of has ever been written—I mean the law-copyists, or scriveners. I have known very many of them, professionally and privately, and, if I pleased, could relate divers histories at which good-natured gentlemen might smile and sentimental souls might weep. But I waive the biographies of all other scriveners for a few passages in the life of Bartleby, who was a scrivener, the strangest I ever saw or heard of. While of other law-copyists I might write the complete life, of Bartleby nothing of that sort can be done. I believe that no materials exist for a full and satisfactory biography of this man. It is an irreparable loss to literature. Bartleby was one of those beings of whom nothing is ascertainable except from the original sources, and, in his case, those are very small. What my own astonished eyes saw of Bartleby, *that* is all I know of him, except, indeed, one vague report, which will appear in the sequel.

Ere introducing the scrivener as he first appeared to me, it is fit I make some mention of myself, my employees, my business, my chambers and general surroundings, because some such description is indispensable to an adequate understanding of the chief character about to be presented. *Imprimis:* I am a man who, from his youth upwards, has been filled with a profound conviction that the easiest way of life is the best. Hence, though I belong to a profession proverbially energetic and nervous even to turbulence at times, yet nothing of that sort have I ever suffered to invade my peace. I am one of those unambitious lawyers who never addresses a jury or in any way draws down public applause, but, in the cool tranquillity of a snug retreat, do a snug business among rich men's bonds, and mortgages, and title deeds. All who know me consider me an eminently *safe* man. The late John Jacob Astor, a personage little given to poetic enthusiasm, had no hesitation in pronouncing my first grand point to be prudence, my next, method. I do not speak it in vanity, but simply record the fact that I was not unemployed in my profession by the late John Jacob Astor, a name which, I admit, I love to repeat, for it hath a rounded and orbicular sound to it, and rings like unto bullion. I will freely add that I was not insensible to the late John Jacob Astor's good opinion.

Some time prior to the period at which this little history begins my avocations had been largely increased. The good old office, now extinct in the State of New York, of a Master in Chancery, had been conferred upon me. It was not a very arduous office, but very pleasantly remunerative. I seldom lose my temper, much more seldom indulge in dangerous indignation at wrongs and outrages, but, I must be permitted to be rash here, and declare that I consider the sudden and violent abrogation of the office of Master in Chancery, by the new Constitution, as a——premature act, inasmuch as I had counted upon a life lease of the profits, whereas I only received those of a few short years. But this is by the way.

My chambers were upstairs at No.—Wall Street. At one end they looked upon the white wall of the interior of a spacious skylight shaft, penetrating the building from top to bottom.

This view might have been considered rather tame than otherwise, deficient in what landscape painters call "life." But, if so, the view from the other end of my chambers offered at least a contrast, if nothing more. In that direction, my windows commanded an unobstructed view of a lofty brick wall, black by age and everlasting shade, which wall required no spyglass to bring out its lurking beauties, but, for the benefit of all nearsighted spectators, was pushed up to within ten feet of my windowpanes. Owing to the great height of the surrounding buildings, and my chambers' being on the second floor, the interval between this wall and mine not a little resembled a huge square cistern.

At the period just preceding the advent of Bartleby, I had two persons as copyists in my employment, and a promising lad as an office boy. First, Turkey; second, Nippers; third, Ginger Nut. These may seem names the like of which are not usually found in the Directory. In truth, they were nicknames, mutually conferred upon each other by my three clerks, and were deemed expressive of their respective persons or characters. Turkey was a short, pursy Englishman, of about my own age—that is, somewhere not far from sixty. In the morning, one might say, his face was of a fine florid hue, but after twelve o'clock, meridian—his dinner hour—it blazed like a grate full of Christmas coals; and continued blazing—but, as it were, with a gradual wane—till six o'clock P.M., or thereabouts; after which I saw no more of the proprietor of the face, which, gaining its meridian with the sun, seemed to set with it, to rise, culminate, and decline the following day, with the like regularity and undiminished glory. There are many singular coincidences I have known in the course of my life, not the least among which was the fact, that, exactly when Turkey displayed his fullest beams from his red and radiant countenance, just then, too, at that critical moment, began the daily period when I considered his business capacities as seriously disturbed for the remainder of the twenty-four hours. Not that he was absolutely idle or averse to business then; far from it. The difficulty was, he was apt to be altogether too energetic. There was a strange, inflamed, flurried, flighty recklessness of activity about him. He would be incautious in dipping his pen into his inkstand. All his blots upon my documents were dropped there after twelve o'clock, meridian. Indeed, not only would he be reckless and sadly given to making blots in the afternoon, but some days he went further and was rather noisy. At such times, too, his face flamed with augmented blazonry, as if cannel coal had been heaped on anthracite. He made an unpleasant racket with his chair; spilled his sandbox; in mending his pens, impatiently split them all to pieces and threw them on the floor in a sudden passion; stood up and leaned over his table, boxing his papers about in a most indecorous manner, very sad to behold in an elderly man like him. Nevertheless, as he was in many ways a most valuable person to me, and all the time before twelve o'clock, meridian, was the quickest, steadiest creature, too, accomplishing a great deal of work in a style not easily to be matched—for these reasons I was willing to overlook his eccentricities, though indeed, occasionally, I remonstrated with him. I did this very gently, however, because, though the civilest, nay, the blandest and most reverential of men in the morning, yet, in the afternoon he was disposed, upon provocation, to be slightly rash with his tongue—in fact, insolent. Now, valuing his morning services as I did, and resolved not to lose them—yet, at the same time, made uncomfortable by his inflamed ways after twelve o'clock—and being a man of peace, unwilling by my admonitions to call forth unseemly retorts from him, I took upon me one Saturday noon (he was always worse on Saturdays) to hint to him, very kindly, that perhaps, now that he was growing old, it might be well to abridge his labors; in short, he need not come to my chambers after twelve o'clock, but, dinner over, had best go home to his lodgings, and rest himself till teatime. But no; he insisted upon his afternoon devotions. His countenance became intolerably fervid, as he oratorically assured me—gesticulating with a long ruler at the other end of the room—that if his services in the morning were useful, how indispensable, then, in the afternoon?

"With submission, sir," said Turkey, on this occasion, "I consider myself your right-hand man. In the morning I but marshal and deploy my columns, but in the afternoon I put myself at their head, and gallantly charge the foe, thus"—and he made a violent thrust with the ruler.

"But the blots, Turkey," intimated I.

"True; but, with submission, sir, behold these hairs! I am getting old. Surely, sir, a blot or two of a warm afternoon is not to be severely urged against gray hairs. Old age—even if it blot the page—is honorable. With submission, sir, we *both* are getting old."

This appeal to my fellow feeling was hardly to be resisted. At all events, I saw that go he would not. So, I made up my mind to let him stay, resolving, nevertheless, to see to it that, during the afternoon, he had to do with my less important papers.

Nippers, the second on my list, was a whiskered, sallow, and upon the whole rather piratical-looking young man of about five and twenty. I always deemed him the victim of two evil powers—ambition and indigestion. The ambition was evinced by a certain impatience of the duties of a mere copyist, an unwarrantable usurpation of strictly professional affairs, such as the original drawing up of legal documents.

The indigestion seemed betokened in an occasional nervous testiness and grinning irritability, causing the teeth to audibly grind together over mistakes committed in copying; unnecessary maledictions, hissed rather than spoken, in the heat of business; and especially by a continual discontent with the height of the table where he worked. Though of a very ingenious, mechanical turn, Nippers could never get this table to suit him. He put chips under it, blocks of various sorts, bits of pasteboard, and at last went so far as to attempt an exquisite adjustment by final pieces of folded blotting paper. But no invention would answer. If, for the sake of easing his back, he brought the table lid at a sharp angle well up towards his chin, and wrote there like a man using the steep roof of a Dutch house for his desk, then he declared that it stopped the circulation in his arms. If now he lowered the table to his waistbands and stooped over it in writing, then there was a sore aching in his back. In short, the truth of the matter was Nippers knew not what he wanted. Or, if he wanted anything, it was to be rid of a scrivener's table altogether. Among the manifestations of his diseased ambition was a fondness he had for receiving visits from certain ambiguous-looking fellows in seedy coats, whom he called his clients. Indeed, I was aware that not only was he, at times, considerable of a ward politician, but he occasionally did a little business at the Justices' courts, and was not unknown on the steps of the Tombs. I have good reason to believe, however, that one individual who called upon him at my chambers, and who, with a grand air, he insisted was his client, was no other than a dun, and the alleged title deed, a bill. But, with all his failings, and the annoyances he caused me, Nippers, like his compatriot Turkey, was a very useful man to me; wrote a neat, swift hand; and, when he chose, was not deficient in a gentlemanly sort of deportment. Added to this, he always dressed in a gentlemanly sort of way; and so, incidentally, reflected credit upon my chambers. Whereas, with respect to Turkey, I had much ado to keep him from being a reproach to me. His clothes were apt to look oily, and smell of eating-houses. He wore his pantaloons very loose and baggy in summer. His coats were execrable, his hat not to be handled. But while the hat was a thing of indifference to me, inasmuch as his natural civility and deference, as a dependent Englishman, always led him to doff it the moment he entered the room, yet his coat was another matter. Concerning his coats, I reasoned with him, but with no effect. The truth was, I suppose, that a man with so small an income could not afford to sport such a lustrous face and a lustrous coat at one and the same time. As Nippers once observed,

Turkey's money went chiefly for red ink. One winter day, I presented Turkey with a highly respectable-looking coat of my own—a padded gray coat of a most comfortable warmth, and which buttoned straight up from the knee to the neck. I thought Turkey would appreciate the favor and abate his rashness and obstreperousness of afternoons. But no; I verily believe that buttoning himself up in so downy and blanket-like a coat had a pernicious effect upon him—upon the same principle that too much oats are bad for horses. In fact, precisely as a rash, restive horse is said to feel his oats, so Turkey felt his coat. It made him insolent. He was a man whom prosperity harmed.

Though, concerning the self-indulgent habits of Turkey, I had my own private surmises, yet, touching Nippers, I was well persuaded that, whatever might be his faults in other respects, he was, at least, a temperate young man. But indeed, nature herself seemed to have been his vintner, and, at his birth, charged him so thoroughly with an irritable, brandy-like disposition that all subsequent potations were needless. When I consider how, amid the stillness of my chambers, Nippers would sometimes impatiently rise from his seat, and, stooping over his table, spread his arms wide apart, seize the whole desk, and move it, and jerk it, with a grim, grinding motion on the floor, as if the table were a perverse voluntary agent, intent on thwarting and vexing him, I plainly perceive that, for Nippers, brandy-and-water were altogether superfluous.

It was fortunate for me that, owing to its peculiar cause—indigestion—the irritability and consequent nervousness of Nippers were mainly observable in the morning, while in the afternoon he was comparatively mild. So that, Turkey's paroxysms only coming on about twelve o'clock, I never had to do with their eccentricities at one time. Their fits relieved each other, like guards. When Nipper's was on, Turkey's was off; and vice versa. This was a good natural arrangement, under the circumstances.

Ginger Nut, the third on my list, was a lad some twelve years old. His father was a carman, ambitious of seeing his son on the bench instead of a cart before he died. So he sent him to my office, as student at law, errand boy, cleaner and sweeper, at the rate of one dollar a week. He had a little desk to himself, but he did not use it much. Upon inspection, the drawer exhibited a great array of the shells of various sorts of nuts. Indeed, to this quick-witted youth, the whole noble science of the law was contained in a nutshell. Not the least among the employments of Ginger Nut, as well as one which he discharged with the most alacrity, was his duty as cake and apple purveyor for Turkey and Nippers. Copying law papers being proverbially a dry, husky sort of business, my two scriveners were fain to moisten their mouths very often with Spitzenbergs, to be had at the numerous stalls nigh the Custom House and Post Office. Also, they sent Ginger Nut very frequently for that peculiar cake—small, flat, round, and very spicy—after which he had been named by them. Of a cold morning, when business was but dull, Turkey would gobble up scores of these cakes, as if they were mere wafers—indeed, they sell them at the rate of six or eight for a penny—the scrape of his pen blending with the crunching of the crisp particles in his mouth. Of all the fiery afternoon blunders and flurried rashnesses of Turkey was his once moistening a ginger cake between his lips, and clapping it on to a mortgage for a seal. I came within an ace of dismissing him then. But he mollified me by making an Oriental bow, and saying:

"With submission, sir, it was generous of me to find you in stationery on my own account."

Now my original business—that of a conveyancer and title hunter, and drawer-up of recondite documents of all sorts—was considerably increased by receiving the Master's office. There was now great work for scriveners. Not only must I push the clerks already with me, but I must have additional help.

In answer to my advertisement, a motionless young man one morning stood upon my office threshold, the door being open, for it was summer. I can see that figure now—pallidly neat, pitiably respectable, incurably forlorn! It was Bartleby.

After a few words touching his qualifications, I engaged him, glad to have among my corps of copyists a man of so singularly sedate an aspect, which I thought might operate beneficially upon the flighty temper of Turkey and the fiery one of Nippers.

I should have stated before that ground-glass folding doors divided my premises into two parts, one of which was occupied by my scriveners, the other by myself. According to my humor, I threw open these doors or closed them. I resolved to assign Bartleby a corner by the folding doors, but on my side of them, so as to have this quiet man within easy call, in case any trifling thing was to be done. I placed his desk close up to a small side window in that part of the room, a window which originally had afforded a lateral view of certain grimy back yards and bricks, but which, owing to subsequent erections, commanded at present no view at all, though it gave some light. Within three feet of the panes was a wall, and the light came down from far above, between two lofty buildings, as from a very small opening in a dome. Still further to a satisfactory arrangement, I procured a high green folding screen, which might entirely isolate Bartleby from my sight, though not remove him from my voice. And thus, in a manner, privacy and society were conjoined.

At first, Bartleby did an extraordinary quantity of writing. As if long famishing for something to copy, he seemed to gorge himself on my documents. There was no pause for digestion. He ran a day and night line, copying by sunlight and by candlelight. I should have been quite delighted with his application, had he been cheerfully industrious. But he wrote on silently, palely, mechanically.

It is, of course, an indispensable part of a scrivener's business to verify the accuracy of his copy, word by word. Where there are two or more scriveners in an office, they assist each other in this examination, one reading from the copy, the other holding the original. It is a very dull, wearisome, and lethargic affair. I can readily imagine that, to some sanguine temperaments, it would be altogether intolerable. For example, I cannot credit that the mettlesome poet, Byron, would have contentedly sat down with Bartleby to examine a law document of, say five hundred pages, closely written in a crimpy hand.

Now and then, in the haste of business, it had

been my habit to assist in comparing some brief document myself, calling Turkey or Nippers for this purpose. One object I had in placing Bartleby so handy to me behind the screen was to avail myself of his services on such trivial occasions. It was on the third day, I think, of his being with me, and before any necessity had arisen for having his own writing examined, that, being much hurried to complete a small affair I had in hand, I abruptly called to Bartleby. In my haste and natural expectancy of instant compliance, I sat with my head bent over the original on my desk, and my right hand sideways, and somewhat nervously extended with the copy, so that, immediately upon emerging from his retreat, Bartleby might snatch it and proceed to business without the least delay.

In this very attitude did I sit when I called to him, rapidly stating what it was I wanted him to do—namely, to examine a small paper with me. Imagine my surprise, nay, my consternation, when, without moving from his privacy, Bartleby, in a singularly mild, firm voice, replied, "I would prefer not to."

I sat awhile in perfect silence, rallying my stunned faculties. Immediately it occurred to me that my ears had deceived me, or Bartleby had entirely misunderstood my meaning. I repeated my request in the clearest tone I could assume;

but in quite as clear a one came the previous reply, "I would prefer not to."

"Prefer not to," echoed I, rising in high excitement, and crossing the room with a stride. "What do you mean? Are you moon-struck? I want you to help me compare this sheet here—take it," and I thrust it towards him.

"I would prefer not to," said he.

I looked at him steadfastly. His face was leanly composed; his gray eyes dimly calm. Not a wrinkle of agitation rippled him. Had there been the least uneasiness, anger, impatience or impertinence in his manner; in other words, had there been anything ordinarily human about him, doubtless I should have violently dismissed him from the premises. But as it was I should have as soon thought of turning my pale plaster-of-paris bust of Cicero out of doors. I stood gazing at him awhile, as he went on with his own writing, and then reseated myself at my desk. This is very strange, thought I. What had one best do? But my business hurried me. I concluded to forget the matter for the present, reserving it for my future leisure. So calling Nippers from the other room, the paper was speedily examined.

A few days after this, Bartleby concluded four lengthy documents, being quadruplicates of a week's testimony taken before me in my High Court of Chancery. It became necessary to examine them. It was an important suit, and great accuracy was imperative. Having all things arranged, I called Turkey, Nippers, and Ginger Nut from the next room, meaning to place the four copies in the hands of my four clerks, while I should read from the original. Accordingly, Turkey, Nippers, and Ginger Nut had taken their seats in a row, each with his document in his hand, when I called to Bartleby to join this interesting group.

"Bartleby! quick, I am waiting."

I heard a slow scrape of his chair legs on the uncarpeted floor, and soon he appeared standing at the entrance of his hermitage.

"What is wanted?" said he, mildly.

"The copies, the copies," said I, hurriedly. "We are going to examine them. There—" and I held towards him the fourth quadruplicate.

"I would prefer not to," he said, and gently disappeared behind the screen.

For a few moments I was turned into a pillar of salt, standing at the head of my seated column of clerks. Recovering myself, I advanced towards the screen and demanded the reason for such extraordinary conduct.

"*Why* do you refuse?"

"I would prefer not to."

With any other man I should have flown outright into a dreadful passion, scorned all further words, and thrust him ignominiously from my presence. But there was something about Bartleby that not only strangely disarmed me, but, in a wonderful manner, touched and disconcerted me. I began to reason with him.

"These are your own copies we are about to examine. It is labor saving to you, because one examination will answer for your four papers. It is common usage. Every copyist is bound to help examine his copy. Is it not so? Will you not speak? Answer!"

"I prefer not to," he replied in a flutelike tone. It seemed to me that, while I had been addressing him, he carefully revolved every statement that I made; fully comprehended the meaning; could not gainsay the irresistible conclusion; but, at the same time, some paramount consideration prevailed with him to reply as he did.

"You are decided, then, not to comply with my request—a request made according to common usage and common sense?"

He briefly gave me to understand that on that point my judgment was sound. Yes: his decision was irreversible.

It is not seldom the case that, when a man is browbeaten in some unprecedented and violently unreasonable way, he begins to stagger in his own plainest faith. He begins, as it were, vaguely to surmise that, wonderful as it may be, all the justice and all the reason is on the other side. Accordingly, if any disinterested persons are present, he turns to them for some reinforcement for his own faltering mind.

"Turkey," said I, "what do you think of this? Am I not right?"

"With submission, sir," said Turkey, in his blandest tone, "I think that you are."

"Nippers," said I, "what do *you* think of it?"

"I think I should kick him out of the office."

(The reader of nice perceptions will here perceive that, it being morning, Turkey's answer is couched in polite and tranquil terms, but Nippers replies in ill-tempered ones. Or, to repeat a previous sentence, Nippers's ugly mood was on duty, and Turkey's off.)

"Ginger Nut," said I, willing to enlist the smallest suffrage in my behalf, "what do *you* think of it?"

"I think, sir, he's a little *luny,*" replied Ginger Nut, with a grin.

"You hear what they say," said I, turning towards the screen, "come forth and do your duty."

But he vouchsafed no reply. I pondered a moment in sore perplexity. But once more business hurried me. I determined again to postpone the consideration of this dilemma to my future leisure. With a little trouble we made out to examine the papers without Bartleby, though at every page or two Turkey deferentially dropped his opinion that this proceeding was quite out of the common; while Nippers, twitching in his chair with a dyspeptic nervousness, ground out between his set teeth occasional hissing maledictions against the stubborn oaf behind the screen. And for his (Nippers's) part, this was the first and the last time he would do another man's business without pay.

Meanwhile Bartleby sat in his hermitage, oblivious to everything but his own peculiar business there.

Some days passed, the scrivener being employed upon another lengthy work. His late remarkable conduct led me to regard his ways narrowly. I observed that he never went to dinner; indeed, that he never went anywhere. As yet I had never, of my personal knowledge, known him to be outside of my office. He was a perpetual sentry in the corner. At about eleven o'clock, though, in the morning, I noticed that Ginger Nut would advance towards the opening in Bartleby's screen, as if silently beckoned thither by a gesture invisible to me where I sat. The boy would then leave the office jingling a few pence, and reappear with a handful of gingernuts, which he delivered in the hermitage, receiving two of the cakes for his trouble.

He lives, then, on gingernuts, thought I; never eats a dinner, properly speaking; he must be a vegetarian, then; but no, he never eats even vegetables, he eats nothing but gingernuts. My mind then ran on in reveries concerning the probable effects upon the human constitution of living entirely on gingernuts. Gingernuts are so called because they contain ginger as one of their peculiar constituents, and the final flavoring one. Now, what was ginger? A hot, spicy thing. Was Bartleby hot and spicy? Not at all. Ginger, then, had no effect upon Bartleby. Probably he preferred it should have none.

Nothing so aggravates an earnest person as a passive resistance. If the individual so resisted be of a not inhumane temper, and the resisting one perfectly harmless in his passivity, then, in the better moods of the former, he will endeavor charitably to construe to his imagination what proves impossible to be solved by his judgment. Even so, for the most part, I regarded Bartleby and his ways. Poor fellow! thought I, he means no mischief; it is plain he intends no insolence; his aspect sufficiently evinces that his eccentricities are involuntary. He is useful to me. I can get along with him. If I turn him away, the chances are he will fall in with some less indulgent employer, and then he will be rudely treated, and perhaps driven forth miserably to starve. Yes. Here I can cheaply purchase a delicious self-approval. To befriend Bartleby, to humor him in his strange willfulness, will cost me little or nothing, while I lay up in my soul what will eventually prove a sweet morsel for my conscience. But this mood was not invariable with me. The passiveness of Bartleby sometimes irritated me. I felt strangely goaded on to encounter him in new opposition—to elicit some angry spark from him answerable to my own. But, indeed, I might as well have essayed to strike fire with my knuckles against a bit of Windsor soap. But one afternoon the evil impulse in me mastered me, and the following little scene ensued:

"Bartleby," said I, "when those papers are all copied, I will compare them with you."

"I would prefer not to."

"How? Surely you do not mean to persist in that mulish vagary?"

No answer.

I threw open the folding doors near by, and, turning upon Turkey and Nippers, exclaimed:

"Bartleby a second time says he won't examine his papers. What do you think of it, Turkey?"

It was afternoon, be it remembered. Turkey sat glowing like a brass boiler, his bald head steaming, his hands reeling among his blotted papers.

"Think of it?" roared Turkey. "I think I'll just step behind his screen and black his eyes for him!"

So saying, Turkey rose to his feet and threw his arms into a pugilistic position. He was hurrying away to make good his promise when I de-tained him, alarmed at the effect of incautiously rousing Turkey's combativeness after dinner.

"Sit down, Turkey," said I, "and hear what Nippers has to say. What do you think of it, Nippers? Would I not be justified in immediately dismissing Bartleby?"

"Excuse me, that is for you to decide, sir. I think his conduct quite unusual, and indeed, unjust, as regards Turkey and myself. But it may only be a passing whim."

"Ah," exclaimed I, "you have strangely changed your mind, then—you speak very gently of him now."

"All beer," cried Turkey; "gentleness is effects of beer—Nippers and I dined together today. You see how gentle *I* am, sir. Shall I go and black his eyes?"

"You refer to Bartleby, I suppose. No, not today, Turkey," I replied; "pray, put up your fists."

I closed the doors and again advanced towards Bartleby. I felt additional incentives tempting me to my fate. I burned to be rebelled against again. I remembered that Bartleby never left the office.

"Bartleby," said I, "Ginger Nut is away; just step around to the Post Office, won't you? (it was but a three minutes' walk), and see if there is anything for me."

"I would prefer not to."

"You *will* not?"

"I *prefer* not."

I staggered to my desk and sat there in a deep study. My blind inveteracy returned. Was there any other thing in which I could procure myself to be ignominiously repulsed by this lean, penniless wight?—my hired clerk? What added thing is there, perfectly reasonable, that he will be sure to refuse to do?

"Bartleby!"

No answer.

"Bartleby," in a louder voice.

No answer.

"Bartleby," I roared.

Like a very ghost, agreeably to the laws of magical invocation, at the third summons he appeared at the entrance of his hermitage.

"Go to the next room, and tell Nippers to come to me."

"I prefer not to," he respectfully and slowly said, and mildly disappeared.

"Very good, Bartleby," said I, in a quiet sort of serenely severe, self-possessed tone, intimating the unalterable purpose of some terrible retribution very close at hand. At the moment I half intended something of the kind. But upon the whole, as it was drawing towards my dinner hour, I thought it best to put on my hat and walk home for the day, suffering much from perplexity and distress of mind.

Shall I acknowledge it? The conclusion of this whole business was that it soon became a fixed fact of my chambers, that a pale young scrivener by the name of Bartleby had a desk there; that he copied for me at the usual rate of four cents a folio (one hundred words); but he was permanently exempt from examining the work done by him, that duty being transferred to Turkey and Nippers, out of compliment, doubtless, to their superior acuteness; moreover, said Bartleby was never, on any account, to be dispatched on the most trivial errand of any sort; and that even if entreated to take upon him such a matter, it was generally understood that he would "prefer not to"—in other words, that he would refuse point-blank.

As days passed on, I became considerably reconciled to Bartleby. His steadiness, his freedom from all dissipation, his incessant industry (except when he chose to throw himself into a standing revery behind his screen), his great stillness, his unalterableness of demeanor under all circumstances, made him a valuable acquisition. One prime thing was this—*he was always there*—first in the morning, continually through the day, and the last at night. I had a singular confidence in his honesty. I felt my most precious papers perfectly safe in his hands. Sometimes, to be sure, I could not, for the very soul of me, avoid falling into sudden spasmodic passions with him. For it was exceeding difficult to bear in mind all the time those strange peculiarities, privileges, and unheard-of exemptions, forming the tacit stipulations on Bartleby's part under which he remained in my office. Now and then, in the eagerness of dispatching pressing business, I would inadvertently summon Bartleby, in a short, rapid tone, to put his finger, say, on the incipient tie of a bit of red tape with which I was about compressing some papers. Of course, from behind the screen the usual answer, "I prefer not to," was sure to come; and then, how could a human creature, with the common infirmities of our nature, refrain from bitterly exclaiming upon such perverseness—such unreasonableness? However, every added repulse of this sort which I received only tended to lessen the probability of my repeating the inadvertence.

Here it must be said that, according to the custom of most legal gentlemen occupying chambers in densely populated law buildings, there were several keys to my door. One was kept by a woman residing in the attic, which person weekly scrubbed and daily swept and dusted my apartments. Another was kept by Turkey for convenience' sake. The third I sometimes carried in my own pocket. The fourth I knew not who had.

Now, one Sunday morning I happened to go

to Trinity Church, to hear a celebrated preacher, and finding myself rather early on the ground I thought I would walk around to my chambers for a while. Luckily I had my key with me, but upon applying it to the lock, I found it resisted by something inserted from the inside. Quite surprised, I called out, when to my consternation a key was turned from within, and, thrusting his lean visage at me, and holding the door ajar, the apparition of Bartleby appeared, in his shirt sleeves, and otherwise in a strangely tattered deshabille, saying quietly that he was sorry, but he was deeply engaged just then, and—preferred not admitting me at present. In a brief word or two, he moreover added, that perhaps I had better walk around the block two or three times, and by that time he would probably have concluded his affairs.

Now, the utterly unsurmised appearance of Bartleby, tenanting my law chambers of a Sunday morning, with his cadaverously gentlemanly *nonchalance,* yet withal firm and self-possessed, had such a strange effect upon me that incontinently I slunk away from my own door and did as desired. But not without sundry twinges of impotent rebellion against the mild effrontery of this unaccountable scrivener. Indeed, it was his wonderful mildness, chiefly, which not only disarmed me but unmanned me, as it were. For I consider that one, for the time, is sort of unmanned when he tranquilly permits his hired clerk to dictate to him and order him away from his own premises. Furthermore, I was full of uneasiness as to what Bartleby could possibly be doing in my office in his shirt sleeves, and in an otherwise dismantled condition, of a Sunday morning. Was anything amiss going on? Nay, that was out of the question. It was not to be thought of for a moment that Bartleby was an immoral person. But what could he be doing there?—copying? Nay again, whatever might be his eccentricities, Bartleby was an eminently decorous person. He would be the last man to sit down to his desk in any state approaching to nudity. Besides, it was Sunday; and there was something about Bartleby that forbade the supposition that he would by any secular occupation violate the proprieties of the day.

Nevertheless, my mind was not pacified, and, full of a restless curiosity, at last I returned to the door. Without hindrance I inserted my key, opened it, and entered. Bartleby was not to be seen. I looked round anxiously, peeped behind his screen, but it was very plain that he was gone. Upon more closely examining the place, I surmised that for an indefinite period Bartleby must have ate, dressed, and slept in my office, and that, too, without plate, mirror, or bed. The cushioned seat of a rickety old sofa in one corner bore the faint impress of a lean, reclining form. Rolled away under his desk I found a blanket; under the empty grate, a blacking box and brush; on a chair, a tin basin, with soap and a ragged towel; in a newspaper a few crumbs of gingernuts and a morsel of cheese. Yes, thought I, it is evident enough that Bartleby has been making his home here, keeping bachelor's hall all by himself. Immediately then the thought came sweeping across me, what miserable friendlessness and loneliness are here revealed. His poverty is great, but his solitude, how horrible! Think of it. Of a Sunday, Wall Street is deserted as Petra, and every night of every day it is an emptiness. This building, too, which of week-days hums with industry and life, at nightfall echoes with sheer vacancy, and all through Sunday is forlorn. And here Bartleby makes his home, sole spectator of a solitude which he has seen all populous—a sort of innocent and transformed Marius brooding among the ruins of Carthage!

For the first time in my life a feeling of overpowering stinging melancholy seized me. Before, I had never experienced aught but a not unpleasing sadness. The bond of a common humanity now drew me irresistibly to gloom. A fraternal melancholy! For both I and Bartleby were sons of Adam. I remembered the bright silks and sparkling faces I had seen that day, in gala trim, swan-like sailing down the Mississippi of Broadway; and I contrasted them with the pallid copyist, and thought to myself, Ah, happiness courts the light, so we deem the world is gay, but misery hides aloof, so we deem that misery there is none. These sad fancyings—chimeras, doubtless, of a sick and silly brain—led on to other and more special thoughts, concerning the eccentricities of Bartleby. Presentiments of strange discoveries hovered round me. The scrivener's pale form appeared to me laid out, among uncaring strangers in its shivering winding sheet.

Suddenly I was attracted by Bartleby's closed desk, the key in open sight left in the lock.

I mean no mischief, seek the gratification of no heartless curiosity, thought I; besides, the desk is mine, and its contents, too, so I will make bold to look within. Everything was methodically arranged, the papers smoothly placed. The pigeonholes were deep, and, removing the files of documents, I groped into their recesses. Presently I felt something there, and dragged it out. It was an old bandanna handkerchief, heavy and knotted. I opened it, and saw it was a savings bank.

I now recalled all the quiet mysteries which I had noted in the man. I remembered that he never spoke but to answer; that, though at intervals he had considerable time to himself, yet I had never seen him reading—no, not even a newspaper; that for long periods he would stand looking out, at his pale window behind the screen, upon the dead brick wall; I was quite sure he never visited any refectory or eating-house, while his pale face clearly indicated that he never drank beer like Turkey, or tea and coffee even, like other men; that he never went anywhere in particular that I could learn; never went out for a walk, unless, indeed, that was the case at present; that he had declined telling who he was, or whence he came, or whether he had any relatives in the world; that though so thin and pale, he never complained of ill health. And more than all I remembered a certain unconscious air of pallid—how shall I call it?—of pallid haughtiness, say, or rather an austere reserve about him, which had positively awed me into my tame compliance with his eccentricities, when I had feared to ask him to do the slightest incidental thing for me, even though I might know, from his long-continued motionlessness, that behind his screen he must be standing in one of those dead-wall reveries of his.

Revolving all these things, and coupling them with the recently discovered fact that he made my office his constant abiding place and home, and not forgetful of his morbid moodiness—revolving all these things, a prudential feeling began to steal over me. My first emotions had been those of pure melancholy and sincerest pity; but just in proportion as the forlornness of Bartleby grew and grew to my imagination, did that same melancholy merge into fear, that pity into repulsion. So true it is, and so terrible too, that up to a certain point the thought or sight of misery enlists our best affections; but, in certain special cases, beyond that point it does not. They err who would assert that invariably this is owing to the inherent selfishness of the human heart. It rather proceeds from a certain hopelessness of remedying excessive and organic ill. To a sensitive being, pity is not seldom pain. And when at last it is perceived that such pity cannot lead to effectual succor, common sense bids the soul be rid of it. What I saw that morning persuaded me that the scrivener was the victim of innate and incurable disorder. I might give alms to his body, but his body did not pain him—it was his soul that suffered, and his soul I could not reach.

I did not accomplish the purpose of going to Trinity Church that morning. Somehow, the things I had seen disqualified me for the time from churchgoing. I walked homeward, thinking what I would do with Bartleby. Finally, I resolved upon this—I would put certain calm questions to him the next morning, touching his history, etc., and if he declined to answer them openly and unreservedly (and I supposed he would prefer not), then to give him a twenty dollar bill over and above whatever I might owe him, and tell him his services were no longer required; but that if in any other way I could assist him, I would be happy to do so, especially if he desired to return to his native place, wherever that might be, I would willingly help to defray the expenses. Moreover, if, after reaching home, he found himself at any time in want of aid, a letter from him would be sure of a reply.

The next morning came.

"Bartleby," said I, gently calling to him behind his screen.

No reply.

"Bartleby," said I, in a still gentler tone, "come here; I am not going to ask you to do anything you would prefer not to do—I simply wish to speak to you."

Upon this he noiselessly slid into view.

"Will you tell me, Bartleby, where you were born?"

"I would prefer not to."

"Will you tell me *anything* about yourself?"

"I would prefer not to."

"But what reasonable objection can you have to speak to me? I feel friendly towards you."

He did not look at me while I spoke, but kept his glance fixed upon my bust of Cicero, which, as I then sat, was directly behind me, some six inches above my head.

"What is your answer, Bartleby," said I, after waiting a considerable time for a reply, during which his countenance remained immovable, only there was the faintest conceivable tremor of the white attenuated mouth.

"At present I prefer to give no answer," he said, and retired into his hermitage.

It was rather weak in me I confess, but his manner, on this occasion, nettled me. Not only did there seem to lurk in it a certain calm disdain, but his perverseness seemed ungrateful, considering the undeniable good usage and indulgence he had received from me.

Again I sat ruminating what I should do. Mortified as I was at his behavior, and resolved as I had been to dismiss him when I entered my office, nevertheless I strangely felt something superstitious knocking at my heart, and forbidding me to carry out my purpose, and denouncing me for a villain if I dared to breathe one bitter word against this forlornest of mankind. At last, familiarly drawing my chair behind his screen, I sat down and said: "Bartleby, never mind, then, about revealing your history; but let me entreat you, as a friend, to comply as far as may be with the usages of this office. Say now, you will help to examine papers tomorrow or next day: in short, say now, that in a day or two you will begin to be a little reasonable:—say so, Bartleby."

"At present I would prefer not to be a little reasonable," was his mildly cadaverous reply.

Just then the folding doors opened and Nippers approached. He seemed suffering from an unusually bad night's rest, induced by severer indigestion than common. He overheard those final words of Bartleby.

"*Prefer not,* eh?" gritted Nippers—"I'd *prefer* him, if I were you, sir," addressing me—"I'd *prefer* him; I'd give him preferences, the stubborn mule! What is it, sir, pray, that he *prefers* not to do now?"

Bartleby moved not a limb.

"Mr. Nippers," said I, "I'd prefer that you would withdraw for the present."

Somehow, of late, I had got into the way of involuntarily using this word "prefer" upon all sorts of not exactly suitable occasions. And I trembled to think that my contact with the scrivener had already and seriously affected me in a mental way. And what further and deeper aberration might it not yet produce? This apprehension had not been without efficacy in determining me to summary measures.

As Nippers, looking very sour and sulky, was departing, Turkey blandly and deferentially approached.

"With submission, sir," said he, "yesterday I was thinking about Bartleby here, and I think that if he would but prefer to take a quart of good ale every day, it would do much towards mending him, and enabling him to assist in examining his papers."

"So you have got the word, too," said I, slightly excited.

"With submission, what word, sir?" asked Turkey, respectfully crowding himself into the contracted space behind the screen, and by so doing making me jostle the scrivener. "What word, sir?"

"I would prefer to be left alone here," said Bartleby, as if offended at being mobbed in his privacy.

"*That's* the word, Turkey," said I—"*that's* it."

"Oh, *prefer?* oh yes—queer word. I never use it myself. But, sir, as I was saying, if he would but prefer——"

"Turkey," interrupted I, "you will please withdraw."

"Oh certainly, sir, if you prefer that I should."

As he opened the folding door to retire, Nippers at his desk caught a glimpse of me, and asked whether I would prefer to have a certain paper copied on blue paper or white. He did not in the least roguishly accent the word prefer. It was plain that it involuntarily rolled from his tongue. I thought to myself, surely I must get rid of a demented man, who already has in some degree turned the tongues, if not the heads, of myself and clerks. But I thought it prudent not to break the dismission at once.

The next day I noticed that Bartleby did nothing but stand at his window in his dead-wall reverie. Upon asking him why he did not write, he said that he had decided upon doing no more writing.

"Why, how now? what next?" exclaimed I, "do no more writing?"

"No more."

"And what is the reason?"

"Do you not see the reason for yourself?" he indifferently replied.

I looked steadfastly at him, and perceived that his eyes looked dull and glazed. Instantly it occurred to me that his unexampled diligence in copying by his dim window for the first few weeks of his stay with me might have temporarily impaired his vision.

I was touched. I said something in condolence with him. I hinted that of course he did wisely in abstaining from writing for a while; and urged him to embrace that opportunity of taking wholesome exercise in the open air. This, however, he did not do. A few days after this, my other clerks being absent, and being in a great hurry to dispatch certain letters by the mail, I thought that, having nothing else earthly to do, Bartleby would surely be less inflexible than usual, and carry these letters to the Post Office.

But he blankly declined. So, much to my inconvenience, I went myself.

Still added days went by. Whether Bartleby's eyes improved or not, I could not say. To all appearance, I thought they did. But when I asked him if they did, he vouchsafed no answer. At all events, he would do no copying. At last, in reply to my urgings, he informed me that he had permanently given up copying.

"What!" exclaimed I; "suppose your eyes should get entirely well—better than ever before—would you not copy then?"

"I have given up copying," he answered, and slid aside.

He remained as ever, a fixture in my chamber. Nay—if that were possible—he became still more of a fixture than before. What was to be done? He would do nothing in the office; why should he stay there? In plain fact, he had now become a millstone to me, not only useless as a necklace, but afflictive to bear. Yet I was sorry for him. I speak less than truth when I say that, on his own account, he occasioned me uneasiness. If he would but have named a single relative or friend, I would instantly have written and urged their taking the poor fellow away to some convenient retreat. But he seemed alone, absolutely alone in the universe. A bit of wreck in the mid-Atlantic. At length, necessities connected with my business tyrannized over all other considerations. Decently as I could, I told Bartleby that in six days' time he must unconditionally leave the office. I warned him to take measures, in the interval, for procuring some other abode. I offered to assist him in this endeavor, if he himself would but take the first step towards a removal. "And when you finally quit me, Bartleby," added I, "I shall see that you go not away entirely unprovided. Six days from this hour, remember."

At the expiration of that period, I peeped behind the screen, and lo! Bartleby was there.

I buttoned up my coat, balanced myself, advanced slowly towards him, touched his shoulder, and said, "The time has come; you must quit this place; I am sorry for you; here is money; but you must go."

"I would prefer not," he replied, with his back still towards me.

"You *must*."

He remained silent.

Now I had an unbounded confidence in this man's common honesty. He had frequently restored to me sixpences and shillings carelessly dropped upon the floor, for I am apt to be very reckless in such shirt-button affairs. The proceeding, then, which followed will not be deemed extraordinary.

"Bartleby," said I, "I owe you twelve dollars on account; here are thirty-two; the odd twenty are yours—Will you take it?" and I handed the bills towards him.

But he made no motion.

"I will leave them here, then," putting them under a weight on the table. Then taking my hat and cane and going to the door, I tranquilly turned and added—"After you have removed your things from these offices, Bartleby, you will of course lock the door—since everyone is now gone for the day but you—and if you please, slip your key underneath the mat, so that I may have it in the morning. I shall not see you again; so good-bye to you. If, hereafter, in your new place of abode, I can be of any service to you, do not fail to advise me by letter. Good-bye, Bartleby, and fare you well."

But he answered not a word; like the last column of some ruined temple, he remained standing mute and solitary in the middle of the otherwise deserted room.

As I walked home in a pensive mood, my vanity got the better of my pity. I could not but highly plume myself on my masterly management in getting rid of Bartleby. Masterly I call it, and such it must appear to any dispassionate thinker. The beauty of my procedure seemed to consist in its perfect quietness. There was no vulgar bullying, no bravado of any sort, no choleric hectoring, and striding to and fro across the apartment, jerking out vehement commands for Bartleby to bundle himself off with his beggarly traps. Nothing of the kind. Without loudly bidding Bartleby depart—as an inferior genius might have done—I *assumed* the ground that depart he must, and upon that assumption built all I had to say. The more I thought over my procedure, the more I was charmed with it. Nevertheless, next morning, upon awakening, I had my doubts—I had somehow slept off the fumes of vanity. One of the coolest and wisest hours a man has is just after he awakes in the morning. My procedure seemed as sagacious as ever—but only in theory. How it would prove in practice—there was the rub. It was truly a beautiful thought to have assumed Bartleby's departure; but, after all, that assumption was simply my own, and none of Bartleby's. The great point was, not whether I had assumed that he would quit me, but whether he would prefer so to do. He was more a man of preferences than assumptions.

After breakfast, I walked downtown, arguing the probabilities pro and con. One moment I thought it would prove a miserable failure, and Bartleby would be found all alive at my office as usual; the next moment it seemed certain that I should find his chair empty. And so I kept veering about. At the corner of Broadway and Canal Street, I saw quite an excited group of people standing in earnest conversation.

"I'll take odds he doesn't," said a voice as I passed.

"Doesn't go?—done!" said I, "put up your money."

I was instinctively putting my hand in my pocket to produce my own, when I remembered that this was an election day. The words I had overheard bore no reference to Bartleby but to the success or nonsuccess of some candidate for the mayoralty. In my intent frame of mind, I had, as it were, imagined that all Broadway shared in my excitement, and were debating the same question with me. I passed on, very thankful that the uproar of the street screened my momentary absent-mindedness.

As I had intended, I was earlier than usual at my office door. I stood listening for a moment. All was still. He must be gone. I tried the knob. The door was locked. Yes, my procedure had worked to a charm; he indeed must be vanished. Yet a certain melancholy mixed with this: I was almost sorry for my brilliant success. I was fumbling under the door mat for the key, which Bartleby was to have left there for me, when accidentally my knee knocked against a panel, producing a summoning sound, and in response a voice came to me from within—"Not yet; I am occupied."

It was Bartleby.

I was thunderstruck. For an instant I stood

like the man who, pipe in mouth, was killed one cloudless afternoon long ago in Virginia by summer lightning; at his own warm open window he was killed, and remained leaning out there upon the dreamy afternoon, till someone touched him, when he fell.

"Not gone!" I murmured at last. But again obeying that wondrous ascendancy which the inscrutable scrivener had over me, and from which ascendancy, for all my chafing, I could not completely escape, I slowly went downstairs and out into the street, and while walking round the block considered what I should next do in this unheard-of perplexity. Turn the man out by an actual thrusting I could not; to drive him away by calling him hard names would not do; calling in the police was an unpleasant idea; and yet, permit him to enjoy his cadaverous triumph over me—this, too, I could not think of. What was to be done? or, if nothing could be done, was there anything further that I could *assume* in the matter? Yes, as before I had prospectively assumed that Bartleby would depart, so now I might retrospectively assume that departed he was. In the legitimate carrying out of this assumption I might enter my office in a great hurry, and, pretending not to see Bartleby at all, walk straight against him as if he were air. Such a proceeding would in a singular degree have the appearance of a home thrust. It was hardly possible that Bartleby could withstand such an application of the doctrine of assumptions. But upon second thoughts the success of the plan seemed rather dubious. I resolved to argue the matter over with him again.

"Bartleby," said I, entering the office, with a quietly severe expression, "I am seriously displeased. I am pained, Bartleby. I had thought better of you. I had imagined you of such a gentlemanly organization that in any delicate dilemma a slight hint would suffice—in short, an assumption. But it appears I am deceived. Why," I added, unaffectedly starting, "you have not even touched that money yet," pointing to it, just where I had left it the evening previous.

He answered nothing.

"Will you, or will you not, quit me?" I now demanded in a sudden passion, advancing close to him.

"I would prefer *not* to quit you," he replied, gently emphasizing the *not*.

"What earthly right have you to stay here? Do you pay any rent? Do you pay my taxes? Or is this property yours?"

He answered nothing.

"Are you ready to go on and write now? Are your eyes recovered? Could you copy a small paper for me this morning? or help examine a few lines? or step round to the Post Office? In a word, will you do anything at all, to give a coloring to your refusal to depart the premises?"

He silently retired into his hermitage.

I was now in such a state of nervous resentment that I thought it but prudent to check myself at present from further demonstrations. Bartleby and I were alone. I remembered the tragedy of the unfortunate Adams and the still more unfortunate Colt in the solitary office of the latter; and how poor Colt, being dreadfully incensed by Adams, and imprudently permitting himself to get wildly excited, was at unawares hurried into his fatal act—an act which certainly no man could possibly deplore more than the actor himself. Often it had occurred to me in my ponderings upon the subject that had that altercation taken place in the public street, or at a private residence, it would not have terminated as it did. It was the circumstance of being alone in a solitary office, upstairs, of a building entirely unhallowed by humanizing domestic associations—an uncarpeted office, doubtless, of a dusty, haggard sort of appearance—this it must have been which greatly helped to enhance the irritable desperation of the hapless Colt.

But when this old Adam of resentment rose in me and tempted me concerning Bartleby, I grappled him and threw him. How? Why, simply by recalling the divine injunction: "A new commandment give I unto you, that ye love one another." Yes, this it was that saved me. Aside from higher considerations, charity often operates as a vastly wise and prudent principle—a great safeguard to its possessor. Men have committed murder for jealousy's sake, and anger's sake, and hatred's sake, and selfishness' sake, and spiritual pride's sake; but no man that ever I heard of ever committed a diabolical murder for sweet charity's sake. Mere self-interest, then, if no better motive can be enlisted, should, especially with high-tempered men, prompt all beings to charity and philanthropy. At any rate, upon the occasion in question, I strove to drown my exasperated feelings towards the scrivener by benevolently construing his conduct. Poor fellow, poor fellow! thought I, he don't mean anything, and besides, he has seen hard times, and ought to be indulged.

I endeavored, also, immediately to occupy myself, and at the same time to comfort my despondency. I tried to fancy that in the course of the morning, at such time as might prove agreeable to him, Bartleby, of his own free accord, would emerge from his hermitage and take up some decided line of march in the direction of the door. But no. Half-past twelve o'clock came; Turkey began to glow in the face, overturn his inkstand, and become generally obstreperous; Nippers abated down into quietude and courtesy; Ginger Nut munched his noon apple; and Bartleby remained standing at his window in one of his profoundest dead-wall reveries. Will it be credited? Ought I to acknowledge it? That afternoon I left the office without saying one further word to him.

Some days now passed during which, at leisure intervals, I looked a little into "Edwards on the Will," and "Priestley on Necessity." Under the circumtances, those books induced a salutary feeling. Gradually I slid into the persuasion that these troubles of mine touching the scrivener had been all predestinated from eternity, and Bartleby was billeted upon me for some mysterious purpose of an all-wise Providence, which it was not for a mere mortal like me to fathom. Yes, Bartleby, stay there behind your screen, thought I; I shall persecute you no more; you are harmless and noiseless as any of these old chairs; in short, I never feel so private as when I know you are here. At last I see it, I feel it; I penetrate to the predestinated purpose of my life. I am content. Others may have loftier parts to enact; but my mission in this world, Bartleby, is to furnish you with office room for such period as you may see fit to remain.

I believe that this wise and blessed frame of mind would have continued with me had it not been for the unsolicited and uncharitable remarks obtruded upon me by my professional friends who visited the rooms. But thus it often is that the constant friction of illiberal minds wears out at last the best resolves of the more generous. Though to be sure, when I reflected upon it it was not strange that people entering my office should be struck by the peculiar aspect of the unaccountable Bartleby, and so be tempted to throw out some sinister observations concerning him. Sometimes an attorney having business with me, and calling at my office, and finding no one but the scrivener there, would undertake to obtain some sort of precise information from him touching my whereabouts; but without heeding his idle talk, Bartleby would remain standing immovable in the middle of the room. So, after contemplating him in that position for a time, the attorney would depart no wiser than he came.

Also, when a reference was going on, and the room full of lawyers and witnesses, and business driving fast, some deeply-occupied legal gentleman present, seeing Bartleby wholly unemployed, would request him to run round to his (the legal gentleman's) office and fetch some papers for him. Thereupon Bartleby would tranquilly decline, and yet remain idle as before. Then the lawyer would give a great stare, and turn to me. And what could I say? At last I was made aware that all through the circle of my professional acquaintance a whisper of wonder was running round, having reference to the strange creature I kept at my office. This worried me very much. And as the idea came upon me of his possibly turning out a long-lived man, and keep occupying my chambers, and denying my authority; and perplexing my visitors; and scandalizing my professional reputation; and casting a general gloom over the premises; keeping soul and body together to the last upon his savings (for doubtless he spent but half a dime a day), and in the end perhaps outlive me, and claim possession of my office by right of his perpetual occupancy—as all these dark anticipations crowded upon me more and more, and my friends continually intruded their relentless remarks upon the apparition in my room, a great change was wrought in me. I resolved to gather all my faculties together and forever rid me of this intolerable incubus.

Ere revolving any complicated project, however, adapted to this end, I first simply suggested to Bartleby the propriety of his permanent departure. In a calm and serious tone, I commended the idea to his careful and mature consideration. But, having taken three days to meditate upon it, he apprised me, that his original determination remained the same; in short, that he still preferred to abide with me.

What shall I do? I now said to myself, buttoning up my coat to the last button. What shall I do? what ought I to do? what does conscience say I *should* do with this man, or, rather, ghost. Rid myself of him, I must; go, he shall. But how? You will not thrust him, the poor, pale, passive mortal—you will not thrust such a helpless creature out of your door? you will not dishonor yourself by such cruelty? No, I will not, I cannot do that. Rather would I let him live and die here, and then mason up his remains in the wall. What, then, will you do? For all your coaxing, he will not budge. Bribes he leaves under your own paperweight on your table; in short, it is quite plain that he prefers to cling to you.

Then something severe, something unusual, must be done. What! surely you will not have him collared by a constable, and commit his innocent pallor to the common jail? And upon what ground could you procure such a thing to be done?—a vagrant, is he? What! he a vagrant, a wanderer, who refuses to budge? It is because he will *not* be a vagrant, then, that you seek to count him *as* a vagrant. This is too absurd. No visible means of support: there I have him. Wrong again: for indubitably he *does* support himself, and that is the only unanswerable proof that any man can show of his possessing the means so to do. No more, then. Since he will not quit me, I must quit him. I will change my offices; I will move elsewhere, and give him fair notice that if I find him on my new premises I will then proceed against him as a common trespasser.

Acting accordingly, next day I thus addressed him: "I find these chambers too far from the City Hall; the air is unwholesome. In a word, I propose to remove my offices next week, and shall no longer require your services. I tell you this now, in order that you may seek another place."

He made no reply, and nothing more was said.

On the appointed day I engaged carts and men, proceeded to my chambers, and, having but little furniture, everything was removed in a few hours. Throughout, the scrivener remained standing behind the screen, which I directed to be removed the last thing. It was withdrawn; and, being folded up like a huge folio, left him the motionless occupant of a naked room. I stood in the entry watching him a moment, while something from within me upbraided me.

I re-entered, with my hand in my pocket—and—and my heart in my mouth.

"Good-bye, Bartleby; I am going—good-bye; and God some way bless you; and take that," slipping something in his hand. But it dropped upon the floor, and then—strange to say—I tore myself from him whom I had so longed to be rid of.

Established in my new quarters, for a day or two I kept the door locked, and started at every footfall in the passages. When I returned to my rooms after any little absence, I would pause at the threshold for an instant and attentively listen ere applying my key. But these fears were needless. Bartleby never came nigh me.

I thought all was going well, when a perturbed-looking stranger visited me, inquiring whether I was the person who had recently occupied rooms at No.—Wall Street.

Full of forebodings, I replied that I was.

"Then, sir," said the stranger, who proved a lawyer, "you are responsible for the man you left there. He refuses to do any copying; he refuses to do anything; he says he prefers not to; and he refuses to quit the premises."

"I am very sorry, sir," said I, with assumed tranquillity, but an inward tremor, "but, really, the man you allude to is nothing to me—he is no relation or apprentice of mine, that you should hold me responsible for him."

"In mercy's name, who is he?"

"I certainly cannot inform you. I know nothing about him. Formerly I employed him as a copyist; but he has done nothing for me now for some time past."

"I shall settle him, then—good morning, sir."

Several days passed, and I heard nothing more; and, though I often felt a charitable prompting to call at the place and see poor Bartleby, yet a certain squeamishness, of I know not what, withheld me.

All is over with him, by this time, thought I at last, when, through another week, no further intelligence reached me. But, coming to my room the day after, I found several persons waiting at my door in a high state of nervous excitement.

"That's the man—here he comes," cried the foremost one, whom I recognized as the lawyer who had previously called upon me alone.

"You must take him away, sir, at once," cried a portly person among them, advancing upon me, and whom I knew to be the landlord of No.—Wall Street. "These gentlemen, my tenants, cannot stand it any longer; Mr. B——," pointing to the lawyer, "has turned him out of his room, and he now persists in haunting the building generally, sitting upon the banisters of the stairs by day, and sleeping in the entry by night. Everybody is concerned; clients are leaving the offices; some fears are entertained of a mob; something you must do, and that without delay."

Aghast at this torrent, I fell back before it, and would fain have locked myself in my new quarters. In vain I persisted that Bartleby was nothing to me—no more than to anyone else. In vain—I was the last person known to have anything to do with him, and they held me to the terrible account. Fearful, then, of being exposed in the papers (as one person present obscurely threatened), I considered the matter, and at length said that if the lawyer would give me a confidential interview with the scrivener, in his (the lawyer's) own room, I would, that afternoon, strive my best to rid them of the nuisance they complained of.

Going up stairs to my old haunt, there was Bartleby silently sitting upon the banister at the landing.

"What are you doing here, Bartleby?" said I.

"Sitting upon the banister," he mildly replied.

I motioned him into the lawyer's room, who then left us.

"Bartleby," said I, "are you aware that you are the cause of great tribulation to me, by persisting in occupying the entry after being dismissed from the office?"

No answer.

"Now one of two things must take place. Either you must do something, or something must be done to you. Now what sort of business would you like to engage in? Would you like to re-engage in copying for someone?"

"No; I would prefer not to make any change."

"Would you like a clerkship in a dry-goods store?"

"There is too much confinement about that.

No, I would not like a clerkship; but I am not particular."

"Too much confinement," I cried; "why you keep yourself confined all the time!"

"I would prefer not to take a clerkship," he rejoined, as if to settle that little item at once.

"How would a bartender's business suit you? There is no trying of the eyesight in that."

"I would not like it at all; though, as I said before, I am not particular."

His unwonted wordiness inspirited me. I returned to the charge.

"Well, then, would you like to travel through the country collecting bills for the merchants? That would improve your health."

"No, I would prefer to be doing something else."

"How, then, would going as a companion to Europe, to entertain some young gentleman with your conversation—how would that suit you?"

"Not at all. It does not strike me that there is anything definite about that. I like to be stationary. But I am not particular."

"Stationary you shall be, then," I cried, now losing all patience, and, for the first time in all my exasperating connection with him, fairly flying into a passion. "If you do not go away from these premises before night, I shall feel bound—indeed, I *am* bound—to—to—to quit the premises myself!" I rather absurdly concluded, knowing not with what possible threat to try to frighten his immobility into compliance. Despairing of all further efforts, I was precipitately leaving him, when a final thought occurred to me—one which had not been wholly unindulged before.

"Bartleby," said I, in the kindest tone I could assume under such exciting circumstances, "will you go home with me now—not to my office, but my dwelling—and remain there till we can conclude upon some convenient arrangement for you at our leisure? Come, let us start now, right away."

"No; at present I would prefer not to make any change at all."

I answered nothing, but, effectually dodging everyone by the suddenness and rapidity of my flight, rushed from the building, ran up Wall Street towards Broadway, and, jumping into the first omnibus, was soon removed from pursuit. As soon as tranquillity returned, I distinctly perceived that I had now done all that I possibly could, both in respect to the demands of the landlord and his tenants, and with regard to my own desire and sense of duty, to benefit Bartleby, and shield him from rude persecution. I now strove to be entirely carefree and quiescent, and my conscience justified me in the attempt, though, indeed, it was not so successful as I could have wished. So fearful was I of being again hunted out by the incensed landlord and his exasperated tenants that, surrendering my business to Nippers for a few days, I drove about the upper part of the town and through the suburbs in my rockaway; crossed over to Jersey City and Hoboken, and paid fugitive visits to Manhattanville and Astoria. In fact, I almost lived in my rockaway for the time.

When again I entered my office, lo, a note from the landlord lay upon the desk. I opened it with trembling hands. It informed me that the writer had sent to the police, and had Bartleby removed to the Tombs as a vagrant. Moreover, since I knew more about him than anyone else, he wished me to appear at that place and make a suitable statement of the facts. These tidings had a conflicting effect upon me. At first I was indignant, but at last almost approved. The landlord's energetic, summary disposition had led him to adopt a procedure which I do not think I would have decided upon myself; and yet, as a last resort, under such peculiar circumstances, it seemed the only plan.

As I afterwards learned, the poor scrivener, when told that he must be conducted to the Tombs, offered not the slightest obstacle, but, in his pale, unmoving way, silently acquiesced.

Some of the compassionate and curious bystanders joined the party, and, headed by one of the constables arm in arm with Bartleby, the silent procession filed its way through all the noise, and heat, and joy of the roaring thoroughfares at noon.

The same day I received the note, I went to the Tombs, or, to speak more properly, the Halls of Justice. Seeking the right officer, I stated the purpose of my call, and was informed that the individual I described was indeed within. I then assured the functionary that Bartleby was a perfectly honest man, and greatly to be compassionated, however unaccountably eccentric. I narrated all I knew, and closed by suggesting the idea of letting him remain in as indulgent confinement as possible till something less harsh might be done—though, indeed, I hardly knew what. At all events, if nothing else could be decided upon, the almshouse must receive him. I then begged to have an interview.

Being under no disgraceful charge, and quite serene and harmless in all his ways, they had permitted him freely to wander about the prison, and, especially, in the inclosed grass-platted yards thereof. And so I found him there, standing all alone in the quietest of the yards, his face towards a high wall, while all around, from the narrow slits of the jail windows, I thought I saw peering out upon him the eyes of murderers and thieves.

"Bartleby!"

"I know you," he said, without looking round—"and I want nothing to say to you."

"It was not I that brought you here, Bartleby," said I, keenly pained at his implied suspicion. "And, to you, this should not be so vile a place. Nothing reproachful attaches to you by being here. And see, it is not so sad a place as one might think. Look, there is the sky, and here is the grass."

"I know where I am," he replied, but would say nothing more, and so I left him.

As I entered the corridor again, a broad meat-like man in an apron accosted me, and, jerking his thumb over his shoulder, said—"Is that your friend?"

"Yes."

"Does he want to starve? If he does, let him live on the prison fare, that's all."

"Who are you?" asked I, not knowing what to make of such an unofficially speaking person in such a place.

"I am the grubman. Such gentlemen as have friends here hire me to provide them with something good to eat."

"Is this so?" said I, turning to the turnkey.

He said it was.

"Well, then," said I, slipping some silver into the grubman's hands (for so they called him), "I want you to give particular attention to my friend there; let him have the best dinner you can get. And you must be as polite to him as possible."

"Introduce me, will you?" said the grubman, looking at me with an expression which seemed to say he was all impatience for an opportunity to give a specimen of his breeding.

Thinking it would prove of benefit to the scrivener, I acquiesced, and, asking the grubman his name, went up with him to Bartleby.

"Bartleby, this is a friend; you will find him very useful to you."

"Your sarvant, sir, your sarvant," said the grubman, making a low salutation behind his apron. "Hope you find it pleasant here, sir; nice grounds—cool apartments—hope you'll stay with us sometime—try to make it agreeable. What will you have for dinner today?"

"I prefer not to dine today," said Bartleby, turning away. "It would disagree with me; I am unused to dinners." So saying, he slowly moved to the other side of the inclosure and took up a position fronting the dead-wall.

"How's this?" said the grubman, addressing me with a stare of astonishment. "He's odd, ain't he?"

"I think he is a little deranged," said I, sadly.

"Deranged? deranged is it? Well, now, upon my word, I thought that friend of yourn was a gentleman forger; they are always pale and genteel-like, them forgers. I can't help pity 'em—

can't help it, sir. Did you know Monroe Edwards?" he added, touchingly, and paused. Then, laying his hand piteously on my shoulder, sighed, "He died of consumption at Sing-Sing. So you weren't acquainted with Monroe?"

"No, I was never socially acquainted with any forgers. But I cannot stop longer. Look to my friend yonder. You will not lose by it. I will see you again."

Some few days after this, I again obtained admission to the Tombs, and went through the corridors in quest of Bartleby; but without finding him.

"I saw him coming from his cell not long ago," said a turnkey, "maybe he's gone to loiter in the yards."

So I went in that direction.

"Are you looking for the silent man?" said another turnkey, passing me. "Yonder he lies—sleeping in the yard there. 'Tis not twenty minutes since I saw him lie down."

The yard was entirely quiet. It was not accessible to the common prisoners. The surrounding walls, of amazing thickness, kept off all sounds behind them. The Egyptian character of the masonry weighed upon me with its gloom. But a soft imprisoned turf grew underfoot. The heart of the eternal pyramids, it seemed, wherein, by some strange magic, through the clefts, grass-seed, dropped by birds, had sprung.

Strangely huddled at the base of the wall, his knees drawn up and lying on his side, his head touching the cold stones, I saw the wasted Bartleby. But nothing stirred. I paused, then went close up to him; stooped over, and saw that his dim eyes were open; otherwise he seemed profoundly sleeping. Something prompted me to touch him. I felt his hand, when a tingling shiver ran up my arm and down my spine to my feet.

The round face of the grubman peered upon me now. "His dinner is ready. Won't he dine today, either? Or does he live without dining?"

"Lives without dining," said I, and closed the eyes.

"Eh!—He's asleep, ain't he?"

"With kings and counselors," murmured I.

• • •

There would seem little need for proceeding further in this history. Imagination will readily supply the meager recital of poor Bartleby's interment. But, ere parting with the reader, let me say that if this little narrative has sufficiently interested him to awaken curiosity as to who Bartleby was, and what manner of life he led prior to the present narrator's making his acquaintance, I can only reply that in such curiosity I fully share, but am wholly unable to gratify it. Yet here I hardly know whether I should divulge one little item of rumor which came to my ear a few months after the scrivener's decease. Upon what basis it rested, I could never ascertain, and hence how true it is I cannot now tell. But, inasmuch as this vague report has not been without a certain suggestive interest to me, however said, it may prove the same with some others, and so I will briefly mention it. The report was this: that Bartleby had been a subordinate clerk in the Dead Letter Office at Washington, from which he had been suddenly removed by a change in the administration. When I think over this rumor, hardly can I express the emotions which seize me. Dead letters! does it not sound like dead men? Conceive a man by nature and misfortune prone to a pallid hopelessness, can any business seem more fitted to heighten it than that of continually handling these dead letters, and assorting them for the flames? For by the cartload they are annually burned. Sometimes from out the folded paper the pale clerk takes a ring—the finger it was meant for, perhaps, moulders in the grave; a bank note sent in swiftest charity—he whom it would relieve nor eats nor hungers any more; pardon for those who died despairing; hope for those who died unhoping; good tidings for those who died stifled by unrelieved calamities. On errands of life, these letters speed to death.

Ah, Bartleby! Ah, humanity!

The Outcasts of Poker Flat
by Bret Harte

As Mr. John Oakhurst, gambler, stepped into the main street of Poker Flat on the morning of the twenty-third of November, 1850, he was conscious of a change in its moral atmosphere since the preceding night. Two or three men, conversing earnestly together, ceased as he approached, and exchanged significant glances. There was a Sabbath lull in the air, which, in a settlement unused to Sabbath influences, looked ominous.

Mr. Oakhurst's calm, handsome face betrayed small concern in these indications. Whether he was conscious of any predisposing cause, was another question. "I reckon they're after somebody," he reflected; "likely it's me." He returned to his pocket the handkerchief with which he had been whipping away the red dust of Poker Flat from his neat boots, and quietly discharged his mind of any further conjecture.

In point of fact, Poker Flat was "after somebody." It had lately suffered the loss of several thousand dollars, two valuable horses, and a prominent citizen. It was experiencing a spasm of virtuous reaction, quite as lawless and ungovernable as any of the acts that had provoked it. A secret committee had determined to rid the town of all improper persons. This was done permanently in regard of two men who were then hanging from the boughs of a sycamore in the gulch, and temporarily in the banishment of certain other objectionable characters. I regret to say that some of these were ladies. It is but due to the sex, however, to state that their impropriety was professional, and it was only in such easily established standards of evil that Poker Flat ventured to sit in judgment.

Mr. Oakhurst was right in supposing that he was included in this category. A few of the committee had urged hanging him as a possible example, and a sure method of reimbursing themselves from his pockets of the sums he had won from them. "It's agin justice," said Jim Wheeler, "to let this yer young man from Roaring Camp—an entire stranger—carry away our money." But a crude sentiment of equity residing in the breasts of those who had been fortunate enough to win from Mr. Oakhurst overruled this narrower local prejudice.

Mr. Oakhurst received his sentence with philosophic calmness, none the less coolly that he was aware of the hesitation of his judges. He was too much of a gambler not to accept Fate. With him life was at best an uncertain game, and he recognized the usual percentage in favor of the dealer.

A party of armed men accompanied the deported wickedness of Poker Flat to the outskirts of the settlement. Besides Mr. Oakhurst, who was known to be a coolly desperate man, and for whose intimidation the armed escort was intended, the expatriated party consisted of a young woman familiarly known as "The Duchess;" another who had bore the title of "Mother Shipton;" and "Uncle Billy," a suspected sluice-robber and confirmed drunkard. The cavalcade provoked no comments from the spectators, nor was any word uttered by the escort. Only when the gulch which marked the uttermost limit of Poker Flat was reached, the leader spoke briefly and to the point. The exiles were forbidden to return at the peril of their lives.

As the escort disappeared, their pent-up feelings found vent in a few hysterical tears from the Duchess, some bad language from Mother Shipton, and a Parthian volley of expletives from Uncle Billy. The philosophic Oakhurst alone remained silent. He listened calmly to Mother Shipton's desire to cut somebody's heart out, to the repeated statements of the Duchess that she would die in the road, and to the alarming oaths that seemed to be bumped out of

Uncle Billy as he rode forward. With the easy good-humor characteristic of his class, he insisted upon exchanging his own riding-horse, "Five Spot," for the sorry mule which the Duchess rode. But even this act did not draw the party into any closer sympathy. The young woman readjusted her somewhat draggled plumes with a feeble, faded coquetry; Mother Shipton eyed the possessor of "Five Spot" with malevolence; and Uncle Billy included the whole party in one sweeping anathema.

The road to Sandy Bar—a camp that, not having as yet experienced the regenerating influences of Poker Flat, consequently seemed to offer some invitation to the emigrants—lay over a steep mountain range. It was distant a day's severe travel. In that advanced season, the party soon passed out of the moist, temperate regions of the foot-hills into the dry, cold, bracing air of the Sierras. The trail was narrow and difficult. At noon the Duchess, rolling out of her saddle upon the ground, declared her intention of going no farther, and the party halted.

The spot was singularly wild and impressive. A wooded amphitheatre, surrounded on three sides by precipitous cliffs of naked granite, sloped gently toward the crest of another precipice that overlooked the valley. It was, undoubtedly, the most suitable spot for a camp, had camping been advisable. But Mr. Oakhurst knew that scarcely half the journey to Sandy Bar was accomplished, and the party were not equipped or provisioned for delay. This fact he pointed out to his companions curtly, with a philosophic commentary on the folly of "throwing up their hand before the game was played out." But they were furnished with liquor, which in this emergency stood them in place of food, fuel, rest and prescience. In spite of his remonstrances, it was not long before they were more or less under its influence. Uncle Billy passed rapidly from a bellicose state into one of stupor, the Duchess became maudlin, and Mother Shipton snored. Mr. Oakhurst alone remained erect, leaning against a rock, calmly surveying them.

Mr. Oakhurst did not drink. It interfered with a profession which required coolness, impassiveness, and presence of mind, and, in his own language, he "couldn't afford it." As he gazed at his recumbent fellow-exiles, the loneliness begotten of his pariah-trade, his habits of life, his very vices, for the first time seriously oppressed him. He bestirred himself in dusting his black clothes, washing his hands and face, and other acts characteristic of his studiously neat habits, and for a moment forgot his annoyance. The thought of deserting his weaker and more pitiable companions never perhaps occurred to him. Yet he could not help feeling the want of that excitement which, singularly enough, was most conducive to that calm equanimity for which he was notorious. He looked at the gloomy walls that rose a thousand feet sheer above the circling pines around him; at the sky, ominously clouded; at the valley below, already deepening into shadow. And, doing so, suddenly he heard his own name called.

A horseman slowly ascended the trail. In the fresh, open face of the new-comer, Mr. Oakhurst recognized Tom Simson, otherwise known as "The Innocent" of Sandy Bar. He had met him some months before over a "little game," and had, with perfect equanimity, won the entire fortune—amounting to some forty dollars—of that guileless youth. After the game was finished, Mr. Oakhurst drew the youthful speculator behind the door, and thus addressed him: "Tommy, you're a good little man, but you can't gamble worth a cent. Don't try it over again." He then handed him his money back, pushed him gently from the room, and so made a devoted slave of Tom Simson.

There was a remembrance of this in his boyish and enthusiastic greeting of Mr. Oakhurst. He had started, he said, to go to Poker Flat to seek his fortune. "Alone?" No, not exactly alone; in fact (a giggle), he had run away with Piney Woods. Didn't Mr. Oakhurst remember Piney? She that used to wait on the table at the

Temperance House? They had been engaged a long time, but old Jake Woods had objected, and so they had run away, and were going to Poker Flat to be married; and here they were. And they were tired out, and how lucky it was they had found a place to camp and company. All this the Innocent delivered rapidly, while Piney, a stout, comely damsel of fifteen, emerged from behind the pine-tree, where she had been blushing unseen, and rode to the side of her lover.

Mr. Oakhurst seldom troubled himself with sentiment, still less with propriety; but he had a vague idea that the situation was not fortunate. He retained, however, his presence of mind sufficiently to kick Uncle Billy, who was about to say something, and Uncle Billy was sober enough to recognize in Mr. Oakhurst's kick a superior power that would not bear trifling. He then endeavored to dissuade Tom Simson from delaying further, but in vain. He even pointed out the fact that there was no provision, nor means of making a camp. But, unluckily, the Innocent met this objection by assuring the party that he was provided with an extra mule loaded with provisions, and by the discovery of a rude attempt at a log-house near the trail. "Piney can stay with Mrs. Oakhurst," said the Innocent, pointing to the Duchess, "and I can shift for myself."

Nothing but Mr. Oakhurst's admonishing foot saved Uncle Billy from bursting into a roar of laughter. As it was, he felt compelled to retire up the cañon until he could recover his gravity. There he confided the joke to the tall pine-trees, with many slaps of his leg, contortions of his face, and the usual profanity. But when he returned to the party, found them seated by a fire—for the air had grown strangely chill, and the sky overcast—in apparently amicable conversation. Piney was actually talking in an impulsive, girlish fashion to the Duchess, who was listening with an interest and animation she had not shown for many days. The Innocent was holding forth, apparently with equal effect, to Mr. Oakhurst and Mother Shipton, who was actually relaxing into amiability. "Is this yer a d—d picnic?" said Uncle Billy, with inward scorn, as he surveyed the sylvan group, the glancing firelight, and the tethered animals in the foreground. Suddenly an idea mingled with the alcoholic fumes that disturbed his brain. It was apparently of a jocular nature, for he felt impelled to slap his leg again and cram his fist into his mouth.

As the shadows crept slowly up the mountain, a slight breeze rocked the tops of the pine-trees, and moaned through their long and gloomy aisles. The ruined cabin, patched and covered with pine-boughs, was set apart for the ladies.

As the lovers parted, they unaffectedly exchanged a kiss, so honest and sincere that it might have been heard above the swaying pines. The frail Duchess and the malevolent Mother Shipton were probably too stunned to remark upon this last evidence of simplicity, and so turned without a word to the hut. The fire was replenished, the men lay down before the door, and in a few minutes were asleep.

Mr. Oakhurst was a light sleeper. Toward morning he awoke benumbed and cold. As he stirred the dying fire, the wind, which was now blowing strongly, brought to his cheek that which caused the blood to leave it—snow!

He started to his feet with the intention of awakening the sleepers, for there was no time to lose. But turning to where Uncle Billy had been lying, he found him gone. A suspicion leaped to his brain and a curse to his lips. He ran to the spot where the mules had been tethered; they were no longer there. The tracks were already rapidly disappearing in the snow.

The momentary excitement brought Mr. Oakhurst back to the fire with his usual calm. He did not waken the sleepers. The Innocent slumbered peacefully, with a smile on his good-humored, freckled face; the virgin Piney slept beside her frailer sisters as sweetly as though attended by celestial guardians, and Mr. Oakhurst, drawing his blanket over his shoulders, stroked his mustaches and waited for the dawn. It came slowly in a whirling mist of snow-flakes that dazzled and confused the eye. What could be seen of the landscape appeared magically changed. He looked over the valley, and summed up the present and future in two words—"snowed in!"

A careful inventory of the provisions, which, fortunately for the party, had been stored within the hut, and so escaped the felonious fingers of Uncle Billy, disclosed the fact that with care and prudence they might last ten days longer. "That is," said Mr. Oakhurst *sotto voce* to the Innocent, "if you're willing to board us. If you ain't—and perhaps you'd better not—you can wait till Uncle Billy gets back with provisions." For some occult reason Mr. Oakhurst could not bring himself to disclose Uncle Billy's rascality, and so offered the hypothesis that he had wandered from the camp and had accidentally stampeded the animals. He dropped a warning to the Duchess and Mother Shipton, who of course knew the facts of their associate's defection. "They'll find out the truth about us *all* when they find out anything," he added significantly, "and there's no good frightening them now."

Tom Simson not only put all his worldly store at the disposal of Mr. Oakhurst, but seemed to enjoy the prospect of their enforced seclusion. "We'll have a good camp for a week, and then the snow'll melt, and we'll all go back together." The cheerful gaiety of the young man, and Mr. Oakhurst's calm, infected the others. The Innocent, with the aid of pine-boughs, extemporized a thatch for the roofless cabin, and the Duchess directed Piney in the rearrangement of the interior with a taste and tact that opened the blue eyes of that provincial maiden to their fullest extent. "I reckon now you're used to fine things at Poker Flat," said Piney. The Duchess turned away sharply to conceal something that reddened her cheeks through its professional tint, and Mother Shipton requested Piney not to "chatter." But when Mr. Oakhurst returned from a weary search for the trail, he heard the sound of happy laughter echoed from the rocks. He stopped in some alarm, and his thoughts first naturally reverted to the whiskey, which he had prudently cached. "And yet it don't somehow sound like whiskey," said the gambler. It was not until he caught sight of the blazing fire through the still blinding storm and the group around it, that he settled to the conviction that it was "square fun."

Whether Mr. Oakhurst had cached his cards with the whiskey as something debarred the free access of the community, I cannot say. It was certain that, in Mother Shipton's words, he "didn't say cards once" during that evening. Haply the time was beguiled by an accordion, produced somewhat ostentatiously by Tom Simson from his pack. Notwithstanding some difficulties attending the manipulation of this instrument, Piney Woods managed to pluck several reluctant melodies from its keys, to an accompaniment by the Innocent on a pair of bone castanets. But the crowning festivity of the evening was reached in a rude camp-meeting hymn, which the lovers, joining hands, sang with great earnestness and vociferation. I fear that a certain defiant tone and Covenanter's swing to its chorus, rather than any devotional quality, caused it speedily to infect the others, who at last joined in the refrain:—

"I'm proud to live in the service of the Lord,
And I'm bound to die in His army."

The pines rocked, the storm eddied and whirled above the miserable group, and the flames of their altar leaped heavenward, as if in token of the vow.

At midnight the storm abated, the rolling clouds parted, and the stars glittered keenly above the sleeping camp. Mr. Oakhurst, whose professional habits had enabled him to live on the smallest possible amount of sleep, in dividing the watch with Tom Simson, somehow managed to take upon himself the greater part of that duty. He excused himself to the Innocent by saying that he had "often been a week without sleep." "Doing what?" asked Tom. "Poker!" replied Oakhurst, sententiously; "when a man gets a streak of luck—nigger-luck—he don't get tired. The luck gives in first. Luck," continued the gambler, reflectively, "is a mighty queer thing. All you know about it for certain is that it's bound to change. And it's finding out when it's going to change that makes you. We've had a streak of bad luck since we left Poker Flat—you come along, and slap you get into it, too. If you can hold your cards right along you're all right. For," added the gambler, with cheerful irrelevance—

"'I'm proud to live in the service of the Lord,
And I'm bound to die in His army.'"

The third day came, and the sun, looking through the white-curtained valley, saw the outcasts divide their slowly decreasing store of provisions for the morning meal. It was one of the peculiarities of that mountain climate that its rays diffused a kindly warmth over the wintry landscape, as if in regretful commiseration of the past. But it revealed drift on drift of snow piled high around the hut—a hopeless, uncharted, trackless sea of white lying below the rocky shores to which the castaways still clung. Through the marvelously clear air the smoke of the pastoral village of Poker Flat rose miles away. Mother Shipton saw it, and from a remote pinnacle of her rocky fastness, hurled in that direction a final malediction. It was her last vituperative attempt, and perhaps for that reason was invested with a certain degree of sublimity. It did her good, she privately informed the Duchess. "Just you go out there and cuss, and see." She then set herself to the task of amusing "the child," as she and the Duchess were pleased to call Piney. Piney was no chicken, but it was a soothing and original theory of the pair thus to account for the fact that she didn't swear and wasn't improper.

When night crept up again through the gorges, the reedy notes of the accordion rose and fell in fitful spasms and long-drawn gasps by the flickering camp-fire. But music failed to fill entirely the aching void left by insufficient food, and a new diversion was proposed by Piney—storytelling. Neither Mr. Oakhurst nor his female companions caring to relate their personal experiences, this plan would have failed, too, but for the Innocent. Some months before he had chanced upon a stray copy of Mr. Pope's ingenious translation of the Iliad. He now proposed to narrate the principal incidents of that poem—having thoroughly mastered the argument and fairly forgotten the words—in the current vernacular of Sandy Bar. And so for the rest of that night the Homeric demigods again walked the earth. Trojan bully and wily Greek wrestled in the winds, and the great pines in the cañon seemed to bow to the wrath of the son of Peleus. Mr. Oakhurst listened with quiet satisfaction. Most especially was he interested in the fate of "Ash-heels," as the Innocent persisted in denominating the "swift-footed Achilles."

So with small food and much of Homer and the accordion, a week passed over the heads of the outcasts. The sun again forsook them, and again from leaden skies the snow-flakes were sifted over the land. Day by day closer around them drew the snowy circle, until at last they looked from their prison over drifted walls of dazzling white, that towered twenty feet above their heads. It became more and more difficult to replenish their fires, even from the fallen trees beside them, now half hidden in the drifts. And yet no one complained. The lovers turned from the dreary prospect, and looked into each other's eyes, and were happy. Mr. Oakhurst settled himself coolly to the losing game before him. The Duchess, more cheerful than she had been, assumed the care of Piney. Only Mother Shipton—once the strongest of the party—seemed to sicken and fade. At midnight on the tenth day she called Oakhurst to her side. "I'm going," she said, in a voice of querulous weakness, "but don't say anything about it. Don't waken the kids. Take the bundle from under my head, and open it." Mr. Oakhurst did so. It contained Mother Shipton's rations for the last week, untouched. "Give 'em to the child," she said, pointing to the sleeping Piney. "You've starved yourself," said the gambler. "That's what they call it," said the woman, querulously, as she lay down again, and, turning her face to the wall, passed quietly away.

The accordion and the bones were put aside that day, and Homer was forgotten. When the body of Mother Shipton had been committed to the snow, Mr. Oakhurst took the Innocent aside, and showed him a pair of snow-shoes, which he had fashioned from the old pack-saddle. "There's one chance in a hundred to save her yet," he said, pointing to Piney; "but it's there," he added, pointing toward Poker Flat. "If you can reach there in two days she's safe." "And you?" asked Tom Simson. "I'll stay here," was the curt reply.

The lovers parted with a long embrace. "You are not going, too?" said the Duchess, as she saw Mr. Oakhurst apparently waiting to accompany him. "As far as the cañon," he replied. He turned suddenly, and kissed the Duchess, leaving her pallid face aflame, and her trembling limbs rigid with amazement.

Night came, but not Mr. Oakhurst. It brought the storm again and the whirling snow. Then the Duchess, feeding the fire, found that some one had quietly piled beside the hut enough fuel to last a few days longer. The tears rose to her eyes, but she hid them from Piney.

The women slept but little. In the morning, looking into each other's faces, they read their fate. Neither spoke; but Piney, accepting the position of the stronger, drew near and placed her arm around the Duchess's waist. They kept this attitude for the rest of the day. That night the storm reached its greatest fury, and, rending asunder the protecting pines, invaded the very hut.

Toward morning they found themselves unable to feed the fire, which gradually died away. As the embers slowly blackened, the Duchess crept closer to Piney, and broke the silence of many hours: "Piney, can you pray?" "No, dear," said Piney, simply. The Duchess, without knowing exactly why, felt relieved, and, putting her head upon Piney's shoulder, spoke no more. And so reclining, the younger and purer pillowing the head of her soiled sister upon her virgin breast, they fell asleep.

The wind lulled as if it feared to waken them. Feathery drifts of snow, shaken from the long pine-boughs, flew like white-winged birds, and settled about them as they slept. The moon through the rifted clouds looked down upon what had been the camp. But all human stain, all trace of earthly travail, was hidden beneath the spotless mantle mercifully flung from above.

They slept all that day and the next, nor did

they waken when voices and footsteps broke the silence of the camp. And when pitying fingers brushed the snow from their wan faces, you could scarcely have told, from the equal peace that dwelt upon them, which was she that had sinned. Even the law of Poker Flat recognized this, and turned away, leaving them still locked in each other's arms.

But at the head of the gulch, on one of the largest pine-trees, they found the deuce of clubs pinned to the bark with a bowie-knife. It bore the following, written in pencil, in a firm hand:—

†

BENEATH THIS TREE
LIES THE BODY
OF
JOHN OAKHURST,
WHO STRUCK A STREAK OF BAD LUCK
ON THE 23RD OF NOVEMBER, 1850,
AND
HANDED IN HIS CHECKS
ON THE 7TH DECEMBER, 1850.

ǂ

And pulseless and cold, with a Derringer by his side and a bullet in his heart, though still calm as in life, beneath the snow lay he who was at once the strongest and yet the weakest of the outcasts of Poker Flat.

An Occurrence at Owl Creek Bridge

by Ambrose Bierce

I

A man stood upon a railroad bridge in northern Alabama, looking down into the swift water twenty feet below. The man's hands were behind his back, the wrists bound with a cord. A rope closely encircled his neck. It was attached to a stout cross-timber above his head and the slack fell to the level of his knees. Some loose boards laid upon the sleepers supporting the metals of the railway supplied a footing for him and his executioners—two private soldiers of the Federal army, directed by a sergeant who in civil life may have been a deputy sheriff. At a short remove upon the same temporary platform was an officer in the uniform of his rank, armed. He was a captain. A sentinel at each end of the bridge stood with his rifle in the position known as "support," that is to say, vertical in front of the left shoulder, the hammer resting on the forearm thrown straight across the chest—a formal and unnatural position, enforcing an erect carriage of the body. It did not appear to be the duty of these two men to know what was occurring at the centre of the bridge; they merely blockaded the two ends of the foot planking that traversed it.

Beyond one of the sentinels nobody was in sight; the railroad ran straight away into a forest for a hundred yards, then, curving, was lost to view. Doubtless there was an outpost farther along. The other bank of the stream was open ground—a gentle acclivity topped with a stockade of vertical tree trunks, loopholed for rifles, with a single embrasure through which protruded the muzzle of a brass cannon commanding the bridge. Midway of the slope between the bridge and fort were the spectators—a single company of infantry in line, at "parade rest," the butts of the rifles on the ground, the barrels inclining slightly backward against the right shoulder, the hands crossed upon the stock. A lieutenant stood at the right of the line, the point of his sword upon the ground, his left hand resting upon his right. Excepting the group of four at the centre of the bridge, not a man moved. The company faced the bridge, staring stonily, motionless. The sentinels, facing the banks of the stream, might have been statues to adorn the bridge. The captain stood with folded arms, silent, observing the work of his subordinates, but making no sign. Death is a dignitary who when he comes announced is to be received with formal manifestations of respect, even by those most familiar with him. In the code of military etiquette silence and fixity are forms of deference.

The man who was engaged in being hanged was apparently about thirty-five years of age. He was a civilian, if one might judge from his habit, which was that of a planter. His features were good—a straight nose, firm mouth, broad forehead, from which his long, dark hair was combed straight back, falling behind his ears to the collar of his well-fitting frock-coat. He wore a mustache and pointed beard, but no whiskers; his eyes were large and dark gray, and had a kindly expression which one would hardly have expected in one whose neck was in the hemp. Evidently this was no vulgar assassin. The liberal military code makes provision for hanging many kinds of persons, and gentlemen are not excluded.

The preparations being complete, the two private soldiers stepped aside and each drew away the plank upon which he had been standing. The sergeant turned to the captain, saluted and placed himself immediately behind that officer, who in turn moved apart one pace. These movements left the condemned man and the sergeant standing on the two ends of the same plank, which spanned three of the cross-ties of the bridge. The end upon which the civilian stood almost, but not quite, reached a fourth. This plank had been held in place by the weight of the captain; it was now held by that of the sergeant. At a signal from the former the latter would step aside, the plank would tilt and the condemned man go down between two ties. The arrangement commended itself to his judgment as simple and effective. His face had not been covered nor his eyes bandaged. He looked a moment at his "unsteadfast footing," then let his gaze wander to the swirling water of the stream racing madly beneath his feet. A piece of dancing driftwood caught his attention and his eyes followed it down the current. How slowly it appeared to move! What a sluggish stream!

He closed his eyes in order to fix his last thoughts upon his wife and children. The water, touched to gold by the early sun, the brooding mists under the banks at some distance down the stream, the fort, the soldiers, the piece of drift—all had distracted him. And now he became conscious of a new disturbance. Striking through the thought of his dear ones was a sound which he could neither ignore nor understand, a sharp, distinct, metallic percussion like the stroke of a blacksmith's hammer upon the anvil; it had the same ringing quality. He wondered what it was, and whether immeasurably distant or near by—it seemed both. Its recurrence was regular, but as slow as the tolling of a death knell. He awaited each stroke with impatience and—he knew not why—apprehension. The intervals of silence grew progressively longer; the delays became maddening. With their greater infrequency the sounds increased in strength and sharpness. They hurt his ear like the thrust of a knife; he feared he would shriek. What he heard was the ticking of his watch.

He unclosed his eyes and saw again the water below him. "If I could free my hands," he thought, "I might throw off the noose and spring into the stream. By diving I could evade the bullets and, swimming vigorously, reach the bank, take to the woods and get away home. My home, thank God, is as yet outside their lines; my wife and little ones are still beyond the invader's farthest advance."

As these thoughts, which have here to be set down in words, were flashed into the doomed man's brain rather than evolved from it the captain nodded to the sergeant. The sergeant stepped aside.

II

Peyton Farquhar was a well-to-do planter, of an old and highly respected Alabama family. Being a slave owner and like other slave owners a politician he was naturally an original secessionist and ardently devoted to the Southern cause. Circumstances of an imperious nature, which it is unnecessary to relate here, had prevented him from taking service with the gallant army that had fought the disastrous campaigns ending with the fall of Corinth, and he chafed under the inglorious restraint, longing for the release of his energies, the larger life of the soldier, the opportunity for distinction. That opportunity, he felt, would come, as it comes to all in war time. Meanwhile he did what he could. No service was too humble for him to perform in aid of the South, no adventure too perilous for him to undertake if consistent with the character of a civilian who was at heart a soldier, and who in good faith and without too much qualification assented to at least a part of the frankly villainous dictum that all is fair in love and war.

One evening while Farquhar and his wife were sitting on a rustic bench near the entrance to his grounds, a gray-clad soldier rode up to the gate and asked for a drink of water. Mrs. Farquhar was only too happy to serve him with her own white hands. While she was fetching the water her husband approached the dusty horseman and inquired eagerly for news from the front.

"The Yanks are repairing the railroads," said the man, "and are getting ready for another advance. They have reached the Owl Creek bridge, put it in order and built a stockade on the north bank. The commandant has issued an order, which is posted everywhere, declaring that any civilian caught interfering with the railroad, its bridges, tunnels or trains will be summarily hanged. I saw the order."

"How far is it to the Owl Creek bridge?" Farquhar asked.

"About thirty miles."

"Is there no force on this side the creek?"

"Only a picket post half a mile out, on the railroad, and a single sentinel at this end of the bridge."

"Suppose a man—a civilian and student of hanging—should elude the picket post and perhaps get the better of the sentinel," said Farquhar, smiling, "what could he accomplish?"

The soldier reflected. "I was there a month ago," he replied. "I observed that the flood of last winter had lodged a great quantity of driftwood against the wooden pier at this end of the bridge. It is now dry and would burn like tow."

The lady had now brought the water, which the soldier drank. He thanked her ceremoniously, bowed to her husband and rode away. An hour later, after nightfall, he repassed the plantation, going northward in the direction from which he had come. He was a Federal scout.

III

As Peyton Farquhar fell straight downward through the bridge he lost consciousness and was as one already dead. From this state he was awakened—ages later, it seemed to him—by the pain of a sharp pressure upon his throat, followed by a sense of suffocation. Keen, poignant agonies seemed to shoot from his neck downward through every fibre of his body and limbs. These pains appeared to flash along well-defined lines of ramification and to beat with an inconceivably rapid periodicity. They seemed like streams of pulsating fire heating him to an intolerable temperature. As to his head, he was conscious of nothing but a feeling of fulness—of congestion. These sensations were unaccompanied by thought. The intellectual part of his nature was already effaced; he had power only to feel, and feeling was torment. He was conscious of motion. Encompassed in a luminous cloud, of which he was now merely the fiery heart, without material substance, he swung through unthinkable arcs of oscillation, like a vast pendulum. Then all at once, with terrible suddenness, the light about him shot upward with the noise of a loud plash; a frightful roaring was in his ears, and all was cold and dark. The power of thought was restored; he knew that the rope had broken and he had fallen into the stream. There was no additional strangulation; the noose about his neck was already suffocating him and kept the water from his lungs. To die of hanging at the bottom of a river!—the idea seemed to him ludicrous. He opened his eyes in the darkness and saw above him a gleam of light, but how distant, how inaccessible! He was still sinking, for the light became fainter and fainter until it was a mere glimmer. Then it began to grow and brighten, and he knew that he was rising toward the surface—knew it with reluctance, for he was now very comfortable. "To be hanged and drowned," he thought, "that is not so bad; but I do not wish to be shot. No; I will not be shot; that is not fair."

He was not conscious of an effort, but a sharp pain in his wrist apprised him that he was trying to free his hands. He gave the struggle his attention, as an idler might observe the feat of a juggler, without interest in the outcome. What splendid effort!—what magnificent, what superhuman strength! Ah, that was a fine endeavor! Bravo! The cord fell away; his arms parted and floated upward, the hands dimly seen on each side in the growing light. He watched them with a new interest as first one and then the other pounced upon the noose at his neck. They tore it away and thrust it fiercely aside, its undulations resembling those of a water-snake. "Put it back, put it back!" He thought he shouted these words to his hands, for the undoing of the noose had been succeeded by the direst pang that he had yet experienced. His neck ached horribly; his brain was on fire; his heart, which had been fluttering faintly, gave a great leap, trying to force itself out at his mouth. His whole body was racked and wrenched with an insupportable anguish! But his disobedient hands gave no heed to the command. They beat the water vigorously with quick, downward strokes, forcing him to the surface. He felt his head emerge; his eyes were blinded by the sunlight; his chest expanded convulsively, and with a supreme and crowning agony his lungs engulfed a great draught of air, which instantly he expelled in a shriek!

He was now in full possession of his physical senses. They were, indeed, preternaturally keen and alert. Something in the awful disturbance of his organic system had so exalted and refined them that they made record of things never before perceived. He felt the ripples upon his face and heard their separate sounds as they struck. He looked at the forest on the bank of the stream, saw the individual trees, the leaves and the veining of each leaf—saw the very insects upon them: the locusts, the brilliant-bodied flies, the gray spiders stretching their webs from twig to twig. He noted the prismatic colors in all the dewdrops upon a million blades of grass. The humming of the gnats that danced above the eddies of the stream, the beating of the dragon-flies' wings, the strokes of the water-spiders' legs, like oars which had lifted their boat—all these made audible music. A fish slid along beneath his eyes and he heard the rush of its body parting the water.

He had come to the surface facing down the stream; in a moment the visible world seemed to wheel slowly round, himself the pivotal point, and he saw the bridge, the fort, the soldiers upon the bridge, the captain, the sergeant, the two privates, his executioners. They were in silhouette against the blue sky. They shouted and gesticulated, pointing at him. The captain had drawn his pistol, but did not fire; the others were unarmed. Their movements were grotesque and horrible, their forms gigantic.

Suddenly he heard a sharp report and something struck the water smartly within a few inches of his head, spattering his face with spray. He heard a second report, and saw one of the sentinels with his rifle at his shoulder, a light cloud of blue smoke rising from the muzzle. The man in the water saw the eye of the man on the bridge gazing into his own through the sights of the rifle. He observed that it was a gray eye and remembered having read that gray eyes were keenest, and that all famous marksmen had them. Nevertheless, this one had missed.

A counter-swirl had caught Farquhar and turned him half round; he was again looking into the forest on the bank opposite the fort. The sound of a clear, high voice in a monotonous singsong now rang out behind him and came across the water with a distinctness that pierced and subdued all other sounds, even the beating of the ripples in his ears. Although no soldier, he had frequented camps enough to know the dread significance of that deliberate, drawling, aspirated chant; the lieutenant on shore was taking a part in the morning's work. How coldly and pitilessly—with what an even, calm intonation, presaging, and enforcing tranquillity in the men—with what accurately measured intervals fell those cruel words:

"Attention, company! . . . Shoulder arms! . . . Ready! . . . Aim! . . . Fire!"

Farquhar dived—dived as deeply as he could. The water roared in his ears like the voice of Niagara, yet he heard the dulled thunder of the volley and, rising again toward the surface, met shining bits of metal, singularly flattened, oscillating slowly downward. Some of them touched him on the face and hands, then fell away, continuing their descent. One lodged between his collar and neck; it was uncomfortably warm and he snatched it out.

As he rose to the surface, gasping for breath, he saw that he had been a long time under water; he was perceptibly farther down stream—nearer to safety. The soldiers had almost finished reloading; the metal ramrods flashed all at once in the sunshine as they were drawn from the barrels, turned in the air, and thrust into their sockets. The two sentinels fired again, independently and ineffectually.

The hunted man saw all this over his shoulder; he was now swimming vigorously with the current. His brain was as energetic as his arms and legs; he thought with the rapidity of lightning.

"The officer," he reasoned, "will not make that martinet's error a second time. It is as easy to dodge a volley as a single shot. He has probably already given the command to fire at will. God help me, I cannot dodge them all!"

An appalling plash within two yards of him was followed by a loud, rushing sound, *diminuendo,* which seemed to travel back through the air to the fort and died in an explosion which stirred the very river to its deeps! A rising sheet of water curved over him, fell down upon him, blinded him, strangled him! The cannon had taken a hand in the game. As he shook his head free from the commotion of the smitten water he heard the deflected shot humming through the air ahead, and in an instant it was cracking and smashing the branches in the forest beyond.

"They will not do that again," he thought; "the next time they will use a charge of grape. I must keep my eye upon the gun; the smoke will apprise me—the report arrives too late; it lags behind the missile. That is a good gun."

Suddenly he felt himself whirled round and

round—spinning like a top. The water, the banks, the forests, the now distant bridge, fort and men—all were commingled and blurred. Objects were represented by their colors only; circular horizontal streaks of color—that was all he saw. He had been caught in a vortex and was being whirled on with a velocity of advance and gyration that made him giddy and sick. In a few moments he was flung upon the gravel at the foot of the left bank of the stream—the southern bank—and behind a projecting point which concealed him from his enemies. The sudden arrest of his motion, the abrasion of one of his hands on the gravel, restored him, and he wept with delight. He dug his fingers into the sand, threw it over himself in handfuls and audibly blessed it. It looked like diamonds, rubies, emeralds; he could think of nothing beautiful which it did not resemble. The trees upon the bank were giant garden plants; he noted a definite order in their arrangement, inhaled the fragrance of their blooms. A strange, roseate light shone through the spaces among their trunks and the wind made in their branches the music of æolian harps. He had no wish to perfect his escape—was content to remain in that enchanting spot until retaken.

A whiz and rattle of grapeshot among the branches high above his head roused him from his dream. The baffled cannoneer had fired him a random farewell. He sprang to his feet, rushed up the sloping bank, and plunged into the forest.

All that day he traveled, laying his course by the rounding sun. The forest seemed interminable; nowhere did he discover a break in it, not even a woodman's road. He had not known that he lived in so wild a region. There was something uncanny in the revelation.

By nightfall he was fatigued, footsore, famishing. The thought of his wife and children urged him on. At last he found a road which led him in what he knew to be the right direction. It was as wide and straight as a city street, yet it seemed untraveled. No fields bordered it, no dwelling anywhere. Not so much as the barking of a dog suggested human habitation. The black bodies of the trees formed a straight wall on both sides, terminating on the horizon in a point, like a diagram in a lesson in perspective. Overhead, as he looked up through this rift in the wood, shone great golden stars looking unfamiliar and grouped in strange constellations. He was sure they were arranged in some order which had a secret and malign significance. The wood on either side was full of singular noises, among which—once, twice, and again—he distinctly heard whispers in an unknown tongue.

His neck was in pain and lifting his hand to it found it horribly swollen. He knew that it had a circle of black where the rope had bruised it. His eyes felt congested; he could no longer close them. His tongue was swollen with thirst; he relieved its fever by thrusting it forward from between his teeth into the cold air. How softly the turf had carpeted the untraveled avenue—he could no longer feel the roadway beneath his feet!

Doubtless, despite his suffering, he had fallen asleep while walking, for now he sees another scene—perhaps he was merely recovered from a delirium. He stands at the gate of his own home. All is as he left it, and all bright and beautiful in the morning sunshine. He must have traveled the entire night. As he pushes open the gate and passes up the wide white walk, he sees a flutter of female garments; his wife, looking fresh and cool and sweet, steps down from the veranda to meet him. At the bottom of the steps she stands waiting, with a smile of ineffable joy, an attitude of matchless grace and dignity. Ah, how beautiful she is! He springs forward with extended arms. As he is about to clasp her he feels a stunning blow upon the back of the neck; a blinding white light blazes all about him with a sound like the shock of a cannon—then all is darkness and silence!

Peyton Farquhar was dead; his body, with a broken neck, swung gently from side to side beneath the timbers of the Owl Creek bridge.

The Revolt of "Mother"

by Mary E. Wilkins Freeman

"Father!"

"What is it?"

"What are them men diggin' over there in the field for?"

There was a sudden dropping and enlarging of the lower part of the old man's face, as if some heavy weight had settled therein; he shut his mouth tight, and went on harnessing the great bay mare. He hustled the collar on to her neck with a jerk.

"Father!"

The old man slapped the saddle upon the mare's back.

"Look here, father, I want to know what them men are diggin' over in the field for, an' I'm goin' to know."

"I wish you'd go into the house, mother, an' 'tend to your own affairs," the old man said then. He ran his words together, and his speech was almost as inarticulate as a growl.

But the woman understood; it was her most

native tongue. "I ain't goin' into the house till you tell me what them men are doin' over there in the field," said she.

Then she stood waiting. She was a small woman, short and straight-waisted like a child in her brown cotton gown. Her forehead was mild and benevolent between the smooth curves of gray hair; there were meek downward lines about her nose and mouth; but her eyes, fixed upon the old man, looked as if the meekness had been the result of her own will, never of the will of another.

They were in the barn, standing before the wide-open doors. The spring air, full of the smell of growing grass and unseen blossoms, came in their faces. The deep yard in front was littered with farm-wagons and piles of wood; on the edges, close to the fence and the house, the grass was a vivid green, and there were some dandelions.

The old man glanced doggedly at his wife as he tightened the last buckles on the harness. She looked as immovable to him as one of the rocks in his pasture-land, bound to the earth with generations of blackberry vines. He slapped the reins over the horse, and started forth from the barn.

"*Father!*" said she.

The old man pulled up. "What is it?"

"I want to know what them men are diggin' over there in that field for."

"They're diggin' a cellar, I s'pose, if you've got to know."

"A cellar for what?"

"A barn."

"A barn? You ain't goin' to build a barn over there where we was goin' to have a house, father?"

The old man said not another word. He hurried the horse into the farm wagon, and clattered out of the yard, jouncing as sturdily on his seat as a boy.

The woman stood a moment looking after him, then she went out of the barn across a corner of the yard to the house. The house, standing at right angles with the great barn and a long reach of sheds and out-buildings, was infinitesimal compared with them. It was scarcely as commodious for people as the little boxes under the barn eaves were for doves.

A pretty girl's face, pink and delicate as a flower, was looking out of one of the house windows. She was watching three men who were digging over in the field which bounded the yard near the road line. She turned quietly when the woman entered.

"What are they diggin' for, mother?" said she. "Did he tell you?"

"They're diggin' for—a cellar for a new barn."

"Oh, mother, he ain't goin' to build another barn?"

"That's what he says."

A boy stood before the kitchen glass combing his hair. He combed slowly and painstakingly, arranging his brown hair in a smooth hillock over his forehead. He did not seem to pay any attention to the conversation.

"Sammy, did you know father was going to build a new barn?" asked the girl.

The boy combed assiduously.

"Sammy!"

He turned, and showed a face like his father's under his smooth crest of hair. "Yes, I s'pose I did," he said, reluctantly.

"How long have you known it?" asked his mother.

"'Bout three months, I guess."

"Why didn't you tell of it?"

"Didn't think 'twould do no good."

"I don't see what father wants another barn for," said the girl, in her sweet, slow voice. She turned again to the window, and stared out at the digging men in the field. Her tender, sweet face was full of a gentle distress. Her forehead was as bald and innocent as a baby's, with the light hair strained back from it in a row of curl-papers. She was quite large, but her soft curves did not look as if they covered muscles.

Her mother looked sternly at the boy. "Is he goin' to buy more cows?" said she.

The boy did not reply; he was tying his shoes.

"Sammy, I want you to tell me if he's goin' to buy more cows."

"I s'pose he is."

"How many?"

"Four, I guess."

His mother said nothing more. She went into the pantry and there was a clatter of dishes. The boy got his cap from a nail behind the door, took an old arithmetic from the shelf, and started for school. He was lightly built, but clumsy. He went out of the yard with a curious spring in the hips, that made his loose home-made jacket tilt up in the rear.

The girl went to the sink, and began to wash the dishes that were piled up there. Her mother came promptly out of the pantry, and shoved her aside. "You wipe 'em," said she; "I'll wash. There's a good many this mornin'."

The mother plunged her hands vigorously into the water, the girl wiped the plates slowly and dreamily. "Mother," said she, "don't you think it's too bad father's goin' to build that new barn, much as we need a decent house to live in?"

Her mother scrubbed a dish fiercely. "You ain't found out yet we're women-folks, Nanny Penn," said she. "You ain't seen enough of men-folks yet to. One of these days you'll find it out, an' then you'll know that we know only what men-folks think we do, so far as any use of it goes, an' how we'd ought to reckon men-folks in with Providence, an' not complain of what they do any more than we do of the weather."

"I don't care; I don't believe George is anything like that, anyhow," said Nanny. Her delicate face flushed pink, her lips pouted softly, as if she were going to cry.

"You wait an' see. I guess George Eastman ain't no better than other men. You hadn't ought to judge father, though. He can't help it, 'cause he don't look at things jest the way we do. An' we've been pretty comfortable here, after all. The roof don't leak—ain't never but once—that's one thing. Father kept it shingled right up."

"I do wish we had a parlor."

"I guess it won't hurt George Eastman any to come to see you in a nice clean kitchen. I guess a good many girls don't have as good a place as this. Nobody's ever heard me complain."

"I ain't complained either, mother."

"Well, I don't think you'd better, a good father an' a good home as you've got. S'pose your father made you go out an' work for your livin'? Lots of girls have to that ain't no stronger an' better able to than you be."

Sarah Penn washed the frying-pan with a conclusive air. She scrubbed the outside of it as faithfully as the inside. She was a masterly keeper of her box of a house. Her one living-room never seemed to have in it any of the dust which the friction of life with inanimate matter produces. She swept, and there seemed to be no dirt to go before the broom; she cleaned, and one could see no difference. She was like an artist so perfect that he has apparently no art. Today she got out a mixing bowl and a board, and rolled some pies, and there was no more flour upon her than upon her daughter who was doing finer work. Nanny was to be married in the fall, and she was sewing on some white cambric and embroidery. She sewed industriously while her mother cooked; her soft milk-white hands and wrists showed whiter than her delicate work.

"We must have the stove moved out in the shed before long," said Mrs. Penn. "Talk about not havin' things, it's been a real blessin' to be able to put a stove up in that shed in hot weather. Father did one good thing when he fixed that stove-pipe out there."

Sarah Penn's face as she rolled her pies had that expression of meek vigor which might have characterized one of the New Testament saints. She was making mince-pies. Her husband, Adoniram Penn, liked them better than any other kind. She baked twice a week. Adoniram often liked a piece of pie between meals. She hurried this morning. It had been later than usual when she began, and she wanted to have a pie baked for dinner. However deep a resentment she might be forced to hold against her husband, she would never fail in sedulous attention to his wants.

Nobility of character manifests itself at loopholes when it is not provided with large doors. Sarah Penn's showed itself today in flaky dishes of pastry. So she made the pies faithfully, while across the table she could see, when she glanced up from her work, the sight that rankled in her patient and steadfast soul—the digging of the cellar of the new barn in the place where Adoniram forty years ago had promised her their new house should stand.

The pies were done for dinner. Adoniram and Sammy were home a few minutes after twelve o'clock. The dinner was eaten with serious haste. There was never much conversation at the table in the Penn family. Adoniram asked a blessing, and they ate promptly, then rose up and went about their work.

Sammy went back to school, taking soft sly lopes out of the yard like a rabbit. He wanted a game of marbles before school, and feared his father would give him some chores to do. Adoniram hastened to the door and called after him, but he was out of sight.

"I don't see what you let him go for, mother," said he. "I wanted him to help me unload that wood."

Adoniram went to work out in the yard unloading wood from the wagon. Sarah put away the dinner dishes, while Nanny took down her curl-papers and changed her dress. She was going down to the store to buy some more embroidery and thread.

When Nanny was gone, Mrs. Penn went to the door. "Father!" she called.

"Well, what is it?"

"I want to see you jest a minute, father."

"I can't leave this wood nohow. I've got to git it unloaded an' go for a load of gravel afore two o'clock. Sammy had ought to helped me. You hadn't ought to let him go to school so early."

"I want to see you jest a minute."

"I tell ye I can't, nohow, mother."

"Father, you come here." Sarah Penn stood in the door like a queen; she held her head as if it bore a crown; there was that patience which makes authority royal in her voice. Adoniram went.

Mrs. Penn led the way into the kitchen, and pointed to a chair. "Sit down, father," said she; "I've got somethin' I want to say to you."

He sat down heavily; his face was quite stolid, but he looked at her with restive eyes. "Well, what is it, mother?"

"I want to know what you're buildin' that new barn for, father?"

"I ain't got nothin' to say about it."

"It can't be you think you need another barn?"

"I tell ye I ain't got nothin' to say about it, mother; an' I ain't goin' to say nothin'."

"Be you goin' to buy more cows?"

Adoniram did not reply; he shut his mouth tight.

"I know you be, as well as I want to. Now, father, look here"—Sarah Penn had not sat down; she stood before her husband in the humble fashion of a Scripture woman—"I'm goin' to talk real plain to you: I never have sence I married you, but I'm goin' to now. I ain't never complained, an' I ain't goin' to complain now, but I'm goin' to talk plain. You see this room here, father; you look at it well. You see there ain't no carpet on the floor, an' you see the paper is all dirty, an' droppin' off the walls. We ain't had no new paper on it for ten year, an' then I put it on myself an' it didn't cost but ninepence a roll. You see this room, father; it's all the one I've had to work in an' eat in an' sit in sence we was married. There ain't another woman in the whole town whose husband ain't got half the means you have but what's got better. It's all the room Nanny's got to have her company in; an' there ain't one of her mates but what's got better, an' their fathers not so able as hers is. It's all the room she'll have to be married in. What would you have thought, father, if we had had our weddin' in a room no better than this? I was married in my mother's parlor, with a carpet on the floor, an' stuffed furniture, an' a mahogany card-table. An' this is all the room my daughter will have to be married in. Look here, father!"

Sarah Penn went across the room as though it were a tragic stage. She flung open a door and disclosed a tiny bedroom, only large enough for a bed and bureau, with a path between. "There, father," said she—"there's all the room I've had to sleep in forty year. All my children were born there—the two that died, an' the two that's livin'. I was sick with a fever there."

She stepped to another door and opened it. It led into the small, ill-lighted pantry. "Here," said she, "is all the buttery I've got—every place I've got for my dishes to set away my victuals in, an' to keep my milk-pans in. Father, I've been takin' care of the milk of six cows in this place, an' now you're goin' to build a new barn, an' keep more cows, an' give me more to do in it."

She threw open another door. A narrow crooked flight of stairs wound upward from it. "There, father!" said she, "I want you to look at the stairs that go up to them two unfinished chambers that are all the places our son an' daughter have had to sleep in all their lives. There ain't a prettier girl in town nor a more ladylike one than Nanny, an' that's the place she has to sleep in. It ain't so good as your horse's stall; it ain't so warm an' tight."

Sarah Penn went back and stood before her

husband. “Now, father,” said she, “I want to know if you think you’re doin’ right an’ accordin’ to what you profess. Here, when we was married, forty year ago, you promised me faithful that we should have a new house built in that lot over in the field before the year was out. You said you had money enough, an’ you wouldn’t ask me to live in no such place as this. It is forty year now, an’ you’ve been makin’ more money, an’ I’ve been savin’ of it for you ever since, an’ you ain’t built no house yet. You’ve built sheds an’ cow-houses an’ one new barn, an’ now you’re goin’ to build another. Father, I want to know if you think it’s right. You’re lodgin’ your dumb beasts better than you are your own flesh an’ blood. I want to know if you think it’s right.”

“I ain’t got nothin’ to say.”

“You can’t say nothin’ without ownin’ it ain’t right, father. An’ there’s another thing—I ain’t complained; I’ve got along forty year, an’ I s’pose I should forty more, if it wa’n’t for that—if we don’t have another house, Nanny she can’t live with us after she’s married. She’ll have to go somewheres else to live away from us, an’ it don’t seem as if I could have it so, noways, father. She wa’n’t ever strong. She’s got considerable color, but there wa’n’t never any backbone to her. I’ve always took the heft of everything off her, an’ she ain’t fit to keep house an’ do everything herself. She’ll be all worn out inside of a year.

Think of her doin' all the washin' an' ironin' an' bakin' with them soft white hands an' arms, an' sweepin'! I can't have it so, noways, father."

Mrs. Penn's face was burning; her mild eyes gleamed. She had pleaded her little cause like a Webster; she had ranged from severity to pathos; but her opponent employed that obstinate silence which makes eloquence futile with mocking echoes. Adoniram arose clumsily.

"Father, ain't you got nothin' to say?" said Mrs. Penn.

"I've got to go off after that load of gravel. I can't stan' here talkin' all day."

"Father, won't you think it over, an' have a house built there instead of a barn?"

"I ain't got nothin' to say."

Adoniram shuffled out. Mrs. Penn went into her bedroom. When she came out, her eyes were red. She had a roll of unbleached cotton cloth. She spread it out on the kitchen table, and began cutting out some shirts for her husband. The men over in the field had a team to help them this afternoon; she could hear their halloos. She had a scanty pattern for the shirts; she had to plan and piece the sleeves.

Nanny came home with her embroidery, and sat down with her needle-work. She had taken down her curl-papers, and there was a soft roll of fair hair like an aureole over her forehead; her face was as delicately fine and clear as porcelain. Suddenly she looked up, and the tender red flamed all over her face and neck. "Mother," said she.

"What say?"

"I've been thinking—I don't see how we're goin' to have any—wedding in this room. I'd be ashamed to have his folks come if we didn't have anybody else."

"Mebbe we can have some new paper before then; I can put it on. I guess you won't have no call to be ashamed of your belongin's."

"We might have the wedding in the new barn," said Nanny, with gentle pettishness. "Why, mother, what makes you look so?"

Mrs. Penn had started, and was staring at her with a curious expression. She turned again to her work, and spread out a pattern carefully on the cloth. "Nothin'," said she.

Presently Adoniram clattered out of the yard in his two-wheeled dump cart, standing as proudly upright as a Roman charioteer. Mrs. Penn opened the door and stood there a minute looking out; the halloos of the men sounded louder.

It seemed to her all through the spring months that she heard nothing but the halloos and the noises of saws and hammers. The new barn grew fast. It was a fine edifice for this little village. Men came on pleasant Sundays, in their meeting suits and clean shirt bosoms, and stood around it admiringly. Mrs. Penn did not speak of it, and Adoniram did not mention it to her, although sometimes, upon a return from inspecting it, he bore himself with injured dignity.

"It's a strange thing how your mother feels about the new barn," he said, confidentially, to Sammy one day.

Sammy only grunted after an odd fashion for a boy; he had learned it from his father.

The barn was all completed ready for use by the third week in July. Adoniram had planned to move his stock in on Wednesday; on Tuesday he received a letter which changed his plans. He came in with it early in the morning. "Sammy's been to the post-office," said he, "an' I've got a letter from Hiram." Hiram was Mrs. Penn's brother, who lived in Vermont.

"Well," said Mrs. Penn, "what does he say about the folks?"

"I guess they're all right. He says he thinks if I come up country right off there's a chance to buy jest the kind of a horse I want." He stared reflectively out of the window at the new barn.

Mrs. Penn was making pies. She went on clapping the rolling-pin into the crust, although she was very pale, and her heart beat loudly.

"I dun' know but what I'd better go," said Adoniram. "I hate to go off jest now, right in the midst of hayin', but the ten-acre lot's cut, an' I guess Rufus an' the others can git along without me three or four days. I can't get a horse round here to suit me, nohow, an' I've got to have another for all that wood-haulin' in the fall. I told Hiram to watch out, an' if he got wind of a good horse to let me know. I guess I'd better go."

"I'll get out your clean shirt an' collar," said Mrs. Penn calmly.

She laid out Adoniram's Sunday suit and his clean clothes on the bed in the little bedroom. She got his shaving-water and razor ready. At last she buttoned on his collar and fastened his black cravat.

Adoniram never wore his collar and cravat except on extra occasions. He held his head high, with a rasped dignity. When he was all ready, with his coat and hat brushed, and a lunch of pie and cheese in a paper bag, he hesitated on the threshold of the door. He looked at his wife, and his manner was defiantly apologetic. "*If* them cows come today, Sammy can drive 'em into the new barn," said he; "an' when they bring the hay up, they can pitch it in there."

"Well," replied Mrs. Penn.

Adoniram set his shaven face ahead and started. When he had cleared the door-step, he turned and looked back with a kind of nervous solemnity. "I shall be back by Saturday if nothin' happens," said he.

"Do be careful, father," returned his wife.

She stood in the door with Nanny at her elbow and watched him out of sight. Her eyes had a strange, doubtful expression in them; her peaceful forehead was contracted. She went in, and about her baking again. Nanny sat sewing. Her wedding day was drawing nearer, and she was getting pale and thin with her steady sewing. Her mother kept glancing at her.

"Have you got that pain in your side this mornin'?" she asked.

"A little."

Mrs. Penn's face, as she worked, changed, her perplexed forehead smoothed, her eyes were steady, her lips firmly set. She formed a maxim for herself, although incoherently with her unlettered thoughts. "Unsolicited opportunities are the guide-posts of the Lord to the new roads of life," she repeated in effect, and she made up her mind to her course of action.

"S'posin' I *had* wrote to Hiram," she muttered once, when she was in the pantry—"s'posin' I had wrote, an' asked him if he knew of any horse? But I didn't, an' father's goin' wa'n't none of my doin'. It looks like a providence." Her voice rang out quite loud at the last.

"What you talkin' about, mother?" called Nanny.

"Nothin'."

Mrs. Penn hurried her baking; at eleven o'clock it was all done. The load of hay from the west field came slowly down the cart track, and drew up at the new barn. Mrs. Penn ran out. "Stop!" she screamed—"stop!"

The men stopped and looked; Sammy upreared from the top of the load, and stared at his mother.

"Stop!" she cried out again. "Don't you put the hay in that barn; put it in the old one."

"Why, he said to put it in here," returned one of the hay-makers, wonderingly. He was a young man, a neighbor's son, whom Adoniram hired by the year to help on the farm.

"Don't you put the hay in the new barn; there's room enough in the old one, ain't there?" said Mrs. Penn.

"Room enough," returned the hired man, in his thick, rustic tones. "Didn't need the new barn, nohow, far as room's concerned. Well, I s'pose he changed his mind." He took hold of the horses' bridles.

Mrs. Penn went back to the house. Soon the kitchen windows were darkened, and a fragrance like warm honey came into the room.

Nanny laid down her work. "I thought father wanted them to put the hay into the new barn?" she said, wonderingly.

"It's all right," replied her mother.

Sammy slid down from the load of hay, and came in to see if dinner was ready.

"I ain't goin' to get a regular dinner today, as

long as father's gone," said his mother. "I've let the fire go out. You can have some bread an' milk an' pie. I thought we could get along." She set out some bowls of milk, some bread, and a pie on the kitchen table. "You'd better eat your dinner now," said she. "You might jest as well get through with it. I want you to help me afterward."

Nanny and Sammy stared at each other. There was something strange in their mother's manner. Mrs. Penn did not eat anything herself. She went into the pantry, and they heard her moving dishes while they ate. Presently she came out with a pile of plates. She got the clothes-basket out of the shed, and packed them in it. Nanny and Sammy watched. She brought out cups and saucers, and put them in with the plates.

"What you goin' to do, mother?" inquired Nanny, in a timid voice. A sense of something unusual made her tremble, as if it were a ghost. Sammy rolled his eyes over his pie.

"You'll see what I'm goin' to do," replied Mrs. Penn. "If you're through, Nanny, I want you to go up-stairs an' pack up your things; an' I want you, Sammy, to help me take down the bed in the bedroom."

"Oh, mother, what for?" gasped Nanny.

"You'll see."

During the next few hours a feat was performed by this simple, pious New England mother which was equal in its way to Wolfe's storming of the Heights of Abraham. It took no more genius and audacity of bravery for Wolfe to cheer his wondering soldiers up those steep precipices, under the sleeping eyes of the enemy, than for Sarah Penn, at the head of her children, to move all her little household goods into the new barn while her husband was away.

Nanny and Sammy followed their mother's instructions without a murmur; indeed, they were overawed. There is a certain uncanny and superhuman quality about all such purely original undertakings as their mother's was to them. Nanny went back and forth with her light loads, and Sammy tugged with sober energy.

At five o'clock in the afternoon the little house in which the Penns had lived for forty years had emptied itself into the new barn.

Every builder builds somewhat for unknown purposes, and is in a measure a prophet. The architect of Adoniram Penn's barn, while he designed it for the comfort of four-footed animals, had planned better than he knew for the comfort of humans. Sarah Penn saw at a glance its possibilities. Those great box-stalls, with quilts hung before them, would make better bedrooms than the one she had occupied for forty years, and there was a tight carriage-room. The harness-room, with its chimney and shelves, would make a kitchen of her dreams. The great middle space would make a parlor, by-and-by, fit for a palace. Up-stairs there was as much room as down. With partitions and windows, what a house would there be! Sarah looked at the row of stanchions before the allotted space for cows, and reflected that she would have her front entry there.

At six o'clock the stove was up in the harness-room, the kettle was boiling, and the table set for tea. It looked almost as home-like as the abandoned house across the yard had ever done. The young hired man milked, and Sarah directed him calmly to bring the milk to the new barn. He came gaping, dropping little blots of foam from the brimming pails on the grass. Before the next morning he had spread the story of Adoniram Penn's wife moving into the new barn all over the little village. Men assembled in the store and talked it over, women with shawls over their heads scuttled into each other's houses before their work was done. Any deviation from the ordinary course of life in this quiet town was enough to stop all progress in it. Everybody paused to look at the staid, independent figure on the side track. There was a difference of opinion with regard to her. Some held her to be insane; some, of a lawless and rebellious spirit.

Friday the minister went to see her. It was in

the forenoon, and she was at the barn door shelling pease for dinner. She looked up and returned his salutation with dignity, then she went on with her work. She did not invite him in. The saintly expression of her face remained fixed, but there was an angry flush over it.

The minister stood awkwardly before her, and talked. She handled the pease as if they were bullets. At last she looked up, and her eyes showed the spirit that her meek front had covered for a lifetime.

"There ain't no use talkin', Mr. Hersey," said she. "I've thought it all over an' over, an' I believe I'm doin' what's right. I've made it the subject of prayer, an' it's betwixt me an' the Lord an' Adoniram. There ain't no call for nobody else to worry about it."

"Well, of course, if you have brought it to the Lord in prayer, and feel satisfied that you are doing right, Mrs. Penn," said the minister, helplessly. His thin gray-bearded face was pathetic. He was a sickly man; his youthful confidence had cooled; he had to scourge himself up to some of his pastoral duties as relentlessly as a Catholic ascetic, and then he was prostrated by the smart.

"I think it's right jest as much as I think it was right for our forefathers to come over from the old country, 'cause they didn't have what belonged to 'em," said Mrs. Penn. She arose. The barn threshold might have been Plymouth Rock from her bearing. "I don't doubt you mean well, Mr. Hersey," said she, "but there are things people hadn't ought to interfere with. I've been a member of the church for over forty year. I've got my own mind an' my own feet, an' I'm goin' to think my own thoughts an' go my own ways, an' nobody but the Lord is goin' to dictate to me unless I've a mind to have him. Won't you come in an' set down? How is Mis' Hersey?"

"She is well, I thank you," replied the minister. He added some more perplexed apologetic remarks; then he retreated.

He could expound the intricacies of every character study in the Scriptures, he was competent to grasp the Pilgrim Fathers and all historical innovators, but Sarah Penn was beyond him. He could deal with primal cases, but parallel ones worsted him. But, after all, although it was aside from his province, he wondered more how Adoniram Penn would deal with his wife than how the Lord would. Everybody shared the wonder. When Adoniram's four new cows arrived, Sarah ordered three to be put in the old barn, the other in the house shed where the cooking-stove had stood. That added to the excitement. It was whispered that all four cows were domiciled in the house.

Toward sunset on Saturday, when Adoniram was expected home, there was a knot of men in the road near the new barn. The hired man had milked, but he still hung around the premises. Sarah Penn had supper all ready. There were brown-bread and baked beans and a custard pie; it was the supper that Adoniram loved on a Saturday night. She had on a clean calico, and she bore herself imperturbably. Nanny and Sammy kept close at her heels. Their eyes were large, and Nanny was full of nervous tremors. Still there was to them more pleasant excitement than anything else. An inborn confidence in their mother over their father asserted itself.

Sammy looked out of the harness-room window. "There he is," he announced, in an awed whisper. He and Nanny peeped around the casing. Mrs. Penn kept on about her work. The children watched Adoniram leave the new horse standing in the drive while he went to the house door. It was fastened. Then he went around to the shed. That door was seldom locked, even when the family was away. The thought how her father would be confronted by the cow flashed upon Nanny. There was a hysterical sob in her throat. Adoniram emerged from the shed and stood looking about in a dazed fashion. His lips moved; he was saying something, but they could not hear what it was. The hired man was peeping around a corner of the old barn, but nobody saw him.

Adoniram took the new horse by the bridle

and led him across the yard to the new barn. Nanny and Sammy slunk close to their mother. The barn doors rolled back, and there stood Adoniram, with the long mild face of the great Canadian farm horse looking over his shoulder.

Nanny kept behind her mother, but Sammy stepped suddenly forward, and stood in front of her.

Adoniram stared at the group. "What on airth you all down here for?" said he. "What's the matter over to the house?"

"We've come here to live, father," said Sammy. His shrill voice quavered out bravely.

"What"—Adoniram sniffed—"what is it smells like cookin'?" said he. He stepped forward and looked in the open door of the harness-room. Then he turned to his wife. His old bristling face was pale and frightened. "What on airth does this mean, mother?" he gasped.

"You come in here, father," said Sarah. She led the way into the harness-room and shut the door. "Now, father," said she, "you needn't be scared. I ain't crazy. There ain't nothin' to be upset over. But we've come here to live, an' we're goin' to live here. We've got jest as good a right here as new horses an' cows. The house wa'n't fit for us to live in any longer, an' I made up my mind I wa'n't goin' to stay there. I've done my duty by you forty year, an' I'm goin' to do it now; but I'm goin' to live here. You've got to put in some windows and partitions; an' you'll have to buy some furniture."

"Why, mother!" the old man gasped.

"You'd better take your coat off an' get washed—there's the wash-basin—an' then we'll have supper."

"Why, mother!"

Sammy went past the window, leading the new horse to the old barn. The old man saw him, and shook his head speechlessly. He tried to take off his coat, but his arms seemed to lack the power. His wife helped him. She poured some water into the tin basin, and put in a piece of soap. She got the comb and brush, and smoothed his thin gray hair after he had washed. Then she put the beans, hot bread, and tea on the table. Sammy came in, and the family drew up. Adoniram sat looking dazedly at his plate, and they waited.

"Ain't you goin' to ask a blessin', father?" said Sarah.

And the old man bent his head and mumbled.

All through the meal he stopped eating at intervals, and stared furtively at his wife; but he ate well. The home food tasted good to him, and his old frame was too sturdily healthy to be affected by his mind. But after supper he went out and sat down on the step of the smaller door at the right of the barn, through which he had meant his Jerseys to pass in stately file, but which Sarah designed for her front house-door, and he leaned his head on his hands.

After the supper dishes were cleared away and the milk-pans washed, Sarah went out to him. The twilight was deepening. There was a clear green glow in the sky. Before them stretched the smooth level of field; in the distance was a cluster of hay-stacks like the huts of a village; the air was very cool and calm and sweet. The landscape might have been an ideal one of peace.

Sarah bent over and touched her husband on one of his thin, sinewy shoulders. "Father!"

The old man's shoulders heaved: he was weeping.

"Why, don't do so, father," said Sarah.

"I'll—put up the—partitions, an'—everything you—want, mother."

Sarah put her apron up to her face; she was overcome by her own triumph.

Adoniram was like a fortress whose walls had no active resistance, and went down the instant the right besieging tools were used. "Why, mother," he said, hoarsely, "I hadn't no idee you was so set on't as all this comes to."

The Yellow Wall-Paper

by Charlotte Perkins Gilman

It is very seldom that mere ordinary people like John and myself secure ancestral halls for the summer.

A colonial mansion, a hereditary estate, I would say a haunted house, and reach the height of romantic felicity—but that would be asking too much of fate!

Still I will proudly declare that there is something queer about it.

Else, why should it be let so cheaply? And why have stood so long untenanted?

John laughs at me, of course, but one expects that in marriage.

John is practical in the extreme. He has no patience with faith, an intense horror of superstition, and he scoffs openly at any talk of things not to be felt and seen and put down in figures.

John is a physician, and *perhaps*—(I would not say it to a living soul, of course, but this is dead paper and a great relief to my mind—) *perhaps* that is one reason I do not get well faster.

You see he does not believe I am sick!

And what can one do?

If a physician of high standing, and one's own husband, assures friends and relatives that there is really nothing the matter with one but temporary nervous depression—a slight hysterical tendency—what is one to do?

My brother is also a physician, and also of high standing, and he says the same thing.

So I take phosphates or phosphites—whichever it is, and tonics, and journeys, and air, and exercise, and am absolutely forbidden to "work" until I am well again.

Personally, I disagree with their ideas.

Personally, I believe that congenial work, with excitement and change, would do me good.

But what is one to do?

I did write for a while in spite of them; but it *does* exhaust me a good deal—having to be so sly about it, or else meet with heavy opposition.

I sometimes fancy that in my condition if I had less opposition and more society and stimulus—but John says the very worst thing I can do is to think about my condition, and I confess it always makes me feel bad.

So I will let it alone and talk about the house.

The most beautiful place! It is quite alone, standing well back from the road, quite three miles from the village. It makes me think of English places that you read about, for there are hedges and walls and gates that lock, and lots of separate little houses for the gardeners and people.

There is a *delicious* garden! I never saw such a garden—large and shady, full of box-bordered paths, and lined with long grape-covered arbors with seats under them.

There were greenhouses, too, but they are all broken now.

There was some legal trouble, I believe, something about the heirs and coheirs; anyhow, the place has been empty for years.

That spoils my ghostliness, I am afraid, but I don't care—there is something strange about the house—I can feel it.

I even said so to John one moonlight evening, but he said what I felt was a *draught,* and shut the window.

I get unreasonably angry with John sometimes. I'm sure I never used to be so sensitive. I think it is due to this nervous condition.

But John says if I feel so, I shall neglect proper self-control; so I take pains to control myself—before him, at least, and that makes me very tired.

I don't like our room a bit. I wanted one down-stairs that opened on the piazza and had roses all over the window, and such pretty old-fashioned chintz hangings! but John would not hear of it.

He said there was only one window and not room for two beds, and no near room for him if he took another.

He is very careful and loving, and hardly lets me stir without special direction.

I have a schedule prescription for each hour in the day; he takes all care from me, and so I feel basely ungrateful not to value it more.

He said we came here solely on my account, that I was to have perfect rest and all the air I could get. "Your exercise depends on your strength, my dear," said he, "and your food somewhat on your appetite; but air you can absorb all the time." So we took the nursery at the top of the house.

It is a big, airy room, the whole floor nearly, with windows that look all ways, and air and sunshine galore. It was nursery first and then playroom and gymnasium, I should judge; for the windows are barred for little children, and there are rings and things in the walls.

The paint and paper look as if a boys' school had used it. It is stripped off—the paper—in great patches all around the head of my bed, about as far as I can reach, and in a great place on the other side of the room low down. I never saw a worse paper in my life.

One a those sprawling flamboyant patterns committing every artistic sin.

It is dull enough to confuse the eye in following, pronounced enough to constantly irritate and provoke study, and when you follow the lame uncertain curves for a little distance they suddenly commit suicide—plunge off at outrageous angles, destroy themselves in unheard of contradictions.

The color is repellant, almost revolting; a smouldering unclean yellow, strangely faded by the slow-turning sunlight.

It is a dull yet lurid orange in some places, a sickly sulphur tint in others.

No wonder the children hated it! I should hate it myself if I had to live in this room long.

There comes John, and I must put this away,—he hates to have me write a word.

* * *

We have been here two weeks, and I haven't felt like writing before, since that first day.

I am sitting by the window now, up in this atrocious nursery, and there is nothing to hinder my writing as much as I please, save lack of strength.

John is away all day, and even some nights when his cases are serious.

I am glad my case is not serious!

But these nervous troubles are dreadfully depressing.

John does not know how much I really suffer. He knows there is no *reason* to suffer, and that satisfies him.

Of course it is only nervousness. It does weigh on me so not to do my duty in any way!

I meant to be such a help to John, such a real rest and comfort, and here I am a comparative burden already!

Nobody would believe what an effort it is to do what little I am able,—to dress and entertain, and order things.

It is fortunate Mary is so good with the baby. Such a dear baby!

And yet I *cannot* be with him, it makes me so nervous.

I suppose John never was nervous in his life. He laughs at me so about this wall-paper!

At first he meant to repaper the room, but afterwards he said that I was letting it get the better of me, and that nothing was worse for a nervous patient than to give way to such fancies.

He said that after the wall-paper was changed it would be the heavy bedstead, and then the barred windows, and then that gate at the head of the stairs, and so on.

"You know the place is doing you good," he said, "and really, dear, I don't care to renovate the house just for a three months' rental."

"Then do let us go down-stairs," I said, "there are such pretty rooms there."

Then he took me in his arms and called me a blessed little goose, and said he would go down cellar, if I wished, and have it whitewashed into the bargain.

But he is right enough about the beds and windows and things.

It is an airy and comfortable room as any one need wish, and, of course, I would not be so silly as to make him uncomfortable just for a whim.

I'm really getting quite fond of the big room, all but that horrid paper.

Out of one window I can see the garden, those mysterious deep-shaded arbors, the riotous old-fashioned flowers, and bushes and gnarly trees.

Out of another I get a lovely view of the bay and a little private wharf belonging to the estate. There is a beautiful shaded lane that runs down there from the house. I always fancy I see people walking in these numerous paths and arbors, but John has cautioned me not to give way to fancy in the least. He says that with my imaginative power and habit of story-making, a nervous weakness like mine is sure to lead to all manner of excited fancies, and that I ought to use my will and good sense to check the tendency. So I try.

I think sometimes that if I were only well enough to write a little it would relieve the press of ideas and rest me.

But I find I get pretty tired when I try.

It is so discouraging not to have any advice and companionship about my work. When I get really well, John says we will ask Cousin Henry and Julia down for a long visit; but he says he would as soon put fireworks in my pillow-case as to let me have those stimulating people about now.

I wish I could get well faster.

But I must not think about that. This paper looks to me as if it *knew* what a vicious influence it had!

There is a recurrent spot where the pattern lolls like a broken neck and two bulbous eyes stare at you upside down.

I get positively angry with the impertinence of it and the everlastingness. Up and down and sideways they crawl, and those absurd, unblinking eyes are everywhere There is one place where two breadths didn't match, and the eyes go all up and down the line, one a little higher than the other.

I never saw so much expression in an inanimate thing before, and we all know how much expression they have! I used to lie awake as a child and get more entertainment and terror out of blank walls and plain furniture than most children could find in a toy-store.

I remember what a kindly wink the knobs of our big, old bureau used to have, and there was one chair that always seemed like a strong friend.

I used to feel that if any of the other things looked too fierce I could always hop into that chair and be safe.

The furniture in this room is no worse than inharmonious, however, for we had to bring it all from down-stairs. I suppose when this was used as a playroom they had to take the nursery things out, and no wonder! I never saw such ravages as the children have made here.

The wall-paper, as I said before, is torn off in spots, and it sticketh closer than a brother—they must have had perseverance as well as hatred.

Then the floor is scratched and gouged and splintered, the plaster itself is dug out here and there, and this great heavy bed which is all we found in the room, looks as if it had been through the wars.

But I don't mind it a bit—only the paper.

There comes John's sister. Such a dear girl as she is, and so careful of me! I must not let her find me writing.

She is a perfect and enthusiastic housekeeper, and hopes for no better profession. I verily believe she thinks it is the writing which made me sick!

But I can write when she is out, and see her a long way off from these windows.

There is one that commands the road, a lovely shaded winding road, and one that just looks off over the country. A lovely country, too, full of great elms and velvet meadows.

This wall-paper has a kind of sub-pattern in a different shade, a particularly irritating one, for you can only see it in certain lights, and not clearly then.

But in the places where it isn't faded and where the sun is just so—I can see a strange, provoking, formless sort of figure, that seems to skulk about behind that silly and conspicuous front design.

There's sister on the stairs!

* * *

Well, the Fourth of July is over! The people are all gone and I am tired out. John thought it might do me good to see a little company, so we just had mother and Nellie and the children down for a week.

Of course I didn't do a thing. Jennie sees to everything now.

But it tired me all the same.

John says if I don't pick up faster he shall send me to Weir Mitchell in the fall.

But I don't want to go there at all. I had a friend who was in his hands once, and she says he is just like John and my brother, only more so!

Besides, it is such an undertaking to go so far.

I don't feel as if it was worth while to turn my hand over for anything, and I'm getting dreadfully fretful and querulous.

I cry at nothing, and cry most of the time.

Of course I don't when John is here, or anybody else, but when I am alone.

And I am alone a good deal just now. John is kept in town very often by serious cases, and Jennie is good and lets me alone when I want her to.

So I walk a little in the garden or down that lovely lane, sit on the porch under the roses, and lie down up here a good deal.

I'm getting really fond of the room in spite of the wall-paper. Perhaps *because* of the wall-paper.

It dwells in my mind so!

I lie here on this great immovable bed—it is nailed down, I believe—and follow that pattern about by the hour. It is as good as gymnastics, I assure you. I start, we'll say, at the bottom, down in the corner over there where it has not been touched, and I determine for the thousandth time that I *will* follow that pointless pattern to some sort of a conclusion.

I know a little of the principle of design, and I know this thing was not arranged on any laws of radiation, or alternation, or repetition, or symmetry, or anything else that I ever heard of.

It is repeated, of course, by the breadths, but not otherwise.

Looked at in one way each breadth stands alone, the bloated curves and flourishes—a kind of "debased Romanesque" with *delirium tremens*—go waddling up and down in isolated columns of fatuity.

But, on the other hand, they connect diagonally, and the sprawling outlines run off in great slanting waves of optic horror, like a lot of wallowing seaweeds in full chase.

The whole thing goes horizontally, too, at least it seems so, and I exhaust myself in trying to distinguish the order of its going in that direction.

They have used a horizontal breadth for a frieze, and that adds wonderfully to the confusion.

There is one end of the room where it is almost intact, and there, when the crosslights fade and the low sun shines directly upon it, I can almost fancy radiation after all,—the interminable grotesque seem to form around a common center and rush off in headlong plunges of equal distraction.

It makes me tired to follow it. I will take a nap I guess.

* * *

I don't know why I should write this.

I don't want to.

I don't feel able.

And I know John would think it absurd. But I *must* say what I feel and think in some way—it is such a relief!

But the effort is getting to be greater than the relief.

Half the time now I am awfully lazy, and lie down ever so much.

John says I mustn't lose my strength, and has me take cod liver oil and lots of tonics and things, to say nothing of ale and wine and rare meat.

Dear John! He loves me very dearly, and hates to have me sick. I tried to have a real earnest reasonable talk with him the other day, and tell him how I wish he would let me go and make a visit to Cousin Henry and Julia.

But he said I wasn't able to go, nor able to stand it after I got there; and I did not make out a very good case for myself, for I was crying before I had finished.

It is getting to be a great effort for me to think straight. Just this nervous weakness I suppose.

And dear John gathered me up in his arms, and just carried me upstairs and laid me on the bed, and sat by me and read to me till it tired my head.

He said I was his darling and his comfort and all he had, and that I must take care of myself for his sake, and keep well.

He says no one but myself can help me out of it, that I must use my will and self-control and not let any silly fancies run away with me.

There's one comfort, the baby is well and happy, and does not have to occupy this nursery with the horrid wall-paper.

If we had not used it, that blessed child would have! What a fortunate escape! Why, I wouldn't have a child of mine, an impressionable little thing, live in such a room for worlds.

I never thought of it before, but it is lucky that John kept me here after all, I can stand it so much easier than a baby, you see.

Of course I never mention it to them any more—I am too wise,—but I keep watch of it all the same.

There are things in that paper that nobody knows but me, or ever will.

Behind that outside pattern the dim shapes get clearer every day.

It is always the same shape, only very numerous.

And it is like a woman stooping down and creeping about behind that pattern. I don't like it a bit. I wonder—I begin to think—I wish John would take me away from here!

* * *

It is so hard to talk with John about my case, because he is so wise, and because he loves me so.

But I tried it last night.

It was moonlight. The moon shines in all around just as the sun does.

I hate to see it sometimes, it creeps so slowly, and always comes in by one window or another.

John was asleep and I hated to waken him, so I kept still and watched the moonlight on that undulating wall-paper till I felt creepy.

The faint figure behind seemed to shake the pattern, just as if she wanted to get out.

I got up softly and went to feel and see if the paper *did* move, and when I came back John was awake.

"What is it, little girl?" he said. "Don't go walking about like that—you'll get cold."

I thought it was a good time to talk, so I told him that I really was not gaining here, and that I wished he would take me away.

"Why darling!" said he, "our lease will be up in three weeks, and I can't see how to leave before.

"The repairs are not done at home, and I cannot possibly leave town just now. Of course if you were in any danger, I could and would, but you really are better, dear, whether you can see it or not. I am a doctor, dear, and I know. You are gaining flesh and color, your appetite is better, I feel really much easier about you."

"I don't weigh a bit more," said I, "nor as

much; and my appetite may be better in the evening when you are here, but it is worse in the morning when you are away!"

"Bless her little heart!" said he with a big hug, "she shall be as sick as she pleases! But now let's improve the shining hours by going to sleep, and talk about it in the morning!"

"And you won't go away?" I asked gloomily.

"Why, how can I, dear? It is only three weeks more and then we will take a nice little trip of a few days while Jennie is getting the house ready. Really dear you are better!"

"Better in body perhaps—" I began, and stopped short, for he sat up straight and looked at me with such a stern, reproachful look that I could not say another word.

"My darling," said he, "I beg of you, for my sake and for our child's sake, as well as for your own, that you will never for one instant let that idea enter your mind! There is nothing so dangerous, so fascinating, to a temperament like yours. It is a false and foolish fancy. Can you not trust me as a physician when I tell you so?"

So of course I said no more on that score, and we went to sleep before long. He thought I was asleep first, but I wasn't, and lay there for hours trying to decide whether that front pattern and the back pattern really did move together or separately.

* * *

On a pattern like this, by daylight, there is a lack of sequence, a defiance of law, that is a constant irritant to a normal mind.

The color is hideous enough, and unreliable enough, and infuriating enough, but the pattern is torturing.

You think you have mastered it, but just as you get well underway in following, it turns a back-somersault and there you are. It slaps you in the face, knocks you down, and tramples upon you. It is like a bad dream.

The outside pattern is a florid arabesque, reminding one of a fungus. If you can imagine a toadstool in joints, an interminable string of toadstools, budding and sprouting in endless convolutions—why, that is something like it.

That is, sometimes!

There is one marked peculiarity about this paper, a thing nobody seems to notice but myself, and that is that it changes as the light changes.

When the sun shoots in through the east window—I always watch for that first long, straight ray—it changes so quickly that I never can quite believe it.

That is why I watch it always.

By moonlight—the moon shines in all night when there is a moon—I wouldn't know it was the same paper.

At night in any kind of light, in twilight, candlelight, lamplight, and worst of all by moonlight, it becomes bars! The outside pattern I mean, and the woman behind it is as plain as can be.

I didn't realize for a long time what the thing was that showed behind, that dim sub-pattern, but now I am quite sure it is a woman.

By daylight she is subdued, quiet. I fancy it is the pattern that keeps her so still. It is so puzzling. It keeps me quiet by the hour.

I lie down ever so much now. John says it is good for me, and to sleep all I can.

Indeed he started the habit by making me lie down for an hour after each meal.

It is a very bad habit I am convinced, for you see I don't sleep.

And that cultivates deceit, for I don't tell them I'm awake—O no!

The fact is I am getting a little afraid of John.

He seems very queer sometimes, and even Jennie has an inexplicable look.

It strikes me occasionally, just as a scientific hypothesis,—that perhaps it is the paper!

I have watched John when he did not know I was looking, and come into the room suddenly on the most innocent excuses, and I've caught him several times *looking at the paper!* And Jennie too. I caught Jennie with her hand on it once.

She didn't know I was in the room, and when I asked her in a quiet, a very quiet voice, with the most restrained manner possible, what she was doing with the paper—she turned around as if she had been caught stealing, and looked quite angry—asked me why I should frighten her so!

Then she said that the paper stained everything it touched, that she had found yellow smooches on all my clothes and John's, and she wished we would be more careful!

Did not that sound innocent? But I know she was studying that pattern, and I am determined that nobody shall find it out but myself!

* * *

Life is very much more exciting now than it used to be. You see I have something more to expect, to look forward to, to watch. I really do eat better, and am more quiet than I was.

John is so pleased to see me improve! He laughed a little the other day, and said I seemed to be flourishing in spite of my wall-paper.

I turned it off with a laugh. I had no intention of telling him it was *because* of the wall-paper—he would make fun of me. He might even want to take me away.

I don't want to leave now until I have found it out. There is a week more, and I think that will be enough.

* * *

I'm feeling ever so much better! I don't sleep much at night, for it is so interesting to watch developments; but I sleep a good deal in the daytime.

In the daytime it is tiresome and perplexing.

There are always new shoots on the fungus, and new shades of yellow all over it. I cannot keep count of them, though I have tried conscientiously.

It is the strangest yellow, that wall-paper! It makes me think of all the yellow things I ever saw—not beautiful ones like buttercups, but old foul, bad yellow things.

But there is something else about that paper—the smell! I noticed it the moment we came into the room, but with so much air and sun it was not bad. Now we have had a week of fog and rain, and whether the windows are open or not, the smell is here.

It creeps all over the house.

I find it hovering in the dining-room, skulking in the parlor, hiding in the hall, lying in wait for me on the stairs.

It gets into my hair.

Even when I go to ride, if I turn my head suddenly and surprise it—there is that smell!

Such a peculiar odor, too! I have spent hours in trying to analyze it, to find what it smelled like.

It is not bad—at first, and very gentle, but quite the subtlest, most enduring odor I ever met.

In this damp weather it is awful, I wake up in the night and find it hanging over me.

It used to disturb me at first. I thought seriously of burning the house—to reach the smell.

But now I am used to it. The only thing I can think of that it is like is the *color* of the paper! A yellow smell.

There is a very funny mark on this wall, low down, near the mopboard. A streak that runs round the room. It goes behind every piece of furniture, except the bed, a long, straight, even *smooch,* as if it had been rubbed over and over.

I wonder how it was done and who did it, and what they did it for. Round and round and round—round and round and round—it makes me dizzy!

* * *

I really have discovered something at last.

Through watching so much at night, when it changes so, I have finally found out.

The front pattern *does* move—and no wonder! The woman behind shakes it!

Sometimes I think there are a great many women behind, and sometimes only one, and she crawls around fast, and her crawling shakes it all over.

Then in the very bright spots she keeps still, and in the very shady spots she just takes hold of the bars and shakes them hard.

And she is all the time trying to climb through. But nobody could climb through that pattern—it strangles so; I think that is why it has so many heads.

They get through, and then the pattern strangles them off and turns them upside down, and makes their eyes white!

If those heads were covered or taken off it would not be half so bad.

* * *

I think that woman gets out in the daytime!

And I'll tell you why—privately—I've seen her!

I can see her out of every one of my windows!

It is the same woman, I know, for she is always creeping, and most women do not creep by daylight.

I see her in that long shaded lane, creeping up and down. I see her in those dark grape arbors, creeping all around the garden.

I see her on that long road under the trees, creeping along, and when a carriage comes she hides under the blackberry vines.

I don't blame her a bit. It must be very humiliating to be caught creeping by daylight!

I always lock the door when I creep by daylight. I can't do it at night, for I know John would suspect something at once.

And John is so queer now, that I don't want to irritate him. I wish he would take another room! Besides, I don't want anybody to get that woman out at night but myself.

I often wonder if I could see her out of all the windows at once.

But, turn as fast as I can, I can only see out of one at one time.

And though I always see her, she *may* be able to creep faster than I can turn!

I have watched her sometimes away off in the open country, creeping as fast as a cloud shadow in a high wind.

* * *

If only that top pattern could be gotten off from the under one! I mean to try it, little by little.

I have found out another funny thing, but I shan't tell it this time! It does not do to trust people too much.

There are only two more days to get this paper off, and I believe John is beginning to notice. I don't like the look in his eyes.

And I heard him ask Jennie a lot of professional questions about me. She had a very good report to give.

She said I slept a good deal in the daytime.

John knows I don't sleep very well at night, for all I'm so quiet!

He asked me all sorts of questions, too, and pretended to be very loving and kind.

As if I couldn't see through him!

Still, I don't wonder he acts so, sleeping under this paper for three months.

It only interests me, but I feel sure John and Jennie are secretly affected by it.

* * *

Hurrah! This is the last day, but it is enough. John is to stay in town over night, and won't be out until this evening.

Jennie wanted to sleep with me—the sly thing! but I told her I should undoubtedly rest better for a night all alone.

That was clever, for really I wasn't alone a bit! As soon as it was moonlight and that poor thing began to crawl and shake the pattern, I got up and ran to help her.

I pulled and she shook, I shook and she pulled, and before morning we had peeled off yards of that paper.

A strip about as high as my head and half around the room.

And then when the sun came and that awful pattern began to laugh at me, I declared I would finish it today!

We go away tomorrow, and they are moving all my furniture down again to leave things as they were before.

Jennie looked at the wall in amazement, but I told her merrily that I did it out of pure spite at the vicious thing.

She laughed and said she wouldn't mind doing it herself, but I must not get tired.

How she betrayed herself that time!

But I am here, and no person touches this paper but me,—not *alive!*

She tried to get me out of the room—it was too patent! But I said it was so quiet and empty and clean now that I believed I would lie down again and sleep all I could; and not to wake me even for dinner—I would call when I woke.

So now she is gone, and the servants are gone, and the things are gone, and there is nothing left but that great bedstead nailed down, with the canvas mattress we found on it.

We shall sleep down-stairs to-night, and take the boat home tomorrow.

I quite enjoy the room, now it is bare again.

How those children did tear about here!

This bedstead is fairly gnawed!

But I must get to work.

I have locked the door and thrown the key down into the front path.

I don't want to go out, and I don't want to have anybody come in, till John comes.

I want to astonish him.

I've got a rope up here that even Jennie did not find. If that woman does get out, and tries to get away, I can tie her!

But I forgot I could not reach far without anything to stand on!

This bed will *not* move!

I tried to lift and push it until I was lame, and then I got so angry I bit off a little piece at one corner—but it hurt my teeth.

Then I peeled off all the paper I could reach

standing on the floor. It sticks horribly and the pattern just enjoys it! All those strangled heads and bulbous eyes and waddling fungus growths just shriek with derision!

I am getting angry enough to do something desperate. To jump out of the window would be admirable exercise, but the bars are too strong even to try.

Besides I wouldn't do it. Of course not. I know well enough that a step like that is improper and might be misconstrued.

I don't like to *look* out of the windows even—there are so many of those creeping women, and they creep so fast.

I wonder if they all come out of that wall-paper as I did?

But I am securely fastened now by my well-hidden rope—you don't get *me* out in the road there!

I suppose I shall have to get back behind the pattern when it comes night, and that is hard!

It is so pleasant to be out in this great room and creep around as I please!

I don't want to go outside. I won't, even if Jennie asks me to.

For outside you have to creep on the ground, and everything is green instead of yellow.

But here I can creep smoothly on the floor, and my shoulder just fits in that long smooch around the wall, so I cannot lose my way.

Why there's John at the door!

It is no use, young man, you can't open it!

How he does call and pound!

Now he's crying for an axe.

It would be a shame to break down that beautiful door!

"John dear!" said I in the gentlest voice, "the key is down by the front steps, under a plantain leaf!"

That silenced him for a few moments.

Then he said—very quietly indeed—"Open the door, my darling!"

"I can't," said I. "The key is down by the front door under a plantain leaf!"

And then I said it again, several times, very gently and slowly, and said it so often that he had to go and see, and he got it of course, and came in. He stopped short by the door.

"What is the matter?" he cried. "For God's sake, what are you doing!"

I kept on creeping just the same, but I looked at him over my shoulder.

"I've got out at last," said I, "in spite of you and Jane. And I've pulled off most of the paper, so you can't put me back!"

Now why should that man have fainted? But he did, and right across my path by the wall, so that I had to creep over him every time!

The £1,000,000 Bank-Note
by Mark Twain

When I was twenty-seven years old, I was a mining-broker's clerk in San Francisco, and an expert in all the details of stock traffic. I was alone in the world, and had nothing to depend upon but my wits and a clean reputation; but these were setting my feet in the road to eventual fortune, and I was content with the prospect.

My time was my own after the afternoon board, Saturdays, and I was accustomed to put it in on a little sail-boat on the bay. One day I ventured too far, and was carried out to sea. Just at nightfall, when hope was about gone, I was picked up by a small brig which was bound for London. It was a long and stormy voyage, and they made me work my passage without pay, as a common sailor. When I stepped ashore in London my clothes were ragged and shabby, and I had only a dollar in my pocket. This money fed and sheltered me twenty-four hours.

During the next twenty-four I went without food and shelter.

About ten o'clock on the following morning, seedy and hungry, I was dragging myself along Portland Place, when a child that was passing, towed by a nurse-maid, tossed a luscious big pear—minus one bite—into the gutter. I stopped, of course, and fastened my desiring eye on that muddy treasure. My mouth watered for it, my stomach craved it, my whole being begged for it. But every time I made a move to get it some passing eye detected my purpose, and of course I straightened up then, and looked indifferent, and pretended that I hadn't been thinking about the pear at all. This same thing kept happening and happening, and I couldn't get the pear. I was just getting desperate enough to brave all the shame, and to seize it, when a window behind me was raised, and a gentleman spoke out of it, saying:

"Step in here, please."

I was admitted by a gorgeous flunkey, and shown into a sumptuous room where a couple of elderly gentlemen were sitting. They sent away the servant, and made me sit down. They had just finished their breakfast, and the sight of the remains of it almost overpowered me. I could hardly keep my wits together in the presence of that food, but as I was not asked to sample it, I had to bear my trouble as best I could.

Now, something had been happening there a little before, which I did not know anything about until a good many days afterward, but I will tell you about it now. Those two old brothers had been having a pretty hot argument a couple of days before, and had ended by agreeing to decide it by a bet, which is the English way of settling everything.

You will remember that the Bank of England once issued two notes of a million pounds each, to be used for a special purpose connected with some public transaction with a foreign country. For some reason or other only one of these had been used and canceled; the other still lay in the vaults of the Bank. Well, the brothers, chatting along, happened to get to wondering what might be the fate of a perfectly honest and intelligent stranger who should be turned adrift in London without a friend, and with no money but that million-pound bank-note, and no way to account for his being in possession of it. Brother A said he would starve to death; Brother B said he wouldn't. Brother A said he couldn't offer it at a bank or anywhere else, because he would be arrested on the spot. So they went on disputing till Brother B said he would bet twenty thousand pounds that the man would live thirty days, *anyway,* on that million, and keep out of jail, too. Brother A took him up. Brother B went down to the Bank and bought that note. Just like an Englishman, you see; pluck to the backbone. Then he dictated a letter, which one of his clerks wrote out in a beautiful round hand, and then the two brothers sat at the window a whole day watching for the right man to give it to.

They saw many honest faces go by that were not intelligent enough; many that were intelligent, but not honest enough; many that were both, but the possessors were not poor enough, or, if poor enough, were not strangers. There was always a defect, until I came along; but they agreed that I filled the bill all around; so they elected me unanimously, and there I was now waiting to know why I was called in. They began to ask me questions about myself, and pretty soon they had my story. Finally they told me I would answer their purpose. I said I was sincerely glad, and asked what it was. Then one of them handed me an envelope, and said I would find the explanation inside. I was going to open it, but he said no; take it to my lodgings, and look it over carefully, and not be hasty or rash. I was puzzled, and wanted to discuss the matter a little further, but they didn't; so I took my leave, feeling hurt and insulted to be made the butt of what was apparently some kind of a practical joke, and yet obliged to put up with it, not being in circumstances to resent affronts from rich and strong folk.

I would have picked up the pear now and eaten it before all the world, but it was gone; so I had lost that by this unlucky business, and the thought of it did not soften my feeling toward those men. As soon as I was out of sight of that house I opened my envelope, and saw that it contained money! My opinion of those people changed, I can tell you! I lost not a moment, but shoved note and money into my vest pocket, and broke for the nearest cheap eating-house. Well, how I did eat! When at last I couldn't hold any more, I took out my money and unfolded it, took one glimpse and nearly fainted. Five millions of dollars! Why, it made my head swim.

I must have sat there stunned and blinking at the note as much as a minute before I came rightly to myself again. The first thing I noticed, then, was the landlord. His eye was on the note, and he was petrified. He was worshiping, with all his body and soul, but he looked as if he couldn't stir hand or foot. I took my cue in a moment, and did the only rational thing there was to do. I reached the note towards him, and said, carelessly:

"Give me the change, please."

Then he was restored to his normal condition, and made a thousand apologies for not being able to break the bill, and I couldn't get him to touch it. He wanted to look at it, and keep on looking at it; he couldn't seem to get enough of it to quench the thirst of his eye, but he shrank from touching it as if it had been something too sacred for poor common clay to handle. I said:

"I am sorry if it is an inconvenience, but I must insist. Please change it; I haven't anything else."

But he said that wasn't any matter; he was quite willing to let the trifle stand over till another time. I said I might not be in his neighborhood again for a good while; but he said it was of no consequence, he could wait, and, moreover, I could have anything I wanted, any time I chose, and let the account run as long as I pleased. He said he hoped he wasn't afraid to trust as rich a gentleman as I was, merely because I was of a merry disposition, and chose to play larks on the public in the matter of dress. By this time another customer was entering, and the landlord hinted to me to put the monster out of sight; then he bowed me all the way to the door, and I started straight for that house and those brothers, to correct the mistake which had been made before the police should hunt me up, and help me do it. I was pretty nervous; in fact, pretty badly frightened, though, of course, I was no way in fault; but I knew men well enough to know that when they find they've given a tramp a million-pound bill when they thought it was a one-pounder, they are in a frantic rage against *him* instead of quarreling with their own near-sightedness, as they ought. As I approached the house my excitement began to abate, for all was quiet there, which made me feel pretty sure the blunder was not discovered yet. I rang. The same servant appeared. I asked for those gentlemen.

"They are gone." This in the lofty, cold way of that fellow's tribe.

"Gone? Gone where?"

"On a journey."

"But whereabouts?"

"To the Continent, I think."

"The Continent?"

"Yes, sir."

"Which way—by what route?"

"I can't say, sir."

"When will they be back?"

"In a month, they said."

"A month! Oh, this is awful! Give me *some* sort of idea of how to get a word to them. It's of the last importance."

"I can't, indeed. I've no idea where they've gone, sir."

"Then I must see some member of the family."

"Family's away, too; been abroad months—in Egypt and India, I think."

"Man, there's been an immense mistake made. They'll be back before night. Will you tell them I've been here, and that I will keep coming till it's all made right, and they needn't be afraid?"

"I'll tell them, if they come back, but I am not expecting them. They said you would be here in an hour to make inquiries, but I must tell you it's all right, they'll be here on time and expect you."

So I had to give it up and go away. What a riddle it all was! I was like to lose my mind. They would be here "on time." What could that mean? Oh, the letter would explain, maybe. I had forgotten the letter; I got it out and read it. This is what it said:

You are an intelligent and honest man, as one may see by your face. We conceive you to be poor and a stranger. Enclosed you will find a sum of money. It is lent to you for thirty days, without interest. Report at this house at the end of that time. I have a bet on you. If I win it you shall have any situation that is in my gift—any, that is, that you shall be able to prove yourself familiar with and competent to fill.

No signature, no address, no date.

Well, here was a coil to be in! You are posted on what had preceded all this, but I was not. It was just a deep, dark puzzle to me. I hadn't the least idea what the game was, nor whether harm was meant me or a kindness. I went into a park, and sat down to try to think it out, and to consider what I had best do.

At the end of an hour my reasonings had crystallized into this verdict.

Maybe those men mean me well, maybe they mean me ill; no way to decide that—let it go. They've got a game, or a scheme, or an experiment, of some kind on hand; no way to determine what it is—let it go. There's a bet on me; no way to find out what it is—let it go. That disposes of the indeterminable quantities; the remainder of the matter is tangible, solid, and may be classed and labeled with certainty. If I ask the Bank of England to place this bill to the credit of the man it belongs to, they'll do it, for they know him, although I don't; but they will ask me how I came in possession of it, and if I tell the truth they'll put me in the asylum, naturally, and a lie will land me in jail. The same result would follow if I tried to bank the bill anywhere or to borrow money on it. I have got to carry this immense burden around until those men come back, whether I want to or not. It is useless to me, as useless as a handful of ashes, and yet I must take care of it, and watch over it, while I beg my living. I couldn't *give* it away, if I should try, for neither honest citizen nor highwayman would accept it or meddle with it for anything. Those brothers are safe. Even if I lose their bill, or burn it, they are still safe, because they can stop payment, and the bank will make them whole; but meantime I've got to do a month's suffering without wages or profit—unless I help win that bet, whatever it may be, and get that situation that I am promised. I *should* like to get that; men of their sort have situations in their gift that are worth having.

I got to thinking a good deal about that situation. My hopes began to rise high. Without doubt the salary would be large. It would begin in a month; after that I should be all right. Pretty soon I was feeling first rate. By this time I was tramping the streets again. The sight of a tailor-shop gave me a sharp longing to shed my rags, and to clothe myself decently once more. Could I afford it? No; I had nothing in the world but a million pounds. So I forced myself to go on by. But soon I was drifting back again. The temptation persecuted me cruelly. I must have passed that shop back and forth six times during that manful struggle. At last I gave in; I had to. I asked if they had a misfit suit that had been thrown on their hands. The fellow I spoke to nodded his head toward another fellow, and gave me no answer. I went to the indicated fellow, and he indicated another fellow with *his* head, and no words. I went to him, and he said:

"'Tend to you presently."

I waited till he was done with what he was at, then he took me into a back room, and overhauled a pile of rejected suits, and selected the rattiest one for me. I put it on. It didn't fit, and wasn't in any way attractive, but it was new, and I was anxious to have it; so I didn't find any fault, but said, with some diffidence:

"It would be an accommodation to me if you could wait some days for the money. I haven't any small change about me."

The fellow worked up a most sarcastic expression of countenance, and said:

"Oh, you haven't? Well, of course, I didn't expect it. I'd only expect gentlemen like you to carry large change."

I was nettled, and said:

"My friend, you shouldn't judge a stranger always by the clothes he wears. I am quite able to pay for this suit; I simply didn't wish to put you to the trouble of changing a large note."

He modified his style a little at that, and said, though still with something of an air:

"I didn't mean any particular harm, but as long as rebukes are going, I might say it wasn't quite your affair to jump to the conclusion that we couldn't change any note that you might happen to be carrying around. On the contrary, we *can*."

I handed the note to him, and said:

"Oh, very well; I apologize."

He received it with a smile, one of those large smiles which goes all around over, and have folds in them, and wrinkles, and spirals, and look like the place where you have thrown a brick in a pond; and then in the act of his taking a glimpse of the bill this smile froze solid, and turned yellow, and looked like those wavy, wormy spreads of lava which you find hardened on little levels on the side of Vesuvius. I never before saw a smile caught like that, and perpetuated. The man stood there holding the bill, and looking like that, and the proprietor hustled up to see what was the matter, and said, briskly:

"Well, what's up? what's the trouble? what's wanting?"

I said: "There isn't any trouble. I'm waiting for my change."

"Come, come; get him his change, Tod; get him his change."

Tod retorted: "Get him his change! It's easy to say, sir; but look at the bill yourself."

The proprietor took a look, gave a low, eloquent whistle, then made a dive for the pile of rejected clothing, and began to snatch it this way and that, talking all the time excitedly, and as if to himself:

"Sell an eccentric millionaire such an unspeakable suit as that! Tod's a fool—a born fool. Always doing something like this. Drives every millionaire away from this place, because he can't tell a millionaire from a tramp, and never could. Ah, here's the thing I am after. Please get those things off, sir, and throw them in the fire. Do me the favor to put on this shirt and this suit; it's just the thing, the very thing—plain, rich, modest, and just ducally nobby; made to order for a foreign prince—you may know him, sir, his Serene Highness the Hospodar of Halifax; had to leave it with us and take a mourning-suit because his mother was going to die—which she didn't. But that's all right; we can't always have things the way we—that is, the way they—there! trousers all right, they fit you to a charm, sir; now the waistcoat; aha, right again! now the coat—lord! look at that, now! Perfect—the whole thing! I never saw such a triumph in all my experience."

I expressed my satisfaction.

"Quite right, sir, quite right; it'll do for a makeshift, I'm bound to say. But wait till you see what we'll get up for you on your own measure. Come, Tod, book and pen; get at it. Length of leg, 32"—and so on. Before I could get in a word he had measured me, and was giving orders for dress-suits, morning suits, shirts, and all sorts of things. When I got a chance I said:

"But, my dear sir, I *can't* give these orders, unless you can wait indefinitely, or change the bill."

"Indefinitely! It's a weak word, sir, a weak word. Eternally—*that's* the word, sir. Tod, rush these things through, and send them to the gentleman's address without any waste of time. Let the minor customers wait. Set down the gentleman's address and—"

"I'm changing my quarters. I will drop in and leave the new address."

"Quite right, sir, quite right. One moment—let me show you out, sir. There—good day, sir, good day."

Well, don't you see what was bound to happen? I drifted naturally into buying whatever I wanted, and asking for change. Within a week I was sumptuously equipped with all needful comforts and luxuries, and was housed in an expensive private hotel in Hanover Square. I took my dinners there, but for breakfast I stuck by Harris's humble feeding-house, where I had got my first meal on my million-pound bill. I was the making of Harris. The fact had gone all abroad that the foreign crank who carried million-pound bills in his vest pocket was the patron saint of the place. That was enough. From being a poor, struggling, little hand-to-mouth enterprise, it had become celebrated, and overcrowded with customers. Harris was so grateful that he forced loans upon me, and would not be denied; and so, pauper as I was, I had money to spend, and was living like the rich and the great. I judged that there was going to be a crash by and by, but I was in now and must swim across or drown. You see there was just that element of impending disaster to give a serious side, a sober side, yes, a tragic side, to a state of things which would otherwise have been purely ridiculous. In the night, in the dark, the tragedy part was always to the front, and always warning, always threatening; and so I moaned and tossed, and sleep was hard to find. But in the cheerful daylight the tragedy element faded out and disappeared, and I walked on air, and was happy to giddiness, to intoxication, you may say.

And it was natural; for I had become one of the notorieties of the metropolis of the world, and it turned my head, not just a little, but a good deal. You could not take up a newspaper, English, Scotch, or Irish, without finding in it one or more references to the "vest-pocket million-pounder" and his latest doings and sayings. At first, in these mentions, I was at the bottom of the personal-gossip column; next, I was listed above the knights, next above the baronets, next above the barons, and so on, and so on, climbing steadily, as my notoriety augmented, until I reached the highest altitude possible, and there I remained, taking precedence of all dukes not royal, and of all ecclesiastics except the primate of all England. But mind, this was not fame; as yet I had achieved only notoriety. Then came the climaxing stroke—the accolade, so to speak—which in a single instant transmuted the perishable dross of notoriety into the enduring gold of fame: *Punch* caricatured me! Yes, I was a made man now; my place was established. I might be joked about still, but reverently, not hilariously, not rudely; I could be smiled at, but not laughed at. The time for that had gone by. *Punch* pictured me all a-flutter with rags, dickering with a beef-eater for the Tower of London. Well, you can imagine how it was with a young fellow who had never been taken notice of before, and now all of a sudden couldn't say a thing that wasn't taken up and repeated everywhere; couldn't stir abroad without constantly overhearing the remark flying from lip to lip, "There he goes; that's him!" couldn't take his breakfast without a crowd to look on; couldn't appear in an opera-box without concentrating there the fire of a thousand lorgnettes. Why, I just swam in glory all day long—that is the amount of it.

You know, I even kept my old suit of rags, and every now and then appeared in them, so as to have the old pleasure of buying trifles, and being insulted, and then shooting the scoffer dead with the million-pound bill. But I couldn't keep that up. The illustrated papers made the outfit so familiar that when I went out in it I was at once recognized and followed by a crowd, and if I attempted a purchase the man would offer me his whole shop on credit before I could pull my note on him.

About the tenth day of my fame I went to fulfil my duty to my flag by paying my respects to the American minister. He received me with the enthusiasm proper in my case, upbraided me for being so tardy in my duty, and said that there was only one way to get his forgiveness, and that was to take the seat at his dinner-party that night made vacant by the illness of one of his guests. I said I would, and we got to talking. It turned out that he and my father had been schoolmates in boyhood, Yale students together later, and always warm friends up to my father's death. So then he required me to put in at his house all the odd time I might have to spare, and I was very willing, of course.

In fact, I was more than willing; I was glad. When the crash should come, he might somehow be able to save me from total destruction; I didn't know how, but he might think of a way, maybe. I couldn't venture to unbosom myself to him at this late date, a thing which I would have been quick to do in the beginning of this awful career of mine in London. No, I couldn't venture it now; I was in too deep; that is, too deep for me to be risking revelations to so new a friend, though not clear beyond my depth, as *I* looked at it. Because, you see, with all my borrowing, I was carefully keeping within my means—I mean within my salary. Of course, I couldn't *know* what my salary was going to be, but I had a good enough basis for an estimate in the fact that if I won the bet I was to have *choice* of any situation in that rich old gentleman's gift provided I was competent—and I should certainly prove competent; I hadn't any doubt about that. And as to the bet, I wasn't worrying about that; I had always been lucky. Now my estimate of the salary was six hundred to a thousand a year; say, six hundred for the first year, and so on up year by year, till I struck the upper figure by proved merit. At present I was only in debt for my first year's salary. Everybody had been trying to lend me money, but I had fought off the most of them on one pretext or another; so this indebtedness represented only £300 borrowed money, the other £300 represented my keep and my purchases. I believed my second year's salary would carry me through the rest of the month if I went on being cautious and economical, and I intended to look sharply out for that. My month ended, my employer back from his journey, I should be all right once more, for I should at once divide the two years' salary among my creditors by assignment, and get right down to my work.

It was a lovely dinner-party of fourteen. The Duke and Duchess of Shoreditch, and their daughter the Lady Anne-Grace-Eleanor-Celeste-and-so-forth-and-so-forth-de-Bohun, the Earl and Countess of Newgate, Viscount

Cheapside, Lord and Lady Blatherskite, some untitled people of both sexes, the minister and his wife and daughter, and his daughter's visiting friend, an English girl of twenty-two, named Portia Langham, whom I fell in love with in two minutes, and she with me—I could see it without glasses. There was still another guest, an American—but I am a little ahead of my story. While the people were still in the drawing-room, whetting up for dinner, and coldly inspecting the late comers, the servant announced:

"Mr. Lloyd Hastings."

The moment the usual civilities were over, Hastings caught sight of me, and came straight with cordially outstretched hand; then stopped short when about to shake, and said, with an embarrassed look:

"I beg your pardon, sir, I thought I knew you."

"Why, you do know me, old fellow."

"No. Are *you* the—the—"

"Vest-pocket monster? I am, indeed. Don't be afraid to call me by my nickname; I'm used to it."

"Well, well, well, this is a surprise. Once or twice I've seen your own name coupled with the nickname, but it never occurred to me that *you* could be the Henry Adams referred to. Why, it isn't six months since you were clerking away for Blake Hopkins in Frisco on a salary, and sitting up nights on an extra allowance, helping me arrange and verify the Gould and Curry Extension papers and statistics. The idea of your being in London, and a vast millionaire, and a colossal celebrity! Why, it's the Arabian Nights come again. Man, I can't take it in at all; can't realize it; give me time to settle the whirl in my head."

"The fact is, Lloyd, you are no worse off than I am. I can't realize it myself."

"Dear me, it *is* stunning, now isn't it? Why, it's just three months today since we went to the Miners' restaurant—"

"No; the What Cheer."

"Right, it *was* the What Cheer; went there at two in the morning, and had a chop and coffee after a hard six-hours grind over those Extension papers, and I tried to persuade you to come to London with me, and offered to get leave of absence for you and pay all your expenses, and give you something over if I succeeded in making the sale; and you would not listen to me, said I wouldn't succeed, and you couldn't afford to lose the run of business and be no end of time getting the hang of things again when you got back home. And yet here you are. How odd it all is! How did you happen to come, and whatever *did* give you this incredible start?"

"Oh, just an accident. It's a long story—a romance, a body may say. I'll tell you all about it, but not now."

"When?"

"The end of this month."

"That's more than a fortnight yet. It's too much of a strain on a person's curiosity. Make it a week."

"I can't. You'll know why, by and by. But how's the trade getting along?"

His cheerfulness vanished like a breath, and he said with a sigh:

"You were a true prophet, Hal, a true prophet. I wish I hadn't come. I don't want to talk about it."

"But you must. You must come and stop with me to-night, when we leave here, and tell me all about it."

"Oh, may I? Are you in earnest?" and the water showed in his eyes.

"Yes; I want to hear the whole story, every word."

"I'm so grateful! Just to find a human interest once more, in some voice and in some eye, in me and affairs of mine, after what I've been through here—lord! I could go down on my knees for it!"

He gripped my hand hard, and braced up, and was all right and lively after that for the dinner—which didn't come off. No; the usual thing happened, the thing that is always happening under that vicious and aggravating English system—the matter of precedence couldn't be settled, and so there was no dinner. Englishmen always eat dinner before they go out to dinner, because *they* know the risks they are running; but nobody ever warns the stranger, and so he walks placidly into the trap. Of course, nobody was hurt this time, because we had all been to dinner, none of us being novices excepting Hastings, and he having been informed by the minister at the time that he invited him that in deference to the English custom he had not provided any dinner. Everybody took a lady and processioned down to the dining-room because it is usual to go through the motions; but there the dispute began. The Duke of Shoreditch wanted to take precedence, and sit at the head of the table, holding that he outranked a minister who represented merely a nation and not a monarch; but I stood for my rights, and refused to yield. In the gossip column I ranked all dukes not royal, and said so, and claimed precedence of this one. It couldn't be settled, of course, struggle as we might and did, he finally (and injudiciously) trying to play birth and antiquity, and I "seeing" his Conqueror and "raising" him with Adam, whose direct posterity I was, as shown by my name, while *he* was of a collateral branch, as shown by *his,* and by his recent Norman origin; so we all processioned back to the drawing-room again and had a perpendicular lunch—plate of sardines and a strawberry, and you group yourself and stand up and eat it. Here the religion of precedence is not so strenuous; the two persons of highest rank chuck up a shilling, the one that wins has first go at his strawberry, and the loser gets the shilling. The next two chuck up, then the next two, and so on. After refreshment, tables were brought, and we all played cribbage, sixpence a game. The English never play any game for amusement. If they can't make something or lose something—they don't care which—they won't play.

We had a lovely time; certainly two of us had, Miss Langham and I. I was so bewitched with her that I couldn't count my hands if they went above a double sequence; and when I struck home I never discovered it, and started up the outside row again, and would have lost the game every time, only the girl did the same, she being in just my condition, you see; and consequently neither of us ever got out, or cared to wonder why we didn't; we only just knew we were happy, and didn't wish to know anything else, and didn't want to be interrupted. And I *told* her—I did, indeed—told her I loved her; and she—well, she blushed till her hair turned red, but she liked it; she *said* she did. Oh, there was never such an evening! Every time I pegged I put on a postscript; every time she pegged she acknowledged receipt of it, counting the hands the same. Why,

I couldn't even say "Two for his heels" without adding, "*My,* how sweet you do look!" and she would say, "Fifteen two, fifteen four, fifteen six, and a pair are eight, and eight are sixteen—*do* you think so?"—peeping out aslant from under her lashes, you know, so sweet and cunning. Oh, it was just *too*-too!

Well, I was perfectly honest and square with her; told her I hadn't a cent in the world but just the million-pound note she'd heard so much talk about, and *it* didn't belong to me, and that started her curiosity; and then I talked low, and told her the whole history right from the start, and it nearly killed her laughing. What in the nation she could find to laugh about *I* couldn't see, but there it was; every half-minute some new detail would fetch her, and I would have to stop as much as a minute and a half to give her a chance to settle down again. Why, she laughed herself lame—she did, indeed; I never saw anything like it. I mean I never saw a painful story—a story of a person's troubles and worries and fears—produce just *that* kind of effect before. So I loved her all the more, seeing she could be so cheerful when there wasn't anything to be cheerful about; for I might soon need that kind of wife, you know, the way things looked. Of course, I told her we should have to wait a couple of years, till I could catch up on my salary; but she didn't mind that, only she hoped

I would be as careful as possible in the matter of expenses, and not let them run the least risk of trenching on our third year's pay. Then she began to get a little worried, and wondered if we were making any mistake, and starting the salary on a higher figure for the first year than I would get. This was good sense, and it made me feel a little less confident than I had been feeling before; but it gave me a good business idea, and I brought it frankly out.

"Portia, dear, would you mind going with me that day, when I confront those old gentlemen?"

She shrank a little, but said:

"N-o; if my being with you would help hearten you. But—would it be quite proper, do you think?"

"No, I don't know that it would—in fact, I'm afraid it wouldn't; but, you see, there's so *much* dependent upon it that—"

"Then I'll go anyway, proper or improper," she said, with a beautiful and generous enthusiasm. "Oh, I shall be so happy to think I'm helping!"

"Helping, dear? Why, you'll be doing it all. You're so beautiful and so lovely and so winning, that with you there I can pile our salary up till I break those good old fellows, and they'll never have the heart to struggle."

Sho! you should have seen the rich blood mount, and her happy eyes shine!

"You wicked flatterer! There isn't a word of truth in what you say, but still I'll go with you. Maybe it will teach you not to expect other people to look with your eyes."

Were my doubts dissipated? Was my confidence restored? You may judge by this fact: privately I raised my salary to twelve hundred the first year on the spot. But I didn't tell her; I saved it for a surprise.

All the way home I was in the clouds, Hastings talking, I not hearing a word. When he and I entered my parlor, he brought me to myself with his fervent appreciations of my manifold comforts and luxuries.

"Let me just stand here a little and look my fill. Dear me! it's a palace—it's just a palace! And in it everything a body *could* desire, including cozy coal fire and supper standing ready. Henry, it doesn't merely make me realize how rich you are; it makes me realize, to the bone, to the marrow, how poor I am—how poor I am, and how miserable, how defeated, routed, annihilated!"

Plague take it! this language gave me the cold shudders. It scared me broad awake, and made me comprehend that I was standing on a half-inch crust, with a crater underneath. *I* didn't know I had been dreaming—that is, I hadn't been allowing myself to know it for a while back; but *now*—oh, dear! Deep in debt, not a cent in the world, a lovely girl's happiness or woe in my hands, and nothing in front of me but a salary which might never—oh, *would* never—materialize! Oh, oh, oh! I am ruined past hope! nothing can save me!

"Henry, the mere unconsidered drippings of your daily income would—"

"Oh, my daily income! Here, down with this hot Scotch, and cheer up your soul. Here's with you! Or, no—you're hungry; sit down and—"

"Not a bite for me; I'm past it. I can't eat, these days; but I'll drink with you till I drop. Come!"

"Barrel for barrel, I'm with you! Ready? Here we go! Now, then, Lloyd, unreel your story while I brew."

"Unreel it? What, again?"

"Again? What do you mean by that?"

"Why, I mean do you want to hear it *over* again?"

"Do I want to hear it *over* again? This *is* a puzzler. Wait; don't take any more of that liquid. You don't need it."

"Look here, Henry, you alarm me. Didn't I tell you the whole story on the way here?"

"You?"

"Yes, I."

"I'll be hanged if I heard a word of it."

"Henry, this is a serious thing. It troubles me. What did you take up yonder at the minister's?"

Then it all flashed on me, and I owned up like a man.

"I took the dearest girl in this world—prisoner!"

So then he came with a rush, and we shook, and shook, and shook till our hands ached; and he didn't blame me for not having heard a word of a story which had lasted while we walked three miles. He just sat down then, like the patient, good fellow he was, and told it all over again. Synopsized, it amounted to this: He had come to England with what he thought was a grand opportunity; he had an "option" to sell the Gould and Curry Extension for the "locators" of it, and keep all he could get over a million dollars. He had worked hard, had pulled every wire he knew of, had left no honest expedient untried, had spent nearly all the money he had in the world, had not been able to get a solitary capitalist to listen to him, and his option would run out at the end of the month. In a word, he was ruined. Then he jumped up and cried out:

"Henry, you can save me! You can save me, and you're the only man in the universe that can. Will you do it? *Won't* you do it?"

"Tell me how. Speak out, my boy."

"Give me a million and my passage home for my 'option'! Don't, *don't* refuse!"

I was in a kind of agony. I was right on the

point of coming out with the words, "Lloyd, I'm a pauper myself—absolutely penniless, and in *debt.*" But a white-hot idea came flaming through my head, and I gripped my jaws together, and calmed myself down till I was as cold as a capitalist. Then I said, in a commercial and self-possessed way:

"I will save you, Lloyd—"

"Then I'm already saved! God be merciful to you forever! If ever I—"

"Let me finish, Lloyd. I will save you, but not in that way; for that would not be fair to you, after your hard work, and the risks you've run. I don't need to buy mines; I can keep my capital moving, in a commercial center like London, without that; it's what I'm at, all the time; but here is what I'll do. I know all about that mine, of course; I know its immense value, and can swear to it if anybody wishes it. You shall sell out inside of the fortnight for three millions cash, using my name freely, and we'll divide, share and share alike."

Do you know, he would have danced the furniture to kindling-wood in his insane joy, and broken everything on the place, if I hadn't tripped him up and tied him.

Then he lay there, perfectly happy, saying:

"I may use your name! Your name—think of it! Man, they'll flock in droves, these rich Londoners; they'll *fight* for that stock! I'm a made man, I'm a made man forever, and I'll never forget you as long as I live!"

In less than twenty-four hours London was abuzz! I hadn't anything to do, day after day, but sit at home, and say to all comers:

"Yes; I told him to refer to me. I know the man, and I know the mine. His character is above reproach, and the mine is worth far more than he asks for it."

Meantime I spent all my evenings at the minister's with Portia. I didn't say a word to her about the mine; I saved it for a surprise. We talked salary; never anything but salary and love; sometimes love, sometimes salary, sometimes love and salary together. And my! the interest the minister's wife and daughter took in our little affair, and the endless ingenuities they invented to save us from interruption, and to keep the minister in the dark and unsuspicious—well, it was just lovely of them!

When the month was up at last, I had a million dollars to my credit in the London and County Bank, and Hastings was fixed in the same way. Dressed at my level best, I drove by the house in Portland Place, judged by the look of things that my birds were home again, went on towards the minister's and got my precious, and we started back, talking salary with all our might. She was so excited and anxious that it made her just intolerably beautiful. I said:

"Dearie, the way you're looking it's a crime to strike for a salary a single penny under three thousand a year."

"Henry, Henry, you'll ruin us!"

"Don't you be afraid. Just keep up those looks, and trust to me. It'll all come out right."

So, as it turned out, I had to keep bolstering up *her* courage all the way. She kept pleading with me, and saying:

"Oh, please remember that if we ask for too much we may get no salary at all; and then what will become of us, with no way in the world to earn our living?"

We were ushered in by that same servant, and there they were, the two old gentlemen. Of course, they were surprised to see that wonderful creature with me, but I said:

"It's all right, gentlemen; she is my future stay and helpmate."

And I introduced them to her, and called them by name. It didn't surprise them; they knew I would know enough to consult the directory. They seated us, and were very polite to me, and very solicitous to relieve her from embarrassment, and put her as much at her ease as they could. Then I said:

"Gentlemen, I am ready to report."

"We are glad to hear it," said *my* man, "for now we can decide the bet which my brother Abel and I made. If you have won for me, you shall have any situation in my gift. Have you the million-pound note?"

"Here it is, sir," and I handed it to him.

"I've won!" he shouted, and slapped Abel on the back. "*Now* what do you say, brother?"

"I say he *did* survive, and I've lost twenty thousand pounds. I never would have believed it."

"I've a further report to make," I said, "and a pretty long one. I want you to let me come soon, and detail my whole month's history; and I promise you it's worth hearing. Meantime, take a look at that."

"What, man! Certificate of deposit for £200,000. Is it yours?"

"Mine. I earned it by thirty days' judicious use of that little loan you let me have. And the only use I made of it was to buy trifles and offer the bill in change."

"Come, this is astonishing! It's incredible, man!"

"Never mind, I'll prove it. Don't take my word unsupported."

But now Portia's turn was come to be surprised. Her eyes were spread wide, and she said:

"Henry, is that really your money? Have you been fibbing to me?"

"I have, indeed, dearie. But you'll forgive me, *I* know."

She put up an arch pout, and said:

"Don't you be so sure. You are a naughty thing to deceive me so!"

"Oh, you'll get over it, sweetheart, you'll get over it; it was only fun, you know. Come, let's be going."

"But wait, wait! The situation, you know. I want to give you the situation," said my man.

"Well," I said, "I'm just as grateful as I can be, but really I don't want one."

"But you can have the very choicest one in my gift."

"Thanks again, with all my heart; but I don't even want *that* one."

"Henry, I'm ashamed of you. You don't half thank the good gentleman. May I do it for you?"

"Indeed, you shall, dear, if you can improve it. Let us see you try."

She walked to my man, got up in his lap, put her arm round his neck, and kissed him right on the mouth. Then the two old gentlemen shouted with laughter, but I was dumfounded, just petrified, as you may say. Portia said:

"Papa, he has said you haven't a situation in your gift that he'd take; and I feel just as hurt as—"

"My darling, is that your papa?"

"Yes; he's my step-papa, and the dearest one that ever was. You understand now, don't you, why I was able to laugh when you told me at the minister's, not knowing my relationships, what trouble and worry papa's and Uncle Abel's scheme was giving you?"

Of course, I spoke right up now, without any fooling, and went straight to the point.

"Oh, my dearest dear sir, I want to take back what I said. You *have* got a situation open that I want."

"Name it."

"Son-in-law."

"Well, well, well! But you know, if you haven't ever served in that capacity, you, of course, can't furnish recommendations of a sort to satisfy the conditions of the contract, and so—"

"Try me—oh, do, I beg of you! Only just try me thirty or forty years, and if—"

"Oh, well, all right; it's but a little thing to ask, take her along."

Happy, we two? There are not words enough in the unabridged to describe it. And when London got the whole history, a day or two later, of my month's adventures with that bank-note, and how they ended, did London talk, and have a good time? Yes.

My Portia's papa took that friendly and hospitable bill back to the Bank of England and cashed it; then the Bank canceled it and made him a present of it, and he gave it to us at our wedding, and it has always hung in its frame in the sacredest place in our home ever since. For it gave me my Portia. But for it I could not have remained in London, would not have appeared at the minister's, never should have met her. And so I always say, "Yes, it's a million-pounder, as you see; but it never made but one purchase in its life, and *then* got the article for only about a tenth part of its value."

The Open Boat
by Stephen Crane

A Tale Intended to be after the Fact: Being the Experience of Four Men from the Sunk Steamer COMMODORE

I

None of them knew the color of the sky. Their eyes glanced level, and were fastened upon the waves that swept toward them. These waves were of the hue of slate, save for the tops, which were of foaming white, and all of the men knew the colors of the sea. The horizon narrowed and widened, and dipped and rose, and at all times its edge was jagged with waves that seemed thrust up in points like rocks.

Many a man ought to have a bathtub larger than the boat which here rode upon the sea. These waves were most wrongfully and barbarously abrupt and tall, and each froth-top was a problem in small-boat navigation.

The cook squatted in the bottom, and looked with both eyes at the six inches of gunwale which separated him from the ocean. His sleeves were rolled over his fat forearms, and the two flaps of his unbuttoned vest dangled as he bent to bail out the boat. Often he said, "Gawd! that was a narrow clip." As he remarked it he invariably gazed eastward over the broken sea.

The oiler, steering with one of the two oars in the boat, sometimes raised himself suddenly to keep clear of water that swirled in over the stern. It was a thin little oar, and it seemed often ready to snap.

The correspondent, pulling at the other oar, watched the waves and wondered why he was there.

The injured captain, lying in the bow, was at this time buried in that profound dejection and indifference which comes, temporarily at least, to even the bravest and most enduring when, willy-nilly, the firm fails, the army loses, the ship goes down. The mind of the master of a vessel is rooted deep in the timbers of her, though he command for a day or a decade; and this captain had on him the stern impression of a scene in the grays of dawn of seven turned faces, and later a stump of a topmast with a white ball on it, that slashed to and fro at the waves, went low and lower, and down. Thereafter there was something strange in his voice. Although steady, it was deep with mourning, and of a quality beyond oration or tears.

"Keep'er a little more south, Billie," said he.

"A little more south, sir," said the oiler in the stern.

A seat in this boat was not unlike a seat upon a bucking broncho, and by the same token a broncho is not much smaller. The craft pranced and reared and plunged like an animal. As each wave came, and she rose for it, she seemed like a horse making at a fence outrageously high. The manner of her scramble over these walls of water is a mystic thing, and, moreover, at the top of them were ordinarily these problems in white water, the foam racing down from the summit of each wave requiring a new leap, and a leap from the air. Then, after scornfully bumping a crest, she would slide and race and splash down a long incline, and arrive bobbing and nodding in front of the next menace.

A singular disadvantage of the sea lies in the fact that after successfully surmounting one wave you discover that there is another behind it just as important and just as nervously anxious to do something effective in the way of swamping boats. In a ten-foot dinghy one can get an idea of the resources of the sea in the line of waves that is not probable to the average experience, which is never at sea in a dinghy. As each slaty wall of water approached, it shut all else from the view of the men in the boat, and it was not difficult to imagine that this particular wave was the final outburst of the ocean, the last effort of the grim water. There was a terrible grace in the move of the waves, and they came in silence, save for the snarling of the crests.

In the wan light the faces of the men must have been gray. Their eyes must have glinted in strange ways as they gazed steadily astern. Viewed from a balcony, the whole thing would doubtless have been weirdly picturesque. But the men in the boat had no time to see it, and if they had had leisure, there were other things to occupy their minds. The sun swung steadily up the sky, and they knew it was broad day because the color of the sea changed from slate to emerald-green streaked with amber lights, and the foam was like tumbling snow. The process of the breaking day was unknown to them. They were aware only of this effect upon the color of the waves that rolled toward them.

In disjointed sentences the cook and the correspondent argued as to the difference between a life-saving station and a house of refuge. The cook had said: "There's a house of refuge just north of the Mosquito Inlet Light, and as soon as they see us they'll come off in their boat and pick us up."

"As soon as who see us?" said the correspondent.

"The crew," said the cook.

"Houses of refuge don't have crews," said the correspondent. "As I understand them, they are only places where clothes and grub are stored for the benefit of shipwrecked people. They don't carry crews."

"Oh, yes, they do," said the cook.

"No, they don't," said the correspondent.

"Well, we're not there yet, anyhow," said the oiler, in the stern.

"Well," said the cook, "perhaps it's not a house of refuge that I'm thinking of as being near Mosquito Inlet Light; perhaps it's a life-saving station."

"We're not there yet," said the oiler in the stern.

II

As the boat bounced from the top of each wave the wind tore through the hair of the hatless men, and as the craft plopped her stern down again the spray slashed past them. The crest of each of these waves was a hill, from the top of which the men surveyed for a moment a broad tumultuous expanse, shining and wind-riven. It was probably splendid, it was probably glorious, this play of the free sea, wild with lights of emerald and white and amber.

"Bully good thing it's an onshore wind," said

the cook. "If not, where would we be? Wouldn't have a show."

"That's right," said the correspondent.

The busy oiler nodded his assent.

Then the captain, in the bow, chuckled in a way that expressed humor, contempt, tragedy, all in one. "Do you think we've got much of a show now, boys?" said he.

Whereupon the three were silent, save for a trifle of hemming and hawing. To express any particular optimism at this time they felt to be childish and stupid, but they all doubtless possessed this sense of the situation in their minds. A young man thinks doggedly at such times. On the other hand, the ethics of their condition was decidedly against any open suggestion of hopelessness. So they were silent.

"Oh, well," said the captain, soothing his children, "we'll get ashore all right."

But there was that in his tone which made them think; so the oiler quoth, "Yes! If this wind holds!"

The cook was bailing. "Yes! if we don't catch hell in the surf."

Canton-flannel gulls flew near and far. Sometimes they sat down on the sea, near patches of brown seaweed that rolled over the waves with a movement like carpets on a line in a gale. The birds sat comfortably in groups, and they were envied by some in the dinghy, for the wrath of the sea was no more to them than it was to a covey of prairie chickens a thousand miles inland. Often they came very close and stared at the men with black bead-like eyes. At these times they were uncanny and sinister in their unblinking scrutiny, and the men hooted angrily at them, telling them to be gone. One came, and evidently decided to alight on the top of the captain's head. The bird flew parallel to the boat and did not circle, but made short sidelong jumps in the air in chicken fashion. His black eyes were wistfully fixed upon the captain's head. "Ugly brute," said the oiler to the bird. "You look as if you were made with a jackknife." The cook and the correspondent swore darkly at the creature. The captain naturally wished to knock it away with the end of the heavy painter, but he did not dare do it, because anything resembling an emphatic gesture would have capsized this freighted boat, and so, with his open hand, the captain gently and carefully waved the gull away. After it had been discouraged from the pursuit the captain breathed easier on account of his hair, and others breathed easier because the bird struck their minds at this time as being somehow grewsome and ominous.

In the meantime the oiler and the correspondent rowed. And also they rowed. They sat together in the same seat, and each rowed an oar. Then the oiler took both oars; then the correspondent took both oars; then the oiler; then the correspondent. They rowed and they rowed. The very ticklish part of the business was when the time came for the reclining one in the stern to take his turn at the oars. By the very last star of truth, it is easier to steal eggs from under a hen than it was to change seats in the dinghy. First the man in the stern slid his hand along the thwart and moved with care, as if he were of Sèvres. Then the man in the rowing-seat slid his hand along the other thwart. It was all done with the most extraordinary care. As the two sidled past each other, the whole party kept watchful eyes on the coming wave, and the captain cried: "Look out, now! Steady, there!"

The brown mats of seaweed that appeared from time to time were like islands, bits of earth. They were traveling, apparently, neither one way nor the other. They were, to all intents, stationary. They informed the men in the boat that it was making progress slowly toward the land.

The captain, rearing cautiously in the bow after the dinghy soared on a great swell, said that he had seen the lighthouse at Mosquito Inlet. Presently the cook remarked that he had seen it. The correspondent was at the oars then, and for some reason he too wished to look at the lighthouse; but his back was toward the far shore and the waves were important, and for some time he could not seize an opportunity to turn his head.

But at last there came a wave more gentle than the others, and when at the crest of it he swiftly scoured the western horizon.

"See it?" said the captain.

"No," said the correspondent, slowly; "I didn't see anything."

"Look again," said the captain. He pointed. "It's exactly in that direction."

At the top of another wave, the correspondent did as he was bid, and this time his eyes chanced on a small, still thing on the edge of the swaying horizon. It was precisely like the point of a pin. It took an anxious eye to find a lighthouse so tiny.

"Think we'll make it, Captain?"

"If this wind holds and the boat don't swamp, we can't do much else," said the captain.

The little boat, lifted by each towering sea and splashed viciously by the crests, made progress that in the absence of seaweed was not apparent to those in her. She seemed just a wee thing wallowing, miraculously top up, at the mercy of five oceans. Occasionally a great spread of water, like white flames, swarmed into her.

"Bail her, cook," said the captain, serenely.

"All right, Captain," said the cheerful cook.

III

It would be difficult to describe the subtle brotherhood of men that was here established on the seas. No one said that it was so. No one mentioned it. But it dwelt in the boat, and each man felt it warm him. They were a captain, an oiler, a cook, and a correspondent, and they were friends—friends in a more curiously iron-bound degree than may be common. The hurt captain, lying against the water jar in the bow, spoke always in a low voice and calmly; but he could never command a more ready and swiftly obedient crew than the motley three of the dinghy. It was more than a mere recognition of what was best for the common safety. There was surely in it a quality that was personal and heartfelt. And after this devotion to the commander of the boat, there was this comradeship, that the correspondent, for instance, who had been taught to be cynical of men, knew even at the time was the best experience of his life. But no one said that it was so. No one mentioned it.

"I wish we had a sail," remarked the captain. "We might try my overcoat on the end of an oar and give you two boys a chance to rest." So the cook and the correspondent held the mast and spread wide the overcoat; the oiler steered; and the little boat made good way with her new rig. Sometimes the oiler had to scull sharply to keep a sea from breaking into the boat, but otherwise sailing was a success.

Meanwhile the lighthouse had been growing slowly larger. It had now almost assumed color, and appeared like a little gray shadow on the sky. The man at the oars could not be prevented from turning his head rather often to try for a glimpse of this little gray shadow.

At last, from the top of each wave, the men in the tossing boat could see land. Even as the lighthouse was an upright shadow on the sky, this land seemed but a long black shadow on the sea. It certainly was thinner than paper. "We must be about opposite New Smyrna," said the cook, who had coasted this shore often in schooners. "Captain, by the way, I believe they abandoned that lifesaving station there about a year ago."

"Did they?" said the captain.

The wind slowly died away. The cook and the correspondent were not now obliged to slave in order to hold high the oar. But the waves continued their old impetuous swooping at the dinghy, and the little craft, no longer under way, struggled woundily over them. The oiler or the correspondent took the oars again.

Shipwrecks are *apropos* of nothing. If men could only train for them and have them occur when the men had reached pink condition, there would be less drowning at sea. Of the four in the dinghy none had slept any time worth mentioning for two days and two nights previous to embarking in the dinghy, and in the excitement of clambering about the deck of a foundering ship they had also forgotten to eat heartily.

For these reasons, and for others, neither the oiler nor the correspondent was fond of rowing at this time. The correspondent wondered ingenuously how in the name of all that was sane could there be people who thought it amusing to row a boat. It was not an amusement; it was a diabolical punishment, and even a genius of mental aberrations could never conclude that it was anything but a horror to the muscles and a crime against the back. He mentioned to the boat in general how the amusement of rowing struck him, and the weary-faced oiler smiled in full sympathy. Previously to the foundering, by the way, the oiler had worked a double watch in the engine room of the ship.

"Take her easy now, boys," said the captain. "Don't spend yourselves. If we have to run a surf you'll need all your strength, because we'll sure have to swim for it. Take your time."

Slowly the land arose from the sea. From a black line it became a line of black and a line of white—trees and sand. Finally the captain said that he could make out a house on the shore. "That's the house of refuge, sure," said the cook. "They'll see us before long, and come out after us."

The distant lighthouse reared high. "The keeper ought to be able to make us out now, if he's looking through a glass," said the captain. "He'll notify the lifesaving people."

"None of those other boats could have got ashore to give word of the wreck," said the oiler, in a low voice, "else the lifeboat would be out hunting us."

Slowly and beautifully the land loomed out of the sea. The wind came again. It had veered from the northeast to the southeast. Finally a new sound struck the ears of the men in the boat. It was the low thunder of the surf on the shore. "We'll never be able to make the lighthouse now," said the captain. "Swing her head a little more north, Billie."

"A little more north, sir," said the oiler.

Whereupon the little boat turned her nose once more down the wind, and all but the oarsman watched the shore grow. Under the influence of this expansion doubt and direful apprehension were leaving the minds of the men. The management of the boat was still most absorbing, but it could not prevent a quiet cheerfulness. In an hour, perhaps, they would be ashore.

Their backbones had become thoroughly used to balancing in the boat, and they now rode this wild colt of a dinghy like circus men. The correspondent thought that he had been drenched to the skin, but happening to feel in the top pocket of his coat, he found therein eight cigars. Four of them were soaked with seawater; four were perfectly scatheless. After a search, somebody produced three dry matches;

and thereupon the four waifs rode impudently in their little boat and, with an assurance of an impending rescue shining in their eyes, puffed at the big cigars, and judged well and ill of all men. Everybody took a drink of water.

IV

"Cook," remarked the captain, "there don't seem to be any signs of life about your house of refuge."

"No," replied the cook. "Funny they don't see us!"

A broad stretch of lowly coast lay before the eyes of the men. It was of low dunes topped with dark vegetation. The roar of the surf was plain, and sometimes they could see the white lip of a wave as it spun up the beach. A tiny house was blocked out black upon the sky. Southward, the slim lighthouse lifted its little gray length.

Tide, wind, and waves were swinging the dinghy northward. "Funny they don't see us," said the men.

The surf's roar was here dulled, but its tone was nevertheless thunderous and mighty. As the boat swam over the great rollers the men sat listening to this roar. "We'll swamp sure," said everybody.

It is fair to say here that there was not a life-saving station within twenty miles in either direction; but the men did not know this fact, and in consequence they made dark and opprobrious remarks concerning the eyesight of the nation's lifesavers. Four scowling men sat in the dinghy and surpassed records in the invention of epithets.

"Funny they don't see us."

The light-heartedness of a former time had completely faded. To their sharpened minds it was easy to conjure pictures of all kinds of incompetency and blindness and, indeed, cowardice. There was the shore of the populous land, and it was bitter and bitter to them that from it came no sign.

"Well," said the captain, ultimately, "I suppose we'll have to make a try for ourselves. If we stay out here too long, we'll none of us have strength left to swim after the boat swamps."

And so the oiler, who was at the oars, turned the boat straight for the shore. There was a sudden tightening of muscles. There was some thinking.

"If we don't all get ashore," said the captain—"if we don't all get ashore, I suppose you fellows know where to send news of my finish?"

They then briefly exchanged some addresses and admonitions. As for the reflections of the men, there was a great deal of rage in them. Perchance they might be formulated thus: "If I am going to be drowned—if I am going to be drowned—if I am going to be drowned, why, in the name of the seven mad gods who rule the sea, was I allowed to come thus far and contemplate sand and trees? Was I brought here merely to have my nose dragged away as I was about to nibble the sacred cheese of life? It is preposterous. If this old ninny-woman, Fate, cannot do better than this, she should be deprived of the management of men's fortunes. She is an old hen who knows not her intention. If she has decided to drown me, why did she not do it in the beginning and save me all this trouble? The whole affair is absurd. . . . But no; she cannot mean to drown me. She dare not drown me. She cannot drown me. Not after all this work." Afterward the man might have had an impulse to shake his fist at the clouds. "Just you drown me, now, and then hear what I call you!"

The billows that came at this time were more formidable. They seemed always just about to break and roll over the little boat in a turmoil of foam. There was a preparatory and long growl in the speech of them. No mind unused to the sea would have concluded that the dinghy could ascend these sheer heights in time. The shore was still afar. The oiler was a wily surfman. "Boys," he said swiftly, "she won't live three minutes more, and we're too far out to swim. Shall I take her to sea again, Captain?"

"Yes; go ahead!" said the captain.

This oiler, by a series of quick miracles and fast and steady oarsmanship, turned the boat in the middle of the surf and took her safely to sea again.

There was a considerable silence as the boat bumped over the furrowed sea to deeper water. Then somebody in gloom spoke: "Well, anyhow, they must have seen us from the shore by now."

The gulls went in slanting flight up the wind toward the gray, desolate east. A squall, marked by dingy clouds and clouds brick-red, like smoke from a burning building, appeared from the southeast.

"What do you think of those lifesaving people? Ain't they peaches?"

"Funny they haven't seen us."

"Maybe they think we're out here for sport! Maybe they think we're fishin'. Maybe they think we're damned fools."

It was a long afternoon. A changed tide tried to force them southward, but wind and wave said northward. Far ahead, where coastline, sea, and sky formed their mighty angle, there were little dots which seemed to indicate a city on the shore.

"St. Augustine?"

The captain shook his head. "Too near Mosquito Inlet."

And the oiler rowed, and then the correspondent rowed; then the oiler rowed. It was a weary business. The human back can become the seat of more aches and pains than are registered in books for the composite anatomy of a regiment. It is a limited area, but it can become the theater of innumerable muscular conflicts, tangles, wrenches, knots, and other comforts.

"Did you ever like to row, Billie?" asked the correspondent.

"No," said the oiler; "hang it!"

When one exchanged the rowing-seat for a place in the bottom of the boat, he suffered a bodily depression that caused him to be careless of everything save an obligation to wiggle one finger. There was cold seawater swashing to and fro in the boat, and he lay in it. His head, pillowed on a thwart, was within an inch of the swirl of a wave-crest, and sometimes a particularly obstreperous sea came inboard and drenched him once more. But these matters did not annoy him. It is almost certain that if the boat had capsized he would have tumbled comfortably out upon the ocean as if he felt sure it was a great soft mattress.

"Look! There's a man on the shore!"

"Where?"

"There! See 'im? See 'im?"

"Yes, sure! He's walking along."

"Now he's stopped. Look! He's facing us!"

"He's waving at us!"

"So he is! By thunder!"

"Ah, now we're all right! Now we're all right! There'll be a boat out here for us in half an hour."

"He's going on. He's running. He's going up to that house there."

The remote beach seemed lower than the sea, and it required a searching glance to discern the little black figure. The captain saw a floating stick and they rowed to it. A bath towel was by some weird chance in the boat, and, tying this on the stick, the captain waved it. The oarsman did not dare turn his head, so he was obliged to ask questions.

"What's he doing now?"

"He's standing still again. He's looking, I think. . . . There he goes again—toward the house. . . . Now he's stopped again."

"Is he waving at us?"

"No, not now; he was, though."

"Look! There comes another man!"

"He's running."

"Look at him go, would you!"

"Why, he's on a bicycle. Now he's met the other man. They're both waving at us. Look!"

"There comes something up the beach."

"What the devil is that thing?"

"Why, it looks like a boat."

"Why, certainly, it's a boat."

"No; it's on wheels."

"Yes, so it is. Well, that must be the lifeboat. They drag them along shore on a wagon."

"That's the lifeboat, sure."

"No, by God, it's—it's an omnibus."

"I tell you it's a lifeboat."

"It is not! It's an omnibus. I can see it plain. See? One of these big hotel omnibuses."

"By thunder, you're right. It's an omnibus, sure as fate. What do you suppose they are doing with an omnibus? Maybe they are going around collecting the life-crew, hey?"

"That's it, likely. Look! There's a fellow waving a little black flag. He's standing on the steps of the omnibus. There come those other two fellows. Now they're all talking together. Look at the fellow with the flag. Maybe he ain't waving it!"

"That ain't a flag, is it? That's his coat. Why, certainly, that's his coat."

"So it is; it's his coat. He's taken it off and is waving it around his head. But would you look at him swing it!"

"Oh, say, there isn't any lifesaving station there. That's just a winter-resort hotel omnibus that has brought over some of the boarders to see us drown."

"What's that idiot with the coat mean? What's he signaling, anyhow?"

"It looks as if he were trying to tell us to go north. There must be a lifesaving station up there."

"No; he thinks we're fishing. Just giving us a merry hand. See? Ah, there, Willie!"

"Well, I wish I could make something out of those signals. What do you suppose he means?"

"He don't mean anything; he's just playing."

"Well, if he'd just signal us to try the surf again, or to go to sea and wait, or go north, or go south, or go to hell, there would be some reason in it. But look at him! He just stands there and keeps his coat revolving like a wheel. The ass!"

"There come more people."

"Now there's quite a mob. Look! Isn't that a boat?"

"Where? Oh, I see where you mean. No, that's no boat."

"That fellow is still waving his coat."

"He must think we like to see him do that. Why don't he quit it? It don't mean anything."

"I don't know. I think he is trying to make us go north. It must be that there's a lifesaving station there somewhere."

"Say, he ain't tired yet. Look at 'im wave!"

"Wonder how long he can keep that up. He's been revolving his coat ever since he caught sight of us. He's an idiot. Why aren't they getting men to bring a boat out? A fishing boat—one of those big yawls—could come out here all right. Why don't he do something?"

"Oh, it's all right now."

"They'll have a boat out here for us in less than no time, now that they've seen us."

A faint yellow tone came into the sky over the low land. The shadows on the sea slowly deepened. The wind bore coldness with it, and the men began to shiver.

"Holy smoke!" said one, allowing his voice to express his impious mood, "if we keep on monkeying out here! If we've got to flounder out here all night!"

"Oh, we'll never have to stay here all night! Don't you worry. They've seen us now, and it won't be long before they'll come chasing out after us."

The shore grew dusky. The man waving a coat blended gradually into this gloom, and it swallowed in the same manner the omnibus and the group of people. The spray, when it dashed uproariously over the side, made the voyagers shrink and swear like men who were being branded.

"I'd like to catch the chump who waved the coat. I feel like socking him one, just for luck."

"Why? What did he do?"

"Oh, nothing, but then he seemed so damned cheerful."

In the meantime the oiler rowed, and then the correspondent rowed, and then the oiler rowed. Gray-faced and bowed forward, they mechanically, turn by turn, plied the leaden oars. The form of the lighthouse had vanished from the southern horizon, but finally a pale star appeared, just lifting from the sea. The streaked saffron in the west passed before the all-merging darkness, and the sea to the east was black. The land had vanished, and was expressed only by the low and drear thunder of the surf.

"If I am going to be drowned—if I am going to be drowned—if I am going to be drowned, why, in the name of the seven mad gods who rule the sea, was I allowed to come thus far and contemplate sand and trees? Was I brought here merely to have my nose dragged away as I was about to nibble the sacred cheese of life?"

The patient captain, drooped over the water jar, was sometimes obliged to speak to the oarsman.

"Keep her head up! Keep her head up!"

"Keep her head up, sir." The voices were weary and low.

This was surely a quiet evening. All save the oarsman lay heavily and listlessly in the boat's bottom. As for him, his eyes were just capable of noting the tall black waves that swept forward in a most sinister silence, save for an occasional subdued growl of a crest.

The cook's head was on a thwart, and he looked without interest at the water under his nose. He was deep in other scenes. Finally he spoke. "Billie," he murmured, dreamfully, "what kind of pie do you like best?"

V

"Pie!" said the oiler and the correspondent, agitatedly. "Don't talk about those things, blast you!"

"Well," said the cook, "I was just thinking about ham sandwiches, and——"

A night on the sea in an open boat is a long night. As darkness settled finally, the shine of the light, lifting from the sea in the south, changed to full gold. On the northern horizon a new light appeared, a small bluish gleam on the edge of the waters. These two lights were the furniture of the world. Otherwise there was nothing but waves.

Two men huddled in the stern, and distances were so magnificent in the dinghy that the rower was enabled to keep his feet partly warm by thrusting them under his companions. Their legs indeed extended far under the rowing-seat until they touched the feet of the captain forward. Sometimes, despite the efforts of the tired oarsman, a wave came piling into the boat, an icy wave of the night, and the chilling water soaked them anew. They would twist their bodies for a moment and groan, and sleep the dead sleep once more, while the water in the boat gurgled about them as the craft rocked.

The plan of the oiler and the correspondent was for one to row until he lost the ability, and then arouse the other from his seawater couch in the bottom of the boat.

The oiler plied the oars until his head drooped forward, and the overpowering sleep blinded him; and he rowed yet afterward. Then he touched a man in the bottom of the boat, and called his name. "Will you spell me for a little while?" he said meekly.

"Sure, Billie," said the correspondent, awaking and dragging himself to a sitting position. They exchanged places carefully, and the oiler, cuddling down in the seawater at the cook's side, seemed to go to sleep instantly.

The particular violence of the sea had ceased. The waves came without snarling. The obligation of the man at the oars was to keep the boat headed so that the tilt of the rollers would not capsize her, and to preserve her from filling when the crests rushed past. The black waves were silent and hard to be seen in the darkness. Often one was almost upon the boat before the oarsman was aware.

In a low voice the correspondent addressed the captain. He was not sure that the captain was awake, although this iron man seemed to be always awake. "Captain, shall I keep her making for that light north, sir?"

The same steady voice answered him. "Yes. Keep it about two points off the port bow."

The cook had tied a lifebelt around himself in

order to get even the warmth which this clumsy cork contrivance could donate, and he seemed almost stove-like when a rower, whose teeth invariably chattered wildly as soon as he ceased his labor, dropped down to sleep.

The correspondent, as he rowed, looked down at the two men sleeping underfoot. The cook's arm was around the oiler's shoulders, and, with their fragmentary clothing and haggard faces, they were the babes of the sea—a grotesque rendering of the old babes in the wood.

Later he must have grown stupid at his work, for suddenly there was a growling of water, and a crest came with a roar and a swash into the boat, and it was a wonder that it did not set the cook afloat in his lifebelt. The cook continued to sleep, but the oiler sat up, blinking his eyes and shaking with the new cold.

"Oh, I'm awful sorry, Billie," said the correspondent, contritely.

"That's all right, old boy," said the oiler, and lay down again and was asleep.

Presently it seemed that even the captain dozed, and the correspondent thought that he was the one man afloat on all the oceans. The wind had a voice as it came over the waves, and it was sadder than the end.

There was a long, loud swishing astern of the boat, and a gleaming trail of phosphorescence, like blue flame, was furrowed on the black waters. It might have been made by a monstrous knife.

Then there came a stillness, while the correspondent breathed with open mouth and looked at the sea.

Suddenly there was another swish and another long flash of bluish light, and this time it was alongside the boat, and might almost have been reached with an oar. The correspondent saw an enormous fin speed like a shadow through the water, hurling the crystalline spray and leaving the long glowing trail.

The correspondent looked over his shoulder at the captain. His face was hidden, and he seemed to be asleep. He looked at the babes of the sea. They certainly were asleep. So, being bereft of sympathy, he leaned a little way to one side and swore softly into the sea.

But the thing did not then leave the vicinity of the boat. Ahead or astern, on one side or the other, at intervals long or short, fled the long sparkling streak, and there was to be heard the *whirroo* of the dark fin. The speed and power of the thing was greatly to be admired. It cut the water like a gigantic and keen projectile.

The presence of this biding thing did not affect the man with the same horror that it would if he had been a picnicker. He simply looked at the sea dully and swore in an undertone.

Nevertheless, it is true that he did not wish to be alone with the thing. He wished one of his companions to awaken by chance and keep him company with it. But the captain hung motionless over the water jar, and the oiler and the cook in the bottom of the boat were plunged in slumber.

VI

"If I am going to be drowned—if I am going to be drowned—if I am going to be drowned, why, in the name of the seven mad gods who rule the sea, was I allowed to come thus far and contemplate sand and trees?"

During this dismal night, it may be remarked that a man would conclude that it was really the intention of the seven mad gods to drown him, despite the abominable injustice of it. For it was certainly an abominable injustice to drown a man who had worked so hard, so hard. The man felt it would be a crime most unnatural. Other people had drowned at sea since galleys swarmed with painted sails, but still——

When it occurs to a man that nature does not regard him as important, and that she feels she would not maim the universe by disposing of him, he at first wishes to throw bricks at the temple, and he hates deeply the fact that there are no bricks and no temples. Any visible expression of nature would surely be pelleted with his jeers.

Then, if there be no tangible thing to hoot, he feels, perhaps, the desire to confront a personification and indulge in pleas, bowed to one knee, and with hands supplicant, saying, "Yes, but I love myself."

A high cold star on a winter's night is the word he feels that she says to him. Thereafter he knows the pathos of his situation.

The men in the dinghy had not discussed these matters, but each had, no doubt, reflected upon them in silence and according to his mind. There was seldom any expression upon their faces save the general one of complete weariness. Speech was devoted to the business of the boat.

To chime the notes of his emotion, a verse mysteriously entered the correspondent's head. He had even forgotten that he had forgotten this verse, but it suddenly was in his mind.

> A soldier of the Legion lay dying in Algiers;
> There was lack of woman's nursing, there was
>   dearth of woman's tears;
> But a comrade stood beside him, and he took
>   that comrade's hand,
> And he said, "I never more shall see my own,
>   my native land."

In his childhood the correspondent had been made acquainted with the fact that a soldier of the Legion lay dying in Algiers, but he had never regarded the fact as important. Myriads of his schoolfellows had informed him of the soldier's plight, but the dinning had naturally ended by making him perfectly indifferent. He had never considered it his affair that a soldier of the Legion lay dying in Algiers, nor had it appeared to him as a matter for sorrow. It was less to him than the breaking of a pencil's point.

Now, however, it quaintly came to him as a human, living thing. It was no longer merely a picture of a few throes in the breast of a poet, meanwhile drinking tea and warming his feet at the grate; it was an actuality—stern, mournful, and fine.

The correspondent plainly saw the soldier. He lay on the sand with his feet out straight and still. While his pale left hand was upon his chest in an attempt to thwart the going of his life, the blood came between his fingers. In the far Algerian distance, a city of low square forms was set against a sky that was faint with the last sunset hues. The correspondent, plying the oars and dreaming of the slow and slower movements of the lips of the soldier, was moved by a profound and perfectly impersonal comprehension. He was sorry for the soldier of the Legion who lay dying in Algiers.

The thing which had followed the boat and waited had evidently grown bored at the delay. There was no longer to be heard the slash of the cut-water, and there was no longer the flame of the long trail. The light in the north still glimmered, but it was apparently no nearer to the boat. Sometimes the boom of the surf rang in the correspondent's ears, and he turned the craft seaward then and rowed harder. Southward, someone had evidently built a watch fire on the beach. It was too low and too far to be seen, but it made a shimmering, roseate reflection upon the bluff in back of it, and this could be discerned from the boat. The wind came stronger, and sometimes a wave suddenly raged out like a mountain cat, and there was to be seen the sheen and sparkle of a broken crest.

The captain, in the bow, moved on his water jar and sat erect. "Pretty long night," he observed to the correspondent. He looked at the shore. "Those lifesaving people take their time."

"Did you see that shark playing around?"

"Yes, I saw him. He was a big fellow, all right."

"Wish I had known you were awake."

Later the correspondent spoke into the bottom of the boat. "Billie!" There was a slow and gradual disentanglement. "Billie, will you spell me?"

"Sure," said the oiler.

As soon as the correspondent touched the cold comfortable seawater in the bottom of the boat, and had huddled close to the cook's lifebelt he was deep in sleep, despite the fact that his teeth played all the popular airs. This sleep was so good to him that it was but a moment before he heard a voice call his name in a tone that demonstrated the last stages of exhaustion. "Will you spell me?"

"Sure, Billie."

The light in the north had mysteriously vanished, but the correspondent took his course from the wide-awake captain.

Later in the night they took the boat farther out to sea, and the captain directed the cook to take one oar at the stern and keep the boat facing the seas. He was to call out if he should hear the thunder of the surf. This plan enabled the oiler and the correspondent to get respite together. "We'll give those boys a chance to get into shape again," said the captain. They curled down and, after a few preliminary chatterings and trembles, slept once more the dead sleep. Neither knew they had bequeathed to the cook the company of another shark, or perhaps the same shark.

As the boat caroused on the waves, spray occasionally bumped over the side and gave them a fresh soaking, but this had no power to break their repose. The ominous slash of the wind and the water affected them as it would have affected mummies.

"Boys," said the cook, with the notes of every

reluctance in his voice, "she's drifted in pretty close. I guess one of you had better take her to sea again." The correspondent, aroused, heard the crash of the toppled crests.

As he was rowing, the captain gave him some whiskey-and-water, and this steadied the chills out of him. "If I ever get ashore and anybody shows me even a photograph of an oar——"

At last there was a short conversation.

"Billie! . . . Billie, will you spell me?"

"Sure," said the oiler.

VII

When the correspondent again opened his eyes, the sea and the sky were each of the gray hue of the dawning. Later, carmine and gold was painted upon the waters. The morning appeared finally, in its splendor, with a sky of pure blue, and the sunlight flamed on the tips of the waves.

On the distant dunes were set many little black cottages, and a tall white windmill reared above them. No man, nor dog, nor bicycle appeared on the beach. The cottages might have formed a deserted village.

The voyagers scanned the shore. A conference was held in the boat. "Well," said the captain, "if no help is coming, we might better try a run through the surf right away. If we stay out here much longer we will be too weak to do anything for ourselves at all." The others silently acquiesced in this reasoning. The boat was headed for the beach. The correspondent wondered if none ever ascended the tall wind-tower, and if then they never looked seaward. This tower was a giant, standing with its back to the plight of the ants. It represented in a degree, to the correspondent, the serenity of nature amid the struggles of the individual—nature in the wind, and nature in the vision of men. She did not seem cruel to him then, nor beneficent, nor treacherous, nor wise. But she was indifferent, flatly indifferent. It is, perhaps, plausible that a man in this situation, impressed with the unconcern of the universe, should see the innumerable flaws of his life, and have them taste wickedly in his mind, and wish for another chance. A distinction between right and wrong seems absurdly clear to him, then, in this new ignorance of the grave-edge, and he understands that if he were given another opportunity he would mend his conduct and his words, and be better and brighter during an introduction or at a tea.

"Now, boys," said the captain, "she is going to swamp sure. All we can do is to work her in as far as possible, and then when she swamps, pile out and scramble for the beach. Keep cool now, and don't jump until she swamps sure."

The oiler took the oars. Over his shoulders he scanned the surf. "Captain," he said, "I think I'd better bring her about and keep her head-on to the seas and back her in."

"All right, Billie," said the captain. "Back her in." The oiler swung the boat then, and, seated in the stern, the cook and the correspondent were obliged to look over their shoulders to contemplate the lonely and indifferent shore.

The monstrous inshore rollers heaved the boat high until the men were again enabled to see the white sheets of water scudding up the slanted beach. "We won't get in very close," said the captain. Each time a man could wrest his attention from the rollers, he turned his glance toward the shore, and in the expression of the eyes during this contemplation there was a singular quality. The correspondent, observing the others, knew that they were not afraid, but the full meaning of their glances was shrouded.

As for himself, he was too tired to grapple fundamentally with the fact. He tried to coerce his mind into thinking of it, but the mind was dominated at this time by the muscles, and the muscles said they did not care. It merely occurred to him that if he should drown it would be a shame.

There were no hurried words, no pallor, no plain agitation. The men simply looked at the shore. "Now, remember to get well clear of the boat when you jump," said the captain.

Seaward the crest of a roller suddenly fell with

a thunderous crash, and the long white comber came roaring down upon the boat.

"Steady now," said the captain. The men were silent. They turned their eyes from the shore to the comber and waited. The boat slid up the incline, leaped at the furious top, bounced over it, and swung down the long back of the wave. Some water had been shipped, and the cook bailed it out.

But the next crest crashed also. The tumbling, boiling flood of white water caught the boat and whirled it almost perpendicular. Water swarmed in from all sides. The correspondent had his hands on the gunwale at this time, and when the water entered at that place he swiftly withdrew his fingers, as if he objected to wetting them.

The little boat, drunken with this weight of water, reeled and snuggled deeper into the sea.

"Bail her out, cook! Bail her out!" said the captain.

"All right, Captain," said the cook.

"Now, boys, the next one will do for us sure," said the oiler. "Mind to jump clear of the boat."

The third wave moved forward, huge, furious, implacable. It fairly swallowed the dinghy, and almost simultaneously the men tumbled into the sea. A piece of lifebelt had lain in the bottom of the boat, and as the correspondent went overboard he held this to his chest with his left hand.

The January water was icy, and he reflected

immediately that it was colder than he had expected to find it off the coast of Florida. This appeared to his dazed mind as a fact important enough to be noted at the time. The coldness of the water was sad; it was tragic. This fact was somehow mixed and confused with his opinion of his own situation, so that it seemed almost a proper reason for tears. The water was cold.

When he came to the surface he was conscious of little but the noisy water. Afterward he saw his companions in the sea. The oiler was ahead in the race. He was swimming strongly and rapidly. Off to the correspondent's left, the cook's great white and corked back bulged out of the water; and in the rear the captain was hanging with his one good hand to the keel of the overturned dinghy.

There is a certain immovable quality to a shore, and the correspondent wondered at it amid the confusion of the sea.

It seemed also very attractive; but the correspondent knew that it was a long journey, and he paddled leisurely. The piece of life preserver lay under him, and sometimes he whirled down the incline of a wave as if he were on a hand-sled.

But finally he arrived at a place in the sea where travel was beset with difficulty. He did not pause swimming to inquire what manner of current had caught him, but there his progress ceased. The shore was set before him like a bit of scenery on a stage, and he looked at it and understood with his eyes each detail of it.

As the cook passed, much farther to the left, the captain was calling to him, "Turn over on your back, cook! Turn over on your back and use the oar."

"All right, sir." The cook turned on his back, and, paddling with an oar, went ahead as if he were a canoe.

Presently the boat also passed to the left of the correspondent, with the captain clinging with one hand to the keel. He would have appeared like a man raising himself to look over a board fence if it were not for the extraordinary gymnastics of the boat. The correspondent marveled that the captain could still hold to it.

They passed on nearer to shore—the oiler, the cook, the captain—and following them went the water jar, bouncing gaily over the seas.

The correspondent remained in the grip of this strange new enemy—a current. The shore, with its white slope of sand and its green bluff topped with little silent cottages, was spread like a picture before him. It was very near to him then, but he was impressed as one who, in a gallery, looks at a scene from Brittany or Algiers.

He thought: "I am going to drown? Can it be possible? Can it be possible? Can it be possible?"

Perhaps an individual must consider his own death to be the final phenomenon of nature.

But later a wave perhaps whirled him out of this small deadly current, for he found suddenly that he could again make progress toward the shore. Later still he was aware that the captain, clinging with one hand to the keel of the dinghy, had his face turned away from the shore and toward him, and was calling his name. "Come to the boat! Come to the boat!"

In his struggle to reach the captain and the boat, he reflected that when one gets properly wearied drowning must really be a comfortable arrangement—a cessation of hostilities accompanied by a large degree of relief; and he was glad of it, for the main thing in his mind for some moments had been horror of the temporary agony. He did not wish to be hurt.

Presently he saw a man running along the shore. He was undressing with most remarkable speed. Coat, trousers, shirt, everything flew magically off him.

"Come to the boat!" called the captain.

"All right, Captain." As the correspondent paddled, he saw the captain let himself down to bottom and leave the boat. Then the correspondent performed his one little marvel of the voyage. A large wave caught him and flung him with ease and supreme speed completely over the boat and far beyond it. It struck him even then as an event in gymnastics and a true miracle of the sea. An overturned boat in the surf is not a plaything to a swimming man.

The correspondent arrived in water that reached only to his waist, but his condition did not enable him to stand for more than a moment. Each wave knocked him into a heap, and the undertow pulled at him.

Then he saw the man who had been running and undressing, and undressing and running, come bounding into the water. He dragged ashore the cook, and then waded toward the captain, but the captain waved him away and sent him to the correspondent. He was naked—naked as a tree in winter; but a halo was about his head, and he shone like a saint. He gave a strong pull, and a long drag, and a bully heave at the correspondent's hand. The correspondent, schooled in the minor formulæ, said, "Thanks, old man." But suddenly the man cried, "What's that?" He pointed a swift finger. The correspondent said, "Go."

In the shallows, face downward, lay the oiler. His forehead touched sand that was periodically, between each wave, clear of the sea.

The correspondent did not know all that transpired afterward. When he achieved safe ground he fell, striking the sand with each particular part of his body. It was as if he had dropped from a roof, but the thud was grateful to him.

It seems that instantly the beach was populated with men with blankets, clothes, and flasks, and women with coffeepots and all the remedies sacred to their minds. The welcome of the land to the men from the sea was warm and generous; but a still and dripping shape was carried slowly up the beach, and the land's welcome for it could only be the different and sinister hospitality of the grave.

When it came night, the white waves paced to and fro in the moonlight, and the wind brought the sound of the great sea's voice to the men on the shore, and they felt that they could then be interpreters.

A Pair of Silk Stockings

by Kate Chopin

Little Mrs. Sommers one day found herself the unexpected possessor of fifteen dollars. It seemed to her a very large amount of money, and the way in which it stuffed and bulged her worn old *porte-monnaie* gave her a feeling of importance such as she had not enjoyed for years.

The question of investment was one that occupied her greatly. For a day or two she walked about apparently in a dreamy state, but really absorbed in speculation and calculation. She did not wish to act hastily, to do anything she might afterward regret. But it was during the still hours of the night when she lay awake revolving plans in her mind that she seemed to see her way clearly toward a proper and judicious use of the money.

A dollar or two should be added to the price usually paid for Janie's shoes, which would insure their lasting an appreciable time longer than they usually did. She would buy so and so many yards of percale for new shirt waists for the boys and Janie and Mag. She had intended to make the old ones do by skilful patching. Mag should have another gown. She had seen some beautiful patterns, veritable bargains in the shop windows. And still there would be left enough for new stockings—two pairs apiece—and what darning that would save for a while! She would get caps for the boys and sailor-hats for the girls. The vision of her little brood looking fresh and dainty and new for once in their lives excited her and made her restless and wakeful with anticipation.

The neighbors sometimes talked of certain "better days" that little Mrs. Sommers had known before she had ever thought of being Mrs. Sommers. She herself indulged in no such morbid retrospection. She had no time—no second of time to devote to the past. The needs of the present absorbed her every faculty. A vision of the future like some dim, gaunt monster sometimes appalled her, but luckily tomorrow never comes.

Mrs. Sommers was one who knew the value of bargains; who could stand for hours making her way inch by inch toward the desired object that was selling below cost. She could elbow her way if need be; she had learned to clutch a piece of goods and hold it and stick to it with persistence and determination till her turn came to be served, no matter when it came.

But that day she was a little faint and tired. She had swallowed a light luncheon—no! when she came to think of it, between getting the children fed and the place righted, and preparing herself for the shopping bout, she had actually forgotten to eat any luncheon at all!

She sat herself upon a revolving stool before a counter that was comparatively deserted, trying to gather strength and courage to charge through an eager multitude that was besieging breast-works of shirting and figured lawn. An all-gone limp feeling had come over her and she rested her hand aimlessly upon the counter. She wore no gloves. By degrees she grew aware that her hand had encountered something very soothing, very pleasant to touch. She looked down to see that her hand lay upon a pile of silk stockings. A placard near by announced that they had been reduced in price from two dollars and fifty cents to one dollar and ninety-eight cents; and a young girl who stood behind the counter asked her if she wished to examine their line of silk hosiery. She smiled, just as if she had been asked to inspect a tiara of diamonds with the ultimate view of purchasing it. But she went on feeling the soft, sheeny luxurious things—with both hands now, holding them up to see them glisten, and to feel them glide serpent-like through her fingers.

Two hectic blotches came suddenly into her pale cheeks. She looked up at the girl.

"Do you think there are any eights-and-a-half among these?"

There were any number of eights-and-a-half. In fact, there were more of that size than any other. Here was a light-blue pair; there were some lavender, some all black and various shades of tan and gray. Mrs. Sommers selected a black pair and looked at them very long and closely. She pretended to be examining their texture, which the clerk assured her was excellent.

"A dollar and ninety-eight cents," she mused aloud. "Well, I'll take this pair." She handed the girl a five-dollar bill and waited for her change and for her parcel. What a very small parcel it was! It seemed lost in the depths of her shabby old shopping-bag.

Mrs. Sommers after that did not move in the direction of the bargain counter. She took the elevator, which carried her to an upper floor into the region of the ladies' waiting-rooms. Here, in a retired corner, she exchanged her cotton stockings for the new silk ones which she had just bought. She was not going through any acute mental process or reasoning with herself, nor was she striving to explain to her satisfaction the motive of her action. She was not thinking at all. She seemed for the time to be taking a rest from that laborious and fatiguing function and to have abandoned herself to some mechanical impulse that directed her actions and freed her of responsibility.

How good was the touch of the raw silk to her flesh! She felt like lying back in the cushioned chair and reveling for a while in the luxury of it. She did for a little while. Then she replaced her shoes, rolled the cotton stockings together and thrust them into her bag. After doing this she crossed straight over to the shoe department and took her seat to be fitted.

She was fastidious. The clerk could not make her out; he could not reconcile her shoes with her stockings, and she was not too easily pleased. She held back her skirts and turned her feet one way and her head another way as she glanced down at the polished, pointed-tipped boots. Her foot and ankle looked very pretty. She could not realize that they belonged to her and were a part of herself. She wanted an excellent and stylish fit, she told the young fellow who served her, and she did not mind the difference of a dollar or two more in the price so long as she got what she desired.

It was a long time since Mrs. Sommers had been fitted with gloves. On rare occasions when she had bought a pair they were always "bargains," so cheap that it would have been preposterous and unreasonable to have expected them to be fitted to the hand.

Now she rested her elbow on the cushion of the glove counter, and a pretty, pleasant young creature, delicate and deft of touch, drew a long-wristed "kid" over Mrs. Sommers' hand. She smoothed it down over the wrist and buttoned it neatly, and both lost themselves for a second or two in admiring contemplation of the little symmetrical gloved hand. But there were other places where money might be spent.

There were books and magazines piled up in the window of a stall a few paces down the street. Mrs. Sommers bought two high-priced magazines such as she had been accustomed to read in the days when she had been accustomed to other pleasant things. She carried them without wrapping. As well as she could she lifted her skirts at the crossings. Her stockings and boots and well fitting gloves had worked marvels in her bearing—had given her a feeling of assurance, a sense of belonging to the well-dressed multitude.

She was very hungry. Another time she would have stilled the cravings for food until reaching her own home, where she would have brewed herself a cup of tea and taken a snack of anything that was available. But the impulse that was guiding her would not suffer her to entertain any such thought.

There was a restaurant at the corner. She had never entered its doors; from the outside she had sometimes caught glimpses of spotless damask and shining crystal, and soft-stepping waiters serving people of fashion.

When she entered her appearance created no surprise, no consternation, as she had half feared it might. She seated herself at a small table alone, and an attentive waiter at once approached to take her order. She did not want a profusion; she craved a nice and tasty bite—a half dozen blue-points,[1] a plump chop with cress, a something sweet—a crème-frappée, for instance; a glass of Rhine wine, and after all a small cup of black coffee.

While waiting to be served she removed her gloves very leisurely and laid them beside her. Then she picked up a magazine and glanced through it, cutting the pages with a blunt edge of her knife. It was all very agreeable. The damask was even more spotless than it had seemed through the window, and the crystal more sparkling. There were quiet ladies and gentlemen, who did not notice her, lunching at the small tables like her own. A soft, pleasing strain of music could be heard, and a gentle breeze was blowing through the window. She

1. *blue-points*] a type of oyster from Blue Point, Long Island.

tasted a bite, and she read a word or two, and she sipped the amber wine and wiggled her toes in the silk stockings. The price of it made no difference. She counted the money out to the waiter and left an extra coin on his tray, whereupon he bowed before her as before a princess of royal blood.

There was still money in her purse, and her next temptation presented itself in the shape of a matinée poster.

It was a little later when she entered the theatre, the play had begun and the house seemed to her to be packed. But there were vacant seats here and there, and into one of them she was ushered, between brilliantly dressed women who had gone there to kill time and eat candy and display their gaudy attire. There were many others who were there solely for the play and acting. It is safe to say there was no one present who bore quite the attitude which Mrs. Sommers did to her surroundings. She gathered in the whole—stage and players and people in one wide impression, and absorbed it and enjoyed it. She laughed at the comedy and wept—she and the gaudy woman next to her wept over the tragedy. And they talked a little together over it. And the gaudy woman wiped her eyes and sniffled on a tiny square of filmy, perfumed lace and passed little Mrs. Sommers her box of candy.

The play was over, the music ceased, the

crowd filed out. It was like a dream ended. People scattered in all directions. Mrs. Sommers went to the corner and waited for the cable car.

A man with keen eyes, who sat opposite to her, seemed to like the study of her small, pale face. It puzzled him to decipher what he saw there. In truth, he saw nothing—unless he were wizard enough to detect a poignant wish, a powerful longing that the cable car would never stop anywhere, but go on and on with her forever.

The Foreigner

by Sarah Orne Jewett

I

One evening, at the end of August, in Dunnet Landing, I heard Mrs. Todd's firm footstep crossing the small front entry outside my door, and her conventional cough which served as a herald's trumpet, or a plain New England knock, in the harmony of our fellowship.

"Oh, please come in!" I cried, for it had been so still in the house that I supposed my friend and hostess had gone to see one of her neighbors. The first cold northeasterly storm of the season was blowing hard outside. Now and then there was a dash of great raindrops and a flick of wet lilac leaves against the window, but I could hear that the sea was already stirred to its dark depths, and the great rollers were coming in heavily against the shore. One might well believe that Summer was coming to a sad end that night, in the darkness and rain and sudden access of autumnal cold. It seemed as if there must be danger offshore among the outer islands.

"Oh, there!" exclaimed Mrs. Todd, as she entered. "I know nothing ain't ever happened out to Green Island since the world began, but I always do worry about mother in these great gales. You know those tidal waves occur sometimes down to the West Indies, and I get dwellin' on 'em so I can't set still in my chair, nor knit a common row to a stocking. William might get mooning, out in his small bo't, and not observe how the sea was making, an' meet with some accident. Yes, I thought I'd come in and set with you if you wa'n't busy. No, I never feel any concern about 'em in winter 'cause then they're prepared, and all ashore and everything snug. William ought to keep help, as I tell him; yes, he ought to keep help."

I hastened to reassure my anxious guest by saying that Elijah Tilley had told me in the afternoon, when I came along the shore past the fish houses, that Johnny Bowden and the Captain were out at Green Island; he had seen them beating up the bay, and thought they must have put into Burnt Island cove, but one of the lobstermen brought word later that he saw them hauling out at Green Island as he came by, and Captain Bowden pointed ashore and shook his head to say that he did not mean to try to get in. "The old Miranda just managed it, but she will have to stay at home a day or two and put new patches in her sail," I ended, not without pride in so much circumstantial evidence.

Mrs. Todd was alert in a moment. "Then they'll all have a very pleasant evening," she assured me, apparently dismissing all fears of tidal waves and other sea-going disasters. "I was urging Alick Bowden to go ashore some day and see mother before cold weather. He's her own nephew; she sets a great deal by him. And Johnny's a great chum o' William's; don't you know the first day we had Johnny out 'long of us, he took an' give William his money to keep for him that he'd been a-savin', and William showed it to me an' was so affected, I thought he was goin' to shed tears? 'Twas a dollar an' eighty cents; yes, they'll have a beautiful evenin' all together, and like's not the sea'll be flat as a doorstep come morning."

I had drawn a large wooden rocking-chair before the fire, and Mrs. Todd was sitting there jogging herself a little, knitting fast, and wonderfully placid of countenance. There came a fresh gust of wind and rain, and we could feel the small wooden house rock and hear it creak as if it were a ship at sea.

"Lord, hear the great breakers!" exclaimed Mrs. Todd. "How they pound!—there, there! I always run of an idea that the sea knows anger these nights and gets full o' fight. I can hear the rote[1] o' them old black ledges way down the thoroughfare. Calls up all those stormy verses in the Book o' Psalms; David he knew how old sea-goin' folks have to quake at the heart."

I thought as I had never thought before of such anxieties. The families of sailors and coastwise adventurers by sea must always be worrying about somebody, this side of the world or the other. There was hardly one of Mrs. Todd's elder acquaintances, men or women, who had not at some time or other made a sea voyage, and there was often no news until the voyagers themselves came back to bring it.

"There's a roaring high overhead, and a roaring in the deep sea," said Mrs. Todd solemnly, "and they battle together nights like this. No, I couldn't sleep; some women folks always goes right to bed an' to sleep, so's to forget, but 't ain't my way. Well, it's a blessin' we don't all feel alike; there's hardly any of our folks at sea to worry about, nowadays, but I can't help my feelin's, an' I got thinking of mother all alone, if William had happened to be out lobsterin' and couldn't make the cove gettin' back."

"They will have a pleasant evening," I repeated. "Captain Bowden is the best of good company."

"Mother'll make him some pancakes for his

1. *rote*] Sound of the surf on the shore.

supper, like's not," said Mrs. Todd, clicking her knitting needles and giving a pull at her yarn. Just then the old cat pushed open the unlatched door and came straight toward her mistress's lap. She was regarded severely as she stepped about and turned on the broad expanse, and then made herself into a round cushion of fur, but was not openly admonished. There was another great blast of wind overhead, and a puff of smoke came down the chimney.

"This makes me think o' the night Mis' Cap'n Tolland died," said Mrs. Todd, half to herself. "Folks used to say these gales only blew when somebody's a-dyin', or the devil was a-comin' for his own, but the worst man I ever knew died a real pretty mornin' in June."

"You have never told me any ghost stories," said I; and such was the gloomy weather and the influence of the night that I was instantly filled with reluctance to have this suggestion followed. I had not chosen the best of moments; just before I spoke we had begun to feel as cheerful as possible. Mrs. Todd glanced doubtfully at the cat and then at me, with a strange absent look, and I was really afraid that she was going to tell me something that would haunt my thoughts on every dark stormy night as long as I lived.

"Never mind now; tell me tomorrow by daylight, Mrs. Todd," I hastened to say, but she still looked at me full of doubt and deliberation.

"Ghost stories!" she answered. "Yes, I don't know but I've heard a plenty of 'em first an' last. I was just sayin' to myself that this is like the night Mis' Cap'n Tolland died. 'Twas the great line storm in September all of thirty, or maybe forty, year ago. I ain't one that keeps much account o' time."

"Tolland? That's a name I have never heard in Dunnet," I said.

"Then you haven't looked well about the old part o' the buryin' ground, no'theast corner," replied Mrs. Todd. "All their women folks lies there; the sea's got most o' the men. They were a known family o' shipmasters in early times. Mother had a mate, Ellen Tolland, that she mourns to this day; died right in her bloom with quick consumption, but the rest o' that family was all boys but one, and older than she, an' they lived hard seafarin' lives an' all died hard. They were called very smart seamen. I've heard that when the youngest went into one o' the old shippin' houses in Boston, the head o' the firm called out to him: 'Did you say Tolland from Dunnet? That's recommendation enough for any vessel!' There was some o' them old shipmasters as tough as iron, an' they had the name o' usin' their crews very severe, but there wa'n't a man that wouldn't rather sign with 'em an' take his chances, than with the slack ones that didn't know how to meet accidents."

II

There was so long a pause, and Mrs. Todd still looked so absent-minded, that I was afraid she and the cat were growing drowsy together before the fire, and I should have no reminiscences at all. The wind struck the house again, so that we both started in our chairs and Mrs. Todd gave a curious, startled look at me. The cat lifted her head and listened too, in the silence that followed, while after the wind sank we were more conscious than ever of the awful roar of the sea. The house jarred now and then, in a strange, disturbing way.

"Yes, they'll have a beautiful evening out to the island," said Mrs. Todd again; but she did not say it gayly. I had not seen her before in her weaker moments.

"Who was Mrs. Captain Tolland?" I asked eagerly, to change the current of our thoughts.

"I never knew her maiden name; if I ever heard it, I've gone an' forgot; 't would mean nothing to me," answered Mrs. Todd.

"She was a foreigner, an' he met with her out in the Island o' Jamaica. They said she'd been left a widow with property. Land knows what become of it; she was French born, an' her first husband was a Portugee, or somethin'."

I kept silence now, a poor and insufficient question being worse than none.

"Cap'n John Tolland was the least smartest of any of 'em, but he was full smart enough, an' commanded a good brig at the time, in the sugar trade; he'd taken out a cargo o' pine lumber to the islands from somewheres up the river, an' had been loadin' for home in the port o' Kingston, an' had gone ashore that afternoon for his papers, an' remained afterwards 'long of three friends o' his, shipmasters. They was havin' their suppers together in a tavern; 'twas late in the evenin' an' they was more lively than usual, an' felt boyish; and over opposite was another house full o' company, real bright and pleasant lookin', with a lot o' lights, an' they heard somebody singin' very pretty to a guitar. They wa'n't in no go-to-meetin' condition, an' one of 'em, he slapped the table an' said, 'Le' 's go over, an' hear that lady sing!' an' over they all went, good honest sailors, but three sheets in the wind, and stepped in as if they was invited, an' made their bows inside the door, an' asked if they could hear the music; they were all respectable well-dressed men. They saw the woman that had the guitar, an' there was a company a-listenin', regular high binders all of 'em; an' there was a long table all spread out with big candlesticks like little trees o' light, and a sight o' glass an' silver ware; an' part o' the men was young officers in uniform, an' the colored folks was steppin' round servin' 'em, an' they had the lady singin'.

'Twas a wasteful scene, an' a loud talkin' company, an' though they was three sheets in the wind themselves there wa'n't one o' them cap'ns but had sense to perceive it. The others had pushed back their chairs, an' their decanters an' glasses was standin' thick about, an' they was teasin' the one that was singin' as if they'd just got her in to amuse 'em. But they quieted down; one o' the young officers had beautiful manners, an' invited the four cap'ns to join 'em, very polite; 'twas a kind of public house, and after they all heard another song, he come to consult with 'em whether they wouldn't git up and dance a hornpipe or somethin' to the lady's music.

"They was all elderly men an' shipmasters, and owned property; two of 'em was church members in good standin'," continued Mrs. Todd loftily, "an' they wouldn't lend theirselves to no such kickshows as that, an' spite o' bein' three sheets in the wind, as I have once observed; they waved aside the tumblers of wine the young officer was pourin' out for 'em so freehanded, and said they should rather be excused. An' when they all rose, still very dignified, as I've been well informed, and made their partin' bows and was goin' out, them young sports got round 'em an' tried to prevent 'em, and they had to push an' strive considerable, but out they come. There was this Cap'n Tolland and two Cap'n Bowdens, and the fourth was my own father." (Mrs. Todd spoke slowly, as if to impress the value of her authority.) "Two of them was very religious, upright men, but they would have their night off sometimes, all 'o them old-fashioned cap'ns, when they was free of business and ready to leave port.

"An' they went back to their tavern an' got their bills paid, an' set down kind o' mad with everybody by the front windows, mistrusting some o' their tavern charges, like's not, by that time, an' when they got tempered down, they watched the house over across, where the party was.

"There was a kind of grove o' trees between the house an' the road, an' they heard the guitar a-goin' an' a-stoppin' short by turns, and pretty soon somebody began to screech, an' they saw a white dress come runnin' out through the bushes, an' tumbled over each other in their haste to offer help; an' out she come, with the guitar, cryin' into the street, and they just walked off four square with her amongst 'em, down toward the wharves where they felt more to home. They couldn't make out at first what 'twas she spoke,—Cap'n Lorenzo Bowden was well acquainted in Havre an' Bordeaux, an' spoke a poor quality o' French, an' she knew a little mite o' English, but not much; and they come somehow or other to discern that she was in real distress. Her husband and her children had died o' yellow fever; they'd all come up to Kingston from one o' the far Wind'ard Islands to get passage on a steamer to France, an' a negro had stole their money off her husband while he lay sick o' the fever, an' she had been befriended some, but the folks that knew about her had died too; it had been a dreadful run o' the fever that season, an' she fell at last to playin' an' singin' for hire, and for what money they'd throw to her round them harbor houses.

"'Twas a real hard case, an' when them cap'ns made out about it, there wa'n't one that meant to take leave without helpin' of her. They was pretty mellow, an' whatever they might lack o' prudence they more'n made up with charity: they didn't want to see nobody abused, an' she was sort of a pretty woman, an' they stopped in the street then an' there an' drew lots who should take her aboard, bein' all bound home. An' the lot fell to Cap'n Jonathan Bowden who did act discouraged; his vessel had but small accommodations, though he could stow a big freight, an' she was a dreadful slow sailer through bein' square as a box, an' his first wife, that was livin' then, was a dreadful jealous woman. He threw himself right onto the mercy o' Cap'n Tolland."

Mrs. Todd indulged herself for a short time in a season of calm reflection.

"I always thought they'd have done better,

and more reasonable, to give her some money to pay her passage home to France, or wherever she may have wanted to go," she continued.

I nodded and looked for the rest of the story.

"Father told mother," said Mrs. Todd confidentially, "that Cap'n Jonathan Bowden an' Cap'n John Tolland had both taken a little more than usual; I wouldn't have you think, either, that they both wasn't the best o' men, an' they was solemn as owls, and argued the matter between 'em, an' waved aside the other two when they tried to put their oars in. An' spite o' Cap'n Tolland's bein' a settled old bachelor they fixed it that he was to take the prize on his brig; she was a fast sailer, and there was a good spare cabin or two where he'd sometimes carried passengers, but he'd filled 'em with bags o' sugar on his own account an' was loaded very heavy beside. He said he'd shift the sugar an' get along somehow, an' the last the other three cap'ns saw of the party was Cap'n John handing the lady into his bo't, guitar and all, an' off they all set tow'ds their ships with their men rowin' 'em in the bright moonlight down to Port Royal where the anchorage was, an' where they all lay, goin' out with the tide an' mornin' wind at break o' day. An' the others thought they heard music of the guitar, two o' the bo'ts kept well together, but it may have come from another source."

"Well; and then?" I asked eagerly after a

pause. Mrs. Todd was almost laughing aloud over her knitting and nodding emphatically. We had forgotten all about the noise of the wind and sea.

"Lord bless you! he come sailing into Portland with his sugar, all in good time, an' they stepped right afore a justice o' the peace, and Cap'n John Tolland come paradin' home to Dunnet Landin' a married man. He owned one o' them thin, narrow-lookin' houses with one room each side o' the front door, and two slim black spruces spindlin' up against the front windows to make it gloomy inside. There was no horse nor cattle of course, though he owned pasture land, an' you could see rifts o' light right through the barn as you drove by. And there was a good excellent kitchen, but his sister reigned over that; she had a right to two rooms, and took the kitchen an' a bedroom that led out of it; an' bein' given no rights in the kitchen had angered the cap'n so they weren't on no kind o' speakin' terms. He preferred his old brig for comfort, but now and then, between voyages, he'd come home for a few days, just to show he was master over his part o' the house, and show Eliza she couldn't commit no trespass.

"They stayed a little while; 'twas pretty spring weather, an' I used to see Cap'n John rollin' by with his arms full o' bundles from the store, lookin' as pleased and important as a boy; an' then they went right off to sea again, an' was gone a good many months. Next time he left her to live there alone, after they'd stopped at home together some weeks, an' they said she suffered from bein' at sea, but some said that the owners wouldn't have a woman aboard. 'Twas before father was lost on that last voyage of his, an' he said mother went up once or twice to see them. Father said there wa'n't a mite o' harm in her, but somehow or other a sight o' prejudice arose; it may have been caused by the remarks of Eliza an' her feelin's tow'ds her brother. Even my mother had no regard for Eliza Tolland. But mother asked the cap'n's wife to come with her one evenin' to a social circle, that was down to the meetin'-house vestry, so she'd get acquainted a little, an' she appeared very pretty until they started to have some singin' to the melodeon. Mari' Harris an' one o' the younger Caplin girls undertook to sing a duet, an' they sort o' flatted, an' she put her hands right up to her ears, and give a little squeal, an' went quick as could be an' give 'em the right notes, for she could read the music like plain print, an' made 'em try it over again. She was real willin' an' pleasant, but that didn't suit, an' she made faces when they got it wrong. An' then there fell a dead calm, an' we was all settin' round prim as dishes, an' my mother, that never expects ill feelin', asked her if she wouldn't sing somethin', an' up she got,—

poor creatur', it all seems so different to me now,—an' sung a lovely little song standin' in the floor; it seemed to have something gay about it that kept a-repeatin', an' nobody could help keepin' time, an' all of a sudden she looked round at the tables and caught up a tin plate that somebody'd fetched a Washin'ton pie in, an' she begun to drum on it with her fingers like one o' them tambourines, an' went right on singin' faster an' faster, and next minute she began to dance a little pretty dance between the verses, just as light and pleasant as a child. You couldn't help seein' how pretty 'twas; we all got to trottin' a foot, an' some o' the men clapped their hands quite loud, a-keepin' time, 'twas so catchin', an' seemed so natural to her. There wa'n't one of 'em but enjoyed it; she just tried to do her part, an' some urged her on, till she stopped with a little twirl of her skirts an' went to her place again by mother. And I can see mother now, reachin' over an' smilin' and pattin' her hand.

"But next day there was an awful scandal goin' in the parish, an' Mari' Harris reproached my mother to her face, an' I never wanted to see her since, but I've had to a good many times. I said Mis' Tolland didn't intend no impropriety,—I reminded her of David's dancin' before the Lord; but she said such a man as David never would have thought o' dancin' right there in the Orthodox vestry, and she felt I spoke with irreverence.

"And next Sunday Mis' Tolland come walkin' into our meeting but I must say she acted like a cat in a strange garret, and went right out down the aisle with her head in the air, from the pew Deacon Caplin had showed her into. 'Twas just in the beginning of the long prayer. I wished she'd stayed through, whatever her reasons were. Whether she'd expected somethin' different, or misunderstood some o' the pastor's remarks, or what 'twas, I don't really feel able to explain, but she kind o' declared war, at least folks thought so, an' war 'twas from that time. I see she was cryin', or had been, as she passed by me; perhaps bein' in meetin' was what had power to make her feel homesick and strange.

"Cap'n John Tolland was away fittin' out; that next week he come home to see her and say farewell. He was lost with his ship in the Straits of Malacca, and she lived there alone in the old house a few months longer till she died. He left her well off; 'twas said he hid his money about the house and she knew where 'twas. Oh, I expect you've heard that story told over an' over twenty times, since you've been here at the Landin'?"

"Never one word," I insisted.

"It was a good while ago," explained Mrs. Todd, with reassurance. "Yes, it all happened a great while ago."

III

At this moment, with a sudden flaw of the wind, some wet twigs outside blew against the window panes and made a noise like a distressed creature trying to get in. I started with sudden fear, and so did the cat, but Mrs. Todd knitted away and did not even look over her shoulder.

"She was a good-looking woman; yes, I always thought Mis' Tolland was good-looking, though she had, as was reasonable, a sort of foreign cast, and she spoke very broken English, no better than a child. She was always at work about her house, or settin' at a front window with her sewing; she was a beautiful hand to embroider. Sometimes, summer evenings, when the windows was open, she'd set an' drum on her guitar, but I don't know as I ever heard her sing but once after the cap'n went away. She appeared very happy about havin' him, and took on dreadful at partin' when he was down here on the wharf, going back to Portland by boat to take ship for that last v'y'ge. He acted kind of ashamed, Cap'n John did; folks about here ain't so much accustomed to show their feelings. The whistle had blown an' they was waitin' for him to get aboard, an' he was put to it to know what to do and treated her very affectionate in spite of all impatience; but mother happened to be there and she went an' spoke, and I remember what a comfort she seemed to be. Mis' Tolland clung to her then, and she wouldn't give a glance after the boat when it had started, though the captain was very eager a-wavin' to her. She wanted mother to come home with her an' wouldn't let go her hand, and mother had just come in to stop all night with me an' had plenty o' time ashore, which didn't always happen, so they walked off together, an' 'twas some considerable time before she got back.

" 'I want you to neighbor with that poor lonesome creatur',' says mother to me, lookin' reproachful. 'She's a stranger in a strange land,' says mother. 'I want you to make her have a sense that somebody feels kind to her.'

" 'Why, since that time she flaunted out o' meetin', folks have felt she liked other ways better'n our'n,' says I. I was provoked, because I'd had a nice supper ready, an' mother'd let it wait so long 't was spoiled. 'I hope you'll like your supper!' I told her. I was dreadful ashamed afterward of speakin' so to mother.

" 'What consequence is my supper?' says she to me; mother can be very stern,—'or your comfort or mine, beside letting a foreign person an' a stranger feel so desolate; she's done the best a woman could do in her lonesome place, and she asks nothing of anybody except a little common kindness. Think if 't was you in a foreign land!'

"And mother set down to drink her tea, an' I

set down humbled enough over by the wall to wait till she finished. An' I did think it all over, an' next day I never said nothin', but I put on my bonnet, and went to see Mis' Cap'n Tolland, if 't was only for mother's sake. 'Twas about three quarters of a mile up the road here, beyond the school-house. I forgot to tell you that the cap'n had bought out his sister's right at three or four times what 'twas worth, to save trouble, so they'd got clear o' her, an' I went round into the side yard sort o' friendly an' sociable, rather than stop an' deal with the knocker an' the front door. It looked so pleasant an' pretty I was glad I come; she had set a little table for supper, though 'twas still early, with a white cloth on it, right out under an old apple tree close by the house. I noticed 'twas same as with me at home, there was only one plate. She was just coming out with a dish; you couldn't see the door nor the table from the road.

"In the few weeks she'd been there she'd got some bloomin' pinks an' other flowers next the doorstep. Somehow it looked as if she'd known how to make it homelike for the cap'n. She asked me to set down' she was very polite, but she looked very mournful, and I spoke of mother, an' she put down her dish and caught holt o' me with both hands an' said my mother was an angel. When I see the tears in her eyes 't was all right between us, and we were always friendly after that, and mother had us come out and make a little visit that summer; but she come a foreigner and she went a foreigner, and never was anything but a stranger among our folks. She taught me a sight o' things about herbs I never knew before nor since; she was well acquainted with the virtues o' plants. She'd act awful secret about some things too, an' used to work charms for herself sometimes, an' some o' the neighbors told to an' fro after she died that they knew enough not to provoke her, but 'twas all nonsense; 't is the believin' in such things that causes 'em to be any harm, an' so I told 'em," confided Mrs. Todd contemptuously. "That first night I stopped to tea with her she'd cooked some eggs with some herb or other sprinkled all through, and 'twas she that first led me to discern mushrooms; an' she went right down on her knees in my garden here when she saw I had my different officious herbs. Yes, 't was she that learned me the proper use o' parsley too; she was a beautiful cook."

Mrs. Todd stopped talking, and rose, putting the cat gently in the chair, while she went away to get another stick of apple-tree wood. It was not an evening when one wished to let the fire go down, and we had a splendid bank of bright coals. I had always wondered where Mrs. Todd had got such an unusual knowledge of cookery, of the varieties of mushrooms, and the use of sorrel as a vegetable, and other blessings of that sort. I had long ago learned that she could vary her omelettes like a child of France, which was indeed a surprise in Dunnet Landing.

IV

All these revelations were of the deepest interest, and I was ready with a question as soon as Mrs. Todd came in and had well settled the fire and herself and the cat again.

"I wonder why she never went back to France, after she was left alone?"

"She come here from the French islands," explained Mrs. Todd. "I asked her once about her folks, an' she said they were all dead; 'twas the fever took 'em. She made this her home, lonesome as 'twas; she told me she hadn't been in France since she was 'so small,' and measured me off a child o' six. She'd lived right out in the country before, so that part wa'n't unusual to her. Oh yes, there was something very strange about her, and she hadn't been brought up in high circles nor nothing o' that kind. I think she'd been really pleased to have the cap'n marry her an' give her a good home, after all she'd passed through, and leave her free with his money an' all that. An' she got over bein' so strange-looking to me after a while, but 'twas a very singular expression: she wore a fixed smile that wa'n't a smile; there wa'n't no light behind it, same's a lamp can't shine if it ain't lit. I don't know just how to express it, 'twas a sort of made countenance."

One could not help thinking of Sir Philip Sidney's phrase, "A made countenance, between simpering and smiling."

"She took it hard, havin' the captain go off on that last voyage," Mrs. Todd went on. "She said somethin' told her when they was partin' that he would never come back. He was lucky to speak a home-bound ship this side o' the Cape o' Good Hope, an' got a chance to send her a letter, an' that cheered her up. You often felt as if you was dealin' with a child's mind, for all she had so much information that other folks hadn't. I was a sight younger than I be now, and she made me imagine new things, and I got interested watchin' her an' findin' out what she had to say, but you couldn't get to no affectionateness with her. I used to blame me sometimes; we used to be real good comrades goin' off for an afternoon, but I never gave her a kiss till the day she laid in her coffin and it come to my heart there wa'n't no one else to do it."

"And Captain Tolland died," I suggested after a while.

"Yes, the cap'n was lost," said Mrs. Todd, "and of course word didn't come for a good while after it happened. The letter come from the owners to my uncle, Cap'n Lorenzo Bowden, who was in charge of Cap'n Tolland's affairs at home, and he come right up for me an' said I must go with him to the house. I had known what it was to be a widow, myself, for near a year, an' there was plenty o' widow women along this coast that the sea had made desolate, but I never saw a heart break as I did then.

"'Twas this way: we walked together along the road, me an' uncle Lorenzo. You know how it leads straight from just above the schoolhouse to the brook bridge, and their house was just this side o' the brook bridge on the left hand; the cellar's there now, and a couple or three good-sized gray birches growin' in it. And when we come near enough I saw that the best room, this way, where she most never set, was all lighted up, and the curtains up so that the light shone bright down the road, and as we walked, those lights would dazzle and dazzle in my eyes, and I could hear the guitar a-goin', an' she was singin'. She heard our steps with her quick ears and come running to the door with her eyes a-shinin', and all that set look gone out of her face, an' begun to talk French, gay as a bird, an' shook hands and behaved very pretty an' girlish, sayin' 'twas her fête day. I didn't know what she meant then. And she had gone an' put a wreath o' flowers on her hair an' wore a handsome gold chain that the cap'n had given her; an' there she was, poor creatur', makin' believe have a party all alone in her best room; 'twas prim enough to discourage a person, with too many chairs set close to the walls, just as the cap'n's mother had left it, but she had put sort o' long garlands on the walls, droopin' very graceful, and a sight of green boughs in the corners, till it looked lovely, and all lit up with a lot o' candles."

"Oh dear!" I sighed. "Oh, Mrs. Todd, what did you do?"

"She beheld our countenances," answered Mrs. Todd solemnly. "I expect they was telling everything plain enough, but Cap'n Lorenzo spoke the sad words to her as if he had been her father; and she wavered a minute and then over she went on the floor before we could catch hold of her, and then we tried to bring her to herself and failed, and at last we carried her upstairs, an' I told uncle to run down and put out the lights, and then go fast as he could for Mrs. Begg, being very experienced in sickness, an' he so did. I got off her clothes and her poor wreath, and I cried as I done it. We both stayed there that night, and the doctor said 'twas a shock when he come in the morning; he'd been over to Black Island an' had to stay all night with a very sick child."

"You said that she lived alone some time after the news came," I reminded Mrs. Todd then.

"Oh yes, dear," answered my friend sadly, "but it wa'n't what you'd call livin'; no, it was only dyin', though at a snail's pace. She never went out again those few months, but for a while she could manage to get about the house a little, and do what was needed, an' I never let two days go by without seein' her or hearin' from her. She never took much notice as I came an' went except to answer if I asked her anything. Mother was the one who gave her the only comfort."

"What was that?" I asked softly.

"She said that anybody in such trouble ought to see their minister, mother did, and one day she spoke to Mis' Tolland, and found that the poor soul had been believin' all the time that there weren't any priests here. We'd come to know she was a Catholic by her beads and all, and that had set some narrow minds against her. And mother explained it just as she would to a child; and uncle Lorenzo sent word right off somewhere up river by a packet that was bound up the bay, and the first o' the week a priest come by the boat, an' uncle Lorenzo was on the wharf 'tendin' to some business; so they just come up for me, and I walked with him to show him the house. He was a kind-hearted old man; he looked so benevolent an' fatherly I could ha' stopped an' told him my own troubles; yes, I was satisfied when I first saw his face, an' when poor Mis' Tolland beheld him enter the room, she went right down on her knees and clasped her hands together to him as if he'd come to save her life, and he lifted her up and blessed her, an' I left 'em together, and slipped out into the open field and walked there in sight so if they needed to call me, and I had my own thoughts. At last I saw him at the door; he had to catch the return boat. I meant to walk back with him and offer him some supper, but he said no, and said he was comin' again if needed, and signed me to go into the house to her, and shook his head in a way that meant he understood everything. I can see him now; he walked with a cane, rather tired and feeble; I wished somebody would come along, so's to carry him down to the shore.

"Mis' Tolland looked up at me with a new look when I went in, an' she even took hold o' my hand and kept it. He had put some oil on her forehead, but nothing anybody could do would keep her alive very long; 'twas his medicine for the soul rather 'n the body. I helped her to bed, and next morning she couldn't get up to dress her, and that was Monday, and she began to fail, and 't was Friday night she died." (Mrs. Todd spoke with unusual haste and lack of detail.) "Mrs. Begg and I watched with her, and made everything nice and proper, and after all the ill will there was a good number gathered to the funeral. 'Twas in reverend Mr. Bascom's day, and he done very well in his prayer, considering he couldn't fill in with mentioning all the near connections by name as was his habit. He spoke very feeling about her being a stranger and twice widowed, and all he said about her being reared among the heathen was to observe that there might be roads leadin' up to the New Jerusalem from various points. I says to myself that I guessed quite a number must ha' reached there that wa'n't able to set out from Dunnet Landin'!"

Mrs. Todd gave an odd little laugh as she bent toward the firelight to pick up a dropped stitch in her knitting, and then I heard a heartfelt sigh.

"'Twas most forty years ago," she said; "most everybody's gone a'ready that was there that day."

V

Suddenly Mrs. Todd gave an energetic shrug of her shoulders, and a quick look at me, and I saw that the sails of her narrative were filled with a fresh breeze.

"Uncle Lorenzo, Cap'n Bowden that I have referred to"—

"Certainly!" I agreed with eager expectation.

"He was the one that had been left in charge of Cap'n John Tolland's affairs, and had now come to be of unforeseen importance.

"Mrs. Begg an' I had stayed in the house both before an' after Mis' Tolland's decease, and she was now in haste to be gone, having affairs to call her home; but uncle come to me as the exercises was beginning, and said he thought I'd better remain at the house while they went to the buryin' ground. I couldn't understand his reasons, an' I felt disappointed, bein' as near to her as most anybody; 'twas rough weather, so mother couldn't get in, and didn't even hear Mis' Tolland was gone till next day. I just nodded to satisfy him, 'twas'n't no time to discuss anything. Uncle seemed flustered; he'd gone out deep-sea fishin' the day she died, and the storm I told you of rose very sudden, so they got blown off way down the coast beyond Monhegan, and he'd just got back in time to dress himself and come.

"I set there in the house after I'd watched her away down the straight road far's I could see from the door; 'twas a little short walkin' funeral an' a cloudy sky, so everything looked dull an' gray, an' it crawled along all in one piece, same's walking funerals do, an' I wondered how it ever come to the Lord's mind to let her begin down among them gay islands all heat and sun, and end up here among the rocks with a north wind blowin'. 'Twas a gale that begun the afternoon before she died, and had kept blowin' off an' on ever since. I'd thought more than once how glad I should be to get home an' out o' sound o' them black spruces a-beatin' an' scratchin' at the front windows.

"I set to work pretty soon to put the chairs

back, an' set outdoors some that was borrowed, an' I went out in the kitchen, an' I made up a good fire in case somebody come an' wanted a cup o' tea; but I didn't expect any one to travel way back to the house unless 'twas uncle Lorenzo. 'Twas growin' so chilly that I fetched some kindlin' wood and made fires in both the fore rooms. Then I set down an' begun to feel as usual, and I got my knittin' out of a drawer. You can't be sorry for a poor creatur' that's come to the end o' all her troubles; my only discomfort was I thought I'd ought to feel worse at losin' her than I did; I was younger then that I be now. And as I set there, I begun to hear some long notes o' dronin' music from upstairs that chilled me to the bone."

Mrs. Todd gave a hasty glance at me.

"Quick's I could gather me, I went right upstairs to see what 'twas," she added eagerly, "an' 'twas just what I might ha' known. She'd always kept her guitar hangin' right against the wall in her room; 'twas tied by a blue ribbon, and there was a window left wide open; the wind was veerin' a good deal, an' it slanted in and searched the room. The strings was jarrin' yet.

"'Twas growin' pretty late in the afternoon, an' I begun to feel lonesome as I shouldn't now, and I was disappointed at having to stay there, the more I thought it over, but after a while I saw Cap'n Lorenzo polin' back up the road all alone, and when he come nearer I could see he had a bundle under his arm and had shifted his best black clothes for his everyday ones. I run out and put some tea into the teapot and set it back on the stove to draw, an' when he come in I reached down a little jug o' spirits,—Cap'n Tolland had left his house well provisioned as if his wife was goin' to put to sea same's himself, an' there she'd gone an' left it. There was some cake that Mis' Begg an' I had made the day before. I thought that uncle an' me had a good right to the funeral supper, even if there wa'n't any one to join us. I was lookin' forward to my cup o' tea; 'twas beautiful tea out of a green lacquered chest that I've got now."

"You must have felt very tired," said I, eagerly listening.

"I was 'most beat out, with watchin' an' tendin' and all," answered Mrs. Todd, with as much sympathy in her voice as if she were speaking of another person. "But I called out to uncle as he came in, 'Well, I expect it's all over now, an' we've all done what we could. I thought we'd better have some tea or somethin' before we go home. Come right out in the kitchen, sir,' says I, never thinking but we only had to let the fires out and lock up everything safe an' eat our refreshment, an' go home.

" 'I want both of us to stop here tonight,' says uncle, looking at me very important.

"'Oh, what for?' says I, kind o' fretful.

"'I've got my proper reasons,' says uncle. 'I'll see you well satisfied, Almira. Your tongue ain't so easy-goin' as some o' the women folks, an' there's property here to take charge of that you don't know nothin' at all about.'

"'What do you mean?' says I.

"'Cap'n Tolland acquainted me with his affairs; he hadn't no sort o' confidence in nobody but me an' his wife, after he was tricked into signin' that Portland note, an' lost money. An' she didn't know nothin' about business; but what he didn't take to sea to be sunk with him he's hid somewhere in this house. I expect Mis' Tolland may have told you where she kept things?' said uncle.

"I see he was dependin' a good deal on my answer," said Mrs. Todd, "but I had to disappoint him; no, she had never said nothin' to me.

"'Well, then, we've got to make a search,' says he, with considerable relish; but he was all tired and worked up, and we set down to the table, an' he had somethin', an' I took my desired cup o' tea, and then I begun to feel more interested.

"'Where you goin' to look first?' says I, but he give me a short look an' made no answer, an' begun to mix me a very small portion out of the jug, in another glass. I took it to please him; he said I looked tired, speakin' real fatherly, and I did feel better for it, and we set talkin' a few minutes, an' then he started for the cellar, carrying an old ship's lantern he fetched out o' the stairway an' lit.

"'What are you lookin' for, some kind of a chist?' I inquired, and he said yes. All of a sudden it come to me to ask who was the heirs; Eliza Tolland, Cap'n John's own sister, had never demeaned herself to come near the funeral, and uncle Lorenzo faced right about and begun to laugh, sort o' pleased. I thought queer of it; 'twa'n't what he'd taken, which would be nothin' to an old weathered sailor like him.

"'Who's the heir?' says I the second time.

"'Why, it's *you,* Almiry,' says he; and I was so took aback I set right down on the turn o' the cellar stairs.

"'Yes, 'tis,' said uncle Lorenzo. 'I'm glad of it too. Some thought she didn't have no sense but foreign sense, an' a poor stock o' that, but she said you was friendly to her, an' one day after she got news of Tolland's death, an' I had fetched up his will that left everything to her, she said she was goin' to make a writin', so's you could have things after she was gone, an' she give five hundred to me for bein' executor. Square[1] Pease fixed up the paper, an' she signed it; it's all accordin' to law.' "There, I begun to

1. *Square*] Squire.

cry," said Mrs. Todd; "I couldn't help it. I wished I had her back again to do somethin' for, an' to make her know I felt sisterly to her more'n I'd ever showed, an' it come over me 'twas all too late, an' I cried the more, till uncle showed impatience, an' I got up an' stumbled along down cellar with my apern to my eyes the greater part of the time.

"'I'm goin' to have a clean search,' says he; 'you hold the light.' An' I held it and he rummaged in the arches an' under the stairs, an' over in some old closet where he reached out bottles an' stone jugs an' canted some kags an' one or two casks, an' chuckled well when he heard there was somethin' inside,—but there wa'n't nothin' to find but things usual in a cellar, an' then the old lantern was givin' out an' we come away.

"'He spoke to me of a chist, Cap'n Tolland did,' says uncle in a whisper. 'He said a good sound chist was as safe a bank as there was, an' I beat him out of such nonsense, 'count o' fire an' other risks.' 'There's no chist in the rooms above,' says I; 'no, uncle, there ain't no sea-chist, for I've been here long enough to see what there was to be seen.' Yet he wouldn't feel contented till he'd mounted up into the toploft; 'twas one o' them single, hip roofed houses that don't give proper accommodation for a real garret, like Cap'n Littlepage's down here at the Landin'. There was broken furniture and rubbish, an' he let down a terrible sight o' dust into the front entry, but sure enough there wasn't no chist. I had it all to sweep up next day.

"'He must have took it away to sea,' says I to the cap'n, an' even then he didn't want to agree, but we was both beat out. I told him where I'd always seen Mis' Tolland get her money from, and we found much as a hundred dollars there in an old red morocco wallet. Cap'n John had been gone a good while a'ready, and she had spent what she needed. 'Twas in an old desk o' his in the settin' room that we found the wallet."

"At the last minute he may have taken his money to sea," I suggested.

"Oh yes," agreed Mrs. Todd. "He did take considerable to make his venture to bring home, as was customary, an' that was drowned with him as uncle agreed; but he had other property in shipping, and a thousand dollars invested in Portland in a cordage shop, but 'twas about the time shipping begun to decay, and the cordage shop failed, and in the end I wa'n't so rich as I thought I was goin' to be for those few minutes on the cellar stairs. There was an auction that accumulated something. Old Mis' Tolland, the cap'n's mother, had heired some good furniture from a sister: there was above thirty chairs in all, and they're apt to sell well. I got over a thousand dollars when we come to settle up, and I made uncle take his five hundred; he was getting along in years and had met with losses in navigation, and he left it back to me when he died, so I had a real good lift. It all lays in the bank over to Rockland, and I draw my interest fall an' spring, with the little Mr. Todd was able to leave me; but that's kind o' sacred money; 'twas earnt and saved with the hope o' youth, an' I'm very particular what I spent it for. Oh yes, what with ownin' my house, I've been enabled to get along very well, with prudence!" said Mrs. Todd contentedly.

"But there was the house and land," I asked,—"what became of that part of the property?"

Mrs. Todd looked into the fire, and a shadow of disapproval flitted over her face.

"Poor old uncle!" she said, "he got childish about the matter. I was hoping to sell at first, and I had an offer, but he always run of an idea that there was more money hid away, and kept wanting me to delay; an' he used to go up there all alone and search, and dig in the cellar, empty an' bleak as 'twas in winter weather or any time. An' he'd come and tell me he'd dreamed he found gold behind a stone in the cellar wall, or somethin'. And one night we all see the light o' fire up that way, an' the whole Landin' took the road, and run to look, and the Tolland property was all in a light blaze. I expect the old gentleman had dropped fire about; he said he'd been up there to see if everything was safe in the afternoon. As for the land, 'twas so poor that everybody used to have a joke that the Tolland boys preferred to farm the sea instead. It's 'most all grown up to bushes now where it ain't poor water grass in the low places. There's some upland that has a pretty view, after you cross the brook bridge. Years an' years after she died, there was some o' her flowers used to come up an' bloom in the door garden. I brought two or three that was unusual down here; they always come up and remind me of her, constant as the spring. But I never did want to fetch home that guitar, some way or 'nother; I wouldn't let it go at the auction, either. It was hangin' right there in the house when the fire took place. I've got some o' her other little things scattered about the house: that picture on the mantelpiece belonged to her."

I had often wondered where such a picture had come from, and why Mrs. Todd had chosen it; it was a French print of the statue of the Empress Josephine in the Savane at old Fort Royal, in Martinique.

VI

Mrs. Todd drew her chair closer to mine; she held the cat and her knitting with one hand as she moved, but the cat was so warm and so sound asleep that she only stretched a lazy paw in spite of what must have felt like a slight earthquake. Mrs. Todd began to speak almost in a whisper.

"I ain't told you all," she continued; "no, I haven't spoken of all to but very few. The way it came was this," she said solemnly, and then stopped to listen to the wind, and sat for a moment in deferential silence, as if she waited for the wind to speak first. The cat suddenly lifted her head with quick excitement and gleaming eyes, and her mistress was leaning forward toward the fire with an arm laid on either knee, as if they were consulting the glowing coals for some augury. Mrs. Todd looked like an old prophetess as she sat there with the firelight shining on her strong face; she was posed for some great painter. The woman with the cat was as unconscious and as mysterious as any sibyl of the Sistine Chapel.

"There, that's the last struggle o' the gale," said Mrs. Todd, nodding her head with impressive certainty and still looking into the bright embers of the fire. "You'll see!" She gave me another quick glance, and spoke in a low tone as if we might be overheard.

"'Twas such a gale as this the night Mis' Tolland died. She appeared more comfortable the first o' the evenin'; and Mrs. Begg was more spent than I, bein' older, and a beautiful nurse that was the first to see and think of everything, but perfectly quiet an' never asked a useless question. You remember her funeral when you first come to the Landing? And she consented to goin' an' havin' a good sleep while she could, and left me one o' those good little pewter lamps that burnt whale oil an' made plenty o' light in the room, but not too bright to be disturbin'.

"Poor Mis' Tolland had been distressed the night before, an' all that day, but as night came on she grew more and more easy, an' was layin' there asleep; 'twas like settin' by any sleepin' person, and I had none but usual thoughts. When the wind lulled and the rain, I could hear the seas, though more distant than this, and I don't know's I observed any other sound than what the weather made; 'twas a very solemn feelin' night. I set close by the bed; there was times she looked to find somebody when she was awake. The light was on her face, so I could see her plain; there was always times when she wore a look that made her seem a stranger you'd never set eyes on before. I did think what a world it was that her an' me should have come together so, and she had nobody but Dunnet Landin' folks about her in her extremity. 'You're one o' the stray ones, poor creatur',' I said. I remember those very words passin' through my mind, but I saw reason to be glad she had some comforts, and didn't lack friends at the last, though she'd seen misery an' pain. I was glad she was quiet; all day she'd been restless, and we couldn't understand what she wanted from her French speech. We had the window open to give her air, an' now an' then a gust would strike that guitar that was on the wall and set it swinging by the blue ribbon, and soundin' as if somebody begun to play it. I come near takin' it down, but you never know what'll fret a sick person an' put 'em on the rack, an' that guitar was one o' the few things she'd brought with her."

I nodded assent, and Mrs. Todd spoke still lower.

"I set there close by the bed; I'd been through a good deal for some days back, and I thought I might's well be droppin' asleep too, bein' a quick person to wake. She looked to me as if she might last a day longer, certain, now she'd got more comfortable, but I was real tired, an' sort o' cramped as watchers will get, an' a fretful feeling begun to creep over me such as they often do have. If you give way, there ain't no support for the sick person; they can't count on no composure o' their own. Mis' Tolland moved then, a little restless, an' I forgot me quick enough, an' begun to hum out a little part of a hymn tune just to make her feel everything was as usual an' not wake up into a poor uncertainty. All of a sudden she set right up in bed with her eyes wide open, an' I stood an' put my arm behind her; she hadn't moved like that for days. And she reached out both her arms toward the door, an' I looked the way she was lookin' an' I see some one was standin' there against the dark. No,

’t wa’n’t Mis’ Begg; ’twas somebody a good deal shorter than Mis’ Begg. The lamplight struck across the room between us. I couldn’t tell the shape, but ’twas a woman’s dark face lookin’ right at us; ’twa’n’t but an instant I could see. I felt dreadful cold, and my head begun to swim; I thought the light went out; ‘twa’n’t but an instant, as I say, an’ when my sight come back I couldn’t see nothing there. I was one that didn’t know what it was to faint away, no matter what happened; time was I felt above it in others, but ’twas somethin’ that made poor human natur’ quail. I saw very plain while I could see; ’twas a pleasant enough face, shaped somethin’ like Mis’ Tolland’s, and a kind of expectin’ look.

“No, I don’t expect I was asleep,” Mrs. Todd assured me quietly, after a moment’s pause, though I had not spoken. She gave a heavy sigh before she went on. I could see that the recollection moved her in the deepest way.

“I suppose if I hadn’t been so spent an’ quavery with long watchin’, I might have kept my head an’ observed much better,” she added humbly; “but I see all I could bear. I did try to act calm, an’ I laid Mis’ Tolland down on her pillow, an’ I was a-shakin’ as I done it. All she did was to look up to me so satisfied and sort o’ questioning, an I looked back to her.

“ ‘You saw her, didn’t you?’ she says to me, speakin’ perfectly reasonable. ‘ ’T is my mother,’ she says again, very feeble, but lookin' straight up at me, kind of surprised with the pleasure, and smiling as if she saw I was overcome, an' would have said more if she could, but we had hold of hands. I see then her change was comin', but I didn't call Mis' Begg, nor make no uproar. I felt calm then, an' lifted to somethin' different as I never was since. She opened her eyes just as she was goin'—

"'You saw her, didn't you?' she said the second time, an' I says, *'Yes, dear, I did; you ain't never goin' to feel strange an' lonesome no more.'* An' then in a few quiet minutes 'twas all over. I felt they'd gone away together. No, I wa'n't alarmed afterward; 'twas just that one moment I couldn't live under, but I never called it beyond reason I should see the other watcher. I saw plain enough there was somebody there with me in the room.

VII

"'Twas just such a night as this Mis' Tolland died," repeated Mrs. Todd, returning to her usual tone and leaning back comfortably in her chair as she took up her knitting. "'Twas just such a night as this. I've told the circumstances to but very few; but I don't call it beyond reason. When folks is goin' 'tis all natural, and only common things can jar upon the mind. You know plain enough there's somethin' beyond this world; the doors stand wide open. There's somethin' of us that must still live on; we've got to join both worlds together an' live in one but for the other.' The doctor said that to me one day, an' I never could forget it; he said 'twas in one o' his old doctor's books."

We sat together in silence in the warm little room; the rain dropped heavily from the eaves, and the sea still roared, but the high wind had done blowing. We heard the far complaining fog horn of a steamer up the Bay.

"There goes the Boston boat out, pretty near on time," said Mrs. Todd with satisfaction. "Sometimes these late August storms'll sound a good deal worse than they really be. I do hate to hear the poor steamers callin' when they're bewildered in thick nights in winter, comin' on the coast. Yes, there goes the boat; they'll find it rough at sea, but the storm's all over."

The Law of Life
by Jack London

Old Koskoosh listened greedily. Though his sight had long since faded, his hearing was still acute, and the slightest sound penetrated to the glimmering intelligence which yet abode behind the withered forehead, but which no longer gazed forth upon the things of the world. Ah! that was Sit-cum-to-ha, shrilly anathematizing the dogs as she cuffed and beat them into the harnesses. Sit-cum-to-ha was his daughter's daughter, but she was too busy to waste a thought upon her broken grandfather, sitting alone there in the snow, forlorn and helpless. Camp must be broken. The long trail waited while the short day refused to linger. Life called her, and the duties of life, not death. And he was very close to death now.

The thought made the old man panicky for the moment, and he stretched forth a palsied hand which wandered tremblingly over the small heap of dry wood beside him. Reassured that it was indeed there, his hand returned to the shelter of his mangy furs, and he again fell to listening. The sulky crackling of half-frozen hides told him that the chief's moose-skin lodge had been struck, and even then was being rammed and jammed into portable compass. The chief was his son, stalwart and strong, head man of the tribesmen, and a mighty hunter. As the women toiled with the camp luggage, his voice rose, chiding them for their slowness. Old Koskoosh strained his ears. It was the last time he would hear that voice. There went Geehow's lodge! And Tusken's! Seven, eight, nine; only the Shaman's could be still standing. There! They were at work upon it now. He could hear the Shaman grunt as he piled it on the sled. A child whimpered, and a woman soothed it with soft, crooning gutturals. Little Koo-tee, the old man thought, a fretful child, and not over strong. It would die soon, perhaps, and they would burn a hole through the frozen tundra and pile rocks above to keep the wolverines away. Well, what did it matter? A few years at best, and as many an empty belly as a full one. And in the end, Death waited, ever-hungry and hungriest of them all.

What was that? Oh, the men lashing the sleds and drawing tight the thongs. He listened, who would listen no more. The whip-lashes snarled and bit among the dogs. Hear them whine! How they hated the work and the trail! They were off!

Sled after sled churned slowly away into the silence. They were gone. They had passed out of his life, and he faced the last bitter hour alone. No. The snow crunched beneath a moccasin; a man stood beside him; upon his head a hand rested gently. His son was good to do this thing. He remembered other old men whose sons had not waited after the tribe. But his son had. He wandered away into the past, till the young man's voice brought him back.

"Is it well with you?" he asked.

And the old man answered, "It is well."

"There be wood beside you," the younger man continued, "and the fire burns bright. The morning is gray, and the cold has broken. It will snow presently. Even now is it snowing."

"Ay, even now is it snowing."

"The tribesmen hurry. Their bales are heavy, and their bellies flat with lack of feasting. The trail is long and they travel fast. I go now. It is well?"

"It is well. I am as a last year's leaf, clinging lightly to the stem. The first breath that blows, and I fall. My voice is become like an old woman's. My eyes no longer show me the way of my feet, and my feet are heavy, and I am tired. It is well."

He bowed his head in content till the last noise of the complaining snow had died away, and he knew his son was beyond recall. Then his hand crept out in haste to the wood. It alone stood betwixt him and the eternity which yawned in upon him. At last the measure of his life was a handful of faggots. One by one they would go to feed the fire, and just so, step by step, death would creep upon him. When the last stick had surrendered up its heat, the frost would begin to gather strength. First his feet would yield, then his hands; and the numbness would travel, slowly, from the extremities to the body. His head would fall forward upon his knees, and he would rest. It was easy. All men must die.

He did not complain. It was the way of life, and it was just. He had been born close to the earth, close to the earth had he lived, and the law thereof was not new to him. It was the law of all flesh. Nature was not kindly to the flesh. She had no concern for that concrete thing called the individual. Her interest lay in the species, the race. This was the deepest abstraction old Koskoosh's barbaric mind was capable of, but he grasped it firmly. He saw it exemplified in all life. The rise of the sap, the bursting greenness of the willow bud, the fall of the yellow leaf—in this alone was told the whole history. But one task did Nature set the individual. Did he not perform it, he died. Did he perform it, it was all the same, he died. Nature did not care; there were plenty who were obedient, and it was only the obedience in this matter, not the obedient, which lived and lived always. The tribe of Koskoosh was very old. The old men he had known when a boy, had known old men before them. Therefore it was true that the tribe lived, that it stood for the obedience of all its members, way down into the forgotten past, whose very resting places were unremembered. They did not count; they were episodes. They had passed away like clouds from a summer sky. He also was an episode, and would pass away. Nature did not care. To life she set one task, gave one law. To perpetuate was the task of life, its law was death. A maiden was a good creature to look upon, full-breasted and strong, with spring to her step and light in her eyes. But her task was yet before her. The light in her eyes brightened, her step quickened, she was now bold with the young men, now timid, and she gave them of her own unrest. And ever she grew fairer and yet fairer to look upon, till some hunter, able no longer to withhold himself, took her to his lodge to cook and toil for him and to become the mother of his children. And with the coming of her offspring her looks left her. Her limbs dragged and shuffled, her eyes dimmed and bleared, and only the little children found joy against the withered cheek of the old squaw by the fire. Her task was done. But a little while, on the first pinch of famine or the first long trail, and she would be left, even as he had been left, in the snow, with a little pile of wood. Such was the law.

He placed a stick carefully upon the fire and resumed his meditations. It was the same everywhere, with all things. The mosquitoes vanished with the first frost. The little tree-squirrel crawled away to die. When age settled upon the rabbit it became slow and heavy, and could no longer outfoot its enemies. Even the big baldface grew clumsy and blind and quarrelsome, in the end to be dragged down by a handful of yelping huskies. He remembered how he had abandoned his own father on an upper reach of the Klondike one winter, the winter before the missionary came with his talk-books and his box of medicines. Many a time had Koskoosh smacked his lips over the recollection of that box, though now his mouth refused to moisten. The "painkiller" had been especially good. But the missionary was a bother after all, for he brought no meat into the camp, and he ate heartily, and the hunters grumbled. But he chilled his lungs on the divide by the Mayo, and the dogs afterwards nosed the stones away and fought over his bones.

Koskoosh placed another stick on the fire and harked back deeper into the past. There was the time of the Great Famine, when the old men crouched empty-bellied to the fire, and let fall from their lips dim traditions of the ancient day when the Yukon ran wide open for three winters, and then lay frozen for three summers. He had lost his mother in that famine. In the summer the salmon run had failed, and the tribe looked forward to the winter and the coming of the caribou. Then the winter came, but with it there were no caribou. Never had the like been known, not even in the lives of the old men. But the caribou did not come, and it was the seventh year, and the rabbits had not replenished, and the dogs were naught but bundles of bones. And through the long darkness the children wailed and died, and the women, and the old men; and not one in ten of the tribe lived to meet the sun when it came back in the spring. That *was* a famine!

But he had seen times of plenty, too, when the meat spoiled on their hands, and the dogs were fat and worthless with over-eating—times when they let the game go unkilled, and the women were fertile, and the lodges were cluttered with sprawling men-children and women-children. Then it was the men became high-stomached, and revived ancient quarrels, and crossed the divides to the south to kill the Pellys, and to the west that they might sit by the dead fires of the Tananas. He remembered, when a boy, during a time of plenty, when he saw a moose pulled down by the wolves. Zing-ha lay with him in the snow and watched—Zing-ha, who later became the craftiest of hunters, and who, in the end, fell through an air-hole on the Yukon. They found him, a month afterward, just as he had crawled half-way out and frozen stiff to the ice.

But the moose. Zing-ha and he had gone out that day to play at hunting after the manner of their fathers. On the bed of the creek they struck the fresh track of a moose, and with it the tracks of many wolves. "An old one," Zing-ha, who was quicker at reading the sign, said—"an old one who cannot keep up with the herd. The wolves have cut him out from his brothers, and they will never leave him." And it was so. It was their way. By day and by night, never resting, snarling on his heels, snapping at his nose, they would stay by him to the end. How Zing-ha and he felt the blood-lust quicken! The finish would be a sight to see!

Eager-footed, they took the trail, and even he, Koskoosh, slow of sight and an unversed tracker, could have followed it blind, it was so wide. Hot were they on the heels of the chase, reading the grim tragedy, fresh-written, at every step. Now they came to where the moose had made a stand. Thrice the length of a grown man's body, in every direction, had the snow been stamped about and uptossed. In the midst were the deep impressions of the splay-hoofed game, and all about, everywhere, were the lighter footmarks of the wolves. Some, while their brothers harried the kill, had lain to one side and rested. The full-stretched impress of their bodies in the snow was as perfect as though made the moment before. One wolf had been caught in a wild lunge of the maddened victim and trampled to death. A few bones, well picked, bore witness.

Again, they ceased the uplift of their snow-shoes at a second stand. Here the great animal had fought desperately. Twice had he been dragged down, as the snow attested, and twice had he shaken his assailants clear and gained footing once more. He had done his task long since, but none the less was life dear to him. Zing-ha said it was a strange thing, a moose once down to get free again; but this one certainly had. The Shaman would see signs and wonders in this when they told him.

And yet again, they came to where the moose had made to mount the bank and gain the timber. But his foes had laid on from behind, till he reared and fell back upon them, crushing two deep into the snow. It was plain the kill was at hand, for their brothers had left them untouched. Two more stands were hurried past, brief in time-length and very close together. The trail was red now, and the clean stride of the great beast had grown short and slovenly. Then they heard the first sounds of the battle—not the full-throated chorus of the chase, but the short, snappy bark which spoke of close quarters and teeth to flesh. Crawling up the wind, Zing-ha bellied it through the snow, and with him crept he, Koskoosh, who was to be chief of the tribesmen in the years to come. Together they shoved aside the under branches of a young spruce and peered forth. It was the end they saw.

The picture, like all of youth's impressions, was still strong with him, and his dim eyes watched the end played out as vividly as in that far-off time. Koskoosh marveled at this, for in the days which followed, when he was a leader of men and a head of councilors, he had done great deeds and made his name a curse in the mouths of the Pellys, to say naught of the strange white man he had killed, knife to knife, in open fight.

For long he pondered on the days of his youth, till the fire died down and the frost bit deeper. He replenished it with two sticks this time, and gauged his grip on life by what remained. If Sit-cum-to-ha had only remembered her grandfather, and gathered a larger armful, his hours would have been longer. It would have been easy. But she was ever a careless child, and honored not her ancestors from the time the Beaver, son of the son of Zing-ha, first cast eyes upon her. Well, what mattered it? Had he not done likewise in his own quick youth? For a while he listened to the silence. Perhaps the heart of his son might soften, and he would come back with the dogs to take his old father on with the tribe to where the caribou ran thick and the fat hung heavy upon them.

He strained his ears, his restless brain for the moment stilled. Not a stir, nothing. He alone took breath in the midst of the great silence. It was very lonely. Hark! What was that? A chill passed over his body. The familiar, long-drawn howl broke the void, and it was close at hand. Then on his darkened eyes was projected the vision of the moose—the old bull moose—the torn flanks and bloody sides, the riddled mane, and the great branching horns, down low and tossing to the last. He saw the flashing forms of gray, the gleaming eyes, the lolling tongues, the slavered fangs. And he saw the inexorable circle close in till it became a dark point in the midst of the stamped snow.

A cold muzzle thrust against his cheek, and at its touch his soul leaped back to the present. His hand shot into the fire and dragged out a burning faggot. Overcome for the nonce by his hereditary fear of man, the brute retreated, raising a prolonged call to his brothers; and greedily they answered, till a ring of crouching, jaw-slobbered gray was stretched round about. The old man listened to the drawing in of this circle.

He waved his brand wildly, and sniffs turned to snarls; but the panting brutes refused to scatter. Now one wormed his chest forward, dragging his haunches after, now a second, now a third; but never a one drew back. Why should he cling to life? he asked, and dropped the blazing stick into the snow. It sizzled and went out. The circle grunted uneasily, but held its own. Again he saw the last stand of the old bull moose, and Koskoosh dropped his head wearily upon his knees. What did it matter after all? Was it not the law of life?

The Gift of the Magi

by O. Henry

One dollar and eighty-seven cents. That was all. And sixty cents of it was in pennies. Pennies saved one and two at a time by bulldozing the grocer and the vegetable man and the butcher until one's cheeks burned with the silent imputation of parsimony that such close dealing implied. Three times Della counted it. One dollar and eighty-seven cents. And the next day would be Christmas.

There was clearly nothing left to do but flop down on the shabby little couch and howl. So Della did it. Which instigates the moral reflection that life is made up of sobs, sniffles, and smiles, with sniffles predominating.

While the mistress of the home is gradually subsiding from the first stage to the second, take a look at the home. A furnished flat at $8 per week. It did not exactly beggar description, but it certainly had that word on the lookout for the mendicancy squad.

In the vestibule below was a letter-box into which no letter would go, and an electric button from which no mortal finger could coax a ring. Also appertaining thereunto was a card bearing the name "Mr. James Dillingham Young."

The "Dillingham" had been flung to the breeze during a former period of prosperity when its possessor was being paid $30 per week. Now, when the income was shrunk to $20, the letters of "Dillingham" looked blurred, as though they were thinking seriously of contracting to a modest and unassuming D. But whenever Mr. James Dillingham Young came home and reached his flat above he was called "Jim" and greatly hugged by Mrs. James Dillingham Young, already introduced to you as Della. Which is all very good.

Della finished her cry and attended to her cheeks with the powder rag. She stood by the window and looked out dully at a gray cat walking a gray fence in a gray backyard. Tomorrow would be Christmas Day, and she had only $1.87 with which to buy Jim a present. She had been saving every penny she could for months, with this result. Twenty dollars a week doesn't go far. Expenses had been greater than she had calculated. They always are. Only $1.87 to buy a present for Jim. Her Jim. Many a happy hour she had spent planning for something nice for him. Something fine and rare and sterling—

something just a little bit near to being worthy of the honour of being owned by Jim.

There was a pier-glass between the windows of the room. Perhaps you have seen a pier-glass in an $8 flat. A very thin and very agile person may, by observing his reflection in a rapid sequence of longitudinal strips, obtain a fairly accurate conception of his looks. Della, being slender, had mastered the art.

Suddenly she whirled from the window and stood before the glass. Her eyes were shining brilliantly, but her face had lost its colour within twenty seconds. Rapidly she pulled down her hair and let it fall to its full length.

Now, there were two possessions of the James Dillingham Youngs in which they both took a mighty pride. One was Jim's gold watch that had been his father's and his grandfather's. The other was Della's hair. Had the Queen of Sheba lived in the flat across the airshaft, Della would have let her hair hang out the window some day to dry just to depreciate Her Majesty's jewels and gifts. Had King Solomon been the janitor, with all his treasures piled up in the basement, Jim would have pulled out his watch every time he passed, just to see him pluck at his beard from envy.

So now Della's beautiful hair fell about her, rippling and shining like a cascade of brown waters. It reached below her knee and made itself almost a garment for her. And then she did it up again nervously and quickly. Once she faltered for a minute and stood still while a tear or two splashed on the worn red carpet.

On went her old brown jacket; on went her old brown hat. With a whirl of skirts and with the brilliant sparkle still in her eyes, she fluttered out of the door and down the stairs to the street.

Where she stopped the sign read: "Mme. Sofronie. Hair Goods of All Kinds." One flight up Della ran, and collected herself, panting. Madame, large, too white, chilly, hardly looked the "Sofronie."

"Will you buy my hair?" asked Della.

"I buy hair," said Madame. "Take yer hat off and let's have a sight at the looks of it."

Down rippled the brown cascade.

"Twenty dollars," said Madame, lifting the mass with a practised hand.

"Give it to me quick," said Della.

Oh, and the next two hours tripped by on rosy wings. Forget the hashed metaphor. She was ransacking the stores for Jim's present.

She found it at last. It surely had been made for Jim and no one else. There was no other like it in any of the stores, and she had turned all of them inside out. It was a platinum fob chain simple and chaste in design, properly proclaiming its value by substance alone and not by meretricious ornamentation—as all good things should do. It was even worthy of The Watch. As soon as she saw it she knew that it must be Jim's. It was like him. Quietness and value—the description applied to both. Twenty-one dollars they took from her for it, and she hurried home with the 87 cents. With that chain on his watch Jim might be properly anxious about the time in any company. Grand as the watch was, he sometimes looked at it on the sly on account of the old leather strap that he used in place of a chain.

When Della reached home her intoxication gave way a little to prudence and reason. She got out her curling irons and lighted the gas and went to work repairing the ravages made by generosity added to love. Which is always a tremendous task, dear friends—a mammoth task.

Within forty minutes her head was covered with tiny, close-lying curls that made her look wonderfully like a truant schoolboy. She looked at her reflection in the mirror long, carefully, and critically.

"If Jim doesn't kill me," she said to herself, "before he takes a second look at me, he'll say I look like a Coney Island chorus girl. But what could I do—oh! what could I do with a dollar and eighty-seven cents?"

At 7 o'clock the coffee was made and the frying-pan was on the back of the stove hot and ready to cook the chops.

Jim was never late. Della doubled the fob

chain in her hand and sat on the corner of the table near the door that he always entered. Then she heard his step on the stair away down on the first flight, and she turned white for just a moment. She had a habit of saying little silent prayers about the simplest everyday things, and now she whispered: “Please God, make him think I am still pretty.”

The door opened and Jim stepped in and closed it. He looked thin and very serious. Poor fellow, he was only twenty-two—and to be burdened with a family! He needed a new overcoat and he was without gloves.

Jim stepped inside the door, as immovable as a setter at the scent of quail. His eyes were fixed upon Della, and there was an expression in them that she could not read, and it terrified her. It was not anger, nor surprise, nor disapproval, nor horror, nor any of the sentiments that she had been prepared for. He simply stared at her fixedly with that peculiar expression on his face.

Della wriggled off the table and went for him.

“Jim, darling,” she cried, “don’t look at me that way. I had my hair cut off and sold it because I couldn’t have lived through Christmas without giving you a present. It’ll grow out again—you won’t mind, will you? I just had to do it. My hair grows awfully fast. Say ‘Merry Christmas!’ Jim, and let’s be happy. You don’t know what a nice—what a beautiful, nice gift I've got for you."

"You've cut off your hair?" asked Jim, laboriously, as if he had not arrived at that patent fact yet even after the hardest mental labor.

"Cut it off and sold it," said Della. "Don't you like me just as well, anyhow? I'm me without my hair, ain't I?"

Jim looked about the room curiously.

"You say your hair is gone?" he said with an air almost of idiocy.

"You needn't look for it," said Della. "It's sold, I tell you—sold and gone, too. It's Christmas Eve, boy. Be good to me, for it went for you. Maybe the hairs of my head were numbered," she went on with a sudden serious sweetness, "but nobody could ever count my love for you. Shall I put the chops on, Jim?"

Out of his trance Jim seemed quickly to wake. He enfolded his Della. For ten seconds let us regard with discreet scrutiny some inconsequential object in the other direction. Eight dollars a week or a million a year—what is the difference? A mathematician or a wit would give you the wrong answer. The magi brought valuable gifts, but that was not among them. This dark assertion will be illuminated later on.

Jim drew a package from his overcoat pocket and threw it upon the table.

"Don't make any mistake, Dell," he said,

"about me. I don't think there's anything in the way of a haircut or a shave or a shampoo that could make me like my girl any less. But if you'll unwrap that package you may see why you had me going a while at first."

White fingers and nimble tore at the string and paper. And then an ecstatic scream of joy; and then, alas! a quick feminine change to hysterical tears and wails, necessitating the immediate employment of all the comforting powers of the lord of the flat.

For there lay The Combs—the set of combs, side and back, that Della had worshipped for long in a Broadway window. Beautiful combs, pure tortoise shell, with jewelled rims—just the shade to wear in the beautiful vanished hair. They were expensive combs, she knew, and her heart had simply craved and yearned over them without the least hope of possession. And now, they were hers, but the tresses that should have adorned the coveted adornments were gone.

But she hugged them to her bosom, and at length she was able to look up with dim eyes and a smile and say: "My hair grows so fast, Jim!"

And then Della leaped up like a little singed cat and cried, "Oh, oh!"

Jim had not yet seen his beautiful present. She held it out to him eagerly upon her open palm. The dull precious metal seemed to flash with a reflection of her bright and ardent spirit.

"Isn't it a dandy, Jim? I hunted all over town to find it. You'll have to look at the time a hundred times a day now. Give me your watch. I want to see how it looks on it."

Instead of obeying, Jim tumbled down on the couch and put his hands under the back of his head and smiled.

"Dell," said he, "let's put our Christmas presents away and keep 'em a while. They're too nice to use just at present. I sold the watch to get the money to buy your combs. And now suppose you put the chops on."

The magi, as you know, were wise men—wonderfully wise men—who brought gifts to the Babe in the manger. They invented the art of giving Christmas presents. Being wise, their gifts were no doubt wise ones, possibly bearing the privilege of exchange in case of duplication. And here I have lamely related to you the uneventful chronicle of two foolish children in a flat who most unwisely sacrificed for each other the greatest treasures of their house. But in a last word to the wise of these days, let it be said that of all who give gifts these two were the wisest. Of all who give and receive gifts, such as they are wisest. Everywhere they are wisest. They are the magi.

The Jolly Corner
by Henry James

I

"Every one asks me what I 'think' of everything," said Spencer Brydon; "and I make answer as I can—begging or dodging the question, putting them off with any nonsense. It wouldn't matter to any of them really," he went on, "for, even were it possible to meet in that stand-and-deliver way so silly a demand on so big a subject, my 'thoughts' would still be almost altogether about something that concerns only myself." He was talking to Miss Staverton, with whom for a couple of months now he had availed himself of every possible occasion to talk; this disposition and this resource, this comfort and support, as the situation in fact presented itself, having promptly enough taken the first place in the considerable array of rather unattenuated surprises attending his so strangely belated return to America. Everything was somehow a surprise; and that might be natural when one had so long and so consistently neglected everything, taken pains to give surprises so much margin for play. He had given them more than thirty years—thirty-three, to be exact; and they now seemed to him to have organised their performance quite on the scale of that license. He had been twenty-three on leaving New York—he was fifty-six today: unless indeed he were to reckon as he had sometimes, since his repatriation, found himself feeling; in which case he would have lived longer than is often allotted to man. It would have taken a century, he repeatedly said to himself, and said also to Alice Staverton, it would have taken a longer absence and a more averted mind than those even of which he had been guilty, to pile up the differences, the newnesses, the queernesses, above all the bignesses, for the better or the worse, that at present assaulted his vision wherever he looked.

The great fact all the while however had been the incalculability; since he *had* supposed himself, from decade to decade, to be allowing, and in the most liberal and intelligent manner, for brilliancy of change. He actually saw that he had allowed for nothing; he missed what he would have been sure of finding, he found what he would never have imagined. Proportions and values were upside-down; the ugly things he had expected, the ugly things of his far-away youth, when he had too promptly waked up to a sense of the ugly—these uncanny phenomena placed him rather, as it happened, under the charm; whereas the "swagger" things, the modern, the monstrous, the famous things, those he had more particularly, like thousands of ingenuous enquirers every year, come over to see, were exactly his sources of dismay. They were as so many set traps for displeasure, above all for reaction, of which his restless tread was constantly pressing the spring. It was interesting, doubtless, the whole show, but it would have been too disconcerting hadn't a certain finer truth saved the situation. He had distinctly not, in this steadier light, come over *all* for the monstrosities; he had come, not only in the last analysis but quite on the face of the act, under an impulse with which they had nothing to do. He had come—putting the thing pompously—to look at his "property," which he had thus for a third of a century not been within four thousand miles of; or, expressing it less sordidly, he had yielded to the humor of seeing again his house on the jolly corner, as he usually, and quite fondly, described it—the one in which he had first seen the light, in which various members of his family had lived and had died, in which the holidays of his overschooled boyhood had been passed and the few social flowers of his chilled adolescence gathered, and which, alienated then for so long a period, had, through the successive deaths of his two brothers and the termination of old arrangements, come wholly into his hands. He was the owner of another, not quite so "good"—the jolly corner having been, from far back, superlatively extended and consecrated; and the value of the pair represented his main capital, with an income consisting, in these later years, of their respective rents which (thanks precisely to their original excellent type) had never been depressingly low. He could live in "Europe," as he had been in the habit of living, on the product of these flourishing New York leases, and all the better since, that of the second structure, the mere number in its long row, having within a twelvemonth fallen in, renovation at a high advance had proved beautifully possible.

These were items of property indeed, but he had found himself since his arrival distinguishing more than ever between them. The house within the street, two bristling blocks westward, was already in course of reconstruction as a tall mass of flats; he had acceded, some time before, to overtures for this conversion—in which, now that it was going forward, it had been not the least of his astonishments to find himself able, on the spot, and though without a previous ounce of such experience, to participate with a certain intelligence, almost with a certain authority. He had lived his life with his back so turned to such concerns and his face addressed to those of so different an order that he scarce knew what to make of this lively stir, in a compartment of his mind never yet penetrated, of a capacity for business and a sense for construction. These virtues, so common all round him now, had been dormant in his own organism—where it might be said of them perhaps that they had slept the sleep of the just. At present, in the splendid autumn weather—the autumn at least was a pure boon in the terrible place—he loafed about his "work" undeterred, secretly agitated; not in the least "minding" that the whole proposition, as they said, was vulgar and sordid, and ready to climb ladders, to walk the plank, to handle materials and look wise about them, to ask questions, in fine, and challenge explanations and really "go into" figures.

It amused, it verily quite charmed him; and, by the same stroke, it amused, and even more, Alice Staverton, though perhaps charming her perceptibly less. She wasn't however going to be better off for it, as *he* was—and so astonishingly much: nothing was now likely, he knew, even to make her better off than she found herself, in the afternoon of life, as the delicately frugal possessor and tenant of the small house in Irving Place to which she had subtly managed to cling through her almost unbroken New York career. If he knew the way to it now better than to any other address among the dreadful multiplied numberings which seemed to him to reduce the whole place to some vast ledger-page, overgrown, fantastic, of ruled and criss-crossed lines and figures—if he had formed, for his consolation, that habit, it was really not a little because of the charm of his having encountered and recognised, in the vast wilderness of the wholesale, breaking through the mere gross generalisation of wealth and force and success, a small still scene where items and shades, all delicate things, kept the sharpness of the notes of a high voice perfectly trained, and where economy hung about like the scent of a garden. His old friend lived with one maid and herself dusted her relics and trimmed her lamps and polished her silver; she stood off, in the awful modern crush, when she could, but she sallied forth and did battle when the challenge was really to "spirit," the spirit she after all confessed to, proudly and a little shyly, as to that of the better time, that of *their* common, their quite far-away and antediluvian social period and order. She made use of the street-cars when need be, the terrible things that people scrambled for as the panic-stricken at sea scramble for the boats; she affronted, inscrutably, under stress, all the public concussions and ordeals; and yet, with that slim mystifying grace of her appearance, which defied you to say if she were a fair young woman who looked older through trouble, or a fine smooth older one who looked young through successful indifference; with her precious reference, above all, to memories and histories into which he could enter, she was as exquisite for him as some pale pressed flower (a rarity to begin with), and, failing other sweetnesses, she was a sufficient reward of his effort. They had communities of knowledge, "their" knowledge (this discriminating possessive was always on her lips) of presences of the other age, presences all overlaid, in his case, by the experience of a man and the freedom of a wanderer, overlaid by pleasure, by infidelity, by passages of life that were strange and dim to her, just by "Europe" in short, but still unobscured, still exposed and cherished, under that pious visitation of the spirit from which she had never been diverted.

She had come with him one day to see how his "apartment-house" was rising; he had helped her over gaps and explained to her plans, and while they were there had happened to have, before her, a brief but lively discussion with the man in charge, the representative of the building-firm that had undertaken his work. He had found himself quite "standing-up" to this personage over a failure on the latter's part to observe some detail of one of their noted conditions, and had so lucidly urged his case that, besides ever so prettily flushing, at the time, for sympathy in his triumph, she had afterwards said to him (though to a slightly greater effect of irony) that he had clearly for too many years neglected a real gift. If he had but stayed at home he would have anticipated the inventor of the sky-scraper. If he had but stayed at home he would have discovered his genius in time really to start some new variety of awful architectural hare and run it till it burrowed in a gold-mine. He was to remember these words, while the weeks elapsed, for the small silver ring they had sounded over the queerest and deepest of his own lately most disguised and most muffled vibrations.

It had begun to be present to him after the first fortnight, it had broken out with the oddest abruptness, this particular wanton wonderment: it met him there—and this was the image under which he himself judged the matter, or at least, not a little, thrilled and flushed with it—very much as he might have been met by some strange figure, some unexpected occupant, at a turn of one of the dim passages of an empty house. The quaint analogy quite hauntingly remained with him, when he didn't indeed rather improve it by a still intenser form: that of his opening a door behind which he would have made sure of finding nothing, a door into a room shuttered and void, and yet so coming, with a great suppressed start, on some quite erect confronting presence, sometimes planted in the middle of the place and facing him through the dusk. After that visit to the house in construction he walked with his companion to see the other and always so much the better one, which in the eastward direction formed one of the corners, the "jolly" one precisely, of the street now so generally dishonoured and disfigured in its westward reaches, and of the comparatively conservative Avenue. The Avenue still had pretensions, as Miss Staverton said, to decency; the old people had mostly gone, the old names were unknown, and here and there an old association seemed to stray, all vaguely, like some very aged person, out too late, whom you might meet and feel the impulse to watch or follow, in kindness, for safe restoration to shelter.

They went in together, our friends; he admitted himself with his key, as he kept no one there, he explained, preferring, for his reasons, to leave the place empty, under a simple arrangement with a good woman living in the neighbourhood and who came for a daily hour to open windows and dust and sweep. Spencer Brydon had his reasons and was growingly aware of them; they seemed to him better each time he was there, though he didn't name them all to his companion, any more than he told her as yet how often, how quite absurdly often, he himself came. He only let her see for the present, while they walked through the great blank rooms, that absolute vacancy reigned and that, from top to bottom, there was nothing but Mrs. Muldoon's broomstick, in a corner, to tempt the burglar. Mrs. Muldoon was then on the premises, and she loquaciously attended the visitors, preceding them from room to room and pushing back shutters and throwing up sashes—all to show them, as she remarked, how little there was to see. There was little indeed to see in the great gaunt shell where the main dispositions and the general apportionment of space, the style of an age of ampler allowances, had nevertheless for its master their honest pleading message, affecting him as some good old servant's, some lifelong retainer's appeal for a character, or even for a retiring-pension; yet it was also a remark of Mrs. Muldoon's that, glad as she was to oblige him by her noonday round, there was a request she greatly hoped he would never make of her. If he should wish her for any reason to come in after dark she would just tell him, if he "plased," that he must ask it of somebody else.

The fact that there was nothing to see didn't militate for the worthy woman against what one *might* see, and she put it frankly to Miss Staverton that no lady could be expected to like, could she? "scraping up to thim top storeys in the ayvil hours." The gas and the electric light were off the house, and she fairly evoked a gruesome vision of her march through the great gray rooms—so many of them as there were too!—with her glimmering taper. Miss Staverton met her honest glare with a smile and the profession that she herself certainly would recoil from such an adventure. Spencer Brydon meanwhile held his peace—for the moment; the question of the "evil" hours in his old home had already become too grave for him. He had begun some time since to "crape," and he knew just why a packet of candles addressed to that pursuit had been stowed by his own hand, three weeks before, at the back of a drawer of the fine old sideboard that occupied, as a "fixture," the deep recess in the dining-room. Just now he laughed at his companions—quickly however changing the subject; for the reason that, in the first place, his laugh struck him even at that moment as starting the odd echo, the conscious human resonance (he scarce knew how to qualify it) that sounds made while he was there alone sent back to his ear or his fancy; and that, in the second, he imagined Alice Staverton for the instant on the point of asking him, with a divination, if he ever so prowled. There were divinations he was unprepared for, and he had at all events averted enquiry by the time Mrs. Muldoon had left them, passing on to other parts.

There was happily enough to say, on so consecrated a spot, that could be said freely and fairly; so that a whole train of declarations was precipitated by his friend's having herself broken out, after a yearning look round: "But I hope you don't mean they want you to pull *this* to pieces!" His answer came, promptly, with his re-awakened wrath: it was of course exactly what they wanted, and what they were "at" him for, daily, with the iteration of people who couldn't for their life understand a man's liability to decent feelings. He had found the place, just as it stood and beyond what he could express, an interest and a joy. There were values other than the beastly rent-values, and in short, in short—! But it was thus Miss Staverton took him up. "In short you're to make so good a thing of your sky-scraper that, living in luxury on *those* ill-gotten gains, you can afford for a while to be sentimental here!" Her smile had for him, with the words, the particular mild irony with which he found half her talk suffused; an irony without bitterness and that came, exactly, from her having so much imagination—not, like the cheap sarcasms with which one heard most people, about the world of "society," bid for the reputation of cleverness, from nobody's really having any. It was agreeable to him at this very moment to be sure that when he had answered, after a brief demur, "Well yes: so, precisely, you may put it!" her imagination would still do him justice. He explained that even if never a dollar were to come to him from the other house he would nevertheless cherish this one; and he dwelt, further, while they lingered and wandered, on the fact of the stupefaction he was already exciting, the positive mystification he felt himself create.

He spoke of the value of all he read into it, into the mere sight of the walls, mere shapes of the rooms, mere sound of the floors, mere feel, in his hand, of the old silver-plated knobs of the several mahogany doors, which suggested the pressure of the palms of the dead; the seventy years of the past in fine that these things represented, the annals of nearly three generations, counting his grandfather's, the one that had ended there, and the impalpable ashes of his long-extinct youth, afloat in the very air like microscopic motes. She listened to everything; she was a woman who answered intimately but who utterly didn't chatter. She scattered abroad therefore no cloud of words; she could assent, she could agree, above all she could encourage, without doing that. Only at the last she went a little further than he had done himself. "And then how do you know? You may still, after all, want to live here." It rather indeed pulled him up, for it wasn't what he had been thinking, at least in her sense of the words. "You mean I may decide to stay on for the sake of it?"

"Well, *with* such a home—!" But, quite beautifully, she had too much tact to dot so monstrous an *i,* and it was precisely an illustration of the way she didn't rattle. How could any one—of any wit—insist on any one else's "wanting" to live in New York?

"Oh," he said, "I *might* have lived here (since I had my opportunity early in life); I might have put in here all these years. Then everything would have been different enough—and, I dare say, 'funny' enough. But that's another matter. And then the beauty of it—I mean of my perversity, of my refusal to agree to a 'deal'—is just in the total absence of a reason. Don't you see that if I had a reason about the matter at all it would *have* to be the other way, and would then be inevitably a reason of dollars? There are no reasons here *but* of dollars. Let us therefore have none whatever—not the ghost of one."

They were back in the hall then for departure, but from where they stood the vista was large, through an open door, into the great square main saloon, with its almost antique felicity of brave spaces between windows. Her eyes came back from that reach and met his own a moment. "Are you very sure the 'ghost' of one doesn't, much rather, serve—?"

He had a positive sense of turning pale. But it was as near as they were then to come. For he made answer, he believed, between a glare and a grin: "Oh ghosts—of course the place must swarm with them! I should be ashamed of it if it didn't. Poor Mrs. Muldoon's right, and it's why I haven't asked her to do more than look in."

Miss Staverton's gaze again lost itself, and things she didn't utter, it was clear, came and went in her mind. She might even for the minute, off there in the fine room, have imagined some element dimly gathering. Simplified like the death-mask of a handsome face, it perhaps produced for her just then an effect akin to the stir of an expression in the "set" commemorative plaster. Yet whatever her impression may have been she produced instead a vague platitude. "Well, if it were only furnished and lived in—!"

She appeared to imply that in case of its being still furnished he might have been a little less opposed to the idea of a return. But she passed straight into the vestibule, as if to leave her words behind her, and the next moment he had opened the house-door and was standing with her on the steps. He closed the door and, while he re-pocketed his key, looking up and down, they took in the comparatively harsh actuality of the Avenue, which reminded him of the assault of the outer light of the Desert on the traveller emerging from an Egyptian tomb. But he risked before they stepped into the street his gathered answer to her speech. "For me it *is* lived in. For me it *is* furnished." At which it was easy for her to sigh "Ah yes—!" all vaguely and discreetly; since his parents and his favorite sister, to say nothing of other kin, in numbers, had run their course and met their end there. That represented, within the walls, ineffaceable life.

It was a few days after this that, during an hour passed with her again, he had expressed his impatience of the too flattering curiosity—among the people he met—about his appreciation of New York. He had arrived at none at all that was socially producible, and as for that matter of his "thinking" (thinking the better or the worse of anything there) he was wholly taken up with one subject of thought. It was mere vain egoism, and it was moreover, if she liked, a morbid obsession. He found all things come back to the question of what he personally might have been, how he might have led his life and "turned out," if he had not so, at the outset, given it up. And confessing for the first time to the intensity within him of this absurd speculation—which but proved also, no doubt, the habit of too selfishly thinking—he affirmed the impotence there of any other source of interest, any other native appeal. "What would it have made of me, what would it have made of me? I keep for ever wondering, all idiotically; as if I could possibly know! I see what it has made of dozens of others, those I meet, and it positively aches within me, to the point of exasperation, that it would have made something of me as well. Only I can't make out *what,* and the worry of it, the small rage of curiosity never to be satisfied, brings back what I remember to have felt, once or twice, after judging best, for reasons, to burn some important letter unopened. I've been sorry, I've hated it—I've never known what was in the letter. You may of course say it's a trifle—!"

"I don't say it's a trifle," Miss Staverton gravely interrupted.

She was seated by her fire, and before her, on his feet and restless, he turned to and fro between this intensity of his idea and a fitful and unseeing inspection, through his single eye-glass, of the dear little old objects on her chimney-piece. Her interruption made him for an instant look at her harder. "I shouldn't care if you did!" he laughed, however; "and it's only a figure, at any rate, for the way I now feel. *Not* to have followed my perverse young course—and almost in the teeth of my father's curse, as I may say; not to have kept it up, so, 'over there,' from that day to this, without a doubt or a pang; not, above all, to have liked it, to have loved it, so much, loved it, no doubt, with such an abysmal conceit of my own preference: some variation from *that,* I say, must have produced some different effect for my life and for my 'form.' I should have stuck here—if it had been possible; and I was too young, at twenty-three, to judge, *pour deux sous,* whether it *were* possible. If I had waited I might have seen it was, and then I might have been, by staying here, something nearer to one of these types who have been hammered so hard and made so keen by their conditions. It isn't that I admire them so much—the question of any charm in them, or of any charm, beyond that of the rank money-passion, exerted by their conditions *for* them, has nothing to do with the matter: it's only a question of what fantastic, yet perfectly possible, development of my own nature I mayn't have missed. It comes over me that I had then a strange *alter ego* deep down somewhere within me, as the full-blown flower is in the small tight bud, and that I just took the course, I just transferred him to the climate, that blighted him for once and for ever."

"And you wonder about the flower," Miss Staverton said. "So do I, if you want to know; and so I've been wondering these several weeks. I believe in the flower," she continued, "I felt it would have been quite splendid, quite huge and monstrous."

"Monstrous above all!" her visitor echoed; "and I imagine, by the same stroke, quite hideous and offensive."

"You don't believe that," she returned; "if you did you wouldn't wonder. You'd know, and that would be enough for you. What you feel—and what I feel *for* you—is that you'd have had power."

"You'd have liked me that way?" he asked.

She barely hung fire. "How should I not have liked you?"

"I see. You'd have liked me, have preferred me, a billionaire!"

"How should I not have liked you?" she simply again asked.

He stood before her still—her question kept him motionless. He took it in, so much there was of it; and indeed his not otherwise meeting it testified to that. "I know at least what I am," he simply went on; "the other side of the medal's clear enough. I've not been edifying—I believe I'm thought in a hundred quarters to have been barely decent. I've followed strange paths and worshipped strange gods; it must have come to you again and again—in fact you've admitted to me as much—that I was leading, at any time these thirty years, a selfish frivolous scandalous life. And you see what it has made of me."

She just waited, smiling at him. "You see what it has made of *me*."

"Oh you're a person whom nothing can have altered. You were born to be what you are, anywhere, anyway: you've the perfection nothing else could have blighted. And don't you see how, without my exile, I shouldn't have been waiting till now—?" But he pulled up for the strange pang.

"The great thing to see," she presently said, "seems to me to be that it has spoiled nothing. It hasn't spoiled your being here at last. It hasn't spoiled this. It hasn't spoiled your speaking—" She also however faltered.

He wondered at everything her controlled emotion might mean. "Do you believe then—too dreadfully!—that I *am* as good as I might ever have been?"

"Oh no! Far from it!" With which she got up from her chair and was nearer to him. "But I don't care," she smiled.

"You mean I'm good enough?"

She considered a little. "Will you believe it if I say so? I mean will you let that settle your question for you?" And then as if making out in his face that he drew back from this, that he had some idea which, however absurd, he couldn't yet bargain away: "Oh you don't care either—but very differently: you don't care for anything but yourself."

Spencer Brydon recognised it—it was in fact what he had absolutely professed. Yet he importantly qualified. "*He* isn't myself. He's the just so totally other person. But I do want to see him," he added. "And I can. And I shall."

Their eyes met for a minute while he guessed from something in hers that she divined his strange sense. But neither of them otherwise expressed it, and her apparent understanding, with no protesting shock, no easy derision, touched him more deeply than anything yet, constituting for his stifled perversity, on the spot, an element that was like breathable air. What she said however was unexpected. "Well, *I've* seen him."

"You—?"

"I've seen him in a dream."

"Oh a 'dream'—!" It let him down.

"But twice over," she continued. "I saw him as I see you now."

"You've dreamed the same dream—?"

"Twice over," she repeated. "The very same."

This did somehow a little speak to him, as it also gratified him. "You dream about me at that rate?"

"Ah about *him!*" she smiled.

His eyes again sounded her. "Then you know all about him." And as she said nothing more: "What's the wretch like?"

She hesitated, and it was as if he were pressing her so hard that, resisting for reasons of her own, she had to turn away. "I'll tell you some other time!"

II

It was after this that there was most of a virtue for him, most of a cultivated charm, most of a preposterous secret thrill, in the particular form of surrender to his obsession and of address to what he more and more believed to be his privilege. It was what in these weeks he was living for—since he really felt life to begin but after Mrs. Muldoon had retired from the scene and, visiting the ample house from attic to cellar, making sure he was alone, he knew himself in safe possession and, as he tacitly expressed it, let himself go. He sometimes came twice in the twenty-four hours; the moments he liked best were those of gathering dusk, of the short autumn twilight; this was the time of which, again and again, he found himself hoping most. Then he could, as seemed to him, most intimately wander and wait, linger and listen, feel his fine attention, never in his life before so fine, on the pulse of the great vague place: he preferred the lampless hour and only wished he might have prolonged each day the deep crepuscular spell. Later—rarely much before midnight, but then for a considerable vigil—he watched with his glimmering light; moving slowly, holding it high, playing it far, rejoicing above all, as much as he might, in open vistas, reaches of communication between rooms and by passages; the long straight chance or show, as he would have called it, for the revelation he pretended to invite. It was a practice he found he could perfectly "work" without exciting remark; no one was in the least the wiser for it; even Alice Staverton, who was moreover a well of discretion, didn't quite fully imagine.

He let himself in and let himself out with the assurance of calm proprietorship; and accident so far favoured him that, if a fat Avenue "officer" had happened on occasion to see him entering at eleven-thirty, he had never yet, to the best of his belief, been noticed as emerging at two. He walked there on the crisp November nights, arrived regularly at the evening's end; it was as easy to do this after dining out as to take his way to a club or to his hotel. When he left his club, if he hadn't been dining out, it was ostensibly to go to his hotel; and when he left his hotel, if he had spent a part of the evening there, it was ostensibly to go to his club. Everything was easy in fine; everything conspired and promoted: there was truly even in the strain of his experience something that glossed over, something that salved and simplified, all the rest of consciousness. He circulated, talked, renewed, loosely and pleasantly, old relations—met indeed, so far as he could, new expectations and seemed to make out on the whole that in spite of the career, of such different contacts, which he had spoken of to Miss Staverton as ministering so little, for those who might have watched it, to edification, he was positively rather liked than not. He was a dim secondary social success—

and all with people who had truly not an idea of him. It was all mere surface sound, this murmur of their welcome, this popping of their corks—just as his gestures of response were the extravagant shadows, emphatic in proportion as they meant little, of some game of *ombres chinoises.* He projected himself all day, in thought, straight over the bristling line of hard unconscious heads and into the other, the real, the waiting life; the life that, as soon as he had heard behind him the click of his great house-door, began for him, on the jolly corner, as beguilingly as the slow opening bars of some rich music follows the tap of the conductor's wand.

He always caught the first effect of the steel point of his stick on the old marble of the hall pavement, large black-and-white squares that he remembered as the admiration of his childhood and that had then made in him, as he now saw, for the growth of an early conception of style. This effect was the dim reverberating tinkle as of some far-off bell hung who should say where?—in the depths of the house, of the past, of that mystical other world that might have flourished for him had he not, for weal or woe, abandoned it. On this impression he did ever the same thing; he put his stick noiselessly away in a corner—feeling the place once more in the likeness of some great glass bowl, all precious concave crystal, set delicately humming by the play of a moist finger round its edge. The concave crystal held, as it were, this mystical other world, and the indescribably fine murmur of its rim was the sigh there, the scarce audible pathetic wail to his strained ear, of all the old baffled forsworn possibilities. What he did therefore by this appeal of his hushed presence was to wake them into such measure of ghostly life as they might still enjoy. They were shy, all but unappeasably shy, but they weren't really sinister; at least they weren't as he had hitherto felt them—before they had taken the Form he so yearned to make them take, the Form he at moments saw himself in the light of fairly hunting on tiptoe, the points of his evening-shoes, from room to room and from storey to storey.

That was the essence of his vision—which was all rank folly, if one would, while he was out of the house and otherwise occupied, but which took on the last verisimilitude as soon as he was placed and posted. He knew what he meant and what he wanted; it was as clear as the figure on a cheque presented in demand for cash. His *alter ego* "walked"—that was the note of his image of him, while his image of his motive for his own odd pastime was the desire to waylay him and meet him. He roamed, slowly, warily, but all restlessly, he himself did—Mrs. Muldoon had been right, absolutely, with her figure of their "craping"; and the presence he watched for would roam restlessly too. But it would be as cautious and as shifty; the conviction of its probable, in fact its already quite sensible, quite audible evasion of pursuit grew for him from night to night, laying on him finally a rigour to which nothing in his life had been comparable. It had been the theory of many superficially-judging persons, he knew, that he was wasting that life in a surrender to sensations, but he had tasted of no pleasure so fine as his actual tension, had been introduced to no sport that demanded at once the patience and the nerve of this stalking of a creature more subtle, yet at bay perhaps more formidable, than any beast of the forest. The terms, the comparisons, the very practices of the chase positively came again into play; there were even moments when passages of his occasional experience as a sportsman, stirred memories, from his younger time, of moor and mountain and desert, revived for him—and to the increase of his keenness—by the tremendous force of analogy. He found himself at moments—once he had placed his single light on some mantel-shelf or in some recess—stepping back into shelter or shade, effacing himself behind a door or in an embrasure, as he had sought of old the vantage of rock and tree; he found himself holding his breath and living in the joy of the instant, the supreme suspense created by big game alone.

He wasn't afraid (though putting himself the question as he believed gentlemen on Bengal tiger-shoots or in close quarters with the great bear of the Rockies had been known to confess to having put it); and this indeed—since here at least he might be frank!—because of the impression, so intimate and so strange, that he himself produced as yet a dread, produced certainly a strain, beyond the liveliest he was likely to feel. They fell for him into categories, they fairly became familiar, the signs, for his own perception, of the alarm his presence and his vigilance created; though leaving him always to remark, portentously, on his probably having formed a relation, his probably enjoying a consciousness, unique in the experience of man. People enough, first and last, had been in terror of apparitions, but who had ever before so turned the tables and become himself, in the apparitional world, an incalculable terror? He might have found this sublime had he quite dared to think of it; but he didn't too much insist, truly, on that side of his privilege. With habit and repetition he gained to an extraordinary degree the power to penetrate the dusk of distances and the darkness of corners, to resolve back into their innocence the treacheries of uncertain light, the evil-looking forms taken in the gloom by mere shadows, by accidents of the air, by shifting effects of perspective; putting down his dim luminary he could still wander on without it, pass into other rooms and, only knowing it was there behind him in case of need, see his way about, visually project for his purpose a comparative clearness. It made him feel, this acquired faculty, like some monstrous stealthy cat; he wondered if he would have glared at these moments with large shining yellow eyes, and what it mightn't verily be, for the poor hard-pressed *alter ego,* to be confronted with such a type.

He liked however the open shutters; he opened everywhere those Mrs. Muldoon had closed, closing them as carefully afterwards, so that she shouldn't notice: he liked—oh this he did like, and above all in the upper rooms!—the sense of the hard silver of the autumn stars through the window-panes, and scarcely less the flare of the street-lamps below, the white electric lustre which it would have taken curtains to keep out. This was human actual social; this was of the world he had lived in, and he was more at his ease certainly for the countenance, coldly general and impersonal, that all the while and in spite of his detachment it seemed to give him. He had support of course mostly in the rooms at the wide front and the prolonged side; it failed him considerably in the central shades and the parts at the back. But if he sometimes, on his rounds, was glad of his optical reach, so none the less often the rear of the house affected him as the very jungle of his prey. The place was there more subdivided; a large "extension" in particular, where small rooms for servants had been multiplied, abounded in nooks and corners, in closets and passages, in the ramifications especially of an ample back staircase over which he leaned, many a time, to look far down—not deterred from his gravity even while aware that he might, for a spectator, have figured some solemn simpleton playing at hide-and-seek. Outside in fact he might himself make that ironic *rapprochement;* but within the walls, and in spite of the clear windows, his consistency was proof against the cynical light of New York.

It had belonged to that idea of the exasperated consciousness of his victim to become a real test for him; since he had quite put it to himself from the first that, oh distinctly! he could "cultivate" his whole perception. He had felt it as above all open to cultivation—which indeed was but another name for his manner of spending his time. He was bringing it on, bringing it to perfection, by practice; in consequence of which it had grown so fine that he was now aware of impressions, attestations of his general postulate, that couldn't have broken upon him at once. This was the case more specifically with a phenomenon at last quite frequent for him in the upper rooms, the recognition—absolutely unmistakeable, and by a turn dating from a particular hour, his resumption of his campaign after a diplomatic drop, a calculated absence of three nights—of his being definitely followed, tracked at a distance carefully taken and to the express end that he should the less confidently, less arrogantly, appear to himself merely to pursue. It worried, it finally quite broke him up, for it proved, of all the conceivable impressions, the one least suited to his book. He was kept in sight while remaining himself—as regards the essence of his position—sightless, and his only recourse then was in abrupt turns, rapid recoveries of ground. He wheeled about, retracing his steps, as if he might so catch in his face at least the stirred air of some other quick revolution. It was indeed true that his fully dislocalised thought of these manoeuvres recalled to him Pantaloon, at the Christmas farce, buffeted and tricked from behind by ubiquitous Harlequin; but it left intact the influence of the conditions themselves each time he was re-exposed to them, so that in fact this association, had he suffered it to become constant, would on a certain side have but ministered to his intenser gravity. He had made, as I have said, to create on the premises the baseless sense of a reprieve, his three absences; and the result of the third was to confirm the after-effect of the second.

On his return, that night—the night succeeding his last intermission—he stood in the hall and looked up the staircase with a certainty more intimate than any he had yet known. "He's *there,* at the top, and waiting—not, as in general, falling back for disappearance. He's holding his ground, and it's the first time—which is a proof, isn't it? that something has happened for him." So Brydon argued with his hand on the banister and his foot on the lowest stair; in which position he felt as never before the air chilled by his logic. He himself turned cold in it, for he seemed of a sudden to know what now was involved. "Harder pressed?—yes, he takes it in, with its thus making clear to him that I've come, as they say, 'to stay.' He finally doesn't like and can't bear it, in the sense, I mean, that his wrath, his menaced interest, now balances with his dread. I've hunted him till he has 'turned': that, up there, is what has happened—he's the fanged or the antlered animal brought at last to bay." There came to him, as I say—but determined by an influence beyond my notation!—the acuteness of this certainty; under which however the next moment he had broken into a sweat that he would as little have consented to attribute to fear as he would have dared immediately to act upon it for enterprise. It marked none the less a prodigious thrill, a thrill that represented sudden dismay, no doubt, but also represented, and with the selfsame throb, the strangest, the most joyous, possibly the next minute almost the proudest, duplication of consciousness.

"He has been dodging, retreating, hiding, but now, worked up to anger, he'll fight!"—this intense impression made a single mouthful, as it were, of terror and applause. But what was wondrous was that the applause, for the felt fact, was so eager, since, if it was his other self he was running to earth, this ineffable identity was thus in the last resort not unworthy of him. It bristled there—somewhere near at hand, however unseen still—as the hunted thing, even as the trodden worm of the adage *must* at last bristle; and Brydon at this instant tasted probably of a sensation more complex than had ever before found itself consistent with sanity. It was as if it would have shamed him that a character so associated with his own should triumphantly succeed in just skulking, should to the end not risk the open, so that the drop of this danger was, on the spot, a great lift of the whole situation. Yet with another rare shift of the same subtlety he was already trying to measure by how much more he himself might now be in peril of fear; so rejoicing that he could, in another form, actively inspire that fear, and simultaneously quaking for the form in which he might passively know it.

The apprehension of knowing it must after a little have grown in him, and the strangest moment of his adventure perhaps, the most memorable or really most interesting, afterwards, of his crisis, was the lapse of certain instants of concentrated conscious *combat,* the sense of a need to hold on to something, even after the manner of a man slipping and slipping on some awful incline; the vivid impulse, above all, to move, to act, to charge, somehow and upon something—to show himself, in a word, that he wasn't afraid. The state of "holding-on" was thus the state to which he was momentarily reduced; if there had been anything, in the great vacancy, to seize, he would presently have been aware of having clutched it as he might under a shock at home have clutched the nearest chair-back. He had been surprised at any rate—of this he *was* aware—into something unprecedented since his original appropriation of the place; he had closed his eyes, held them tight, for a long minute, as with that instinct of dismay and that terror of vision. When he opened them the room, the other contiguous rooms, extraordinarily, seemed lighter—so light, almost, that at first he took the change for day. He stood firm, however that might be, just where he had paused; his resistance had helped him—it was as if there were something he had tided over. He knew after a little what this was—it had been in the imminent danger of flight. He had stiffened his will against going; without this he would have made for the stairs, and it seemed to him that, still with his eyes closed, he would have descended them, would have known how, straight and swiftly, to the bottom.

Well, as he had held out, here he was—still at the top, among the more intricate upper rooms and with the gauntlet of the others, of all the rest of the house, still to run when it should be his time to go. He would go at his time—only at his time: didn't he go every night very much at the same hour? He took out his watch—there was light for that: it was scarcely a quarter past one, and he had never withdrawn so soon. He reached his lodgings for the most part at two—with his walk of a quarter of an hour. He would wait for the last quarter—he wouldn't stir till then; and he kept his watch there with his eyes on it, reflecting while he held it that this deliberate wait, a wait with an effort, which he recognised, would serve perfectly for the attestation he desired to make. It would prove his courage—unless indeed the latter might most be proved by his budging at last from his place. What he mainly felt now was that, since he hadn't originally scuttled, he had his dignities—which had never in his life seemed so many—all to preserve and to carry aloft. This was before him in truth as a physical image, an image almost worthy of an age of greater romance. That remark indeed glimmered for him only to glow the next instant with a finer light; since what age of romance, after all, could have matched either the state of his mind or, "objectively," as they said, the wonder of his situation? The only difference would have been that, brandishing his dignities over his head as in a parchment scroll, he might then—that is in the heroic time—have proceeded down-stairs with a drawn sword in his other grasp.

At present, really, the light he had set down on the mantel of the next room would have to figure his sword; which utensil, in the course of a minute, he had taken the requisite number of steps to possess himself of. The door between the rooms was open, and from the second another door opened to a third. These rooms, as he remembered, gave all three upon a common corridor as well, but there was a fourth, beyond them, without issue save through the preceding. To have moved, to have heard his step again, was appreciably a help; though even in recognising this he lingered once more a little by the chimney-piece on which his light had rested. When he next moved, just hesitating where to turn, he found himself considering a circumstance that, after his first and comparatively vague apprehension of it, produced in him the start that often attends some pang of recollection, the violent shock of having ceased happily to forget. He had come into sight of the door in which the brief chain of communication ended and which he now surveyed from the nearer threshold, the one not directly facing it. Placed at some distance to the left of this point, it would have admitted him to the last room of the four, the room without other approach or egress, had it not, to his intimate conviction, been closed *since* his former visitation, the matter probably of a quarter of an hour before. He stared with all his eyes at the wonder of the fact, arrested again where he stood and again holding his breath while he sounded its sense. Surely it had been *subsequently* closed—that is it had been on his previous passage indubitably open!

He took it full in the face that something had happened between—that he couldn't not have noticed before (by which he meant on his original tour of all the rooms that evening) that such a barrier had exceptionally presented itself. He had indeed since that moment undergone an agitation so extraordinary that it might have muddled for him any earlier view; and he tried to convince himself that he might perhaps then have gone into the room and, inadvertently, automatically, on coming out, have drawn the door after him. The difficulty was that this exactly was what he never did; it was against his whole policy, as he might have said, the essence of which was to keep vistas clear. He had them from the first, as he was well aware, quite on the brain: the strange apparition, at the far end of one of them, of his baffled "prey" (which had become by so sharp an irony so little the term now to apply!) was the form of success his imagination had most cherished, projecting into it always a refinement of beauty. He had known fifty times the start of perception that had afterwards dropped; had fifty times gasped to himself "There!" under some fond brief hallucination. The house, as the case stood, admirably lent itself; he might wonder at the taste, the native architecture of the particular time, which could rejoice so in the multiplication of doors—the opposite extreme to the modern, the actual almost complete proscription of them; but it had fairly contributed to provoke this obsession of the presence encountered telescopically, as he might say, focussed and studied in diminishing perspective and as by a rest for the elbow.

It was with these considerations that his present attention was charged—they perfectly availed to make what he saw portentous. He *couldn't,* by any lapse, have blocked that aperture; and if he hadn't, if it was unthinkable, why what else was clear but that there had been another agent? Another agent?—he had been catching, as he felt, a moment back, the very breath of him; but when had he been so close as in this simple, this logical, this completely personal act? It was so logical, that is, that one might have *taken* it for personal; yet for what did Brydon take it, he asked himself, while, softly panting, he felt his eyes almost leave their sockets. Ah this time at last they *were,* the two, the opposed projections of him, in presence; and this time, as much as one would, the question of danger loomed. With it rose, as not before, the question of courage—for what he knew the blank face of the door to say to him was "Show us how much you have!" It stared, it glared back at him with that challenge; it put to him the two alternatives: should he just push it open or not? Oh to have this consciousness was to *think*—and to think, Brydon knew, as he stood there, was, with the lapsing moments, not to have acted! Not to have acted—that was the misery and the pang—was even still not to act; was in fact *all* to feel the thing in another, in a new and terrible way. How long did he pause and how long did he debate? There was presently nothing to measure it; for his vibration had already changed—as just by the effect of its intensity. Shut up there, at bay, defiant, and with the prodigy of the thing palpably proveably *done,* thus giving notice like some stark signboard—under that accession of accent the situation itself had turned; and Brydon at last remarkably made up his mind on what it had turned to.

It had turned altogether to a different admonition; to a supreme hint, for him, of the value of Discretion! This slowly dawned, no doubt—for it could take its time; so perfectly, on his threshold, had he been stayed, so little as yet had he either advanced or retreated. It was the strangest of all things that now when, by his taking ten steps and applying his hand to a latch, or even his shoulder and his knee, if necessary, to a panel, all the hunger of his prime need might have been met, his high curiosity crowned, his unrest assuaged—it was amazing, but it was also exquisite and rare, that insistence should have, at a touch, quite dropped from him. Discretion—he jumped at that; and yet not, verily, at such a pitch, because it saved his nerves or his skin, but because, much more valuably, it saved the situation. When I say he "jumped" at it I feel the consonance of this term with the fact that—at the end indeed of I know not how long—he did move again, he crossed straight to the door. He wouldn't touch it—it seemed now that he might *if* he would: he would only just wait there a little, to show, to prove, that he wouldn't. He had thus another station, close to the thin partition by which revelation was denied him; but with his eyes bent and his hands held off in a mere intensity of stillness. He listened as if there had been something to hear, but this attitude, while it lasted, was his own communication. "If you won't then—good: I spare you and I give up. You affect me as by the appeal positively for pity: you convince me that for reasons rigid and sublime—what do I know?—we both of us should have suffered. I respect them then, and, though moved and privileged as I believe, it has never been given to man, I retire, I renounce—never, on my honour, to try again. So rest for ever—and let *me!*"

That, for Brydon was the deep sense of this last demonstration—solemn, measured, directed, as he felt it to be. He brought it to a close, he turned away; and now verily he knew how deeply he had been stirred. He retraced his steps, taking up his candle, burnt, he observed, well-nigh to the socket, and marking again, lighten it as he would, the distinctness of his footfall; after which, in a moment, he knew himself at the other side of the house. He did here what he had not yet done at these hours—he opened half a casement, one of those in the front, and let in the air of the night; a thing he would have taken at any time previous for a sharp rupture of his spell. His spell was broken now, and it didn't matter—broken by his concession and his surrender, which made it idle henceforth that he should ever come back. The empty street—its other life so marked even by the great lamplit vacancy—was within call, within touch; he stayed there as to be in it again, high above it though he was still perched; he watched as for some comforting common fact, some vulgar human note, the passage of a scavenger or a thief, some night-bird however base. He would have blessed that sign of life; he would have welcomed positively the slow approach of his friend the policeman, whom he had hitherto only sought to avoid, and was not sure that if the patrol had come into sight he mightn't have felt the impulse to get into relation with it, to hail it, on some pretext, from his fourth floor.

The pretext that wouldn't have been too silly or too compromising, the explanation that would have saved his dignity and kept his name, in such a case, out of the papers, was not definite to him: he was so occupied with the thought of recording his Discretion—as an effect of the vow he had just uttered to his intimate adversary—that the importance of this loomed large and something had overtaken all ironically his sense of proportion. If there had been a ladder applied to the front of the house, even one of the vertiginous perpendiculars employed by painters and roofers and sometimes left standing overnight, he would have managed somehow, astride of the window-sill, to compass by outstretched leg and arm that mode of descent. If there had been some such uncanny thing as he had found in his room at hotels, a workable fire-escape in the form of notched cable or a canvas shoot, he would have availed himself of it as a proof—well, of his present delicacy. He nursed that sentiment, as the question stood, a little in vain, and even—at the end of he scarce knew, once more, how long—found it, as by the action on his mind of the failure of response of the outer world, sinking back to vague anguish. It seemed to him he had waited an age for some stir of the great grim hush; the life of the town was itself under a spell—so unnaturally, up and down the whole prospect of known and rather ugly objects, the blankness and the silence lasted. Had they ever, he asked himself, the hard-faced houses, which had begun to look livid in the dim dawn, had they ever spoken so little to any need of his spirit? Great builded voids, great crowded stillnesses put on, often, in the heart of cities, for the small hours, a sort of sinister mask, and it was of this large collective negation that Brydon presently became conscious—all the more that the break of day was, almost incredibly, now at hand, proving to him what a night he had made of it.

He looked again at his watch, saw what had become of his time-values (he had taken hours for minutes—not, as in other tense situations, minutes for hours) and the strange air of the streets was but the weak, the sullen flush of a dawn in which everything was still locked up.

His choked appeal from his own open window had been the sole note of life, and he could but break off at last as for a worse despair. Yet while so deeply demoralised he was capable again of an impulse denoting—at least by his present measure—extraordinary resolution; of retracing his steps to the spot where he had turned cold with the extinction of his last pulse of doubt as to there being in the place another presence than his own. This required an effort strong enough to sicken him; but he had his reason, which overmastered for the moment everything else. There was the whole of the rest of the house to traverse, and how should he screw himself to that if the door he had seen closed were at present open? He could hold to the idea that the closing had practically been for him an act of mercy, a chance offered him to descend, depart, get off the ground and never again profane it. This conception held together, it worked; but what it meant for him depended now clearly on the amount of forbearance his recent action, or rather his recent inaction, had engendered. The image of the "presence," whatever it was, waiting there for him to go—this image had not yet been so concrete for his nerves as when he stopped short of the point at which certainty would have come to him. For, with all his resolution, or more exactly with all his dread, he did stop short—he hung back from really seeing.

The risk was too great and his fear too definite: it took at this moment an awful specific form.

He knew—yes, as he had never known anything—that, *should* he see the door open, it would all too abjectly be the end of him. It would mean that the agent of his shame—for his shame was the deep abjection—was once more at large and in general possession; and what glared him thus in the face was the act that this would determine for him. It would send him straight about to the window he had left open, and by that window, be long ladder and dangling rope as absent as they would, he saw himself uncontrollably insanely fatally take his way to the street. The hideous chance of this he at least could avert; but he could only avert it by recoiling in time from assurance. He had the whole house to deal with, this fact was still there; only he now knew that uncertainty alone could start him. He stole back from where he had checked himself—merely to do so was suddenly like safety—and, making blindly for the greater staircase, left gaping rooms and sounding passages behind. Here was the top of the stairs, with a fine large dim descent and three spacious landings to mark off. His instinct was all for mildness, but his feet were harsh on the floors, and, strangely, when he had in a couple of minutes become aware of this, it counted somehow for help. He couldn't have spoken, the tone of his voice would have scared him, and the common conceit or resource of "whistling in the dark" (whether literally or figuratively) have appeared basely vulgar; yet he liked none the less to hear himself go, and when he had reached his first landing—taking it all with no rush, but quite steadily—that stage of success drew from him a gasp of relief.

The house, withal, seemed immense, the scale of space again inordinate; the open rooms, to no one of which his eyes deflected, gloomed in their shuttered state like mouths of caverns; only the high skylight that formed the crown of the deep well created for him a medium in which he could advance, but which might have been, for queerness of colour, some watery underworld. He tried to think of something noble, as that his property was really grand, a splendid possession; but this nobleness took the form too of the clear delight with which he was finally to sacrifice it. They might come in now, the builders, the destroyers—they might come as soon as they would. At the end of two flights he had dropped to another zone, and from the middle of the third, with only one more left, he recognised the influence of the lower windows, of half-drawn blinds, of the occasional gleam of street-lamps, of the glazed spaces of the vestibule. This was the bottom of the sea, which showed an illumination of its own and which he even saw paved—when at a given moment he drew up to sink a long look over the banisters—with the marble squares of his childhood. By that time indubitably he felt, as he might have said in a commoner cause, better; it had allowed him to stop and draw breath, and the ease increased with the sight of the old black-and-white slabs. But what he most felt was that now surely, with the element of impunity pulling him as by hard firm hands, the case was settled for what he might have seen above had he dared that last look. The closed door, blessedly remote now, was still closed—and he had only in short to reach that of the house.

He came down further, he crossed the passage forming the access to the last flight; and if here again he stopped an instant it was almost for the sharpness of the thrill of assured escape. It made him shut his eyes—which opened again to the straight slope of the remainder of the stairs. Here was impunity still, but impunity almost excessive; inasmuch as the side-lights and the high fan-tracery of the entrance were glimmering straight into the hall; an appearance produced, he the next instant saw, by the fact that the vestibule gaped wide, that the hinged halves of the inner door had been thrown far back. Out of that again the *question* sprang at him, making his eyes, as he felt, half-start from his head, as they had done, at the top of the house, before the sign of the other door. If he had left that one open, hadn't he left this one closed, and wasn't he now in *most* immediate presence of some inconceivable occult activity? It was as sharp, the question, as a knife in his side, but the answer hung fire still and seemed to lose itself in the vague darkness to which the thin admitted dawn, glimmering archwise over the whole outer door, made a semicircular margin, a cold silvery nimbus that seemed to play a little as he looked—to shift and expand and contract.

It was as if there had been something within it, protected by indistinctness and corresponding in extent with the opaque surface behind, the painted panels of the last barrier to his escape, of which the key was in his pocket. The indistinctness mocked him even while he stared, affected him as somehow shrouding or challenging certitude, so that after faltering an instant on his step he let himself go with the sense that here *was* at last something to meet, to touch, to take, to know—something all unnatural and dreadful, but to advance upon which was the condition for him either of liberation or of supreme defeat. The penumbra, dense and dark, was the virtual screen of a figure which stood in it as still as some image erect in a niche or as some black-vizored sentinel guarding a treasure. Brydon was to know afterwards, was to recall and make out, the particular thing he had believed during the rest of his descent. He saw, in its great gray glimmering margin, the central vagueness diminish, and he felt it to be taking the very form toward which, for so many days, the passion of his curiosity had yearned. It gloomed, it loomed, it was something, it was somebody, the prodigy of a personal presence.

Rigid and conscious, spectral yet human, a man of his own substance and stature waited there to measure himself with his power to dismay. This only could it be—this only till he recognised, with his advance, that what made the face dim was the pair of raised hands that covered it and in which, so far from being offered in defiance, it was buried as for dark deprecation. So Brydon, before him, took him in; with every fact of him now, in the higher light, hard and acute—his planted stillness, his vivid truth, his grizzled bent head and white masking hands, his queer actuality of evening-dress, of dangling double eye-glass, of gleaming silk lappet and white linen, of pearl button and gold watch-guard and polished shoe. No portrait by a great modern master could have presented him with more intensity, thrust him out of his frame with more art, as if there had been "treatment," of the consummate sort, in his every shade and salience. The revulsion, for our friend, had become, before he knew it, immense—this drop, in the act of apprehension, to the sense of his adversary's inscrutable manœuvre. That meaning at least, while he gaped, it offered him; for he could but gape at his other self in this other anguish, gape as a proof that *he,* standing there for the achieved, the enjoyed, the triumphant life, couldn't be faced in his triumph. Wasn't the proof in the splendid covering hands, strong and completely spread?—so spread and so intentional that, in spite of a special verity that surpassed every other, the fact that one of these hands had lost two fingers, which were reduced to stumps, as if accidentally shot away, the face was effectually guarded and saved.

"Saved," though, *would* it be?—Brydon breathed his wonder till the very impunity of his attitude and the very insistence of his eyes produced, as he felt, a sudden stir which showed the next instant as a deeper portent, which the head raised itself, the betrayal of a braver purpose. The hands, as he looked, began to move, to open; then, as if deciding in a flash, dropped from the face and left it uncovered and presented. Horror, with the sight, had leaped into Brydon's throat, gasping there in a sound he couldn't utter; for the bared identity was too hideous as *his,* and his glare was the passion of his protest. The face, *that* face, Spencer Brydon's?—he searched it still, but looking away from it in dismay and denial, falling straight from his height and sublimity. It was unknown, inconceivable, awful, disconnected from any possibility—! He had been "sold," he inwardly moaned, stalking such game as this: the presence before him was a presence, the horror within him a horror, but the waste of his nights had been only grotesque and the success of his adventure an irony. Such an identity fitted his at *no* point, made its alternative monstrous. A thousand times yes, as it came upon him nearer now—the face was the face of a stranger. It came upon him nearer now, quite as one of those expanding fantastic images projected by the magic lantern of childhood; for the stranger, whoever he might be, evil, odious, blatant, vulgar, had advanced as for aggression, and he knew himself give ground. Then harder pressed still, sick with the force of his shock, and falling back as under the hot breath and the roused passion of a life larger than his own, a rage of personality before which his own collapsed, he felt the whole vision turn to darkness and his very feet give way. His head went round; he was going; he had gone.

III

What had next brought him back, clearly—though after how long?—was Mrs. Muldoon's voice, coming to him from quite near, from so near that he seemed presently to see her as kneeling on the ground before him while he lay looking up at her; himself not wholly on the ground, but half-raised and upheld—conscious, yes, of tenderness of support and, more particularly, of a head pillowed in extraordinary softness and faintly refreshing fragrance. He considered, he wondered, his wit but half at his service; then another face intervened, bending more directly over him, and he finally knew that Alice Staverton had made her lap an ample and perfect cushion to him, and that she had to this end seated herself on the lowest degree of the staircase, the rest of his long person remaining stretched on his old black-and-white slabs. They were cold, these marble squares of his youth; but *he* somehow was not, in this rich return of consciousness—the most wonderful hour, little by little, that he had ever known, leaving him, as it did, so gratefully, so abysmally passive, and yet as with a treasure of intelligence waiting all round him for quiet appropriation; dissolved, he might call it, in the air of the place and producing the golden glow of a late autumn afternoon. He had come back, yes—come back from further away than any man but himself had ever travelled; but it was strange how with this sense what he had come back *to* seemed really the great thing, and as if his prodigious journey had been all for the sake of it. Slowly but surely his consciousness grew, his vision of his state thus completing itself: he had been miraculously *car-*

ried back—lifted and carefully borne as from where he had been picked up, the uttermost end of an interminable gray passage. Even with this he was suffered to rest, and what had now brought him to knowledge was the break in the long mild motion.

It had brought him to knowledge, to knowledge—yes, this was the beauty of his state; which came to resemble more and more that of a man who has gone to sleep on some news of a great inheritance, and then, after dreaming it away, after profaning it with matters strange to it, has waked up again to serenity of certitude and has only to lie and watch it grow. This was the drift of his patience—that he had only to let it shine on him. He must moreover, with intermissions, still have been lifted and borne; since why and how else should he have known himself, later on, with the afternoon glow intenser, no longer at the foot of his stairs—situated as these now seemed at that dark other end of his tunnel—but on a deep window-bench of his high saloon, over which had been spread, couch-fashion, a mantle of soft stuff lined with gray fur that was familiar to his eyes and that one of his hands kept fondly feeling as for its pledge of truth. Mrs. Muldoon's face had gone, but the other, the second he had recognised, hung over him in a way that showed how he was still propped and pillowed. He took it all in, and the more he took it the more it seemed to suffice: he was as much at peace as if he had had food and drink. It was the two women who had found him, on Mrs. Muldoon's having plied, at her usual hour, her latch-key—and on her having above all arrived while Miss Staverton still lingered near the house. She had been turning away, all anxiety, from worrying the vain bell-handle—her calculation having been of the hour of the good woman's visit; but the latter, blessedly, had come up while she was still there, and they had entered together. He had then lain, beyond the vestibule, very much as he was lying now—quite, that is, as he appeared to have fallen, but all so wondrously without bruise or gash; only in a depth of stupor. What he most took in, however, at present, with the steadier clearance, was that Alice Staverton had for a long unspeakable moment not doubted he was dead.

"It must have been that I *was*." He made it out as she held him. "Yes—I can only have died. You brought me literally to life. Only," he wondered, his eyes rising to her, "only, in the name of all the benedictions, how?"

It took her but an instant to bend her face and kiss him, and something in the manner of it, and in the way her hands clasped and locked his head while he felt the cool charity and virtue of her lips, something in all this beatitude somehow answered everything. "And now I keep you," she said.

"Oh keep me, keep me!" he pleaded while her face still hung over him: in response to which it dropped again and stayed close, clingingly close. It was the seal of their situation—of which he tasted the impress for a long blissful moment in silence. But he came back. "Yet how did you know—?"

"I was uneasy. You were to have come, you remember—and you had sent no word."

"Yes, I remember—I was to have gone to you at one today." It caught on to their "old" life and relation—which were so near and so far. "I was still out there in my strange darkness—where was it, what was it? I must have stayed there so long." He could but wonder at the depth and the duration of his swoon.

"Since last night?" she asked with a shade of fear for her possible indiscretion.

"Since this morning—it must have been: the cold dim dawn of today. Where have I been," he vaguely wailed, "where have I been?" He felt her hold him close, and it was as if this helped him now to make in all security his mild moan. "What a long dark day!"

All in her tenderness she had waited a moment. "In the cold dim dawn?" she quavered.

But he had already gone on piecing together the parts of the whole prodigy. "As I didn't turn up you came straight—?"

She barely cast about. "I went first to your hotel—where they told me of your absence. You had dined out last evening and hadn't been back since. But they appeared to know you had been at your club."

"So you had the idea of *this*—?"

"Of what?" she asked in a moment.

"Well—of what has happened."

"I believed at least you'd have been here. I've known, all along," she said, "that you've been coming."

"'Known' it—?"

"Well, I've believed it. I said nothing to you after that talk we had a month ago—but I felt sure. I knew you *would,*" she declared.

"That I'd persist, you mean?"

"That you'd see him."

"Ah but I didn't" cried Brydon with his long wail. "There's somebody—an awful beast; whom I brought, too horribly, to bay. But it's not me."

At this she bent over him again, and her eyes were in his eyes. "No—it's not you." And it was as if, while her face hovered, he might have made out in it, hadn't it been so near, some particular meaning blurred by a smile. "No, thank heaven," she repeated—"it's not you! Of course it wasn't to have been."

"Ah but it *was,*" he gently insisted. And he stared before him now as he had been staring for so many weeks. "I was to have known myself."

"You couldn't!" she returned consolingly. And then reverting, and as if to account further for what she had herself done, "But it wasn't only *that,* that you hadn't been at home," she went on. "I waited till the hour at which we had found Mrs. Muldoon that day of my going with you; and she arrived, as I've told you, while, failing to bring any one to the door, I lingered in my despair on the steps. After a little, if she hadn't come, by such a mercy, I should have found means to hunt her up. But it wasn't," said Alice Staverton, as if once more with her fine intention—"it wasn't only that."

His eyes, as he lay, turned back to her. "What more then?"

She met it, the wonder she had stirred. "In the cold dim dawn, you say? Well, in the cold dim dawn of this morning I too saw you."

"Saw *me*—?"

"Saw *him,*" said Alice Staverton. "It must have been at the same moment."

He lay an instant taking it in—as if he wished to be quite reasonable. "At the same moment?"

"Yes—in my dream again, the same one I've named to you. He came back to me. Then I knew it for a sign. He had come to you."

At this Brydon raised himself; he had to see her better. She helped him when she understood his movement, and he sat up, steadying himself beside her there on the window-bench and with his right hand grasping her left. "*He* didn't come to me."

"You came to yourself," she beautifully smiled.

"Ah I've come to myself now—thanks to you, dearest. But this brute, with his awful face—this brute's a black stranger. He's none of *me,* even as I *might* have been," Brydon sturdily declared.

But she kept the clearness that was like the breath of infallibility. "Isn't the whole point that you'd have been different?"

He almost scowled for it. "As different as *that*—?"

Her look again was more beautiful to him than the things of this world. "Haven't you exactly wanted to know *how* different? So this morning," she said, "you appeared to me."

"Like *him?*"

"A black stranger!"

"Then how did you know it was I?"

"Because, as I told you weeks ago, my mind, my imagination, had worked so over what you might, what you mightn't have been—to show you, you see, how I've thought of you. In the midst of that you came to me—that my wonder might be answered. So I knew," she went on; "and believed that, since the question held you too so fast, as you told me that day, you too would see for yourself. And when this morning I again saw I knew it would be because you had—

and also then, from the first moment, because you somehow wanted me. *He* seemed to tell me of that. So why," she strangely smiled, "shouldn't I like him?"

It brought Spencer Brydon to his feet. "You 'like' that horror—?"

"I *could* have liked him. And to me," she said, "he was no horror. I had accepted him."

"'Accepted'—?" Brydon oddly sounded.

"Before, for the interest of his difference—yes. And as *I* didn't disown him, as *I* knew him—which you at last, confronted with him in his difference, so cruelly didn't, my dear—well, he must have been, you see, less dreadful to me. And it may have pleased him that I pitied him."

She was beside him on her feet, but still holding his hand—still with her arm supporting him. But though it all brought for him thus a dim light, "You 'pitied' him?" he grudgingly, resentfully asked.

"He has been unhappy; he has been ravaged," she said.

"And haven't I been unhappy? Am not I—you've only to look at me!—ravaged?"

"Ah I don't say I like him *better,*" she granted after a thought. "But he's grim, he's worn—and things have happened to him. He doesn't make shift, for sight, with your charming monocle."

"No"—it struck Brydon: "I couldn't have

sported mine 'downtown.' They'd have guyed me there."

"His great convex pince-nez—I saw it, I recognised the kind—is for his poor ruined sight. And his poor right hand—!"

"Ah!" Brydon winced—whether for his proved identity or for his lost fingers. Then, "He has a million a year," he lucidly added. "But he hasn't you."

"And he isn't—no, he isn't—*you!*" she murmured as he drew her to his breast.

A Wagner Matinée

by Willa Cather

I received one morning a letter, written in pale ink on glassy, blue-lined note-paper, and bearing the postmark of a little Nebraska village. This communication, worn and rubbed, looking as if it had been carried for some days in a coat pocket that was none too clean, was from my uncle Howard, and informed me that his wife had been left a small legacy by a bachelor relative, and that it would be necessary for her to go to Boston to attend to the settling of the estate. He requested me to meet her at the station and render her whatever services might be necessary. On examining the date indicated as that of her arrival, I found it to be no later than tomorrow. He had characteristically delayed writing until, had I been away from home for a day, I must have missed my aunt altogether.

The name of my Aunt Georgiana opened before me a gulf of recollection so wide and deep that, as the letter dropped from my hand, I felt suddenly a stranger to all the present conditions of my existence, wholly ill at ease and out of place amid the familiar surroundings of my study. I became, in short, the gangling farmer-boy my aunt had known, scourged with chilblains and bashfulness, my hands cracked and sore from the corn husking. I sat again before her parlour organ, fumbling the scales with my stiff, red fingers, while she, beside me, made canvas mittens for the huskers.

The next morning, after preparing my landlady for a visitor, I set out for the station. When the train arrived I had some difficulty in finding my aunt. She was the last of the passengers to alight, and it was not until I got her into the carriage that she seemed really to recognize me. She had come all the way in a day coach; her linen duster had become black with soot and her black bonnet gray with dust during the journey. When we arrived at my boarding-house the landlady put her to bed at once and I did not see her again until the next morning.

Whatever shock Mrs. Springer experienced at my aunt's appearance, she considerately concealed. As for myself, I saw my aunt's battered figure with that feeling of awe and respect with which we behold explorers who have left their ears and fingers north of Franz-Joseph-Land, or their health somewhere along the Upper Congo. My Aunt Georgiana had been a music teacher at the Boston Conservatory, somewhere back in the latter sixties. One summer, while visiting in the little village among the Green Mountains where her ancestors had dwelt for generations, she had kindled the callow fancy of my uncle, Howard Carpenter, then an idle, shiftless boy of twenty-one. When she returned to her duties in Boston, Howard followed her, and the upshot of this infatuation was that she eloped with him, eluding the reproaches of her family and the criticism of her friends by going with him to the Nebraska frontier. Carpenter, who, of course, had no money, took up a homestead in Red Willow County, fifty miles from the railroad. There they had measured off their land themselves, driving across the prairie in a wagon, to the wheel of which they had tied a red cotton handkerchief, and counting its revolutions. They built a dug-out in the red hillside, one of those cave dwellings whose inmates so often reverted to primitive conditions. Their water they got from the lagoons where the buffalo drank, and their slender stock of provisions was always at the mercy of bands of roving Indians. For thirty years my aunt had not been farther than fifty miles from the homestead.

I owed to this woman most of the good that ever came my way in my boyhood, and had a reverential affection for her. During the years when I was riding herd for my uncle, my aunt, after cooking the three meals—the first of which was ready at six o'clock in the morning—and putting the six children to bed, would often stand until midnight at her ironing-board, with me at the kitchen table beside her, hearing me recite Latin declensions and conjugations, gently shaking me when my drowsy head sank down over a page of irregular verbs. It was to her, at her ironing or mending, that I read my first Shakspere, and her old text-book on mythology was the first that ever came into my empty hands. She taught me my scales and exercises on the little parlour organ which her husband had bought her after fifteen years during which she had not so much as seen a musical instrument. She would sit beside me by the hour, darning and counting, while I struggled with the "Joyous Farmer." She seldom talked to me about music, and I understood why. Once when I had been doggedly beating out some easy passages from an old score of *Euryanthe* I had found among her music books, she came up to me and, putting her hands over my eyes, gently drew my head back upon her shoulder, saying tremulously, "Don't love it so well, Clark, or it may be taken from you."

When my aunt appeared on the morning after her arrival in Boston, she was still in a semi-somnambulant state. She seemed not to realize that she was in the city where she had spent her youth, the place longed for hungrily half a lifetime. She had been so wretchedly train-sick throughout the journey that she had no recollection of anything but her discomfort, and, to all intents and purposes, there were but a few hours of nightmare between the farm in Red Willow County and my study on Newbury Street. I had planned a little pleasure for her that afternoon, to repay her for some of the glorious moments she had given me when we used to milk together in the straw-thatched cowshed and she, because I was more than usually tired, or because her husband had spoken sharply to me, would tell me of the splendid performance of the *Huguenots* she had seen in Paris, in her youth.

At two o'clock the Symphony Orchestra was to give a Wagner program, and I intended to take my aunt; though, as I conversed with her, I grew doubtful about her enjoyment of it. I suggested our visiting the Conservatory and the Common before lunch, but she seemed altogether too timid to wish to venture out. She questioned me absently about various changes in the city, but she was chiefly concerned that she had forgotten to leave instructions about feeding half-skimmed milk to a certain weakling calf, "old Maggie's calf, you know, Clark," she explained, evidently having forgotten how long I had been away. She was further troubled because she had neglected to tell her daughter about the freshly-opened kit of mackerel in the cellar, which would spoil if it were not used directly.

I asked her whether she had ever heard any of the Wagnerian operas, and found that she had not, though she was perfectly familiar with their respective situations, and had once possessed the piano score of *The Flying Dutchman.* I began to think it would be best to get her back to Red Willow County without waking her, and regretted having suggested the concert.

From the time we entered the concert hall, however, she was a trifle less passive and inert, and for the first time seemed to perceive her surroundings. I had felt some trepidation lest she might become aware of her queer, country clothes, or might experience some painful embarrassment at stepping suddenly into the world to which she had been dead for a quarter of a century. But, again, I found how superficially I had judged her. She sat looking about her with eyes as impersonal, almost as stony, as those with which the granite Ramses in a museum watches the froth and fret that ebbs and flows about his pedestal. I have seen this same aloofness in old miners who drift into the Brown hotel at Denver, their pockets full of bullion, their linen soiled, their haggard faces unshaven; standing in the thronged corridors as solitary as though they were still in a frozen camp on the Yukon.

The matinée audience was made up chiefly of women. One lost the contour of faces and figures, indeed any effect of line whatever, and there was only the colour of bodices past counting, the shimmer of fabrics soft and firm, silky and sheer; red, mauve, pink, blue, lilac, purple, écru, rose, yellow, cream, and white, all the colours that an impressionist finds in a sunlit landscape, with here and there the dead shadow of a frock coat. My Aunt Georgiana regarded them as though they had been so many daubs of tube paint on a palette.

When the musicians came out and took their places, she gave a little stir of anticipation, and looked with quickening interest down over the rail at that invariable grouping, perhaps the first wholly familiar thing that had greeted her eye since she had left old Maggie and her weakling calf. I could feel how all those details sank into her soul, for I had not forgotten how they had sunk into mine when I came fresh from ploughing forever and forever between green aisles of corn, where, as in a treadmill, one might walk from daybreak to dusk without perceiving a shadow of change. The clean profiles of the musicians, the gloss of their linen, the dull black of their coats, the beloved shapes of the instruments, the patches of yellow light on the smooth, varnished bellies of the 'cellos and the bass viols in the rear, the restless, wind-tossed forest of fiddle necks and bows—I recalled how, in the first orchestra I ever heard, those long bow-strokes seemed to draw the heart out of me, as a conjurer's stick reels out yards of paper ribbon from a hat.

The first number was the *Tannhauser* overture. When the horns drew out the first strain of the Pilgrim's chorus, Aunt Georgiana clutched my coat sleeve. Then it was I first realized that for her this broke a silence of thirty years. With the battle between the two motives, with the frenzy of the Venusberg theme and its ripping of strings, there came to me an overwhelming sense of the waste and wear we are so powerless to combat; and I saw again the tall, naked house on the prairie, black and grim as a wooden fortress; the black pond where I had learned to swim, its margin pitted with sun-dried cattle tracks; the rain gullied clay banks about the naked house, the four dwarf ash seedlings where the dish-cloths were always hung to dry before the kitchen door. The world there was the flat world of the ancients; to the east, a cornfield that stretched to daybreak; to the west, a corral that reached to sunset; between, the conquests of peace, dearer-bought than those of war.

The overture closed, my aunt released my coat sleeve, but she said nothing. She sat staring dully at the orchestra. What, I wondered, did she get from it? She had been a good pianist in her day, I knew, and her musical education had been broader than that of most music teachers of a quarter of a century ago. She had often told me of Mozart's operas and Meyerbeer's, and I could remember hearing her sing, years ago, certain melodies of Verdi. When I had fallen ill with a fever in her house she used to sit by my cot in the evening—when the cool, night wind blew in through the faded mosquito netting tacked over the window and I lay watching a certain bright star that burned red above the cornfield—and sing "Home to our mountains, O, let us return!" in a way fit to break the heart of a Vermont boy near dead of homesickness already.

I watched her closely through the prelude to *Tristan and Isolde,* trying vainly to conjecture what that seething turmoil of strings and winds might mean to her, but she sat mutely staring at the violin bows that drove obliquely downward, like the pelting streaks of rain in a summer shower. Had this music any message for her? Had she enough left to at all comprehend this power which had kindled the world since she had left it? I was in a fever of curiosity, but Aunt Georgiana sat silent upon her peak in Darien. She preserved this utter immobility throughout the number from *The Flying Dutchman,* though her fingers worked mechanically upon her black dress, as if, of themselves, they were recalling the piano score they had once played. Poor hands! They had been stretched and twisted into mere tentacles to hold and lift and knead with;—on one of them a thin, worn band that had once been a wedding ring. As I pressed and gently quieted one of those groping hands, I remembered with quivering eyelids their services for me in other days.

Soon after the tenor began the "Prize Song," I heard a quick drawn breath and turned to my aunt. Her eyes were closed, but the tears were glistening on her cheeks, and I think, in a moment more, they were in my eyes as well. It never really died, then—the soul which can suffer so excruciatingly and so interminably; it withers to the outward eye only; like that strange moss which can lie on a dusty shelf half a century and yet, if placed in water, grows green again. She wept so throughout the development and elaboration of the melody.

During the intermission before the second half, I questioned my aunt and found that the "Prize Song" was not new to her. Some years before there had drifted to the farm in Red Willow County a young German, a tramp cow-puncher, who had sung in the chorus at Bayreuth when he was a boy, along with the other peasant boys and girls. Of a Sunday morning he used to sit on his gingham-sheeted bed in the hands' bedroom which opened off the kitchen, cleaning the leather of his boots and saddle, singing the "Prize Song," while my aunt went about her work in the kitchen. She had hovered over him until she had prevailed upon him to join the country church, though his sole fitness for this step, in so far as I could gather, lay in his boyish face and his possession of this divine melody. Shortly afterward, he had gone to town on the Fourth of July, been drunk for several days, lost his money at a faro table, ridden a saddled Texas steer on a bet, and disappeared with a fractured collar-bone. All this my aunt told me huskily, wanderingly, as though she were talking in the weak lapses of illness.

"Well, we have come to better things than the old *Trovatore* at any rate, Aunt Georgie?" I queried, with a well meant effort at jocularity.

Her lip quivered and she hastily put her handkerchief up to her mouth. From behind it she murmured, "And you have been hearing this ever since you left me, Clark?" Her question was the gentlest and saddest of reproaches.

The second half of the program consisted of four numbers from the *Ring,* and closed with Siegfried's funeral march. My aunt wept quietly, but almost continuously, as a shallow vessel overflows in a rain-storm. From time to time her dim eyes looked up at the lights, burning softly under their dull glass globes.

The deluge of sound poured on and on; I

never knew what she found in the shining current of it; I never knew how far it bore her, or past what happy islands. From the trembling of her face I could well believe that before the last number she had been carried out where the myriad graves are, into the gray, nameless burying grounds of the sea; or into some world of death vaster yet, where, from the beginning of the world, hope has lain down with hope and dream with dream and, renouncing, slept.

The concert was over; the people filed out of the hall chattering and laughing, glad to relax and find the living level again, but my kinswoman made no effort to rise. The harpist slipped the green felt cover over his instrument; the flute-players shook the water from their mouth-pieces; the men of the orchestra went out one by one, leaving the stage to the chairs and music stands, empty as a winter cornfield.

I spoke to my aunt. She burst into tears and sobbed pleadingly. “I don’t want to go, Clark, I don’t want to go!”

I understood. For her, just outside the concert hall, lay the black pond with the cattle-tracked bluffs; the tall, unpainted house, with weather-curled boards, naked as a tower; the crook-backed ash seedlings where the dish-cloths hung to dry; the gaunt, moulting turkeys picking up refuse about the kitchen door.

The Egg
by Sherwood Anderson

My father was, I am sure, intended by nature to be a cheerful, kindly man. Until he was thirty-four years old he worked as a farm-hand for a man named Thomas Butterworth whose place lay near the town of Bidwell, Ohio. He had then a horse of his own and on Saturday evenings drove into town to spend a few hours in social intercourse with other farm-hands. In town he drank several glasses of beer and stood about in Ben Head's saloon—crowded on Saturday evenings with visiting farm-hands. Songs were sung and glasses thumped on the bar. At ten o'clock father drove home along a lonely country road, made his horse comfortable for the night and himself went to bed, quite happy in his position in life. He had at that time no notion of trying to rise in the world.

It was in the spring of his thirty-fifth year that father married my mother, then a country school-teacher, and in the following spring I came wriggling and crying into the world.

Something happened to the two people. They became ambitious. The American passion for getting up in the world took possession of them.

It may have been that mother was responsible. Being a school-teacher she had no doubt read books and magazines. She had, I presume, read of how Garfield, Lincoln, and other Americans rose from poverty to fame and greatness and as I lay beside her—in the days of her lying-in—she may have dreamed that I would some day rule men and cities. At any rate she induced father to give up his place as a farm-hand, sell his horse and embark on an independent enterprise of his own. She was a tall silent woman with a long nose and troubled gray eyes. For herself she wanted nothing. For father and myself she was incurably ambitious.

The first venture into which the two people went turned out badly. They rented ten acres of poor stony land on Grigg's Road, eight miles from Bidwell, and launched into chicken raising. I grew into boyhood on the place and got my first impressions of life there. From the beginning they were impressions of disaster and if, in my turn, I am a gloomy man inclined to see the darker side of life, I attribute it to the fact that what should have been for me the happy joyous days of childhood were spent on a chicken farm.

One unversed in such matters can have no notion of the many and tragic things that can happen to a chicken. It is born out of an egg, lives for a few weeks as a tiny fluffy thing such as you will see pictured on Easter cards, then becomes hideously naked, eats quantities of corn and meal bought by the sweat of your father's brow, gets diseases called pip, cholera, and other names, stands looking with stupid eyes at the sun, becomes sick and dies. A few hens and now and then a rooster, intended to serve God's mysterious ends, struggle through to maturity. The hens lay eggs out of which come other chickens and the dreadful cycle is thus made complete. It is all unbelievably complex. Most philosophers must have been raised on chicken farms. One hopes for so much from a chicken and is so dreadfully disillusioned. Small chickens, just setting out on the journey of life, look so bright and alert and they are in fact so dreadfully stupid. They are so much like people they mix one up in one's judgments of life. If disease does not kill them they wait until your expectations are thoroughly aroused and then walk under the wheels of a wagon—to go squashed and dead back to their maker. Vermin infest their youth, and fortunes must be spent for curative powders. In later life I have seen how a literature has been built up on the subject of fortunes to be made out of the raising of chickens. It is intended to be read by the gods who have just eaten of the tree of the knowledge of good and evil. It is a hopeful literature and declares that much may be done by simple ambitious people who own a few hens. Do not be led astray by it. It was not written for you. Go hunt for gold on the frozen hills of Alaska, put your faith in the honesty of a politician, believe if you will that the world is daily growing better and that good will triumph over evil, but do not read and believe the literature that is written concerning the hen. It was not written for you.

I, however, digress. My tale does not primarily concern itself with the hen. If correctly told it will center on the egg. For ten years my father and mother struggled to make our chicken farm pay and then they gave up that struggle and began another. They moved into the town of Bidwell, Ohio and embarked in the restaurant business. After ten years of worry with incubators that did not hatch, and with tiny—and in their own way lovely—balls of fluff that passed on into semi-naked pullethood and from that into dead henhood, we threw all aside and packing our belongings on a wagon drove down Griggs's Road toward Bidwell, a tiny caravan of hope looking for a new place from which to start on our upward journey through life.

We must have been a sad looking lot, not, I fancy, unlike refugees fleeing from a battlefield. Mother and I walked in the road. The wagon that contained our goods had been borrowed for the day from Mr. Albert Griggs, a neighbor. Out of its sides stuck the legs of cheap chairs and at the back of the pile of beds, tables, and boxes filled with kitchen utensils was a crate of live chickens, and on top of that the baby carriage in which I had been wheeled about in my infancy. Why we stuck to the baby carriage I don't know. It was unlikely other children would be born and the wheels were broken. People who have few possessions cling tightly to those they have. That is one of the facts that make life so discouraging.

Father rode on top of the wagon. He was then a bald-headed man of forty-five, a little fat and from long association with mother and the chickens he had become habitually silent and discouraged. All during our ten years on the chicken farm he had worked as a laborer on neighboring farms and most of the money he had earned had been spent on remedies to cure chicken diseases, on Wilmer's White Wonder Cholera Cure or Professor Bidlow's Egg Producer or some other preparations that mother found advertised in the poultry papers. There were two little patches of hair on father's head just above his ears. I remember that as a child I used to sit looking at him when he had gone to sleep in a chair before the stove on Sunday afternoons in the winter. I had at that time already begun to read books and have notions of my own and the bald path that led over the top of his head was, I fancied, something like a broad road, such a road as Caesar might have made on which to lead his legions out of Rome and into the wonders of an unknown world. The tufts of hair that grew above father's ears were, I thought, like forests. I fell into a half-sleeping, half-waking state and dreamed I was a tiny thing going along the road into a far beautiful place where there were no chicken farms and where life was a happy eggless affair.

One might write a book concerning our flight from the chicken farm into town. Mother and I walked the entire eight miles—she to be sure that nothing fell from the wagon and I to see the wonders of the world. On the seat of the wagon beside father was his greatest treasure. I will tell you of that.

On a chicken farm where hundreds and even thousands of chickens come out of eggs, surprising things sometimes happen. Grotesques are born out of eggs as out of people. The accident does not often occur—perhaps once in a thousand births. A chicken is, you see, born that has four legs, two pairs of wings, two heads, or what not. The things do not live. They go quickly back to the hand of their maker that has for a moment trembled. The fact that the poor little things could not live was one of the tragedies of life to father. He had some sort of notion that if he could but bring into henhood or roosterhood a five-legged hen or a two-headed rooster his fortune would be made. He dreamed of taking the wonder about the county fairs and of growing rich by exhibiting it to other farm-hands.

At any rate he saved all the little monstrous things that had been born on our chicken farm. They were preserved in alcohol and put each in its own glass bottle. These he had carefully put into a box and on our journey into town it was carried on the wagon seat beside him. He drove the horses with one hand and with the other clung to the box. When we got to our destination the box was taken down at once and the bottles removed. All during our days as keepers of a restaurant in the town of Bidwell, Ohio, the grotesques in their little glass bottles sat on a shelf back of the counter. Mother sometimes protested but father was a rock on the subject of his treasure. The grotesques were, he declared, valuable. People, he said, liked to look at strange and wonderful things.

Did I say that we embarked in the restaurant business in the town of Bidwell, Ohio? I exaggerated a little. The town itself lay at the foot of a low hill and on the shore of a small river. The railroad did not run through the town and the station was a mile away to the north at a place called Pickleville. There had been a cider mill and pickle factory at the station, but before the time of our coming they had both gone out of business. In the morning and in the evening buses came down to the station along a road called Turner's Pike from the hotel on the main street of Bidwell. Our going to the out of the way place to embark in the restaurant business was mother's idea. She talked of it for a year and then one day went off and rented an empty store building opposite the railroad station. It was her idea that the restaurant would be profitable. Traveling men, she said, would be always waiting around to take trains out of town and town people would come to the station to await incoming trains. They would come to the restaurant to buy pieces of pie and drink coffee. Now that I am older I know that she had another motive in going. She was ambitious for me. She wanted me to rise in the world, to get into a town school and become a man of the towns.

At Pickleville father and mother worked hard as they always had done. At first there was the necessity of putting our place into shape to be a restaurant. That took a month. Father built a shelf on which he put tins of vegetables. He painted a sign on which he put his name in large red letters. Below his name was the sharp command—"EAT HERE" that was so seldom obeyed. A show case was bought and filled with cigars and tobacco. Mother scrubbed the floor and the walls of the room. I went to school in the town and was glad to be away from the farm and from the presence of the discouraged, sad-looking chickens. Still I was not very joyous. In the evening I walked home from school along Turner's Pike and remembered the children I had seen playing in the town school yard. A troop of little girls had gone hopping about and singing. I tried that. Down along the frozen road I went hopping solemnly on one leg. "Hippity Hop To The Barber Shop," I sang shrilly. Then I stopped and looked doubtfully about. I was afraid of being seen in my gay mood. It must have seemed to me that I was doing a thing that should not be done by one who, like myself, had been raised on a chicken farm where death was a daily visitor.

Mother decided that our restaurant should remain open at night. At ten in the evening a passenger train went north past our door followed by a local freight. The freight crew had switching to do in Pickleville, and when the work was done they came to our restaurant for hot coffee and food. Sometimes one of them ordered a fried egg. In the morning at four they returned northbound and again visited us. A little trade began to grow up. Mother slept at night and during the day tended the restaurant and fed our boarders while father slept. He slept in the same bed mother had occupied during the night and I went off to the town of Bidwell and to school. During the long nights, while mother and I slept, father cooked meats that were to go into sandwiches for the lunch baskets of our boarders. Then an idea in regard to getting up in the world came into his head. The American spirit took hold of him. He also became ambitious.

In the long nights when there was little to do father had time to think. That was his undoing. He decided that he had in the past been an unsuccessful man because he had not been cheerful enough and that in the future he would adopt a cheerful outlook on life. In the early morning he came upstairs and got into bed with mother. She woke and the two talked. From my bed in the corner I listened.

It was father's idea that both he and mother should try to entertain the people who came to eat at our restaurant. I cannot now remember his words, but he gave the impression of one about to become in some obscure way a kind of public entertainer. When people, particularly young people from the town of Bidwell, came into our place, as on very rare occasions they did, bright entertaining conversation was to be made. From father's words I gathered that something of the jolly innkeeper effect was to be sought. Mother must have been doubtful from the first, but she said nothing discouraging. It was father's notion that a passion for the company of himself and mother would spring up in the breasts of the younger people of the town of Bidwell. In the evening bright happy groups would come singing down Turner's Pike. They would troop shouting with joy and laughter into our place. There would be song and festivity. I do not mean to give the impression that father spoke so elaborately of the matter. He was as I have said an uncommunicative man. "They want some place to go. I tell you they want some place to go," he said over and over. That was as far as he got. My own imagination has filled in the blanks.

For two or three weeks this notion of father's invaded our house. We did not talk much, but in our daily lives tried earnestly to make smiles take the place of glum looks. Mother smiled at the boarders and I, catching the infection, smiled at our cat. Father became a little feverish in his anxiety to please. There was no doubt, lurking somewhere in him, a touch of the spirit of the showman. He did not waste much of his ammunition on the railroad men he served at night, but seemed to be waiting for a young man or woman from Bidwell to come in to show what he could do. On the counter in the restaurant there was a wire basket kept always filled with eggs, and it must have been before his eyes when the idea of being entertaining was born in his brain. There was something pre-natal about the way eggs kept themselves connected with the development of his idea. At any rate an egg ruined his new impulse in life. Late one night I was awakened by a roar of anger coming from father's throat. Both mother and I sat upright in our beds. With trembling hands she lighted a lamp that stood on a table by her head. Downstairs the front door of our restaurant went shut with a bang and in a few minutes father tramped up the stairs. He held an egg in his hand and his hand trembled as though he were having a chill. There was a half insane light in his eyes. As he stood glaring at us I was sure he intended throwing the egg at either mother or me. Then he laid it gently on the table beside the lamp and dropped on his knees beside mother's bed. He began to cry like a boy and I, carried away by his grief, cried with him. The two of us filled the little upstairs room with our wailing voices. It is ridiculous, but of the picture we made I can remember only the fact that mother's hand continually stroked the bald path that ran across the top of his head. I have forgotten what mother said to him and how she induced him to tell her of what had happened down-stairs. His explanation also has gone out of my mind. I remember only my own grief and fright and the shiny path over father's head glowing in the lamp light as he knelt by the bed.

As to what happened down-stairs. For some unexplainable reason I know the story as well as though I had been a witness to my father's discomfiture. One in time gets to know many unexplainable things. On that evening young Joe Kane, son of a merchant of Bidwell, came to Pickleville to meet his father, who was expected on the ten o'clock evening train from the South. The train was three hours late and Joe came into our place to loaf about and to wait for its arrival. The local freight train came in and the freight crew were fed. Joe was left alone in the restaurant with father.

From the moment he came into our place the Bidwell young man must have been puzzled by my father's actions. It was his notion that father was angry at him for hanging around. He noticed that the restaurant keeper was apparently disturbed by his presence and he thought of going out. However, it began to rain and he did not fancy the long walk to town and back. He bought a five-cent cigar and ordered a cup of coffee. He had a newspaper in his pocket and took it out and began to read. "I'm waiting for the evening train. It's late," he said apologetically.

For a long time father, whom Joe Kane had never seen before, remained silently gazing at his visitor. He was no doubt suffering from an attack of stage fright. As so often happens in life he had thought so much and so often of the situation that now confronted him that he was somewhat nervous in its presence.

For one thing, he did not know what to do with his hands. He thrust one of them nervously over the counter and shook hands with Joe Kane. "How-de-do," he said. Joe Kane put his newspaper down and stared at him. Father's eye lighted on the basket of eggs that sat on the counter and he began to talk. "Well," he began hesitatingly, "well, you have heard of Christopher Columbus, eh?" He seemed to be angry. "That Christopher Columbus was a cheat," he declared emphatically. "He talked of making an egg stand on its end. He talked, he did, and then he went and broke the end of the egg."

My father seemed to his visitor to be beside himself at the duplicity of Christopher Columbus. He muttered and swore. He declared it was wrong to teach children that Christopher Columbus was a great man when, after all, he cheated at the critical moment. He had declared he would make an egg stand on end and then when his bluff had been called he had done a trick. Still grumbling at Columbus, father took an egg from the basket on the counter and began to walk up and down. He rolled the egg between the palms of his hands. He smiled genially. He began to mumble words regarding the effect to be produced on an egg by the electricity that comes out of the human body. He declared that without breaking its shell and by virtue of rolling it back and forth in his hands he could stand the egg on its end. He explained that the warmth of his hands and the gentle rolling movement he gave the egg created a new center of gravity, and Joe Kane was mildly interested. "I have handled thousands of eggs," father said. "No one knows more about eggs than I do."

He stood the egg on the counter and it fell on its side. He tried the trick again and again, each time rolling the egg between the palms of his hands and saying the words regarding the wonders of electricity and the laws of gravity. When after a half hour's effort he did succeed in making the egg stand for a moment he looked up to find that his visitor was no longer watching. By the time he had succeeded in calling Joe Kane's attention to the success of his effort the egg had again rolled over and lay on its side.

Afire with the showman's passion and at the same time a good deal disconcerted by the failure of his first effort, father now took the bottles containing the poultry monstrosities down from their place on the shelf and began to show them to his visitor. "How would you like to have seven legs and two heads like this fellow?" he asked, exhibiting the most remarkable of his treasures. A cheerful smile played over his face. He reached over the counter and tried to slap Joe Kane on the shoulder as he had seen men do in

Ben Head's saloon when he was a young farmhand and drove to town on Saturday evenings. His visitor was made a little ill by the sight of the body of the terribly deformed bird floating in the alcohol in the bottle and got up to go. Coming from behind the counter father took hold of the young man's arm and led him back to his seat. He grew a little angry and for a moment had to turn his face away and force himself to smile. Then he put the bottles back on the shelf. In an outburst of generosity he fairly compelled Joe Kane to have a fresh cup of coffee and another cigar at his expense. Then he took a pan and filling it with vinegar, taken from a jug that sat beneath the counter, he declared himself about to do a new trick. "I will heat this egg in this pan of vinegar," he said. "Then I will put it through the neck of a bottle without breaking the shell. When the egg is inside the bottle it will resume its normal shape and the shell will become hard again. Then I will give the bottle with the egg in it to you. You can take it about with you wherever you go. People will want to know how you got the egg in the bottle. Don't tell them. Keep them guessing. That is the way to have fun with this trick."

Father grinned and winked at his visitor. Joe Kane decided that the man who confronted him was mildly insane but harmless. He drank the cup of coffee that had been given him and began to read his paper again. When the egg had been heated in vinegar father carried it on a spoon to the counter and going into a back room got an empty bottle. He was angry because his visitor did not watch him as he began to do his trick, but nevertheless went cheerfully to work. For a long time he struggled, trying to get the egg to go through the neck of the bottle. He put the pan of vinegar back on the stove, intending to reheat the egg, then picked it up and burned his fingers. After a second bath in the hot vinegar, the shell of the egg had been softened a little but not enough for his purpose. He worked and worked and a spirit of desperate determination took possession of him. When he thought that at last the trick was about to be consummated the delayed train came in at the station and Joe Kane started to go nonchalantly out at the door. Father made a last desperate effort to conquer the egg and make it do the thing that would establish his reputation as one who knew how to entertain guests who came into his restaurant. He worried the egg. He attempted to be somewhat rough with it. He swore and the sweat stood out on his forehead. The egg broke under his hand. When the contents spurted over his clothes, Joe Kane, who had stopped at the door, turned and laughed.

A roar of anger rose from my father's throat. He danced and shouted a string of inarticulate words. Grabbing another egg from the basket on the counter, he threw it, just missing the head of the young man as he dodged through the door and escaped.

Father came upstairs to mother and me with an egg in his hand. I do not know what he intended to do. I imagine he had some idea of destroying it, of destroying all eggs, and that he intended to let mother and me see him begin. When, however, he got into the presence of mother, something happened to him. He laid the egg gently on the table and dropped on his knees by the bed as I have already explained. He later decided to close the restaurant for the night and to come upstairs and get into bed. When he did so he blew out the light and after much muttered conversation both he and mother went to sleep. I suppose I went to sleep also, but my sleep was troubled. I awoke at dawn and for a long time looked at the egg that lay on the table. I wondered why eggs had to be and why from the egg came the hen who again laid the egg. The question got into my blood. It has stayed there, I imagine, because I am the son of my father. At any rate, the problem remains unsolved in my mind. And that, I conclude, is but another evidence of the complete and final triumph of the egg—at least as far as my family is concerned.

The Diamond as Big as the Ritz

by F. Scott Fitzgerald

John T. Unger came from a family that had been well known in Hades—a small town on the Mississippi River—for several generations. John's father had held the amateur golf championship through many a heated contest; Mrs. Unger was known "from hot-box to hot-bed," as the local phrase went, for her political addresses; and young John T. Unger, who had just turned sixteen, had danced all the latest dances from New York before he put on long trousers. And now, for a certain time, he was to be away from home. That respect for a New England education which is the bane of all provincial places, which drains them yearly of their most promising young men, had seized upon his parents. Nothing would suit them but that he should go to St. Midas' School near Boston—Hades was too small to hold their darling and gifted son.

Now in Hades—as you know if you ever have been there—the names of the more fashionable preparatory schools and colleges mean very little. The inhabitants have been so long out of the world that, though they make a show of keeping up to date in dress and manners and literature, they depend to a great extent on hearsay, and a function that in Hades would be considered elaborate would doubtless be hailed by a Chicago beef-princess as "perhaps a little tacky."

John T. Unger was on the eve of departure. Mrs. Unger, with maternal fatuity, packed his trunks full of linen suits and electric fans, and Mr. Unger presented his son with an asbestos pocket-book stuffed with money.

"Remember, you are always welcome here," he said. "You can be sure, boy, that we'll keep the home fires burning."

"I know," answered John huskily.

"Don't forget who you are and where you come from," continued his father proudly, "and you can do nothing to harm you. You are an Unger—from Hades."

So the old man and the young shook hands and John walked away with tears streaming from his eyes. Ten minutes later he had passed outside the city limits, and he stopped to glance back for the last time. Over the gates the old-fashioned Victorian motto seemed strangely attractive to him. His father had tried time and time again to have it changed to something with a little more push and verve about it, such as "Hades—Your Opportunity," or else a plain "Welcome" sign set over a hearty handshake pricked out in electric lights. The old motto was a little depressing, Mr. Unger had thought—but now. . . .

So John took his look and then set his face resolutely toward his destination. And, as he turned away, the lights of Hades against the sky seemed full of a warm and passionate beauty.

St. Midas' School is half an hour from Boston in a Rolls-Pierce motor-car. The actual distance will never be known, for no one, except John T. Unger, had ever arrived there save in a Rolls-Pierce and probably no one ever will again. St. Midas' is the most expensive and the most exclusive boys' preparatory school in the world.

John's first two years there passed pleasantly. The fathers of all the boys were money-kings and John spent his summers visiting at fashionable resorts. While he was very fond of all the boys he visited, their fathers struck him as being much of a piece, and in his boyish way he often wondered at their exceeding sameness. When he told them where his home was they would ask jovially, "Pretty hot down there?" and John would muster a faint smile and answer, "It certainly is." His response would have been heartier had they not all made this joke—at best varying it with, "Is it hot enough for you down there?" which he hated just as much.

In the middle of his second year at school, a quiet, handsome boy named Percy Washington had been put in John's form. The newcomer was pleasant in his manner and exceedingly well dressed even for St. Midas', but for some reason he kept aloof from the other boys. The only person with whom he was intimate was John T. Unger, but even to John he was entirely uncommunicative concerning his home or his family. That he was wealthy went without saying, but beyond a few such deductions John knew little of his friend, so it promised rich confectionery for his curiosity when Percy invited him to spend the summer at his home "in the West." He accepted, without hesitation.

It was only when they were in the train that Percy became, for the first time, rather communicative. One day while they were eating lunch in the dining-car and discussing the imperfect characters of several of the boys at school, Percy suddenly changed his tone and made an abrupt remark.

"My father," he said, "is by far the richest man in the world."

"Oh," said John, politely. He could think of

no answer to make to this confidence. He considered "That's very nice," but it sounded hollow and was on the point of saying, "Really?" but refrained since it would seem to question Percy's statement. And such an astounding statement could scarcely be questioned.

"By far the richest," repeated Percy.

"I was reading in the *World Almanac,*" began John, "that there was one man in America with an income of over five million a year and four men with incomes of over three million a year, and——"

"Oh, they're nothing." Percy's mouth was a half-moon of scorn. "Catch-penny capitalists, financial small-fry, petty merchants and money-lenders. My father could buy them out and not know he'd done it."

"But how does he——"

"Why haven't they put down *his* income tax? Because he doesn't pay any. At least he pays a little one—but he doesn't pay any on his *real* income."

"He must be very rich," said John simply. "I'm glad. I like very rich people.

"The richer a fella is, the better I like him." There was a look of passionate frankness upon his dark face. "I visited the Schnlitzer-Murphys last Easter. Vivian Schnlitzer-Murphy had rubies as big as hen's eggs, and sapphires that were like globes with lights inside them——"

"I love jewels," agreed Percy enthusiastically. "Of course I wouldn't want any one at school to know about it, but I've got quite a collection myself. I used to collect them instead of stamps."

"And diamonds," continued John eagerly. "The Schnlitzer-Murphys had diamonds as big as walnuts——"

"That's nothing." Percy had leaned forward and dropped his voice to a low whisper. "That's nothing at all. My father has a diamond bigger than the Ritz-Carlton Hotel."

II

The Montana sunset lay between two mountains like a gigantic bruise from which dark arteries spread themselves over a poisoned sky. An immense distance under the sky crouched the village of Fish, minute, dismal, and forgotten. There were twelve men, so it was said, in the village of Fish, twelve sombre and inexplicable souls who sucked a lean milk from the almost literally bare rock upon which a mysterious populatory force had begotten them. They had become a race apart, these twelve men of Fish, like some species developed by an early whim of nature, which on second thought had abandoned them to struggle and extermination.

Out of the blue-black bruise in the distance crept a long line of moving lights upon the desolation of the land, and the twelve men of Fish gathered like ghosts at the shanty depot to watch the passing of the seven o'clock train, the Transcontinental Express from Chicago. Six times or so a year the Transcontinental Express, through some inconceivable jurisdiction, stopped at the village of Fish, and when this occurred a figure or so would disembark, mount into a buggy that always appeared from out of the dusk, and drive off toward the bruised sunset. The observation of this pointless and preposterous phenomenon had become a sort of cult among the men of Fish. To observe, that was all; there remained in them none of the vital quality of illusion which would make them wonder or speculate, else a religion might have grown up around these mysterious visitations. But the men of Fish were beyond all religion—the barest and most savage tenets of even Christianity could gain no foothold on that barren rock—so there was no altar, no priest, no sacrifice; only each night at seven the silent concourse by the shanty depot, a congregation who lifted up a prayer of dim, anæmic wonder.

On this June night, the Great Brakeman, whom, had they deified any one, they might well have chosen as their celestial protagonist, had ordained that the seven o'clock train should leave its human (or inhuman) deposit at Fish. At two minutes after seven Percy Washington and John T. Unger disembarked, hurried past the spellbound, the agape, the fearsome eyes of the twelve men of Fish, mounted into a buggy which had obviously appeared from nowhere, and drove away.

After half an hour, when the twilight had coagulated into dark, the silent negro who was driving the buggy hailed an opaque body somewhere ahead of them in the gloom. In response to his cry, it turned upon them a luminous disk which regarded them like a malignant eye out of the unfathomable night. As they came closer, John saw that it was the tail-light of an immense automobile, larger and more magnificent than any he had ever seen. Its body was of gleaming metal richer than nickel and lighter than silver, and the hubs of the wheels were studded with iridescent geometric figures of green and yellow—John did not dare to guess whether they were glass or jewel.

Two negroes, dressed in glittering livery such as one sees in pictures of royal processions in London, were standing at attention beside the car and as the two young men dismounted from the buggy they were greeted in some language which the guest could not understand, but which seemed to be an extreme form of the Southern negro's dialect.

"Get in," said Percy to his friend, as their trunks were tossed to the ebony roof of the limousine. "Sorry we had to bring you this far in that buggy, but of course it wouldn't do for the people on the train or those Godforsaken fellas in Fish to see this automobile."

"Gosh! What a car!" This ejaculation was provoked by its interior. John saw that the upholstery consisted of a thousand minute and exquisite tapestries of silk, woven with jewels and embroideries, and set upon a background of cloth of gold. The two armchair seats in which the boys luxuriated were covered with stuff that resembled duvetyn, but seemed woven in numberless colors of the ends of ostrich feathers.

"What a car!" cried John again, in amazement.

"This thing?" Percy laughed. "Why, it's just an old junk we use for a station wagon."

By this time they were gliding along through the darkness toward the break between the two mountains.

"We'll be there in an hour and a half," said Percy, looking at the clock. "I may as well tell you it's not going to be like anything you ever saw before."

If the car was any indication of what John would see, he was prepared to be astonished indeed. The simple piety prevalent in Hades has the earnest worship of and respect for riches as the first article of its creed—had John felt otherwise than radiantly humble before them, his parents would have turned away in horror at the blasphemy.

They had now reached and were entering the break between the two mountains and almost immediately the way became much rougher.

"If the moon shone down here, you'd see that we're in a big gulch," said Percy, trying to peer out of the window. He spoke a few words into the mouthpiece and immediately the footman turned on a search-light and swept the hillsides with an immense beam.

"Rocky, you see. An ordinary car would be knocked to pieces in half an hour. In fact, it'd take a tank to navigate it unless you knew the way. You notice we're going uphill now."

They were obviously ascending, and within a few minutes the car was crossing a high rise, where they caught a glimpse of a pale moon newly risen in the distance. The car stopped suddenly and several figures took shape out of the dark beside it—these were negroes also. Again the two young men were saluted in the same dimly recognizable dialect; then the negroes set to work and four immense cables dangling from overhead were attached with hooks to the hubs of the great jeweled wheels. At a resounding, "Hey-yah!" John felt the car being lifted slowly from the ground—up and up—clear of the tallest rocks on both sides—then higher, until he could see a wavy, moonlit valley stretched out before him in sharp contrast to the quagmire of rocks that they had just left. Only on one side was there still rock—and then suddenly there was no rock beside them or anywhere around.

It was apparent that they had surmounted some immense knife-blade of stone, projecting perpendicularly into the air. In a moment they were going down again, and finally with a soft bump they were landed upon the smooth earth.

"The worst is over," said Percy, squinting out the window. "It's only five miles from here, and our own road—tapestry brick—all the way. This belongs to us. This is where the United States ends, father says."

"Are we in Canada?"

"We are not. We're in the middle of the Montana Rockies. But you are now on the only five square miles of land in the country that's never been surveyed."

"Why hasn't it? Did they forget it?"

"No," said Percy, grinning, "they tried to do it three times. The first time my grandfather corrupted a whole department of the State survey; the second time he had the official maps of the United States tinkered with—that held them for fifteen years. The last time was harder. My father fixed it so that their compasses were in the strongest magnetic field ever artificially set up. He had a whole set of surveying instruments made with a slight defection that would allow for this territory not to appear, and he substituted them for the ones that were to be used. Then he had a river deflected and he had what looked like a village built up on its banks—so that they'd see it, and think it was a town ten miles farther up the valley. There's only one thing my father's afraid of," he concluded, "only one thing in the world that could be used to find us out."

"What's that?"

Percy sank his voice to a whisper.

"Aeroplanes," he breathed. "We've got half a dozen anti-aircraft guns and we've arranged it so far—but there've been a few deaths and a great many prisoners. Not that we mind *that,* you know, father and I, but it upsets mother and the girls, and there's always the chance that some time we won't be able to arrange it."

Shreds and tatters of chinchilla, courtesy clouds in the green moon's heaven, were passing the green moon like precious Eastern stuffs paraded for the inspection of some Tartar Khan. It seemed to John that it was day, and that he was looking at some lads sailing above him in the air, showering down tracts and patent medicine circulars, with their messages of hope for despairing, rockbound hamlets. It seemed to him that he could see them look down out of the clouds and stare—and stare at whatever there was to stare at in this place whither he was bound—What then? Were they induced to land by some insidious device there to be immured far from patent medicines and from tracts until the judgment day—or, should they fail to fall into the trap, did a quick puff of smoke and the sharp round of a splitting shell bring them drooping to earth—and "upset" Percy's mother and sisters. John shook his head and the wraith of a hollow laugh issued silently from his parted lips. What desperate transaction lay hidden here? What a moral expedient of a bizarre Crœsus? What terrible and golden mystery? . . .

The chinchilla clouds had drifted past now and outside the Montana night was bright as day. The tapestry brick of the road was smooth to the tread of the great tires as they rounded a still, moonlit lake; they passed into darkness for a moment, a pine grove, pungent and cool, then they came out into a broad avenue of lawn and John's exclamation of pleasure was simultaneous with Percy's taciturn "We're home."

Full in the light of the stars, an exquisite château rose from the borders of the lake, climbed in marble radiance half the height of an adjoining mountain, then melted in grace, in perfect symmetry, in translucent feminine languor, into the massed darkness of a forest of pine. The many towers, the slender tracery of the sloping parapets, the chiselled wonder of a thousand yellow windows with their oblongs and hectagons and triangles of golden light, the shattered softness of the intersecting planes of star-shine and blue shade, all trembled on John's spirit like a chord of music. On one of the towers, the tallest, the blackest at its base, an arrangement of exterior lights at the top made a sort of floating fairyland—and as John gazed up in warm enchantment the faint acciaccare sound of violins drifted down in a rococo harmony that was like nothing he had ever heard before. Then in a moment the car stopped before wide, high marble steps around which the night air was fragrant with a host of flowers. At the top of the steps two great doors swung silently open and amber light flooded out upon the darkness, silhouetting the figure of an exquisite lady with black, high-piled hair, who held out her arms toward them.

"Mother," Percy was saying, "this is my friend, John Unger, from Hades."

Afterward John remembered that first night as a daze of many colors, of quick sensory impressions, of music soft as a voice in love, and of the beauty of things, lights and shadows, and motions and faces. There was a white-haired man who stood drinking a many-hued cordial from a crystal thimble set on a golden stem. There was a girl with a flowery face, dressed like Titania with braided sapphires in her hair. There was a room where the solid, soft gold of the walls yielded to the pressure of his hand, and a room that was like a platonic conception of the ultimate prison—ceiling, floor, and all, it was lined with an unbroken mass of diamonds, diamonds of every size and shape, until, lit with tall violet lamps in the corners, it dazzled the eyes with a whiteness that could be compared only with itself, beyond human wish or dream.

Through a maze of these rooms the two boys wandered. Sometimes the floor under their feet would flame in brilliant patterns from lighting below, patterns of barbaric clashing colors, of pastel delicacy, of sheer whiteness, or of subtle and intricate mosaic, surely from some mosque on the Adriatic Sea. Sometimes beneath layers of thick crystal he would see blue or green water swirling, inhabited by vivid fish and growths of rainbow foliage. Then they would be treading on furs of every texture and color or along corridors of palest ivory, unbroken as though carved complete from the gigantic tusks of dinosaurs extinct before the age of man. . . .

Then a hazily remembered transition, and they were at dinner—where each plate was of two almost imperceptible layers of solid diamond between which was curiously worked a filigree of emerald design, a shaving sliced from green air. Music, plangent and unobtrusive, drifted down through far corridors—his chair, feathered and curved insidiously to his back, seemed to engulf and overpower him as he drank his first glass of port. He tried drowsily to answer a question that had been asked him, but the honeyed luxury that clasped his body added to the illusion of sleep—jewels, fabrics, wines, and metals blurred before his eyes into a sweet mist. . . .

"Yes," he replied with a polite effort, "it certainly is hot enough for me down there."

He managed to add a ghostly laugh; then, without movement, without resistance, he seemed to float off and away, leaving an iced dessert that was pink as a dream. . . . He fell asleep.

When he awoke he knew that several hours had passed. He was in a great quiet room with ebony walls and a dull illumination that was too faint, too subtle, to be called a light. His young host was standing over him.

"You fell asleep at dinner," Percy was saying. "I nearly did, too—it was such a treat to be comfortable again after this year of school. Servants undressed and bathed you while you were sleeping."

"Is this a bed or a cloud?" sighed John. "Percy, Percy—before you go, I want to apologize."

"For what?"

"For doubting you when you said you had a diamond as big as the Ritz-Carlton Hotel."

Percy smiled.

"I thought you didn't believe me. It's that mountain, you know."

"What mountain?"

"The mountain the château rests on. It's not very big, for a mountain. But except about fifty feet of sod and gravel on top it's solid diamond. *One* diamond, one cubic mile without a flaw. Aren't you listening? Say——"

But John T. Unger had again fallen asleep.

III

Morning. As he awoke he perceived drowsily that the room had at the same moment become dense with sunlight. The ebony panels of one wall had slid aside on a sort of track, leaving his chamber half open to the day. A large negro in a white uniform stood beside his bed.

"Good-evening," muttered John, summoning his brains from the wild places.

"Good-morning, sir. Are you ready for your bath, sir? Oh, don't get up—I'll put you in, if you'll just unbutton your pajamas—there. Thank you, sir."

John lay quietly as his pajamas were removed—he was amused and delighted; he expected to be lifted like a child by this black Gargantua who was tending him, but nothing of the sort happened; instead he felt the bed tilt up slowly on its side—he began to roll, startled at first, in the direction of the wall, but when he reached the wall its drapery gave way, and sliding two yards farther down a fleecy incline he plumped gently into water the same temperature as his body.

He looked about him. The runway or rollway on which he had arrived had folded gently back into place. He had been projected into another chamber and was sitting in a sunken bath with his head just above the level of the floor. All about him, lining the walls of the room and the sides and bottom of the bath itself, was a blue aquarium, and gazing through the crystal surface on which he sat, he could see fish swimming among amber lights and even gliding without curiosity past his outstretched toes, which were separated from them only by the thickness of the crystal. From overhead, sunlight came down through sea-green glass.

"I suppose, sir, that you'd like hot rosewater and soapsuds this morning, sir—and perhaps cold salt water to finish."

The negro was standing beside him.

"Yes," agreed John, smiling inanely, "as you please." Any idea of ordering this bath according to his own meager standards of living would have been priggish and not a little wicked.

The negro pressed a button and a warm rain began to fall, apparently from overhead, but really, so John discovered after a moment, from a fountain arrangement near by. The water turned to a pale rose color and jets of liquid soap spurted into it from four miniature walrus heads at the corners of the bath. In a moment a dozen little paddle-wheels, fixed to the sides, had churned the mixture into a radiant rainbow of pink foam which enveloped him softly with its delicious lightness, and burst in shining, rosy bubbles here and there about him.

"Shall I turn on the moving-picture machine, sir?" suggested the negro deferentially. "There's a good one-reel comedy in this machine today, or I can put in a serious piece in a moment, if you prefer it."

"No, thanks," answered John, politely but firmly. He was enjoying his bath too much to desire any distraction. But distraction came. In a moment he was listening intently to the sound of flutes from just outside, flutes dripping a melody that was like a waterfall, cool and green as the room itself, accompanying a frothy piccolo, in play more fragile than the lace of suds that covered and charmed him.

After a cold salt-water bracer and a cold fresh finish, he stepped out and into a fleecy robe, and upon a couch covered with the same material he was rubbed with oil, alcohol, and spice. Later he sat in a voluptuous chair while he was shaved and his hair was trimmed.

"Mr. Percy is waiting in your sitting-room,"

said the negro, when these operations were finished. "My name is Gygsum, Mr. Unger, sir. I am to see to Mr. Unger every morning."

John walked out into the brisk sunshine of his living-room, where he found breakfast waiting for him and Percy, gorgeous in white kid knickerbockers, smoking in an easy chair.

IV

This is a story of the Washington family as Percy sketched it for John during breakfast.

The father of the present Mr. Washington had been a Virginian, a direct descendant of George Washington, and Lord Baltimore. At the close of the Civil War he was a twenty-five-year-old Colonel with a played-out plantation and about a thousand dollars in gold.

Fitz-Norman Culpepper Washington, for that was the young Colonel's name, decided to present the Virginia estate to his younger brother and go West. He selected two dozen of the most faithful blacks, who, of course, worshipped him, and bought twenty-five tickets to the West, where he intended to take out land in their names and start a sheep and cattle ranch.

When he had been in Montana for less than a month and things were going very poorly indeed, he stumbled on his great discovery. He had lost his way when riding in the hills, and after a day without food he began to grow hungry. As he was without his rifle, he was forced to pursue a squirrel, and in the course of the pursuit he noticed that it was carrying something shiny in its mouth. Just before it vanished into its hole—for Providence did not intend that this squirrel should alleviate his hunger—it dropped its burden. Sitting down to consider the situation Fitz-Norman's eye was caught by a gleam in the grass beside him. In ten seconds he had completely lost his appetite and gained one hundred thousand dollars. The squirrel, which had refused with annoying persistence to become food, had made him a present of a large and perfect diamond.

Late that night he found his way to camp and twelve hours later all the males among his darkies were back by the squirrel hole digging furiously at the side of the mountain. He told them he had discovered a rhinestone mine, and, as only one or two of them had ever seen even a small diamond before, they believed him, without question. When the magnitude of his discovery became apparent to him, he found himself in a quandary. The mountain was *a* diamond—it was literally nothing else but solid diamond. He filled four saddle bags full of glittering samples and started on horseback for St. Paul. There he managed to dispose of half a dozen small stones—when he tried a larger one a storekeeper fainted and Fitz-Norman was arrested as a public disturber. He escaped from jail and caught the train for New York, where he sold a few medium-sized diamonds and received in exchange about two hundred thousand dollars in gold. But he did not dare to produce any exceptional gems—in fact, he left New York just in time. Tremendous excitement had been created in jewelry circles, not so much by the size of his diamonds as by their appearance in the city from mysterious sources. Wild rumors became current that a diamond mine had been discovered in the Catskills, on the Jersey coast, on Long Island, beneath Washington Square. Excursion trains, packed with men carrying picks and shovels, began to leave New York hourly, bound for various neighboring El Dorados. But by that time young Fitz-Norman was on his way back to Montana.

By the end of a fortnight he had estimated that the diamond in the mountain was approximately equal in quantity to all the rest of the diamonds known to exist in the world. There was no valuing it by any regular computation, however, for it was *one solid diamond*—and if it were offered for sale not only would the bottom fall out of the market, but also, if the value should vary with its size in the usual arithmetical progression, there would not be enough gold in the world to buy a tenth part of it. And what could any one do with a diamond that size?

It was an amazing predicament. He was, in one sense, the richest man that ever lived—and yet was he worth anything at all? If his secret should transpire there was no telling to what measures the Government might resort in order to prevent a panic, in gold as well as in jewels. They might take over the claim immediately and institute a monopoly.

There was no alternative—he must market his mountain in secret. He sent South for his younger brother and put him in charge of his colored following—darkies who had never realized that slavery was abolished. To make sure of this, he read them a proclamation that he had composed, which announced that General Forrest had reorganized the shattered Southern armies and defeated the North in one pitched battle. The negroes believed him implicitly. They passed a vote declaring it a good thing and held revival services immediately.

Fitz-Norman himself set out for foreign parts with one hundred thousand dollars and two trunks filled with rough diamonds of all sizes. He sailed for Russia in a Chinese junk and six months after his departure from Montana he was in St. Petersburg. He took obscure lodgings and called immediately upon the court jeweller, announcing that he had a diamond for the Czar. He remained in St. Petersburg for two weeks, in constant danger of being murdered, living from lodging to lodging, and afraid to visit his trunks more than three or four times during the whole fortnight.

On his promise to return in a year with larger and finer stones, he was allowed to leave for India. Before he left, however, the Court Treasurers had deposited to his credit, in American banks, the sum of fifteen million dollars—under four different aliases.

He returned to America in 1868, having been gone a little over two years. He had visited the capitals of twenty-two countries and talked with five emperors, eleven kings, three princes, a shah, a khan, and a sultan. At that time Fitz-Norman estimated his own wealth at one billion dollars. One fact worked consistently against the disclosure of his secret. No one of his larger diamonds remained in the public eye for a week before being invested with a history of enough fatalities, amours, revolutions, and wars to have occupied it from the days of the first Babylonian Empire.

From 1870 until his death in 1900, the history of Fitz-Norman Washington was a long epic in gold. There were side issues, of course—he evaded the surveys, he married a Virginia lady, by whom he had a single son, and he was compelled, due to a series of unfortunate complications, to murder his brother, whose unfortunate habit of drinking himself into an indiscreet stupor had several times endangered their safety. But very few other murders stained these happy years of progress and expansion.

Just before he died he changed his policy, and with all but a few million dollars of his outside wealth bought up rare minerals in bulk, which he deposited in the safety vaults of banks all over the world, marked as bric-à-brac. His son, Braddock Tarleton Washington, followed this policy on an even more tensive scale. The minerals were converted into the rarest of all elements—radium—so that the equivalent of a billion dollars in gold could be placed in a receptacle no bigger than a cigar box.

When Fitz-Norman had been dead three years his son, Braddock, decided that the business had gone far enough. The amount of wealth that he and his father had taken out of the mountain was beyond all exact computation. He kept a note-book in cipher in which he set down the approximate quantity of radium in each of the thousand banks he patronized, and recorded the alias under which it was held. Then he did a very simple thing—he sealed up the mine.

He sealed up the mine. What had been taken out of it would support all the Washingtons yet to be born in unparalleled luxury for generations. His one care must be the protection of his secret, lest in the possible panic attendant on its discovery he should be reduced with all the property-holders in the world to utter poverty.

This was the family among whom John T. Unger was staying. This was the story he heard in his silver-walled living-room the morning after his arrival.

V

After breakfast, John found his way out the great marble entrance, and looked curiously at the scene before him. The whole valley, from the diamond mountain to the steep granite cliff five miles away, still gave off a breath of golden haze which hovered idly above the fine sweep of lawns and lakes and gardens. Here and there clusters of elms made delicate groves of shade, contrasting strangely with the tough masses of pine forest that held the hills in a grip of dark-blue green. Even as John looked he saw three fawns in single file patter out from one clump about a half mile away and disappear with awkward gayety into the black-ribbed half-light of another. John would not have been surprised to see a goat-foot piping his way among the trees or to catch a glimpse of pink nymph-skin and flying yellow hair between the greenest of the green leaves.

In some such cool hope he descended the marble steps, disturbing faintly the sleep of two silky Russian wolfhounds at the bottom, and set off along a walk of white and blue brick that seemed to lead in no particular direction.

He was enjoying himself as much as he was able. It is youth's felicity as well as its insufficiency that it can never live in the present, but must always be measuring up the day against its own radiantly imagined future—flowers and gold, girls and stars, they are only prefigurations and prophecies of that incomparable, unattainable young dream.

John rounded a soft corner where the massed rosebushes filled the air with heavy scent, and struck off across a park toward a patch of moss under some trees. He had never lain upon moss, and he wanted to see whether it was really soft enough to justify the use of its name as an adjective. Then he saw a girl coming toward him over the grass. She was the most beautiful person he had ever seen.

She was dressed in a white little gown that came just below her knees, and a wreath of mignonettes clasped with blue slices of sapphire bound up her hair. Her pink bare feet scattered the dew before them as she came. She was younger than John—not more than sixteen.

"Hello," she cried softly, "I'm Kismine."

She was much more than that to John already. He advanced toward her, scarcely moving as he drew near lest he should tread on her bare toes.

"You haven't met me," said her soft voice. Her

blue eyes added, "Oh, but you've missed a great deal!" . . . "You met my sister, Jasmine, last night. I was sick with lettuce poisoning," went on her soft voice, and her eyes continued, "and when I'm sick I'm sweet—and when I'm well."

"You have made an enormous impression on me," said John's eyes, "and I'm not so slow myself"—"How do you do?" said his voice. "I hope you're better this morning."—"You darling," added his eyes tremulously.

John observed that they had been walking along the path. On her suggestion they sat down together upon the moss, the softness of which he failed to determine.

He was critical about women. A single defect—a thick ankle, a hoarse voice, a glass eye—was enough to make him utterly indifferent. And here for the first time in his life he was beside a girl who seemed to him the incarnation of physical perfection.

"Are you from the East?" asked Kismine with charming interest.

"No," answered John simply. "I'm from Hades."

Either she had never heard of Hades, or she could think of no pleasant comment to make upon it, for she did not discuss it further.

"I'm going East to school this fall," she said. "D'you think I'll like it? I'm going to New York to Miss Bulge's. It's very strict, but you see over the weekends I'm going to live at home with the family in our New York house, because father heard that the girls had to go walking two by two."

"Your father wants you to be proud," observed John.

"We are," she answered, her eyes shining with dignity. "None of us has ever been punished. Father said we never should be. Once when my sister Jasmine was a little girl she pushed him down-stairs and he just got up and limped away.

"Mother was—well, a little startled," continued Kismine, "when she heard that you were from—from where you *are* from, you know. She said that when she was a young girl—but then, you see, she's a Spaniard and old-fashioned."

"Do you spend much time out here?" asked John, to conceal the fact that he was somewhat hurt by this remark. It seemed an unkind allusion to his provincialism.

"Percy and Jasmine and I are here every summer, but next summer Jasmine is going to Newport. She's coming out in London a year from this fall. She'll be presented at court."

"Do you know," began John hesitantly, "you're much more sophisticated than I thought you were when I first saw you?"

"Oh, no, I'm not," she exclaimed hurriedly. "Oh, I wouldn't think of being. I think that sophisticated young people are *terribly* common, don't you? I'm not at all, really. If you say I am, I'm going to cry."

She was so distressed that her lip was trembling. John was impelled to protest:

"I didn't mean that; I only said it to tease you."

"Because I wouldn't mind if I *were,*" she persisted. "but I'm *not.* I'm very innocent and girlish. I never smoke, or drink, or read anything except poetry. I know scarcely any mathematics or chemistry. I dress *very* simply—in fact, I scarcely dress at all. I think sophisticated is the last thing you can say about me. I believe that girls ought to enjoy their youths in a wholesome way."

"I do, too," said John heartily.

Kismine was cheerful again. She smiled at him, and a still-born tear dripped from the corner of one blue eye.

"I like you," she whispered, intimately. "Are you going to spend all your time with Percy while you're here, or will you be nice to me? Just think—I'm absolutely fresh ground. I've never had a boy in love with me in all my life. I've never been allowed even to *see* boys alone—except Percy. I came all the way out here into this grove hoping to run into you, where the family wouldn't be around."

Deeply flattered, John bowed from the hips as he had been taught at dancing school in Hades.

"We'd better go now," said Kismine sweetly. "I have to be with mother at eleven. You haven't asked me to kiss you once. I thought boys always did that nowadays."

John drew himself up proudly.

"Some of them do," he answered, "but not me. Girls don't do that sort of thing—in Hades."

Side by side they walked back toward the house.

VI

John stood facing Mr. Braddock Washington in the full sunlight. The elder man was about forty with a proud, vacuous face, intelligent eyes, and a robust figure. In the mornings he smelt of horses—the best horses. He carried a plain walking-stick of gray birch with a single large opal for a grip. He and Percy were showing John around.

"The slaves' quarters are there." His walking-stick indicated a cloister of marble on their left that ran in graceful Gothic along the side of the mountain. "In my youth I was distracted for a while from the business of life by a period of absurd idealism. During that time they lived in luxury. For instance, I equipped every one of their rooms with a tile bath."

"I suppose," ventured John, with an ingratiating laugh, "that they used the bathtubs to keep coal in. Mr. Schnlitzer-Murphy told me that once he——"

"The opinions of Mr. Schnlitzer-Murphy are of little importance, I should imagine," interrupted Braddock Washington, coldly. "My slaves did not keep coal in their bathtubs. They had orders to bathe every day, and they did. If they hadn't I might have ordered a sulphuric acid shampoo. I discontinued the baths for quite another reason. Several of them caught cold and died. Water is not good for certain races—except as a beverage."

John laughed, and then decided to nod his head in sober agreement. Braddock Washington made him uncomfortable.

"All these negroes are descendants of the ones my father brought North with him. There are about two hundred and fifty now. You notice that they've lived so long apart from the world that their original dialect has become an almost indistinguishable patois. We bring a few of them up to speak English—my secretary and two or three of the house servants.

"This is the golf course," he continued, as they strolled along the velvet winter grass. "It's all a green, you see—no fairway, no rough, no hazards."

He smiled pleasantly at John.

"Many men in the cage, father?" asked Percy suddenly.

Braddock Washington stumbled, and let forth an involuntary curse.

"One less than there should be," he ejaculated darkly—and then added after a moment, "We've had difficulties."

"Mother was telling me," exclaimed Percy, "that Italian teacher——"

"A ghastly error," said Braddock Washington angrily. "But of course there's a good chance that we may have got him. Perhaps he fell somewhere in the woods or stumbled over a cliff. And then there's always the probability that if he did get away his story wouldn't be believed. Nevertheless, I've had two dozen men looking for him in different towns around here."

"And no luck?"

"Some. Fourteen of them reported to my agent that they'd each killed a man answering to that description, but of course it was probably only the reward they were after——"

He broke off. They had come to a large cavity in the earth about the circumference of a merry-go-round and covered by a strong iron grating. Braddock Washington beckoned to John, and pointed his cane down through the grating. John stepped to the edge and gazed. Immediately his ears were assailed by a wild clamor from below.

"Come on down to Hell!"

"Hello, kiddo, how's the air up there?"

"Hey! Throw us a rope!"

"Got an old doughnut, Buddy, or a couple of second-hand sandwiches?"

"Say, fella, if you'll push down that guy you're with, we'll show you a quick disappearance scene."

"Paste him one for me, will you?"

It was too dark to see clearly into the pit below, but John could tell from the coarse optimism and rugged vitality of the remarks and voices that they proceeded from middle-class Americans of the more spirited type. Then Mr. Washington put out his cane and touched a button in the grass, and the scene below sprang into light.

"These are some adventurous mariners who had the misfortune to discover El Dorado," he remarked.

Below them there had appeared a large hollow in the earth shaped like the interior of a bowl. The sides were steep and apparently of polished glass, and on its slightly concave surface stood about two dozen men clad in the half costume, half uniform, of aviators. Their upturned faces, lit with wrath, with malice, with despair, with cynical humor, were covered by long growths of beard, but with the exception of a few who had pined perceptibly away, they seemed to be a well-fed, healthy lot.

Braddock Washington drew a garden chair to the edge of the pit and sat down.

"Well, how are you, boys?" he inquired genially.

A chorus of execration in which all joined except a few too dispirited to cry out, rose up into the sunny air, but Braddock Washington heard it with unruffled composure. When its last echo had died away he spoke again.

"Have you thought up a way out of your difficulty?"

From here and there among them a remark floated up.

"We decided to stay here for love!"

"Bring us up there and we'll find us a way!"

Braddock Washington waited until they were again quiet. Then he said:

"I've told you the situation. I don't want you here. I wish to heaven I'd never seen you. Your own curiosity got you here, and any time that you can think of a way out which protects me and my interests I'll be glad to consider it. But so long as you confine your efforts to digging tunnels—yes, I know about the new one you've started—you won't get very far. This isn't as hard on you as you make it out, with all your howling for the loved ones at home. If you were the type who worried much about the loved ones at home, you'd never have taken up aviation."

A tall man moved apart from the others, and

held up his hand to call his captor's attention to what he was about to say.

"Let me ask you a few questions!" he cried. "You pretend to be a fair-minded man."

"How absurd. How could a man of *my* position be fair-minded toward *you?* You might as well speak of a Spaniard being fair-minded toward a piece of steak."

At this harsh observation the faces of the two dozen steaks fell, but the tall man continued:

"All right!" he cried. "We've argued this out before. You're not a humanitarian and you're not fair-minded, but you're human—at least you say you are—and you ought to be able to put yourself in our place for long enough to think how—how—how——"

"How what?" demanded Washington, coldly.

"—how unnecessary——"

"Not to me."

"Well,—how cruel——"

"We've covered that. Cruelty doesn't exist where self-preservation is involved. You've been soldiers; you know that. Try another."

"Well, then, how stupid."

"There," admitted Washington, "I grant you that. But try to think of an alternative. I've offered to have all or any of you painlessly executed if you wish. I've offered to have your wives, sweethearts, children, and mothers kidnapped and brought out here. I'll enlarge your place down there and feed and clothe you the rest of your lives. If there was some method of producing permanent amnesia I'd have all of you operated on and released immediately, somewhere outside of my preserves. But that's as far as my ideas go."

"How about trusting us not to peach on you?" cried some one.

"You don't proffer that suggestion seriously," said Washington, with an expression of scorn. "I did take out one man to teach my daughter Italian. Last week he got away."

A wild yell of jubilation went up suddenly from two dozen throats and a pandemonium of joy ensued. The prisoners clog-danced and cheered and yodled and wrestled with one another in a sudden uprush of animal spirits. They even ran up the glass sides of the bowl as far as they could, and slid back to the bottom upon the natural cushions of their bodies. The tall man started a song in which they all joined——

"Oh, we'll hang the kaiser
On a sour apple tree——"

Braddock Washington sat in inscrutable silence until the song was over.

"You see," he remarked, when he could gain a modicum of attention. "I bear you no ill-will. I like to see you enjoying yourselves. That's why I didn't tell you the whole story at once. The man—what was his name? Critchtichiello?—was shot by some of my agents in fourteen different places."

Not guessing that the places referred to were cities, the tumult of rejoicing subsided immediately.

"Nevertheless," cried Washington with a touch of anger, "he tried to run away. Do you expect me to take chances with any of you after an experience like that?"

Again a series of ejaculations went up.

"Sure!"

"Would your daughter like to learn Chinese?"

"Hey, I can speak Italian! My mother was a wop."

"Maybe she'd like t'learna speak N'Yawk!"

"If she's the little one with the big blue eyes I can teach her a lot of things better than Italian."

"I know some Irish songs—and I could hammer brass once't."

Mr. Washington reached forward suddenly with his cane and pushed the button in the grass so that the picture below went out instantly, and there remained only that great dark mouth covered dismally with the black teeth of the grating.

"Hey!" called a single voice from below, "you ain't goin' away without givin' us your blessing?"

But Mr. Washington, followed by the two boys, was already strolling on toward the ninth hole of the golf course, as though the pit and its contents were no more than a hazard over which his facile iron had triumphed with ease.

VII

July under the lee of the diamond mountain was a month of blanket nights and of warm, glowing days. John and Kismine were in love. He did not know that the little gold football (inscribed with the legend *Pro deo et patria et St. Mida*) which he had given her rested on a platinum chain next to her bosom. But it did. And she for her part was not aware that a large sapphire which had dropped one day from her simple coiffure was stowed away tenderly in John's jewel box.

Late one afternoon when the ruby and ermine music room was quiet, they spent an hour there together. He held her hand and she gave him such a look that he whispered her name aloud. She bent toward him—then hesitated.

"Did you say 'Kismine'?" she asked softly, "or——"

She had wanted to be sure. She thought she might have misunderstood.

Neither of them had ever kissed before, but in the course of an hour it seemed to make little difference.

The afternoon drifted away. That night when a last breath of music drifted down from the highest tower, they each lay awake, happily dreaming over the separate minutes of the day. They had decided to be married as soon as possible.

VIII

Every day Mr. Washington and the two young men went hunting or fishing in the deep forests or played golf around the somnolent course—games which John diplomatically allowed his host to win—or swam in the mountain coolness of the lake. John found Mr. Washington a somewhat exacting personality—utterly uninterested in any ideas or opinions except his own. Mrs. Washington was aloof and reserved at all times. She was apparently indifferent to her two daughters, and entirely absorbed in her son Percy, with whom she held interminable conversations in rapid Spanish at dinner.

Jasmine, the elder daughter, resembled Kismine in appearance—except that she was somewhat bow-legged, and terminated in large hands and feet—but was utterly unlike her in temperament. Her favorite books had to do with poor girls who kept house for widowed fathers. John learned from Kismine that Jasmine had never recovered from the shock and disappointment caused her by the termination of the World War, just as she was about to start for Europe as a canteen expert. She had even pined away for a time, and Braddock Washington had taken steps to promote a new war in the Balkans—but she had seen a photograph of some wounded Serbian soldiers and lost interest in the whole proceedings. But Percy and Kismine seemed to have inherited the arrogant attitude in all its harsh magnificence from their father. A chaste and consistent selfishness ran like a pattern through their every idea.

John was enchanted by the wonders of the château and the valley. Braddock Washington, so Percy told him, had caused to be kidnapped a landscape gardener, an architect, a designer of state settings, and a French decadent poet left over from the last century. He had put his entire force of negroes at their disposal, guaranteed to supply them with any materials that the world could offer, and left them to work out some ideas of their own. But one by one they had shown their uselessness. The decadent poet had at once begun bewailing his separation from the boulevards in spring—he made some vague remarks about spices, apes, and ivories, but said nothing that was of any practical value. The stage designer on his part wanted to make the whole valley a series of tricks and sensational effects—a state of things that the Washingtons would soon have grown tired of. And as for the architect and the landscape gardener, they thought only in terms of convention. They must make this like this and that like that.

But they had, at least, solved the problem of what was to be done with them—they all went mad early one morning after spending the night in a single room trying to agree upon the location of a fountain, and were now confined comfortably in an insane asylum at Westport, Connecticut.

"But," inquired John curiously, "who did plan all your wonderful reception rooms and halls, and approaches and bathrooms——?"

"Well," answered Percy, "I blush to tell you, but it was a moving-picture fella. He was the only man we found who was used to playing with an unlimited amount of money, though he did tuck his napkin in his collar and couldn't read or write."

As August drew to a close John began to regret that he must soon go back to school. He and Kismine had decided to elope the following June.

"It would be nicer to be married here," Kismine confessed, "but of course I could never get father's permission to marry you at all. Next to that I'd rather elope. It's terrible for wealthy people to be married in America at present—they always have to send out bulletins to the press saying that they're going to be married in remnants, when what they mean is just a peck of old second-hand pearls and some used lace worn once by the Empress Eugénie."

"I know," agreed John fervently. "When I was visiting the Schnlitzer-Murphys, the eldest daughter, Gwendolyn, married a man whose father owns half of West Virginia. She wrote home saying what a tough struggle she was carrying on on his salary as a bank clerk—and then she ended up by saying that 'Thank God, I have four good maids anyhow, and that helps a little.' "

"It's absurd," commented Kismine. "Think of the millions and millions of people in the world, laborers and all, who get along with only two maids."

One afternoon late in August a chance remark of Kismine's changed the face of the entire situation, and threw John into a state of terror.

They were in their favorite grove, and between kisses John was indulging in some romantic forebodings which he fancied added poignancy to their relations.

"Sometimes I think we'll never marry," he said sadly. "You're too wealthy, too magnificent. No one as rich as you are can be like other girls. I should marry the daughter of some well-to-do wholesale hardware man from Omaha or Sioux City, and be content with her half-million."

"I knew the daughter of a wholesale hardware man once," remarked Kismine. "I don't think you'd have been contented with her. She was a friend of my sister's. She visited here."

"Oh, then you've had other guests?" exclaimed John in surprise.

Kismine seemed to regret her words.

"Oh, yes," she said hurriedly, "we've had a few."

"But aren't you—wasn't your father afraid they'd talk outside?"

"Oh, to some extent, to some extent," she answered. "Let's talk about something pleasanter."

But John's curiosity was aroused.

"Something pleasanter!" he demanded. "What's unpleasant about that? Weren't they nice girls?"

To his great surprise Kismine began to weep.

"Yes—th—that's the—the whole t-trouble. I grew qu-quite attached to some of them. So did Jasmine, but she kept inv-viting them anyway. I couldn't under*stand* it."

A dark suspicion was born in John's heart.

"Do you mean that they *told,* and your father had them—removed?"

"Worse than that," she muttered brokenly. "Father took no chances—and Jasmine kept writing them to come, and they had *such* a good time!"

She was overcome by a paroxysm of grief.

Stunned with the horror of this revelation, John sat there open-mouthed, feeling the nerves of his body twitter like so many sparrows perched upon his spinal column.

"Now, I've told you, and I shouldn't have," she said, calming suddenly and drying her dark blue eyes.

"Do you mean to say that your father had them *murdered* before they left?"

She nodded.

"In August usually—or early in September. It's only natural for us to get all the pleasure out of them that we can first."

"How abominable! How—why, I must be going crazy! Did you really admit that——"

"I did," interrupted Kismine, shrugging her shoulders. "We can't very well imprison them like those aviators, where they'd be a continual reproach to us every day. And it's always been made easier for Jasmine and me because father had it done sooner than we expected. In that way we avoided any farewell scene——"

"So you murdered them! Uh!" cried John.

"It was done very nicely. They were drugged while they were asleep—and their families were always told that they died of scarlet fever in Butte."

"But—I fail to understand why you kept on inviting them!"

"I didn't," burst out Kismine. "I never invited one. Jasmine did. And they always had a very good time. She'd give them the nicest presents toward the last. I shall probably have visitors too—I'll harden up to it. We can't let such an inevitable thing as death stand in the way of enjoying life while we have it. Think how lonesome it'd be out here if we never had *any* one. Why, father and mother have sacrificed some of their best friends just as we have."

"And so," cried John accusingly, "and so you were letting me make love to you and pretending to return it, and talking about marriage, all the time knowing perfectly well that I'd never get out of here alive——"

"No," she protested passionately. "Not any more. I did at first. You were here. I couldn't help that, and I thought your last days might as well be pleasant for both of us. But then I fell in love with you, and—and I'm honestly sorry you're going to—going to be put away—though I'd rather you'd be put away than ever kiss another girl."

"Oh, you would, would you?" cried John ferociously.

"Much rather. Besides, I've always heard that a girl can have more fun with a man whom she knows she can never marry. Oh, why did I tell you? I've probably spoiled your whole good time now, and we were really enjoying things when you didn't know it. I knew it would make things sort of depressing for you."

"Oh, you did, did you?" John's voice trembled with anger. "I've heard about enough of this. If you haven't any more pride and decency than to have an affair with a fellow that you know isn't much better than a corpse, I don't want to have any more to do with you!"

"You're not a corpse!" she protested in horror. "You're not a corpse! I won't have you saying that I kissed a corpse!"

"I said nothing of the sort!"

"You did! You said I kissed a corpse!"

"I didn't!"

Their voices had risen, but upon a sudden interruption they both subsided into immediate silence. Footsteps were coming along the path in their direction, and a moment later the rosebushes were parted displaying Braddock Washington, whose intelligent eyes set in his good-looking vacuous face were peering in at them.

"Who kissed a corpse?" he demanded in obvious disapproval.

"Nobody," answered Kismine quickly. "We were just joking."

"What are you two doing here, anyhow?" he demanded gruffly. "Kismine, you ought to be—to be reading or playing golf with your sister.

Go read! Go play golf! Don't let me find you here when I come back!"

Then he bowed at John and went up the path.

"See?" said Kismine crossly, when he was out of hearing. "You've spoiled it all. We can never meet any more. He won't let me meet you. He'd have you poisoned if he thought we were in love."

"We're not, any more!" cried John fiercely, "so he can set his mind at rest upon that. Moreover, don't fool yourself that I'm going to stay around here. Inside of six hours I'll be over those mountains, if I have to gnaw a passage through them, and on my way East."

They had both got to their feet, and at this remark Kismine came close and put her arm through his.

"I'm going, too."

"You must be crazy——"

"Of course I'm going," she interrupted impatiently.

"You most certainly are not. You——"

"Very well," she said quietly, "we'll catch up with father now and talk it over with him."

Defeated, John mustered a sickly smile.

"Very well, dearest," he agreed, with pale and unconvincing affection, "we'll go together."

His love for her returned and settled placidly on his heart. She was his—she would go with him to share his dangers. He put his arms about her and kissed her fervently. After all she loved him; she had saved him, in fact.

Discussing the matter, they walked slowly back toward the château. They decided that since Braddock Washington had seen them together they had best depart the next night. Nevertheless, John's lips were unusually dry at dinner, and he nervously emptied a great spoonful of peacock soup into his left lung. He had to be carried into the turquoise and sable cardroom and pounded on the back by one of the under-butlers, which Percy considered a great joke.

IX

Long after midnight John's body gave a nervous jerk, and he sat suddenly upright, staring into the veils of somnolence that draped the room. Through the squares of blue darkness that were his open windows, he had heard a faint far-away sound that died upon a bed of wind before identifying itself on his memory, clouded with uneasy dreams. But the sharp noise that had succeeded it was nearer, was just outside the room—the click of a turned knob, a footstep, a whisper, he could not tell; a hard lump gathered in the pit of his stomach, and his whole body ached in the moment that he strained agonizingly to hear. Then one of the veils seemed to dissolve, and he saw a vague figure standing by the door, a figure only faintly limned and blocked in upon the darkness, mingled so with the folds of the drapery as to seem distorted, like a reflection seen in a dirty pane of glass.

With a sudden movement of fright or resolution John pressed the button by his bedside, and the next moment he was sitting in the green sunken bath of the adjoining room, waked into alertness by the shock of the cold water which half filled it.

He sprang out, and, his wet pajamas scattering a heavy trickle of water behind him, ran for the aquamarine door which he knew led out onto the ivory landing of the second floor. The door opened noiselessly. A single crimson lamp burning in a great dome above lit the magnificent sweep of the carved stairways with a poignant beauty. For a moment John hesitated, appalled by the silent splendor massed about him, seeming to envelop in its gigantic folds and contours the solitary drenched little figure shivering upon the ivory landing. Then simultaneously two things happened. The door of his own sitting-room swung open, precipitating three naked negroes into the hall—and, as John swayed in wild terror toward the stairway, another door slid back in the wall on the other side of the corridor, and John saw Braddock Washington standing in the lighted lift, wearing a fur coat and a pair of riding boots which reached to his knees and displayed, above, the glow of his rose-colored pajamas.

On the instant the three negroes—John had never seen any of them before, and it flashed through his mind that they must be the professional executioners—paused in their movement toward John, and turned expectantly to the man in the lift, who burst out with an imperious command:

"Get in here! All three of you! Quick as hell!"

Then, within the instant, the three negroes darted into the cage, the oblong of light was blotted out as the lift door slid shut, and John was again alone in the hall. He slumped weakly down against an ivory stair.

It was apparent that something portentous had occurred, something which, for the moment at least, had postponed his own petty disaster. What was it? Had the negroes risen in revolt? Had the aviators forced aside the iron bars of the grating? Or had the men of Fish stumbled blindly through the hills and gazed with bleak, joyless eyes upon the gaudy valley? John did not know. He heard a faint whir of air as the lift whizzed up again, and then, a moment later, as it descended. It was probable that Percy was hurrying to his father's assistance, and it occurred to John that this was his opportunity to join Kismine and plan an immediate escape. He waited until the lift had been silent for several minutes; shivering a little with the night cool that whipped in through his wet pajamas, he returned to his room and dressed himself quickly. Then he mounted a long flight of stairs and turned down the corridor carpeted with Russian sable which led to Kismine's suite.

The door of her sitting-room was open and the lamps were lighted. Kismine, in an angora kimono, stood near the window of the room in a listening attitude, and as John entered noiselessly she turned toward him.

"Oh, it's you!" she whispered, crossing the room to him. "Did you hear them?"

"I heard your father's slaves in my——"

"No," she interrupted excitedly. "Aeroplanes!"

"Aeroplanes? Perhaps that was the sound that woke me."

"There're at least a dozen. I saw one a few moments ago dead against the moon. The guard back by the cliff fired his rifle and that's what roused father. We're going to open on them right away."

"Are they here on purpose?"

"Yes—it's that Italian who got away——"

Simultaneously with her last word, a succession of sharp cracks tumbled in through the open window. Kismine uttered a little cry, took a penny with fumbling fingers from a box on her dresser, and ran to one of the electric lights. In an instant the entire château was in darkness—she had blown out the fuse.

"Come on!" she cried to him. "We'll go up to the roof garden, and watch it from there!"

Drawing a cape about her, she took his hand, and they found their way out the door. It was only a step to the tower lift, and as she pressed the button that shot them upward he put his arms around her in the darkness and kissed her mouth. Romance had come to John Unger at last. A minute later they had stepped out upon the star-white platform. Above, under the misty moon, sliding in and out of the patches of cloud that eddied below it, floated a dozen dark-winged bodies in a constant circling course. From here and there in the valley flashes of fire leaped toward them, followed by sharp detonations. Kismine clapped her hands with pleasure, which, a moment later, turned to dismay as the aeroplanes at some prearranged signal, began to release their bombs and the whole of the valley became a panorama of deep reverberate sound and lurid light.

Before long the aim of the attackers became concentrated upon the points where the anti-aircraft guns were situated, and one of them was almost immediately reduced to a giant cinder to lie smouldering in a park of rosebushes.

"Kismine," begged John, "you'll be glad when I tell you that this attack came on the eve of my murder. If I hadn't heard that guard shoot off his gun back by the pass I should now be stone dead——"

"I can't hear you!" cried Kismine, intent on the scene before her. "You'll have to talk louder!"

"I simply said," shouted John, "that we'd better get out before they begin to shell the château!"

Suddenly the whole portico of the negro quarters cracked asunder, a geyser of flame shot up from under the colonnades, and great fragments of jagged marble were hurled as far as the borders of the lake.

"There go fifty thousand dollars' worth of slaves," cried Kismine, "at prewar prices. So few Americans have any respect for property."

John renewed his efforts to compel her to leave. The aim of the aeroplanes was becoming more precise minute by minute, and only two of the anti-aircraft guns were still retaliating. It was obvious that the garrison, encircled with fire, could not hold out much longer.

"Come on!" cried John, pulling Kismine's arm, "we've got to go. Do you realize that those aviators will kill you without question if they find you?"

She consented reluctantly.

"We'll have to wake Jasmine!" she said, as they hurried toward the lift. Then she added in a sort of childish delight: "We'll be poor, won't we? Like people in books. And I'll be an orphan and utterly free. Free and poor! What fun!" She stopped and raised her lips to him in a delighted kiss.

"It's impossible to be both together," said John grimly. "People have found that out. And I should choose to be free as preferable of the two. As an extra caution you'd better dump the contents of your jewel box into your pockets."

Ten minutes later the two girls met John in the dark corridor and they descended to the main floor of the château. Passing for the last time through the magnificence of the splendid halls, they stood for a moment out on the terrace, watching the burning negro quarters and the flaming embers of two planes which had fallen on the other side of the lake. A solitary gun was still keeping up a sturdy popping, and the attackers seemed timorous about descending lower, but sent their thunderous fireworks in a circle around it, until any chance shot might annihilate its Ethiopian crew.

John and the two sisters passed down the marble steps, turned sharply to the left, and began to ascend a narrow path that wound like a garter about the diamond mountain. Kismine knew a heavily wooded spot half-way up where they could lie concealed and yet be able to observe the wild night in the valley—finally to make an escape, when it should be necessary, along a secret path laid in a rocky gully.

X

It was three o'clock when they attained their destination. The obliging and phlegmatic Jasmine fell off to sleep immediately, leaning against the trunk of a large tree, while John and Kismine sat, his arm around her, and watched the desperate ebb and flow of the dying battle among the ruins of a vista that had been a garden spot that morning. Shortly after four o'clock the last remaining gun gave out a clanging sound and went out of action in a swift tongue of red smoke. Though the moon was down, they saw that the flying bodies were circling closer to the earth. When the planes had made certain that the beleaguered possessed no further resources, they would land and the dark and glittering reign of the Washingtons would be over.

With the cessation of the firing the valley grew quiet. The embers of the two aeroplanes glowed like the eyes of some monster crouching in the grass. The château stood dark and silent, beautiful without light as it had been beautiful in the sun, while the woody rattles of Nemesis filled the air above with a growing and receding complaint. Then John perceived that Kismine, like her sister, had fallen sound asleep.

It was long after four when he became aware of footsteps along the path they had lately followed, and he waited in breathless silence until the persons to whom they belonged had passed the vantage-point he occupied. There was a faint stir in the air now that was not of human origin, and the dew was cold; he knew that the dawn would break soon. John waited until the steps had gone a safe distance up the mountain and were inaudible. Then he followed. About half-way to the steep summit the trees fell away and a hard saddle of rock spread itself over the diamond beneath. Just before he reached this point he slowed down his pace, warned by an animal sense that there was life just ahead of him. Coming to a high boulder, he lifted his head gradually above its edge. His curiosity was rewarded; this is what he saw:

Braddock Washington was standing there motionless, silhouetted against the gray sky without sound or sign of life. As the dawn came up out of the east, lending a cold green color to the earth, it brought the solitary figure into insignificant contrast with the new day.

While John watched, his host remained for a few moments absorbed in some inscrutable contemplation; then he signalled to the two negroes who crouched at his feet to lift the burden which lay between them. As they struggled upright, the first yellow beam of the sun struck through the innumerable prisms of an immense and exquisitely chiselled diamond—and a white radiance was kindled that glowed upon the air like a fragment of the morning star. The bearers staggered beneath its weight for a moment—then their rippling muscles caught and hardened under the wet shine of the skins and the three figures were again motionless in their defiant impotency before the heavens.

After a while the white man lifted his head and slowly raised his arms in a gesture of attention, as one who would call a great crowd to hear—but there was no crowd, only the vast silence of the mountain and the sky, broken by faint bird voices down among the trees. The figure on the saddle of rock began to speak ponderously and with an inextinguishable pride.

"You out there—" he cried in a trembling voice. "You—there—!" He paused, his arms still uplifted, his head held attentively as though he were expecting an answer. John strained his eyes to see whether there might be men coming down the mountain, but the mountain was bare of human life. There was only sky and a mocking flute of wind along the tree-tops. Could Washington be praying? For a moment John wondered. Then the illusion passed—there was something in the man's whole attitude antithetical to prayer.

"Oh, you above there!"

The voice was become strong and confident. This was no forlorn supplication. If anything, there was in it a quality of monstrous condescension.

"You there——"

Words, too quickly uttered to be understood, flowing one into the other. . . . John listened breathlessly, catching a phrase here and there, while the voice broke off, resumed, broke off again—now strong and argumentative, now colored with a slow, puzzled impatience. Then a conviction commenced to dawn on the single listener, and as realization crept over him a spray of quick blood rushed through his arteries. Braddock Washington was offering a bribe to God!

That was it—there was no doubt. The diamond in the arms of his slaves was some advance sample, a promise of more to follow.

That, John perceived after a time, was the thread running through his sentences. Prometheus Enriched was calling to witness forgotten sacrifices, forgotten rituals, prayers obsolete before the birth of Christ. For a while his discourse took the form of reminding God of this gift or that which Divinity had deigned to accept from men—great churches if he would rescue cities from the plague, gifts of myrrh and gold, of human lives and beautiful women and captive armies, of children and queens, of beasts of the forest and field, sheep and goats, harvests and cities, whole conquered lands that had been offered up in lust or blood for His appeasal, buying a meed's worth of alleviation from the Divine wrath—and now he, Braddock Washington, Emperor of Diamonds, king and priest of the age of gold, arbiter of splendor and luxury, would offer up a treasure such as princes before him had never dreamed of, offer it up not in suppliance, but in pride.

He would give to God, he continued, getting down to specifications, the greatest diamond in the world. This diamond would be cut with many more thousand facets than there were leaves on a tree, and yet the whole diamond would be shaped with the perfection of a stone no bigger than a fly. Many men would work upon it for many years. It would be set in a great dome of beaten gold, wonderfully carved and equipped with gates of opal and crusted sapphire. In the middle would be hollowed out a chapel presided over by an altar of iridescent, decomposing, ever-changing radium which would burn out the eyes of any worshipper who lifted up his head from prayer—and on this altar there would be slain for the amusement of the Divine Benefactor any victim He should choose, even though it should be the greatest and most powerful man alive.

In return he asked only a simple thing, a thing

that for God would be absurdly easy—only that matters should be as they were yesterday at this hour and that they should so remain. So very simple! Let but the heavens open, swallowing these men and their aeroplanes—and then close again. Let him have his slaves once more, restored to life and well.

There was no one else with whom he had ever needed to treat or bargain.

He doubted only whether he had made his bribe big enough. God had His price, of course. God was made in man's image, so it had been said: He must have His price. And the price would be rare—no cathedral whose building consumed many years, no pyramid constructed by ten thousand workmen, would be like this cathedral, this pyramid.

He paused here. That was his proposition. Everything would be up to specifications and there was nothing vulgar in his assertion that it would be cheap at the price. He implied that Providence could take it or leave it.

As he approached the end his sentences became broken, became short and uncertain, and his body seemed tense, seemed strained to catch the slightest pressure or whisper of life in the spaces around him. His hair had turned gradually white as he talked, and now he lifted his head high to the heavens like a prophet of old—magnificently mad.

Then, as John stared in giddy fascination, it seemed to him that a curious phenomenon took place somewhere around him. It was as though the sky had darkened for an instant, as though there had been a sudden murmur in a gust of wind, a sound of far-away trumpets, a sighing like the rustle of a great silken robe—for a time the whole of nature round about partook of this darkness; the birds' song ceased; the trees were still, and far over the mountain there was a mutter of dull, menacing thunder.

That was all. The wind died along the tall grasses of the valley. The dawn and the day resumed their place in a time, and the risen sun sent hot waves of yellow mist that made its path bright before it. The leaves laughed in the sun, and their laughter shook the trees until each bough was like a girl's school in fairyland. God had refused to accept the bribe.

For another moment John watched the triumph of the day. Then, turning, he saw a flutter of brown down by the lake, then another flutter, then another, like the dance of golden angels alighting from the clouds. The aeroplanes had come to earth.

John slid off the boulder and ran down the side of the mountain to the clump of trees, where the two girls were awake and waiting for him. Kismine sprang to her feet, the jewels in her pockets jingling, a question on her parted lips, but instinct told John that there was no time for words. They must get off the mountain without losing a moment. He seized a hand of each, and in silence they threaded the tree-trunks, washed with light now and with the rising mist. Behind them from the valley came no sound at all, except the complaint of the peacocks far away and the pleasant undertone of morning.

When they had gone about half a mile, they avoided the park land and entered a narrow path that led over the next rise of ground. At the highest point of this they paused and turned around. Their eyes rested upon the mountainside they had just left—oppressed by some dark sense of tragic impendency.

Clear against the sky a broken, white-haired man was slowly descending the steep slope, followed by two gigantic and emotionless negroes, who carried a burden between them which still flashed and glittered in the sun. Half-way down two other figures joined them—John could see that they were Mrs. Washington and her son, upon whose arm she leaned. The aviators had clambered from their machines to the sweeping lawn in front of the château, and with rifles in hand were starting up the diamond mountain in skirmishing formation.

But the little group of five which had formed farther up and was engrossing all the watchers' attention had stopped upon a ledge of rock. The negroes stooped and pulled up what appeared to be a trap-door in the side of the mountain. Into this they all disappeared, the white-haired man first, then his wife and son, finally the two negroes, the glittering tips of whose jeweled head-dresses caught the sun for a moment before the trap-door descended and engulfed them all.

Kismine clutched John's arm.

"Oh," she cried wildly, "where are they going? What are they going to do?"

"It must be some underground way of escape——"

A little scream from the two girls interrupted his sentence.

"Don't you see?" sobbed Kismine hysterically. "The mountain is wired!"

Even as she spoke John put up his hands to shield his sight. Before their eyes the whole surface of the mountain had changed suddenly to a dazzling burning yellow, which showed up through the jacket of turf as light shows through a human hand. For a moment the intolerable glow continued, and then like an extinguished filament it disappeared, revealing a black waste from which blue smoke arose slowly, carrying off with it what remained of vegetation and of human flesh. Of the aviators there was left neither blood nor bone—they were consumed as completely as the five souls who had gone inside.

Simultaneously, and with an immense concussion, the château literally threw itself into the air, bursting into flaming fragments as it rose, and then tumbling back upon itself in a smoking pile that lay projecting half into the water of the lake. There was no fire—what smoke there was drifted off mingling with the sunshine, and for a few minutes longer a powdery dust of marble drifted from the great featureless pile that had once been the house of jewels. There was no more sound and the three people were alone in the valley.

XI

At sunset John and his two companions reached the high cliff which had marked the boundaries of the Washingtons' dominion, and looking back found the valley tranquil and lovely in the dusk. They sat down to finish the food which Jasmine had brought with her in a basket.

"There!" she said, as she spread the tablecloth and put the sandwiches in a neat pile upon it. "Don't they look tempting? I always think that food tastes better outdoors."

"With that remark," remarked Kismine, "Jasmine enters the middle class."

"Now," said John eagerly, "turn out your pocket and let's see what jewels you brought along. If you made a good selection we three ought to live comfortably all the rest of our lives."

Obediently Kismine put her hand in her pocket and tossed two handfuls of glittering stones before him.

"Not so bad," cried John, enthusiastically. "They aren't very big, but—Hello!" His expression changed as he held one of them up to the declining sun. "Why, these aren't diamonds! There's something the matter!"

"By golly!" exclaimed Kismine, with a startled look. "What an idiot I am!"

"Why, these are rhinestones!" cried John.

"I know." She broke into a laugh. "I opened the wrong drawer. They belonged on the dress of a girl who visited Jasmine. I got her to give them to me in exchange for diamonds. I'd never seen anything but precious stones before."

"And this is what you brought?"

"I'm afraid so." She fingered the brilliants wistfully. "I think I like these better. I'm a little tired of diamonds."

"Very well," said John gloomily. "We'll have to live in Hades. And you will grow old telling incredulous women that you got the wrong drawer. Unfortunately your father's bank-books were consumed with him."

"Well, what's the matter with Hades?"

"If I come home with a wife at my age my

father is just as liable as not to cut me off with a hot coal, as they say down there."

Jasmine spoke up.

"I love washing," she said quietly. "I have always washed my own handkerchiefs. I'll take in laundry and support you both."

"Do they have washwomen in Hades?" asked Kismine innocently.

"Of course," answered John. "It's just like anywhere else."

"I thought—perhaps it was too hot to wear any clothes."

John laughed.

"Just try it!" he suggested. "They'll run you out before you're half started."

"Will father be there?" she asked.

John turned to her in astonishment.

"Your father is dead," he replied somberly. "Why should he go to Hades? You have it confused with another place that was abolished long ago."

After supper they folded up the table-cloth and spread their blankets for the night.

"What a dream it was," Kismine sighed, gazing up at the stars. "How strange it seems to be here with one dress and a penniless fiancé!

"Under the stars," she repeated. "I never noticed the stars before. I always thought of them as great big diamonds that belonged to some one. Now they frighten me. They make me feel that it was all a dream, all my youth."

"It *was* a dream," said John quietly. "Everybody's youth is a dream, a form of chemical madness."

"How pleasant then to be insane!"

"So I'm told," said John gloomily. "I don't know any longer. At any rate, let us love for a while, for a year or so, you and me. That's a form of divine drunkenness that we can all try. There are only diamonds in the whole world, diamonds and perhaps the shabby gift of disillusion. Well, I have that last and I will make the usual nothing of it." He shivered. "Turn up your coat collar, little girl, the night's full of chill and you'll get pneumonia. His was a great sin who first invented consciousness. Let us lose it for a few hours."

So wrapping himself in his blanket he fell off to sleep.